TWISTED LOVE

LAURA CARTER

B

Boldwood

First published in 2016 as *Vengeful Love: Deception*. This edition published in Great Britain in 2025 by Boldwood Books Ltd.

Cover Design by Colin Thomas

Cover Images: Colin Thomas

A CIP catalogue record for this book is available from the British Library.

Paperback ISBN 978-1-80600-086-9

Large Print ISBN 978-1-80600-087-6

Hardback ISBN 978-1-80600-085-2

Trade Paperback ISBN 978-1-80656-080-6

Ebook ISBN 978-1-80600-088-3

Kindle ISBN 978-1-80600-089-0

Audio CD ISBN 978-1-80600-080-7

MP3 CD ISBN 978-1-80600-081-4

Digital audio download ISBN 978-1-80600-082-1

This book is printed on certified sustainable paper. Boldwood Books is dedicated to putting sustainability at the heart of our business. For more information please visit https://www.boldwoodbooks.com/about-us/sustainability/

Boldwood Books Ltd, 23 Bowerdean Street, London, SW6 3TN

www.boldwoodbooks.com

To my professors who probably didn't expect me to use my law degree for this...

1

GREGORY

My Omega tells me it's been less than one minute since I last watched the second hand tick round. Two twenty-three. It's been almost three hours since it happened. Less than three hours since I watched what I've craved for almost three decades unfold. He's dead. The biggest demon in my life has finally been condemned to the pit of flames he deserves. But it's not what I imagined. When I've thought of this day, I've thought that killing him would break the black clouds that have cast a shadow over my existence. Now my black clouds have been replaced with torment.

What have I dragged this sweet girl into? Fuck.

I drag my hands over my tired face, as I sit in this grey, windowless box, not knowing where Scarlett is. She should've stayed clear of me when she had the chance. I should've been fair and stayed away from her. But I couldn't. I sought her out like a vulture seeks its next meal. Those devastating green eyes, the way they turn hazel in a certain light like nothing else I've seen. That unbelievable body. Her skin feels like silk and once you've touched her and tasted her, there's no going back. No other woman could ever be good enough. And she's smart. Too fucking smart for her own good sometimes, and tougher than she thinks. But not in the bedroom. There, she gives herself to me completely, utterly, and I'm desperate to have her all the fucking time. That laugh. I can't help smiling now as I lean forward over the steel table in front of me. Even when she's laughing at something only she finds funny – that happens a lot – I can't help but break my stoicism because it's such a beautiful fucking sound. I've broken her, corrupted her. Since the day she met me, I've turned her world into darkness. I've dragged her down to my level.

Rising from my metal chair, I kick it back against the mirrored wall and pace the concrete floor of my custody cell, my hands deep in the pockets of my blood-stained dinner trousers. *Where is she? What are they doing to her?* She won't break. She's stronger than that. *I* know it but does *she*?

I'm going to fix this. If it's the last thing I do as a free man.

I'll fix this.

The most peculiar pressure builds behind my eyes, making them sting. I can't stand the thought of her trapped in a room like this, like an animal. She'll be cold. She'll be intimidated.

'Fuck! Get a fucking hold of yourself!' I chastise myself through gritted teeth. I need to see her. I need to hold her and make her understand that she's safe. God, that face, that look in her eyes; she was terrified.

There's a short tap on the door before it opens and a tall man wearing a cheap suit walks in. An off-white shirt hugs his middle-aged spread just above the waistline, part-covered by a questionable mustard tie. The cardboard coffee cup in his hand is held as tightly as a full cardboard cup can be held. He's followed by a short woman with her mousey-brown hair in a bun, wearing a black trouser suit and flat, dull leather shoes. She's scowling, brows almost meeting in the middle. She holds one hand on her hip, exposing the gold police badge on her belt.

'Gregory Ryans?'

'Yes,' I say, holding out my hand on instinct.

The man shakes my hand. 'I'm Detective Inspector Barnes and this is my colleague—'

The woman holds out her hand. 'Trina. I'm Trina.'

She's a woman out to deny that this is a man's world but I can tell she's battling with her inner Aphrodite.

I've affected her. Another woman who sees only my looks. Like most women, like all women before Scarlett Heath swanned into my life in her fitted suits with her white-collar sass. She's the only woman who's ever been interested in what's behind my money, face and clothes. A story I can't tell her.

It's unlike Trina to be affected by a man, Barnes's reaction tells me that. It's also obvious that these two people don't see eye to eye.

'It's a pleasure to meet you both,' I say. 'Albeit in the very worst of circumstances.'

Trina flashes a wide, coy smile which she quickly replaces with straight lips.

'Take a seat,' Barnes says, gesturing to the chair that came to rest flush against the mirrored wall. 'You're a Safa.'

Rolling up the sleeves of my crimson-splattered shirt, I sit. His thoughts are written all over his face: South African, angry, volatile. And not afraid of guns. A jury would love the stereotype.

'Do you need someone to look at that?' Barnes asks, pointing to my cut shirt and the slashed skin at my ribs beneath.

'It's been patched up but thank you. Fortunately, it's not as deep as it seems from the mess.'

Barnes nods and pats the recording device on top of the table. 'I'll be recording your statement. We'll start with some basic questions – name, date of birth, that sort of thing – then we'll get to it. Okay?'

I nod, waiting. Barnes hits Record and a digital wheel counts us down to action. He strokes his grey-black beard before he leans back and hangs an elbow over his seat.

'DI Barnes accompanied by Katrina Martin. 2.31 a.m., Sunday, November eighth. Please state your full name and date of birth for the record.'

'Gregory James Ryans. October ninth, 1995.'

'And your address please, Mr Ryans.'

'One, the Shard, London.'

'All right. We were called to your apartment this evening by a member of your Security team, Kenneth Trent. When we arrived, we found two men had been shot, one wounded but alive, the other dead. You were injured and a lady was unharmed. Two other men had arrived, one of whom was Kenneth Trent; both men claim they arrived at the scene after the injuries took place. Does that match your understanding?'

'That's right.'

'Okay. So tell me in your own words what happened tonight. How did you come to be in your apartment and injured?'

'We'd been to a party hosted by my mother at her house in Cobham. It's an annual thing. My mother's a handbag designer; she throws the party every year around fireworks night.'

'Cobham, Surrey?'

'Yes.'

'And when you say "we," who do you mean?'

The image of Scarlett comes to my mind: walking down the stairs, flawless in her black gown, diamonds glimmering around her delicate neck. Her eyes never left mine as she smiled that mesmerising smile, until she reached me. I had to remind myself to breathe. My eyes close as I think of the kiss that followed, her soft lips against mine.

'Mr Ryans?'

'Sorry, it's been a long night. Scarlett Heath. I was at the party with Scarlett Heath and my driver.'

'Jackson?'

He knows him. I nod.

'For the record, please.'

'Yes, Jackson is my driver.'

'We spoke to Geoffrey Jackson and he called himself your bodyguard,' Trina adds. 'Why would you need a bodyguard?'

Clearing my throat, I turn on my best impression of modesty. 'I'm a very wealthy man. Wealth can breed enemies, whether you're a good man or not.'

'Mmhmm, and are you? Are you a good man, Mr Ryans?'

'I'd like to think so.'

'Thank you, Mr Ryans,' Barnes interjects whilst shooting Trina a glare. 'You were at your mother's party, go on.'

Absentmindedly, I rub a hand around the painful ligature bruising around my neck. I need to concentrate. I need to get this right. *God, I need to know where she is. I need to see her.*

'We left the party sometime after eleven, just as the fireworks were starting, maybe closer to midnight.'

Trina frowns. 'You left the firework party before the fireworks started?'

I'd be irritated by her but I'm distracted by the memory of *that* dance and the desire Scarlett and I both had, the urgency we felt to get home. I was desperate to feel her skin on mine, to satisfy my growling erection inside her.

'Yes.' I throw a brief and knowing look at Barnes.

He continues his questions. 'Scarlett Heath is your... girlfriend?'

He startles me. I clear my throat again. 'We know each other romantically.'

Trina rolls her eyes. She's annoyed. Her flushes and smiles are replaced by a moody pout.

'Where did you go when you left the party?'

'Jackson drove us to my apartment. When we got to the car park at the Shard, we noticed that the tyres of my Mercedes had been slashed. I grabbed Scarlett.' *There was no gun*, I remind myself. 'Jackson led the way to the lift vestibule. The door into the lift had been tampered with.'

'We need to check the CCTV,' Trina states, making a note in a small, ring-bound notepad with a cheap, plastic pen.

'That's been done. It's clear.' Barnes briefly casts his attention to me. He knows the tapes were cleaned and probably knows they weren't the only evidence meddled with. I get the feeling he's more than just familiar with Jackson. *Let's see how this pans out.*

'You say the door was tampered with?' Barnes asks.

'Forced open. We took the lift to my floor and when we got out, the door to the apartment was ajar. Jackson kicked it open and was shot as soon as he stepped inside. I think I told Scarlett to look after him, I can't remember exactly, but that's what she did. I knew the intruder had a gun and I knew I could only match that like for like, so I went to the safe and took Jackson's Glock from it.'

Trina jumps in. 'Where exactly is the safe?'

'In my office.'

'Where's that?'

I know what she's getting at; sweat starts to form on my palms but I don't show my nerves. I've spent my life hiding emotions; it's second nature. 'The second floor. Upstairs.'

'Mmhmm. So you, in your frantic state, had time to run upstairs, obtain a gun and come back down. In the meantime, the attacker just, what, hid?'

Bitch. 'With all due respect, Katrina, I don't know what he did. I was upstairs.'

Barnes's lips begin to tip but he puts a closed fist to his mouth until he's composed. 'Go on. You came back downstairs with the gun.'

'Yes. Then I went to find him. There are two rooms off the lounge: a bathroom and a gym. I went into the bathroom where I thought sound was coming from. He came at me, ran at me. We tussled and the mirror broke. He picked up a shard of glass and ripped it into my side.' I raise my arm and remind them both of my injury. 'We kept fighting; somehow, we ended up in the gym room. I tried to kick the guns out of reach but only managed one before he pulled a chain around my neck. I struggled, we were thrashing around, I fell to the floor in the lounge and he was pulling on the chain. I couldn't breathe and I could feel myself slipping; things going dark and blurred. He was killing me. Then I saw the gun I'd kicked, on the floor, just within my reach. Things started to go black. I snatched the gun, and just shot it at him. I didn't aim for his head but that's where the bullet wound up. I was shocked, stunned. I didn't know what to do. I crawled to Jackson and Scarlett and that's when the security guys came in.'

I've done it. It's out there. Now Scarlett just has to keep to the story. I pull my hands through my hair and let my head hang, relieved that my statement is on the record and it's the story I intended to tell.

'Who was the man you killed?' Trina's tone is clipped, offensive.

I sigh. It's still going.

'He was my biological father.'

'And why would your own father want to kill you?'

My dislike of this woman is increasing at a rate of knots. My temper is building. I turn my fist in the palm of my other hand on my lap. 'I bought his company to sell it off.'

'Forgive my naivety, Mr Ryans; I'm not a businesswoman.' The way she uses my name is condescending. 'Surely buying companies happens all the time and people don't kill each other over it.'

It's a statement. Had it been a question, I might've been inclined to enlighten her on how corrupt the world of business can be. But I won't.

'The company was his life, his prize possession, the only thing he's ever treated with respect and cared for.'

'So why would he sell it?'

'Because I offered him an awful lot of money to buy it, Miss Martin, and the other key trait my father possessed was greed.'

'This isn't the first time you've been in a police station, is it?' She catches me off guard and she knows it. A sadistic smile begins to turn on her lips as my jaw drops open and slowly closes again without making a sound.

'To what are you referring, Miss Martin?'

'Oh, there's been more than one other time?'

'Stop playing games, Trina,' Barnes cuts in. 'Ask him a question with purpose or we'll wrap this up.'

She puffs and scowls at her senior. 'You gave a statement once as a boy. In South Africa.'

She's trying to establish motive. It's underhanded, it's dirty, but she's played the game well.

'That has nothing to do with this case.'

'I beg to differ. I think it has a *lot* to do with this case. You once gave a statement that your father—'

'I made a statement as a ten-year-old boy,' I snap, pressing into the table and pushing back my chair. 'I'm thirty years old. I've lived a life since I was that kid. I see what you're doing. I see your game but that ten-year-old boy won't give you a motive. The reason, the *only* reason, I shot a man tonight is because he would have killed me if I hadn't. Am I sorry that a man died tonight? Of course I am. Will it haunt me every day for the rest of my life? Of course it will. But am I sorry that if someone had to die tonight, it wasn't me or, worse still, Jackson or Scarlett? No.'

I rest back into my hard-as-hell seat and soften my tone. *Time to play the man.* I gaze into her eyes until she shifts awkwardly and I wait until her pupils lock on mine. I lure her in. 'I'm just a man, Trina. I took a life to save my own. Don't I deserve to live?'

Her lips part with her breath as she slowly moves her head up and down.

'I'm not the bad guy in this. I can promise you that. Kevin Pearson may have been my father but he was a sinful man. You're about putting bad guys away, aren't you?'

She nods again. She's putty.

I sit back, giving her space to compose herself, glancing at Barnes, who winks very subtly from his left eye.

'We're done here,' he says, turning off the recorder.

I breathe a short sigh of relief.

Trina is quick to make her excuses and exit, no doubt annoyed by her inability to control her pheromones.

'You know Jackson?' I ask Barnes.

'We served together in the military and briefly in the police before he went private. I know what I need to know.' He crosses one heel over his opposite thigh, revealing offensively yellow socks.

'How's it looking?'

He shrugs and rolls a pen between his fingers. 'I can work with self-defence. Jackson's statement matches yours. But the gun is more difficult. It's a bad time politically for gun crime. The Crown Prosecution Service are going to want possession as a minimum, even if they accept self-defence.'

'What can I do?'

'It could cost you.'

I sit up straighter now. 'If there's one thing I've got, it's money, Barnes.'

He nods. 'Jackson said as much. He also said you're a good guy.'

'How is he?'

Barnes shakes his head on a short laugh. 'He's made of stone, that man. Muscle damage only. He was lucky. Had them stitch him up with a shot of the good stuff, no anaesthetic, then he discharged himself. Should be back on his feet soon enough.'

'Sounds like Jackson. And Scarlett, how's she?'

'We haven't spoken to her yet.'

'Where is she? Can I see her?'

He shakes his head. 'We won't be long. She's up next.'

The foreign sensation of pressure begins to build behind my eyes again. I need to sleep.

'Can I trust you, Barnes?'

'Jackson does.'

'I'll take that as a ringing endorsement.'

'Do so. He's a good judge of character.'

'I hope so.'

'You and me both.'

2

SCARLETT

I'm going to hell. The funny thing is, I've never given much thought to whether I believe in God, the Bible, heaven and hell but I suspect I've broken the rules to pass the shiny gate and walk barefoot on the carpet of white cloud. The scary thing is, I don't care why I'm going; I'm only terrified that when I get there, my dad and Gregory might not be waiting.

'Miss Heath!'

Katrina Martin slams a hand on the cold, metal table between us, dragging me from my trance.

'I'm sorry,' I whisper, allowing myself a brief glance upward before settling my eyes on the invisible movie playing out on the surface of the table.

'You were saying?' Her annoyance is obvious.

I don't know what I was saying. I was thinking about my soul, burning alone, but I don't think I said that aloud.

'Scarlett!' she snaps again.

DI Barnes sighs heavily. 'All right, Trina, calm down. She's had a shock and it's the middle of the night.'

His soft tone causes me to search his face. For some unfathomable reason, he's being nice to me. He turns up his lips ever so slightly, comforting me as much as I can or care to be comforted.

'Scarlett, you said you were at the party.'

'We were dancing.' I explain the next half an hour of the party in seconds as

I watch the scene replay in my mind. Gregory's strong hand on my back, pulling me into his firm chest as he moved us around the dance floor, his brown eyes never leaving mine, desire sparking between us. 'We didn't want to stay for the fireworks.'

'And Geoffrey drove you?'

I'd wanted to get in the Bentley and drive to where Gregory could consume me with sheer pleasure. I'd wanted to be held by him and never let go. But the feeling disappeared as soon as we slipped into the back seat of the car. An unsettling eeriness had chilled my bones. Gregory pulled me into him to warm me but I could still feel it, like a presence, something unnerving. 'Yes. He drove us to the Shard, to Gregory's apartment. I've been staying there.'

I stop myself before I tell them *why* I've been staying with Gregory. I promised I would tell them what he told me to say and that's all. I don't have a lawyer. We agreed not to have lawyers at first because we have nothing to hide. That's the story. My mind blurs with confused images: my dad's funeral, me on my knees at his hospital bedside as I realised he'd been murdered, the dark-haired boy from my dreams who watched his father beat his mother half to death.

'Scarlett!' Trina shouts, startling me, causing me to blink my dry eyes quickly.

'Yes.'

'What happened when you got to the Shard?'

'The Shard. We parked and Jackson or Gregory, I don't remember who, one of them noticed the tyres of Gregory's Mercedes had been slashed.'

The hairs on my skin had pricked up. We knew who it was and we knew he was in the vicinity. Gregory told me to take the car and leave but I couldn't, I wouldn't. I couldn't leave Gregory to face Kevin Pearson alone. But there was more than that, something deeper, darker within me that wanted to see the end of my father's killer. Bile rises in my throat and I swallow it down. Gregory took my hand in his, instinctively protecting me, and Jackson pulled his gun from the glove compartment of the Bentley.

Jackson led the way, his gun cocked and raised as we left the basement and rode the lift to the sixty-fourth floor.

'We took the lift to Gregory's floor. Jackson got out first, then Gregory, then me.'

'Nothing else happened in the car park?' Trina queries. 'You noticed the tyres then just left? Jackson or Gregory, they didn't look around the car park? Check for an intruder?'

'I, err, I don't remember. Maybe, I don't think so.'

'So presumably, they weren't taken by surprise?'

'I, err, I'm not sure. I guess they thought it would be best to leave the basement and get to the apartment.'

'You're aware that the man who died tonight was Mr Ryans's father, aren't you?'

'I, err...' We didn't discuss this. My chest begins to throb as my heart rate rises. *They know.* If I say yes, I only confirm what they know. *Don't I?* 'Yes, I know that.'

'Keep going, Scarlett, you're doing well.' DI Barnes casts a warning eye in Katrina's direction. 'So you got out of the lift at the apartment.'

I take a deep breath. *I won't let Gregory down.* I nod.

'For the record, please, Scarlett.'

'Yes, the door was open.'

'Fully open? Wide open?' Katrina jumps in.

This woman is starting to piss me off. 'No,' I snap. 'The door was ajar.'

DI Barnes gives away their position with a subtle nod, letting me know I've said the right thing.

'Jackson kicked open the door and right away, he was shot in the leg. He fell to the floor.' I need to concentrate now. It's time. Gregory went after his father. No, Gregory told me to look after Jackson, then he went after his father. No, Gregory told me to look after Jackson and then he went upstairs. *Damn it!* My eyes are burning under the pressure of the room, the intensity of Katrina's stare, the thought that I might let Gregory and Jackson down. 'Gregory told me to look after Jackson and I did. I tied a tourniquet around his thigh.'

'Where was Gregory?'

'He ran; he left. He went upstairs.'

Katrina snarls. 'He went upstairs? He just left you and Jackson with an armed man who'd already shot one of you? He just went upstairs?'

I look at DI Barnes, begging him with wide eyes for help, but he doesn't jump in; he puts his head down. I'm alone.

'He ran. Like I said. It was all so fast. Next thing I knew, Gregory was back, running through the lounge. Then there was fighting, shouting, tussling. They were in the downstairs bathroom.'

'Who?'

'Gregory, and his father, Pearson. There was banging and smashing, like glass being shattered. Then they burst into the lounge, wrestling, fighting, then into the gym. At some point, a gun slid into the lounge and they followed, struggling. There was a chain, something from the gym, I think, around Gregory's neck. Pearson was strangling him.'

There was a chain around Gregory's neck, his face was red, his eyes were wide, pupils dilated, as he fought for his life. They flipped over and over again, first Gregory on top, then Pearson. The chain stayed pulled tight to his neck. Jackson was shouting at me to do something but I didn't know what to do. I didn't know how to help. I was useless and I was watching the man I love die.

'The chain was so tight on his neck, his muscles were straining, his face was red. Pearson was killing him.'

Gregory thrust an elbow back into his father's throat and took the opportunity to pounce. Towering over him, Gregory thrust his hands around his father's neck, pushing his thumbs into the windpipe. He held his position through kicks and flailing limbs until Pearson stopped moving, lifeless, or so we thought. Gregory slumped back against the wall to catch his breath before checking that I was okay and moving to help Jackson. That's when it happened.

'There was blood. I know now that Gregory had been stabbed with something but when they were struggling, it wasn't obvious who was bleeding. Maybe both of them.'

As Gregory tended to Jackson, I saw Pearson's body twitch. I made steps towards it. I had Jackson's gun in my hand.

'He was dying. Gregory was dying. There was a gun on the floor. That's what Gregory went upstairs for, I realise that now.'

Pearson suddenly sprang up. Grabbing the gun beside him, he raised it and aimed at Gregory.

I had no choice.

'Somehow, Gregory managed to grab a gun from the floor and the rest was so quick. A blur. He—'

I can't do this. I can't do this to him.

'He. Gregory. He.' I take a deep breath and exhale as subtly as I can manage. 'He shot him.'

I shot him. A dry lump forms in my throat; my eyes are on fire. It was him or

Gregory. That's why I took the shot. But right before I did, Gregory wasn't the only man I thought of.

'Just so I can get this straight, Gregory's dying and you and Jackson are watching?' Katrina sits back in her chair and plants one hand firmly on her waist.

'I. We. It wasn't like that. Jackson was injured. What was I supposed to do?'

'Right. And dying Gregory, who earlier left the room and wandered upstairs, suddenly found the strength to pick up a gun and shoot his father through the head?'

I wince at her blunt version of events.

'It wasn't like that. He didn't wander; he ran. And he *was* dying! He was dying and he would be dead now if—' I shake my head and will impending tears not to fall.

'How long have you known Gregory Ryans hated his father?'

'I… I don't—'

'How long, Scarlett?'

'It's not like that.'

Katrina stands, sending her chair crashing against the wall.

'That's enough, Trina!' DI Barnes is on his feet too.

'It's not like what? Why are you protecting him, Scarlett?' She's barking, leaning towards me, both hands on the table, her words wet on my face.

I'm not protecting him. He's protecting me. He's protecting me and you're behaving like he's a murderer. I rise without conscious thought until I'm face to face with her. 'What the fuck did you want him to do? He was going to die! One man in that room was never going to make it out alive and I'll never be sorry that it wasn't the man I love, that it's the fucking bastard who picked the fight!'

She takes a step back from my rage. A sadistic grin starts to rise on her lips. 'Do you know he couldn't even call you his girlfriend? Unrequited love, that's what you're protecting.'

She's a jumped-up, moody bitch and she's trying to rattle me but her words drive a knife through my gut, taking the energy out of my legs, forcing me to sit.

'That. Is. Enough. You want to make your name, Trina, but this isn't the case you're going to use to do it. Get out of here; you're off the case.'

Katrina snaps her head to look at DI Barnes. 'Fuck you!' She marches out of the room, slamming the metal door and causing me to jump as she goes.

I try to calm my heaving chest, taking long inhales. 'It was self-defence. He had no choice,' I mutter, my eyes rising to meet the scrutiny of DI Barnes.

'I know,' he says softly, before pressing the Record button on the digital device and ending the official interrogation.

'Why did she behave like that? What's her problem?'

DI Barnes shakes his head, slowly, thoughtfully. 'You two represent everything she can't stand.'

My hand instinctively rises to stroke the heavy diamond choker around my neck and I look down at my black gown. How perfectly unordinary we must look, giving statements in black tie, smelling of money. Lying to protect our dirty little secret. I want to defend myself. I want to explain that this isn't my life, that I *am* ordinary. But I don't. Instead, I think about the man who borrowed the diamonds around my neck and bought my dress from Harrods.

'Where's Gregory?'

'He's waiting for you.'

'Is he free to go?'

'For now.'

'Even though—'

'You'd both better get out of here before I change my mind and charge his arse.'

'Thank you,' I whisper with more gratitude than he could possibly take from my words.

My weary legs find the strength to stand and move to the door. The corridor is long and grey and closes in on me as I work my way to the guarded double door and the enormity of the night starts to hit me. My entire being aches with pain, sorrow, emptiness. Each step takes me closer to the only person in the world who can make things feel right again.

A guard pushes open the door without speaking and inclines his head for me to walk into the station reception.

Gregory rises from a row of seats, his shirt soiled, his sleeves rolled to his elbows, his hair showing the signs of his stress tell: pulling his fingers through it. His broad shoulders turn slowly to face me, his deep-brown eyes softening when they find me. He's as perfect as ever and I need him. I need to feel his strong arms around me. His shoulders sag and he mouths to me, 'Get here.'

Like he knows I will, I move to him and despite everything, I fall a little deeper.

My heart stops beating and breath leaves my lungs. He places his palms on my cheeks and gently rests his lips on my brow, then pulls me into his hard chest and wraps his arms around me. In the safety of his embrace, my legs finally give way beneath me and I sob, tears streaming down my face as I cling to him. He sweeps me up into his arms and carries me away from the station, away from the nightmare of the last few hours.

'Shh,' he whispers into my ear between soft presses of his lips. I nuzzle further into his neck but my tears don't stop. Everything pours out of me, every emotion I've felt since we met – love, desire, desperation, fear, pain, anger, relief – it all fuels my sobs.

The cold of the dark night bites the naked skin of my arms and chest and harsh reality courses through my bones. 'I could've lost you,' I chug through broken breaths.

He stops, holding us still, until I raise my head. When he can look into my eyes, he inhales deeply, his chest rising against me. 'But you didn't. You saved me, Scarlett. You saved my life.'

Then he kisses me, pressing his lips firmly against mine. My tears stop.

Kenneth climbs out of the Bentley and opens the rear door for Gregory. 'Mr Ryans.'

Gregory doesn't leave me to sit in the front like he might if Jackson was driving. He bends and places me on the back seat then moves around to the other door and joins me.

I look around the Bentley's interior, taking it in, remembering the last time I was in here. Jackson was driving. We were headed into a dark abyss.

I killed a man. I shot him in cold blood. It wasn't premeditated but I'd thought about it before it happened. I said it. I wanted revenge for my dad's death and for the little boy from my dreams. I never really thought I'd do it but I'd wanted him dead.

What's happened to me? Who is this person taking over my body? Where's Scarlett Heath gone? I want her back. I want to go back and find her and tell her to stay. Vomit rises to my throat but just as I think I might be sick, an arm wraps around my cold shoulder and pulls me into warmth. I don't want to think. I need to be numb. I need to clear my mind and not think about what I've become.

Gregory holds me tightly to him as we move through the empty streets of

London, passing only cabs and an occasional off-balance group of drunkenly happy, oblivious people.

'How's Jackson?' Gregory asks quietly, his hand hovering over my ear, shielding me like he thinks I could sleep.

I watch Kenneth through the rear-view mirror as he talks to his boss. 'He's all right. On crutches but discharged himself from hospital. He wants to talk to you.' Kenneth adjusts his position until he can meet my eyes in the mirror. Then he and Gregory exchange unspoken words.

I turn my head into Gregory's side and remember his wound when he winces. Another scar to add to the white gash that runs from his hip to the centre of his lower back and the cigarette burns on his wrist. We've known each other just over a month. Not long enough for him to tell me everything that haunts his sleep. Long enough for our relationship to witness two murders.

'I'm sorry,' I say, raising my head to see his face.

He tries to smile but it's a solemn turn of the lips. He kisses my brow and tugs me back into him.

'How are you fixed for the next few weeks, Ken? I'm going to need a driver until Jackson gets back on his feet.'

'Whatever you need, Mr Ryans.'

Gregory nods subtly. Kenneth is hired but this time, he won't be extra security to protect against the imminent threat of death. I take a tiny comfort from the fact that the little boy I see in my dreams, young Gregory, no longer has to think about that heinous bastard.

We roll up to the basement entrance door and Kenneth slowly moves the Bentley into the underground car park, tracing the journey we made just hours ago. Before the world rocked on its axis and came to rest in a new position. I don't realise I've stopped breathing until Gregory interlaces his fingers in mine and raises the back of my hand to his lips.

'Okay?'

I nod and will myself to smile for him but it doesn't come.

The Mercedes is gone, its usual bay empty. Gregory leaves me just a second whilst he gets out of the car. I need him back. I feel panic tightening my chest, making my heart pound until Kenneth opens my door and Gregory's there again. He holds out a hand and I slip my palm into his firm grip as my unsteady legs step out of the car. Trembling, I stand to face him. He strokes a loose tendril behind my ear.

'Let's go home,' he whispers.

He tugs me gently when I fall behind his stride, turning to watch the empty space the Mercedes has left behind. I close my eyes to see Jackson taking a gun from the glove compartment of the Bentley and Gregory leading me from the car, his body tense, his chiselled jaw set with anger. Now, as we follow Kenneth through the door to the lift vestibule, which still shows signs of tampering.

We ascend in silence. When the lift pings, Kenneth steps to one side to let Gregory lead me out but my legs won't move, remembering what happened the last time we stepped out of the lift on the sixty-fourth floor. I shake my head as Gregory attempts to nudge me forward.

'I can't,' I croak, suppressing the tears that are threatening again.

With two big strides, he moves in front of me, his tall frame sheltering me from the rest of the world. He lifts my chin until I can feel the caress of his breath on my lips. A silent tear slips from my eye when he presses his mouth to mine, trying to kiss away my fear. My arms rise to his shoulders; my fingers lock into his hair. I kiss him back, my tongue slipping into his mouth, trying to think of nothing but thoughts of him. When he pulls away, he rubs away my rogue tear with his thumb and slips his hand back into mine. Armed with the strength he's given me, I follow.

Kenneth holds open the door to the apartment. I want to close the door on reality and be immersed in nothing other than Gregory but we step inside to a lounge full of people, still dressed in their finery. Jackson stands, aided by a crutch under one arm and Sandy's shoulder under the other. Lara and Lawrence stand one after the other. Then Amanda and Williams.

I watch their faces blankly, not knowing how to face them: my childhood nanny and stand-in mum, Gregory's mum and stepdad, my best friend and Gregory's right-hand man. I'm not the Scarlett Heath they know any more. Gregory squeezes my hand but even that won't protect me from the harsh reality staring at me from six pairs of eyes. Lara raises a hand to her chest then, with a sob, makes her way to her son, engulfing him in her arms, weeping into his chest. Amanda raises the tips of her fingers to her lips, her glazed eyes watching me, waiting. I seek out Sandy but shame causes me to look away. As I do so, I find *that* spot. It's clean; the pool of Pearson's blood has disappeared already. The presence of bleach in the air hits me.

'What're you doing here?' Gregory asks Lara. He's hugging her but his words are curt.

'We came as soon as we could.'

'And the party? Do people know?'

'No. It ended as it should.'

I stare at the untarnished floor and the white-washed walls until I can see Pearson's face and the blood spilling from his broken skull. I snap my eyes to the vast skyline of London beyond the wall of windows, set in the darkness. The dark world of the city I've come to live in.

'If you want to keep this quiet, you need to call Sydney to manage the PR, just in case,' Lawrence is saying.

I turn on my stiletto heel and walk through the lounge to the staircase, leaving the room behind me but taking the memories with me.

'I can do that,' Williams offers.

Sickness turns in my stomach as I climb the stairs but this time, there's no Gregory to defeat it and when I reach the landing, I run along the corridor until I'm in the bathroom, retching to rid myself of every sinful thought I've had. My body heaves until I'm spent.

I crawl to the walk-in shower and sink back against the wall, my shoulders pressed to the cold tiles. Reaching an arm up, I turn the shower until hot spray is pouring over me. Pulling my knees into my chest I sit, alone and numb, until Gregory teases me away from the wall and slides behind me, his legs either side of mine. As the shower rains over him, streaks of crimson decorate the water. I watch the swirls darken in colour, the tarnished molecules fighting against the pure.

He holds my back to his warm chest, taking my weight as my body chugs beneath him, choking on soft, endless sobs. He presses his lips to my scalp and releases the catch of the diamond choker around my neck, relieving me of the sparkling stones.

'There's nothing to be afraid of any more,' he whispers into my ear.

He traces his lips along my collarbone, breathing soothingly on my skin. Whilst I'm wrapped in his hold, I believe him. I relax my head back to his shoulder and he twists my chin with his finger until I face him. Closing my eyes, I accept his kiss.

His eyes are still closed when I open mine.

'I could have lost you.'

'But you didn't,' he says, his South African accent strong and sultry through his husky throat.

I pull a hand back through his hair, refusing to tear myself away from the beauty of him. 'I love you so much, it hurts.'

His lips turn just enough that I almost catch a glimpse of the mesmerising half-smile that can melt me. Then he presses his lips firmly against mine and I kiss him back, desperately, roughly, pulling him to me. I'm panting when I eventually peel myself from him.

'Let me clean you,' he says, turning me away from him.

One by one, he removes the pins holding up my hair and releases each curl down my back, intermittently dropping kisses to my shoulders, my darkness lifting a little each time he touches me. When my hair is loose, he puts his hands beneath my arms and lifts me to stand. He unzips my gown and nudges my thighs, encouraging me to step out, then folds the dress in half and casts it to the sink. Two fingers hook into the sides of my French knickers and he slides them down my thighs to the ground.

'Move forward.'

I step under the fiercest part of the shower spray. He removes his shirt and presses his naked chest against my back then massages shampoo into my long, dark hair. I think of nothing but the feel of his fingers and the touch of his skin on mine.

'Turn.'

Facing him, I tilt my head back to let him rinse out the lather, stroking his fingers the full length of the strands. I watch him as he removes his trousers and tight, black boxers in one go, exposing his entire body. I swallow deeply as my gaze wanders the length of his torso to his crotch. He moves to squeeze a bottle of gel onto his palm.

'Lift,' he says, running a hand down my leg.

I raise my leg slightly as he moves the gel around my thigh, down to the tips of my toes, then repeats the same on the other side. He spreads the lather up to my abdomen, his hands drawing circles on my stomach, then he eyes me cautiously, his brows raised. When I nod my head, his hands move up to my breasts, slick and smooth across my skin. My breathing quickens as he cups my plump flesh and teases my hardening nipples. His hands caress my arms, one at a time until they move up my neck and rest on my cheeks, his mouth moving to mine again.

'Your turn,' I say, stepping aside so he switches places with me.

I move my hands across his back, appreciating the firmness of his muscles.

Then pull my fingers down his olive skin, avoiding the waterproof gauze covering his laceration, then slowing my pace to glide my fingertips gently across the scar on the base of his back. His shoulders rise on a deep inhale as I move my hands around his perfect arse and down his thighs. I don't need to tell him to turn; he does it of his own accord. He drinks me in through hooded eyes, his proud erection telling me he wants me every bit as much as I want him.

Stepping into him, I press my chest against his and revel in the feel of his thick length against my abdomen. 'Make me forget, Gregory. Make it all disappear.'

He dips his head a fraction then moves a hand down my body to pick up my thigh. I gasp. I need this. I need the feel and sight of him to replace everything I've seen and felt in the last few hours. He lifts me, my legs locking tightly around his lean waist. He presses me back against the cold tiles of the shower and lowers one leg so I stand on my tiptoes. Then he runs a hand up the side of my body, taking my arms above my head.

'Kiss me,' I beg.

He does. Slowly at first, then passionately, and I match his assault with every shred of emotion I can conjure.

'Please.'

He lifts me onto him, filling me. He holds us still for a moment, his eyes closing, his Adam's apple sliding up and down the taut skin of his throat. Then he draws back slowly and thrusts.

'Scarlett.' My name sounds coarse and indulgent all at once.

Emotions threaten to overwhelm me. I dig my nails angrily into his bare flesh. *I've killed a man.* I clamp my teeth down on his pectoral muscle as he draws out then rams into me again.

'Gregory, again. Harder.'

He pulls out to his tip then thrusts back into me hard, forcing me back against the tiles.

'More,' I beg. Whilst he's driving into me, I can't think.

He goes again, harder, faster, moving in and out of me exactly how I need him until I can feel my clit swelling, my muscles clenching.

My mouth takes his, tongues swirling, lapping as I build, losing my grip on everything except his touch, the feel of him right at the most sensitive spot inside me. My back arches and my swollen breasts press against him, the hard ends desperate to feel the rub of his firm chest. He pulls my lip through his teeth and I match his next drive, forcing him deeper, taking him to the end of me.

He barks my name as my orgasm takes over my body. On one last powerful blow, I feel the force of his warm release inside me and the sight of his strained neck as he throws back his head.

'Thank you,' I whisper, as he presses his lips to my temple and leans against me, the wall taking my weight.

3

'You know why I had to do it,' Gregory says through gritted teeth, as he and Jackson drink coffee at the breakfast bar.

'I know why you *think* you had to do it but I'll never understand it.'

'And I can't explain my need but I have to make this right in a way that means she can move on.'

My heart falls to the pit of my stomach at his words. I suspected I'd fallen too deep too quickly but I've never worried that he doesn't want to be with me. Until now. I pause on the stairs, not knowing whether to continue towards them or run back to the safety of Gregory's bedroom. The floor creaks beneath me as I turn on my bare feet and two sets of eyes regard me.

He knows I overheard, his expressionless face telling me he doesn't know what to do. With all the fake confidence I can muster, I descend the remaining stairs, tucking my shirt into my tapered trousers.

He watches me from his stool on the other side of the breakfast bar as I make my way towards them. He looks tired after a long night and only a few hours' sleep but no less perfect than usual, his tight, black T-shirt fitting exactly the contours of his toned body north of his dark, low-rise jeans. The casual version of the CEO.

'Coffee?'

'Please.'

Gregory pours me a drink from the filter machine of his pristine kitchen and quickly turns his wary eyes back to me like I'm cracked glass, ready to shatter at any moment. I take the cup between my hands and bring it to my nose, inhaling the rich scent. Both men regard me, neither speaking.

'Don't mind me,' I say, wanting them to pick up where they left off.

Looks are exchanged between the three of us but no words are spoken. I refuse to be first; I want to know what they're thinking.

After minutes of exasperating silence, Jackson speaks.

'Scarlett, we need to know what you said to the police.'

It's not what I was expecting. *They don't trust me.* I shake my head, a sharp shake that betrays my irritation – and take my coffee with me to stand in front of the panoramic view across London.

Bright November sun illuminates the skyline and beams down on the River Thames. South Bank is bustling with people enjoying their Sunday, strolling with hot drinks, sitting outside cafés, snapping pictures of London's Tower Bridge and generally going about their lives, as if last night, I didn't kill a man in cold blood.

I killed a man, yet it's Gregory whose suffering has only just begun. I can't let him take the blame. I won't. What if he's convicted? He could go to prison and all these years, all the years he's worked to be free from his father, would be for nothing. He'll be caged like an animal, all because his own blood cursed him the day he was born.

Fire burns in my eyes. I know what I have to do.

'I told them exactly what we agreed.'

I feel rather than hear the relief-filled sighs behind me.

'But,' I take a long, hot gulp of my coffee and brace myself, 'today, I'm going to DI Barnes and I'm telling him the truth.'

I turn to see Jackson off his stool, his body rigid with anger, his eyes crazed. 'You—'

'Jackson!' Gregory snaps. 'Calm down. Scarlett, come over here, please.' He's got his business face on and he's speaking with authority. This is the version of Gregory Ryans people don't refuse.

Jackson's temper doesn't wane. 'Calm down? Are you kidding me? The bobbies should've never been involved in the first place.'

Gregory slams the side of his fist on the breakfast bar, making me jump. 'Jackson, calm down or get out.' They glare at each other, tension palpable, until Jackson takes a seat.

'Then you talk some sense into her.'

'Don't talk about me like I'm not here,' I say more confidently than I feel and sliding onto the stool beside Gregory. 'I understand why you're annoyed, I really do. We had a deal and I'm breaking it but last night, I wasn't thinking straight and now I am.'

Jackson shakes his head.

'I did this. I killed him and I might be going to hell but I won't be dragging anyone down with me.' I drink down the rest of my hot coffee and straighten my back. 'I took the law into my own hands and I should be punished.'

Gregory puts a hand on my thigh and turns me on the stool to face him. 'Scarlett, you don't deserve to be punished for what you did. You saved my life. Do you understand that?' His brown eyes burn into mine. 'I wouldn't be here right now if you hadn't picked up that gun.'

I wince at the thought. 'Don't say that.'

'It's the truth. And I'll never be able to repay that debt to you.'

'Gregory, you don't owe me anything; you never will.'

He holds my gaze and lifts a hand to my cheek as if we're alone in the room. *How can he tell me to move on in one breath and treat me like I'm the centre of his universe in another?* 'I owe you my entire existence, Scarlett, in more ways than one.'

'And I won't let it be taken from you. Not now. Not after everything.' I bring his hand down to my lap, the breakfast bar shielding it from Jackson's view, and run my fingers over the scars on his wrist. 'You've fought long enough to be free.'

He turns his arm, concealing his scars, then pulls me towards him, nestling me between his thighs. 'You amaze me, Scarlett Heath,' he says, tucking my hair behind my ear. 'Everything I've put you through since we met.'

'And as ever, you're giving me whiplash, Gregory Ryans.'

'While I hate to be the one to spoil the party,' Jackson interrupts, 'this just can't happen.'

Gregory lets his shoulders sag. 'She knows that.'

'No. She doesn't,' I say, pulling away from him.

'What if you go to prison, Gregory? Have you thought about that? I would lose you and you might as well have died!'

Gregory jerks his head back, startled.

'I'm sorry, I... I don't even want to think, I can't even think about that. My point is, I couldn't stand to see you go to prison and more to the point, I won't let you to go to prison for something I've done.' The pressure behind my eyes is climbing again and tears are beginning to obscure my vision.

'Hey, come here.' His soft eyes have returned and he pulls me, leaving me no choice but to fall between his thighs again. 'I'm not going to prison. It was self-defence.'

'You don't know that. In the end, the CPS will prosecute. They can't let a gun murder slide in London. They'll pull your reputation to the ground. You could lose your companies. You could lose everything.' The tears come and fall like Niagara. 'I won't let you.'

'I'm not giving you a choice,' he says, wiping my cheeks with his thumbs. 'You haven't done anything wrong. You've done everything right.'

'It's not right.' *I saved you. You were my primary motivation in the moment. But what about the part of me that killed in the name of my dad and that little boy from my subconscious?* 'I need to be tried and if a jury thinks I did the right thing, they'll protect me, but that's not your job.'

'Damn it, Scarlett, no!' He darts up, forcing me to stagger backwards. 'I won't go to prison and this case won't even be tried.'

'But. You. Can't. Be. Sure,' I say angrily, tears still rolling down my face.

'Christ! Stop crying!' He's pissed. Every muscle in his body is tensed, the sinews of his neck are taut and his square jaw is set. He takes a deep breath and rubs a hand over his face. 'Please stop crying. Please. You're killing me.'

His browns soften when he lowers to my level. He takes my hands and puts them around his neck. 'I know that you want to do the right thing. I know that you feel like you've done the wrong thing but you haven't. I've shattered your world, Scarlett. *I* did this to *you*. I brought everything on you and you have to let me protect you now. Trust me. This won't go to trial. It'll be over soon.'

He leads me to the sofa and sits us both down so I'm resting in his lap. Jackson limps to join us and sits onto the coffee table in front of the sofa. 'Scarlett, this is a world you don't know and you don't understand. You need to trust Gregory and me, okay?'

For some unbeknown reason, I do trust them both, so I nod, but it's anything other than okay.

Jackson holds my attention and leans forward, resting his elbows on his knees. 'If you change your story now, I can't help us. You'll put us all in jeopardy and that's just one more charge we'd have to deal with.'

He's right. I couldn't see it before but he's right. If I go to DI Barnes now, I don't just confess that I did wrong; I tell him that Jackson and Gregory lied too.

I sniff back the last of my tears and climb off Gregory's lap. 'I get it.'

'Where're you going?' Gregory asks.

I wipe my cheeks and pull my shoulders back. 'I'm about to hire you the best goddamn KC I know. Get your cheque book ready.'

Gregory stands from the sofa. 'We discussed lawyers last night. Lawyers imply I have something to hide.'

'No, Gregory, lawyers bend the law and by fucking God do you need someone to bend the law right now.'

* * *

'Which one?' I ask, looking around the multitude of GR and GJR number plates in the basement. GR 1. GR 10. GJR 1. GJR 10. GJR 9.

'Lamborghini.' The lights flash on the bright-yellow car when Gregory presses a key in its direction.

I climb – or rather fall – inside and for the brief moment I'm afforded alone, I let my head roll back against the leather seat, trying to absorb everything that's passed in the last twenty-four hours but unable to shift my focus far from the words *she can move on.*

Gregory loosens the buttons of his navy trench coat and slips into the driver seat as if he isn't only inches from the ground. He eases the Lamborghini to motion and my eyes follow the movements of his hands as he sets the car into reverse and manoeuvres out of the car park with just one hand on the wheel. A small move that's irrationally sexy. We drive in painful silence for what feels like an eternity.

'I should probably go to see Sandy later,' I say.

He glances briefly at me before returning his focus to the road ahead. 'Not tonight.'

'I think I should see her sooner rather than later. I've got no idea how she'll react.'

The Lamborghini hurtles into a bus lane before the brakes are slammed, crashing me forward against my seat belt. Gregory's eyes are dark and bulging with fury. When he swallows, his tense jaw releases slightly. He's fighting against rage.

'You understand you can't tell Sandy the truth, don't you?'

I open my mouth but no words materialise.

'Scarlett, you can't tell anyone the truth.'

'But I tell Sandy everything.'

He breathes an exasperated sigh and his near-black irises recede back to brown. 'Everyone you tell is a risk. To us and to themselves.'

'Sandy would never say anything. She might hate me, probably will hate me, but she wouldn't say anything.'

His hand lifts to my cheek and I lean into him. 'Why on earth would she hate you?'

'She practically raised me, Gregory, and she didn't raise a killer.'

He snaps his hand away and throws his head back against his seat, almost inhaling the word, 'Fuck.'

I don't move, not knowing how to react. Then he flicks the car back into gear and swings us back onto the road, driving much faster than is safe or necessary.

'If you tell her, you put her in jeopardy and if you do that to her, you'll despise yourself for it.'

He reverses the car into a space on the road outside Lincoln's Inn, then kills the engine, but neither one of us moves.

'Are we still talking about Sandy?' I ask.

He leans back in his seat and turns his head to look at me. He's so astonishingly beautiful, it makes my stomach ache. Reaching down, he releases my seat belt, then his own. We literally climb out of the car and I move to his side, taking hold of his hand.

'Come here first,' I say, tugging gently, leading us into Lincoln's Inn Field, a small, green sanctuary in the heart of the city. We walk the gravel path, past couples strolling with dogs and resting on benches holding hot drinks to take the chill from their cold hands. 'I could never hate you or despise you and I need you to remember that, no matter what happens.'

Gregory stops us and tucks my hair behind my ear that way he does. 'I'm sorry for everything I've brought on you. I wish I'd killed him so you wouldn't have to keep overthinking this whole thing. I thought I'd killed him and that's how it should've been. I don't want to put you through this any more.'

I swear my heart stops beating in my chest. His words come back to me: *she can move on.* 'Do you want me to move out?'

He hesitates and scrunches his brow. I hold my breath to concentrate on not falling apart.

'Why would I want you to move out?'

'It was only ever temporary. You asked me to move in so you could protect me but that was before. Now there's nothing to protect me from.'

He grasps the sides of my face in his hands and shakes me gently. 'Do you remember what I said to you when I asked you to move in? I told you that I wanted to protect you.'

I nod.

'But I also told you that I never wanted to let you go in case you realised what I was and never came back. Part of me wishes you did want to move out, Scarlett, because getting away from me would be the best thing for you. My life, it's... I'm not the man you deserve. You should have someone who can give you everything you need, someone who can protect you and doesn't operate in the grey.'

I shake my head in his palms and close my eyes.

'I'll never ask you to go. I wish I had the strength to do what's right by you.' He bends slightly and presses his forehead against mine. 'But I just can't let you go.'

'I'll never be sorry I met you. And I'll never hate or despise you. The only thing that scares me is the lengths I'd go to keep you.'

'Jesus, Scarlett, if only you knew...'

'Shh, kiss me.'

His warm, sweet breath caresses my lips before he gives me want I want. He wraps his arms around me and pulls me into his chest. When he eventually frees me of his hold, I fumble with his checkered scarf, arranging it around his neck just so.

'Ready?' he asks.

'Yes.' I slide my hand back into his and we interlace our fingers. 'Gregory, when we meet KC Harrison, you can't tell him anything that he can't defend, okay?'

'You mean that my girlfriend's an assassin?'

As he does so frequently, he takes the air out of my lungs.

He cocks his head to one side and fights a coy smile. 'Too soon?'

'Girlfriend?'

He flashes the most dashing smile I've ever seen and continues his long strides towards Lincoln's Inn. I eventually find my legs and jog, a woman-in-heels-type jog, to catch him up.

'I'm serious. John Harrison's under a duty not to put himself in contempt of court so if you tell him something that would make him lie, he won't be able to defend you.'

* * *

The enormous, red-brick building is the epitome of elegance. Gregory holds open the hefty wood door and we make our way through the grand old corridors adorned with paintings of Lincoln's Inn alumni, judges and King's Counsel.

We follow the gold plaques for *Harrison Chambers* until we arrive at a door with a similar plaque reading *KC Harrison*. Gregory raps twice.

'Come in! Scarlett, nice to see you again.' John extends his hand. I've referred clients to him in the past, but never a boyfriend, funnily enough. 'I dare say it would have been preferable to meet under better circumstances.'

'Yes. John, this is Gregory Ryans.'

The men shake hands, one firm, solid movement. 'Thank you for seeing us on a Sunday, Mr Harrison,' Gregory says.

'Sadly, you can't elect on which day another chap might try to kill you, old boy, can you?' John flicks a hand to the two red, leather armchairs in front of his dark, wooden desk. 'Please do take a seat. You can call me John.'

John unbuttons his pinstripe suit jacket and wiggles the knot of his red tie, a movement that doesn't prevent his shirt collar from digging into the extra roll of skin beneath his chin – a mark of a sedentary profession. He settles back into his chair and rests his hands on top of his rounded belly.

Gregory removes his coat and scarf then straightens the arms of his jumper and crosses one ankle over his opposite thigh. 'Scarlett tells me you're the best, John. What does the best strategy look like for this case?'

'Oh, ho! Young man, I need to hear your tale first. I pride myself on my reputation and I did not create the stature I have by taking on cases I simply cannot win.'

Gregory grunts just loud enough for me to hear in the seat beside him.

'Righty-ho then, from the top, old boy.'

Through clenched teeth, I'm sure I hear Gregory whisper, 'You've got to be fucking kidding me.' But he starts his story. He talks John through the party at Lara's house, the ride home in the Bentley, the slashed tyres, the tampered lift door. He speaks of the lift as if there weren't six million emotions and thoughts circling his body. Then he speaks of Jackson, the shot, running upstairs for a gun. He skims over the tussle with Pearson and describes how he had no choice but to pick up the Glock and shoot him.

John 'ums' and 'ahs' as he listens to the story, not once making a note. When Gregory stops talking, he glances to me from the corner of his eye. I know he's checking that I've kept it together.

'To recap then.' John rolls his index finger across his top lip, then nips his chin between his middle finger and thumb as he speaks. 'You walk into the apartment. Your driver is shot. You tell Scarlett to look after him and, knowing that there is a violent man in the apartment who is most likely intent on killing you and who has already shot a man, you toddle off upstairs to collect a weapon and toddle back down, all the while leaving the attacker free to come after your girlfriend.'

Gregory turns his clenched fist in his other hand and clears his throat. This is going badly.

'He was very quick,' I jump in but I drop my focus to my feet when John glares at me.

'Righty-ho. Now, you have the gun and you go to chase down your attacker. You scuffle and he drops his gun. He injures you with glass from the broken mirror. You somehow fumble your way into the adjacent gym room and the next thing you know, there's a chain around your neck. What was this chain? Where did it come from?'

Gregory swallows slowly and finally unclenches his fist. 'It's a chain that connects a lat pulldown bar to a gym frame.'

'Jolly good. So there you are, a chain around your neck, bursting back into the lounge. You are struggling to breathe, you think you are going to die. Pray tell me where Scarlett and your driver were at this time? I can scarcely believe they stood by, watching you die.'

I stare at the nude patent leather of my shoes. I want to tell him. I want to tell John the truth. I want someone to know.

'Like I said, Jackson was injured. He was shot in the leg. And Scarlett...' He turns to look at me but I can't meet his eye. I don't want him to lie for me. 'Scarlett was taking care of him. She did the right thing to stay back; she could've been hurt otherwise.'

'Mmhmm. I see. Let us move on for now.'

'No,' Gregory snarls. 'Let's move on for good. We won't pursue that line of questioning again.'

John leans back, his leather chair gently rocking, and forms a steeple with the tips of his fingers.

'Let me tell you something, old boy. If, and I say *if*, I agree to defend you, I will be defending *you*. If you intend to hide something from me, if you try to protect another, I will struggle, despite my best efforts, to shield you from a murder charge. Do we understand each other?'

Gregory's chest rises and falls with his slow, shallow breath. He's controlled, measured. CEO mode is activated. 'Mr Harrison, allow me to tell *you* something. I killed a man because he was about to kill me. I killed a man in self-defence. If you can't prevent a charge on those grounds then you surely don't deserve the right to call yourself King's Counsel.'

The two men regard one another thoughtfully then John dips his head. The battle for alpha is over. 'Let us consider your *mens rea*: your state of mind or motive, if you will. The attacker, were you aware of who he was and why he might have wanted to harm you?'

Gregory sits taller in his chair and clenches a fist again, the white of his knuckles fighting to break the surface of his skin. 'His name was Kevin Pearson. He was my biological father.'

'Hmm, yes, you do tend to know the attacker. Not many people strike without cause. So tell me, he hated you because...?'

Gregory rolls his jaw left then right. 'I bought his company with the sole intention of selling it off.'

'A hostile takeover?'

'In more ways than one,' Gregory declares.

'Mmhmm, there we are then: we have your attacker's motive and what about yours? I presume the takeover was intended to punish your father. Give me the facts.'

Gregory bites down on his gums whilst my heart is shattering into a thousand pieces. I don't want him to go through this.

'He beat my mother,' he says, curt and matter-of-fact.

'Mmhmm, go on.'

'That's the story.'

'Give me the detail. The detail is where we hook the jury.'

'That's the story, Mr Harrison, and we'll leave it there. A jury will have to make a decision based on the facts of the night.'

'Young man, I am afraid it just does not work that way. Whether I draw it out of you or the prosecution drag it out of you, if you sit on that stand, your past will become your present and the jury will scrutinise every move you have made and every step you have taken for as many days as you have lived.'

Tears build in my eyes and a lump forms in my throat. I can't put him through that. He won't open up to me, let alone a room full of strangers.

'If the jury explores my past, it will realise that bastard beat my mother and killed... tried to kill me. He deserved to die. How can that go against me?'

'Because you have a motive to kill him,' I croak. 'He hurt you. He hurt someone you love and you wanted him dead. That's not self-defence, Gregory, that's premeditated killing, and a jury will think that should be prosecuted.'

I lock my eyes onto his, trying to make him see that I should be punished. I shot a man because he took my dad's life and turned a gun on the man I love. I killed with motive. Gregory holds my stare. He won't give me permission, not now, not yet.

'She is right, old boy; that is exactly what a jury will see. The fact you're a very wealthy man in a position of power will not lend you sympathy.'

Gregory speaks without taking his eyes from mine. 'Then you'd better make damn sure this case doesn't go to trial, Mr Harrison.'

'Well, let us discuss that. You have not been charged yet, I understand.'

'That's right.'

'That is a good sign. Let me tell you how this works. You see, the police investigate and the Crown Prosecution Service decides whether or not to charge and prosecute.' John rises from his chair and perambulates the chamber's perimeter. 'The decision to prosecute is based on two things.' He raises one finger in the air. 'The first is the evidential test. Remember the CPS is funded by public money, therefore it will only go ahead with a charge and prosecution where it is certain there is sufficient evidence to secure a conviction *and* that the person being charged is the true defendant.'

I shift awkwardly in my seat and feel heat prick my skin under Gregory's oppressive glower.

'Of course, one can have evidence enough to prosecute but believe that there is a true defence. In this case, that would be self-defence. And there you see we have a dilemma, to spend public money or not to spend public money; *that* is the question. If the CPS believes a defence is likely to succeed, it will not and should not waste the good man's taxes. Are you with me?'

Gregory nods once: a curt, businesslike dip of his head.

'The second test,' John begins, even more animated, lifting two fingers into the air, 'is the public interest test. Essentially, the question is, are you a danger to the public? I suspect you would say no. Of course, there is more threat to the public in the case of murder than in the case of petty theft, I am sure you will agree. But that is not to say the CPS will always prosecute a murder. They will think about the victim's family and the impact a decision not to prosecute may have on them.'

Gregory snorts.

'Yes, well, we might not have a problem there. Jolly good. One of the more likely ways to escape prosecution is a lack of evidence but of course you, Scarlett and your driver concur that you did in fact kill a man. And there is the matter of the weapon. The CPS will not look favourably on your weapon of choice.'

'Let's cut to the chase,' Gregory snaps. 'Can you stop this going to trial or not?'

'I do believe, old boy, until you are ready to share your past with me, your best odds are if the CPS chooses not to prosecute your case.'

'And the chances of that happening?'

'I would say sixty/forty on what I have learned today. Sixty/forty against you, that is.'

I close my eyes and will myself to be strong for Gregory.

'That said, often in cases of compelling evidence or where there is a threat to the public, the CPS would decide to charge immediately, which they have not. And, I am the best, old boy. And if there is a man who can prevent a prosecution, it *is* me.'

'How long before they make a decision?' I ask.

'Given they have not made the decision immediately, despite a confession, I would imagine they are waiting for a ballistics report to establish that you are the true defendant, and they may be exploring the strength of a self-defence argument. I can make a call on your behalf but I would hazard a guess at five to seven days for the ballistics report, give or take. If they explore the defence, they will almost certainly look to others in your life to question and establish motive. In this case, the longer it takes to hear from the CPS, the better, I think.'

Five to seven days. Then he could be hauled off in cuffs and tried for my crime.

'What if… what if it goes to trial and we lose?' I croak.

'Scarlett, stop it.'

'No, Gregory, you need to hear this. What's the worst-case scenario, John?'

'Life in prison.'

Despite already knowing the answer to my own question, I'm unable to prevent the erratic beat of my heart and the spinning in my head.

Gregory swallows so hard that I hear it. 'That won't happen. I won't let that happen. Scarlett, listen to me. Open your eyes. Open your eyes and look at me.'

I do as he asks, slowly peeling my eyelids up, my pupils on fire.

'That won't happen,' he says, taking my hand in his.

I nod twice. 'Excuse me, I need the ladies'.'

'Down the hall to the left, Scarlett,' John chirps.

I can feel Gregory watching me as I make to leave the room, nausea making my head spin.

'Now then, old boy, shall we talk figures? I charge by the hour.'

'Let's take 20 per cent off that, John, and call you my defence lawyer.'

'Ten.'

'Fifteen.'

'And I'll shake your hand there, Mr Ryans.'

At least that's something, I think as the door closes behind me; KC John Harrison, the crème de la crème, is willing to stake his reputation on Gregory and our lies.

When I return to the room, the two most important men in my life are standing face to face.

'I'm glad we understand each other,' Gregory says.

John dips his head then turns to me. 'Pleasure to see you again, Scarlett.'

'And you, John, thank you.'

We shake hands then Gregory's palm is on the small of my back, guiding me on a quick march back along the antique corridors to the Lamborghini. He opens the passenger door and closes it behind me once I'm seated. Then he climbs into the driver side, flicks the paddle gears and skids us out of the street at a dangerous speed.

He jabs his fingers at the touch screen in the centre of the dashboard and a dial-out tone fills the sound system, followed by Jackson's voice. 'Everything okay?'

'Are you home?' Gregory asks abruptly.

'On my way back from seeing Sandy; Ken picked me up.'

'We need to talk. I'll be ten.'

'See you then.'

I glance at Gregory's stern face and decide it would be best if I stay quiet. Instead, I watch as we fly through Camden Borough, buildings fading into blurred lines of lights against the already darkening afternoon sky, back to the Southside of the Thames.

Jackson is waiting on a stool at the breakfast bar when we get to the apartment. Gregory takes off his coat and scarf and throws them over the back of another stool. 'Let's go to my office.'

Jackson moves to stand and pushes an arm into his crutch.

'It's fine,' I say, trying to hide the fact that I feel like a patronised child. 'Stay here. I'm going to take a bath.'

I leave them to it, unsure how many more emotional missiles I can withstand in one day.

After squeezing way more bubbles than necessary into the bath, I dim the lights. When the water is almost at the brim, I sink myself under the thick clouds. Adopting the position my yoga teacher makes me take at the beginning of a class, I place my hands on my ribcage and concentrate on expanding my lungs to their full capacity on each inhale. I lie in that position until the water becomes tepid.

Five to seven days. One week, 168 hours, until the damning ballistics report will come.

4

The door to Gregory's apartment is ajar. I move in darkness from the lift, my fingers tightly wrapped around the Glock in my hands. My toes nudge the door, which creaks as it slowly swings open.

'I've been waiting for you.' The male voice is gravelly. I see only the crown of his head, sitting in the black leather chair in the lounge, watching the city below.

My hands are shaking but my legs carry me forward. 'You knew I was coming.'

He turns in the chair to face me, moonlight illuminating his sardonic grin. Kevin Pearson watches me as I move towards him, my gun raised and aimed directly at his skull.

'I've known you were coming since I killed your father.' He laughs, throwing his head back as the malicious sound growls out of his throat. 'Shame. He looked like he could've been a nice man.'

'He was a brilliant man,' I snarl through gritted teeth. 'Not even your life would make up for his. But that won't stop me from taking it.'

He rises from the chair and takes a step towards me. 'Ja, you think you're a strong girl when you're holding a gun. You're not, little girl. You're not.'

He moves a hand quickly behind his back and like lightning, he's aiming a gun at my chest. He clicks off the safety and I know I'm about to...

I jump bolt upright in bed, eyes flying open as I try desperately to fill my lungs. My heart beats hard against my palm on my chest and I pant as I gauge my surroundings and the safety of Gregory's bed. He sleeps, undisturbed by my nightmare.

The floor lighting illuminates my path as I tiptoe from the room and downstairs to the lounge. I open the fridge but instead, make a move for a decanter of Scotch on the bar table in the lounge.

Pouring myself a drink, I sip the burning liquid as my heart rate returns to normal. Then navigating Gregory's sound system, I turn down the volume and select Norah Jones. The warm, smooth sound carries through my mind as I look out over the city.

Would I have taken that shot regardless of whether Kevin Pearson pointed a gun at his son?

I wanted to kill him. I said as much the night of the funeral, right here in this apartment.

A firm palm presses against the small of my back, sending electric bolts through my veins. Gregory peels my fingers from the glass and places it down on the coffee table. Then he presses his chest against my shoulder blades and wraps his arms around my waist.

'I needed to hear some music,' I explain.

He brushes his lips against my collarbone, drawing a line of kisses up my neck. I expose my neck to him further and melt into his hold.

'I'm sorry,' he whispers.

Sorry that you came into my life? Sorry that my dad was murdered? Sorry that I killed a man? Or sorry that I fell in love with you?

'Do you want me to help you forget?'

I squeeze my eyes shut. None of it makes sense. My questions don't have answers but he's the missing link. He's the reason for everything. The only way I can connect the dots between my head and my heart.

I move one hand behind me to his thigh and the other round his neck, slipping my fingers into his hair. Then I turn to look into those mystifying, brown eyes before planting my lips on his. He slides his fingers over my silk nightdress, up the sides of my body, and lifts my arms above my head as he turns me to face him. He's naked but for his tight boxers and I indulge in the sight of him.

Our mouths meet, our tongues tracing each other's lips, tangling in hot wetness. I can already feel desire between my thighs, my body craving his touch, needing him to anchor me. He slides his hands down my nightgown then lifts me and carries me to the sofa. His eyes never leave mine as he lowers me down and nudges my thighs apart with his knees before crawling between them. He brushes his fingers from my chest down to the slit at the thigh of my nightdress. My hips rise towards him as he slides the dress up to my waist, then moves his body over mine until his breath is on my face and he's gazing into my eyes.

'Aurora,' he whispers. 'That's what you are. A mass of light drawn to the magnet of my dark world. Pure. Beautiful. Brave.'

He braces his weight on his forearms and strokes my hair away from my face then brings his mouth down to meet mine. My body dissolves into his and sheer pleasure takes over my mind. As long as I have Gregory, I can cope.

He slips a hand between my thighs, his fingers slick through my readiness. Satisfied, he raises his hips and slides into me in one slow, deliberate move.

A moment of true, honest, unadulterated ignorance of everything but the pleasure of him making me feel whole.

Whether he can say it or not. Whether he even realises it or not. Gregory James Ryans makes love to me the way every woman dreams of being made love to: slowly, savoured, cherished.

We pant through our shared climax then he rests his weight on my chest and nuzzles his head into my neck. 'Lift up,' he says, taking my hands and guiding me to stand.

I mumble as he peels his warmth away from my skin. He shuffles a faux fur cushion to the arm of the leather sofa and lies back, patting the space between his legs for me to fill.

When my back meets his chest, he nuzzles into my neck and whispers, 'Aurora.' His light. His freedom. I will be that again.

I'll be strong for him.

5

'Whoa, sorry! I didn't mean to disturb you.'

Jackson rouses me from the comfort of Gregory's tight embrace on the sofa as he stomps his crutch through the lounge. The sun hasn't yet come up.

'Don't worry, I haven't perfected my aim over distance,' I grumble.

I can't see the smirk on his face but I feel the chug of laughter in Gregory's chest. He squeezes his arms more tightly around me and kisses my temple. I could fool myself into thinking this is a normal day.

'*Pasop Boet*,' he says playfully.

'I'll look out, brother. Control your woman,' Jackson boyishly banters back.

Both men laugh when I sit up, pouting. 'Check the date, guys; misogyny is out.'

'Gym, kid. You don't get a day off just because my leg doesn't work. Let's go.'

Gregory pushes me up with his palms under my arms and places me on my feet. He trails a finger up my arm, leaving goosebumps in his wake, and turns on his knowing half-smile as he slides the rogue strap of my nightdress back up to my collarbone. 'Better.'

I can't resist smiling back at him.

'Aurora,' he whispers, before planting a kiss on my brow.

'Let's go! Let's go!' Jackson shouts, making his way to the gym.

'Ja, ja!' Gregory shouts back in reply, darting up the staircase, three steps per stride. I watch the gym door close behind Jackson and shudder. Out of Gregory's hold, the apartment feels dark and cold. Day two: one day closer to finding out whether Gregory will be charged.

As I fumble around, trying to fathom the coffee machine, a knock on the apartment door makes me jump. The lock clinks and the door begins to open.

I slide open a drawer and reach for the first knife I see, my knuckles white around the handle.

A middle-aged woman steps into the lounge wearing a silver bubble coat and carrying two large bags for life.

'Good morning!' Her voice almost sings from her petite body.

I loosen my grip on the knife and quickly push the drawer closed as she bumps the door shut with her hip, her mousey-blonde hair swinging from her high ponytail as she moves.

'Hi,' I manage, suddenly very aware of the inappropriateness of my skimpy nightdress.

'You must be Scarlett,' she says through a smile. 'Oh my, and as pretty as I imagined.'

My cheeks flush as I fold my arms around my body. 'Erm, thank you, ah... Amy?'

'Oh, silly me!' She lifts her bags with an *umph* and plants them on the granite worktop. 'Yes, I'm Amy. I cook, clean, whatever.' She waves a hand flippantly through the air.

She's Gregory's Sandy... kind of.

'It's nice to meet you,' I offer.

'Here, let me help you with that.' Like a pro who's very familiar with the kitchen, Amy opens the front of the coffee machine, takes small pouches of coffee from a cupboard, fills a jug with water which in turn fills the machine, then pushes a button, springing the filter process to life. 'How do you take it?'

'Just a drop of milk. I can do it,' I say, feeling completely inept.

Amy jumps into action, locating a mug and milk then pouring in coffee. 'Nonsense, that's why I'm here. Now, what would you like for breakfast?'

She takes two cartons of eggs and a huge pack of smoked salmon from one of her bags, then herbs and a fresh carton of milk and places everything in the fridge.

'Gregory likes eggs on a Monday once he's done with the gym and his run but I had a sneaky feeling he might have company for breakfast so I bought bacon, granola, yoghurt and fresh fruit. Oh, and bagels.'

Holding my coffee in two hands, I glance at the items on the bench and to the open fridge. 'I, erm—'

'Listen to me. When I talk too much, just say, "Amy, you're talking too much." You might not want breakfast yet. Do you get ready first? However which way is fine. You just tell me your routine and I'll work around you.' She stands in front of me, smiling expectantly.

'Okay. Coffee is good for now. I'll get dressed then maybe I'll eat with Gregory.'

'Oh, no, not on a Monday, he likes to get started early on a Monday.'

'Right. Okay. So maybe I'll have strawberries and yoghurt when I'm dressed, is that all right?'

Amy chuckles, a sweet sound that makes her nose scrunch and her cheeks widen. 'Yes, yes, yes. Off you pop. It'll be ready when you come back down. If you need anything doing, washing, whatever, just let me know. I'm here every day during the week and sometimes on a weekend if Gregory needs me.'

'How come we haven't met?'

'Well, I've had some time off. I was ready for a break and Gregory was keen for me to take some time off, too.'

He was keeping you safe.

'My kids had holidays from school. He's good like that, lets me have time off when I need it for the kids. Then any time I *have* been here, I'm told you've always been at work.'

'Sounds about right. Thanks for the coffee.'

* * *

Gregory holds his mug part way between the breakfast bar and his lips and stares at me as I make my way down the stairs towards him, my hair hanging across one shoulder as I fasten pearl earrings in place. He's already dressed in a navy suit with a white shirt and crisp, powder-blue tie, his hair damp with product. Casual weekend Gregory is hot but Gregory in a suit... I could take him right here and now.

'Scarlett, hop up here and get your breakfast,' Amy chimes.

I slip onto the stool beside Gregory, adjusting my black skirt to make sure the lace tops of my stockings are covered.

The ringtone of a mobile breaks the peace of the room.

'Ryans!'

I eat my strawberries whilst Gregory takes his call and I'm wrapping myself into my knee-length black coat when he returns.

'Are you sure you're ready for work?' he asks me, dropping his phone into his inside pocket.

'Yes. I'm fine.'

'By that, do you mean you're burying your head in the water?'

I laugh, genuinely, grateful for the short relief, and take a step towards him. 'I *think* you mean burying my head in the sand,' I say, cheekily biting my bottom lip. He moves closer to me until I'm wilting under his scrutiny and the feel of his breath on my skin.

'In South Africa, we might say putting your head in the Great White's jaws.'

'I'd love to.'

He turns his scowl into a beautiful smile, the kind my sexy CEO rarely shares. 'Let's go.'

'We're going together?' I ask.

He cocks his head to one side.

'I guess so,' I mumble, following him to the lift.

We walk out into the biting air, where Kenneth is waiting on the street in the Mercedes. Gregory glares at the driver window and I know he's thinking Jackson would be out of the car and holding the door open by now. Kenneth continues to tap his fingers on the steering wheel in time to whatever he's listening to inside and jumps when Gregory flings open the back door. Lucky for Kenneth, Gregory's phone is screaming for his attention again.

'Ryans!' he snaps into the handset whilst inclining his head to tell me to get into the car. Playful Gregory is lost to the white-collar world. 'Sydney, has Williams briefed you?'

Taking my seat next to him, I scroll through my own emails.

'Right. Yes. I know. Yes. I'll give you the rest when I get to the office. Twenty minutes. No, that's absolutely not acceptable. Sydney, calm down, you'll handle this in the same way you deal with all other PR, negative or otherwise. Okay, I'll have Anya clear my calendar for this morning; make sure you're in my office. My what? *The Times*? Okay, what time? My office? Well, can't they do it in my office? It's an interview; why does it matter where we are? Christ, what kind of photographs? Right, here's what you're going to do. Call them, tell them they come to me or we rearrange. The shots can be taken at my desk. It's not open for discussion.' He hangs up the phone and presses two buttons, then returns the phone to his ear. 'Four rings, Anya. Explain to me why you'd answer my call after four rings. Please tell me your job title. Mmhmm, personal assistant to whom? That's right, which means when I call, you stop talking to Melanie from IT and you answer the phone. Stop, I don't want to hear it. I need you to clear my diary this morning and my interview for *The Times Magazine* will be in my office this afternoon.' He hangs up again and repeats the same process of pressing two buttons and putting the phone to his ear. 'Two rings. Better.'

'Wow, taking no prisoners this morning are you, Mr Ryans?'

The look he casts in my direction tells me he's not in the mood to play. He rests his elbow on the window frame and holds his bent knuckles to his lips, looking out at the flurry of suits and briefcases we pass on the street.

'It's the glass high-rise building just there, Kenneth,' I say, pointing unhelp-fully out my window.

I rummage through my tote for my security pass and take two pound coins from my purse. It occurs to me that I don't know what to do next. *Do I just get out of the car? Do I lean in and give him a peck on the cheek? Do we kiss?* I've never driven to work with a man before, let alone a man who's also my client, and I've certainly never driven to work with a man as complex as Gregory Ryans.

The car stops and I decide that just climbing out and saying goodbye is perhaps the best approach. I open the door myself, Kenneth really not getting how this works, and shuffle my feet to the pavement.

'Where are you going?' Gregory asks.

'To work,' I say, twisting to look at him over my shoulder.

He leans his head to one side and raises a brow. 'Not without giving me a kiss you're not.'

I sigh as if to turn and kiss him is the biggest chore of my life but little men in my stomach are dancing in delight. Lifting my feet back into the car, I press my lips to his. 'Have a good day, Mr Ryans.'

'And you, Miss Heath.'

I'm still smiling when Kenneth pulls away from the kerbside and honks his horn as he weaves into rush-hour traffic.

'I sit every day just waiting for my chance and now you've found yourself a rich man. Tell me I can still hope?'

I smile at Paul sitting on the ground by the entrance to my office block, his plastic cup empty in front of him. He must be freezing. His sleeping bag is wrapped around him and only a piece of cardboard separates his body from the bitterly cold concrete. He's shivering but as charming as always.

I crouch in front of him. 'Did you manage to get a space to sleep last night?' I ask, placing my two pound coins into his cup.

He nods. 'Got a bed.'

'Did you indeed?'

'Sure did, I've been winking at my soup angel. She's falling for me, I know it. She keeps looking out for me.'

'So all that business about still hoping for a chance is rubbish; you've found yourself a soup angel?'

He chuckles, the kind that lifts his shaking shoulders. Though I'm smiling, my heart breaks for Paul, the young man with no home, no possessions and whose story I don't know but who can laugh and smile and be polite despite everything.

I open my bag, not at all worried that he might try anything funny because he never has, and hand him my wool gloves. 'Here, take these. I'm sorry about the bows.'

'I think they'll look good on me.' He smiles.

'Me too.'

He puts on the gloves without delay, wriggling his fingers to stretch the wool. 'Thanks, Scarlett.'

'You're welcome. Happy hunting.'

Making my way to the revolving office doors, I call back to him. 'Paul, hot drinks and food, okay?'

'Sure thing.'

In truth, I don't mind what he spends my two pounds on and I never do because the reality is, my two pounds can't buy him a home and if I was living on the cruel streets of London, I might spend my last penny on a drop of alcohol to numb the pain too.

As the lift doors open, Margaret walks past with a stack of ring binders and I fall into the same stride as her kitten heels.

'Good morning, Scarlett. Your latte is on your desk and I've sorted the paper mail. Only one letter you need to action. I've popped it in your top tray. Did you have a good weekend? How was the big party?'

I stop dead in my tracks, regretting that I haven't had the foresight to prepare a response to simple questions like this. Margaret looks back over her shoulder and I quicken my pace to catch up to her. 'It was fine, thank you. Did you have a nice weekend?'

'Nice but tiring. My daughter brought my grandson to visit and we had a pyjama party on Saturday night. He's a little bundle of treasure and terror all wrapped up in one three-year-old body. Before I forget, Neil Wallace has a brunch with a potential client at the Savoy this morning and he'd like you to go along if you're free.'

'Am I free?'

'You can be if I juggle your diary. You've got a call with the CEO of the Platinum Spring Hotel Group ten until eleven but I've checked your emails and it looks more like a catch-up call than an instruction, so I could bring it forward to nine thirty or bump it to tomorrow, then you could go to the brunch.'

'What time's the table at the Savoy?'

'Eleven.'

'Who booked my meeting with Richard Blakely: him or his PA?'

'His PA.'

'Okay, bump the meeting to tomorrow and let Neil know I can go to brunch, please. Do you know who he's entertaining?'

'I've already printed some information from their website and left it on your desk.'

'What would I do without you, Margaret? You're a star.'

She blushes and rolls her eyes. 'Oh and one more thing: an appointment just came through from Mr Ryans at GJR Enterprises. I haven't accepted it yet but it mentions an interview with *The Times Magazine* at GJR's office; does that ring any bells?'

'I'll deal with that one, thanks, Margaret.'

I take a seat at my desk, dump my laptop into its docking station and fire up my computer, then take a big gulp of latte. As I'm typing my username and password, Amanda struts into my office then plants her hands on the hips of her grey, tailored dress.

'What are you doing here?' She's whispering but her words are fiery.

'Happy Monday to you, too.'

'Scarlett, how aren't you completely freaking out right now? You can't be at work when, after, well, you *know*. I mean, holy shit, how are you?'

My best friend is upset and I know it's not just about me. Saturday was a shock for everyone and only now is it dawning on me that I've spent the last two days thinking about Gregory, Jackson and myself and not about the other people in my life.

'Come here,' I say, rising from my desk and holding out my arms.

Amanda walks straight into me and relaxes into my cuddle.

'Are you okay?'

She pulls back, shaking her head. 'You're asking me if *I'm* okay? Scarlett, babes, stop worrying about other people. Sit.'

Despite how irritating it's becoming to have everyone telling me what to do, I sit and Amanda plonks herself on the desk in front of me. She takes my hand in hers, bracing herself to tell me something I suspect she won't be able to take back.

'Whatever it is, Amanda, don't. Please.'

'No, I'm going to because if I don't, I'm not sure anyone else will.' She takes a deep breath and straightens her back. 'Gregory is bad news, Scarlett.'

'Amanda, I said don't.'

'No. I was never his biggest fan, you know that. He's miserable and arrogant but I could've gotten past that for you. Now, things are different. He's killed a man and—'

'Amanda, stop it.' My tone is low and surprisingly ominous.

'No!' She's standing now. 'You shouldn't be with someone like him. You're nice, you're perfect. You're the person everyone looks to when they need to know what's right and wrong. He's no good for you.'

I rise to confront her, matching her height in my heels. 'That's enough.' The venom in my voice is so unfamiliar, there could be a third person in the room.

'For Christ's sake, Scarlett, he's a murderer!'

My nostrils flare and my eyes feel like they're going to explode. My lungs stretch with each deep draw of breath. 'Get out before I say something I'll regret.'

She stares at me for two seconds more then turns on the pointed toes of her shoes and makes to leave the room.

'What would you have done?' I call after her. 'If you were him, in that room and that sick bastard was going to kill *you*, then *me*, what would you have done?'

She's thinking, turning my words through her mind. I know because she's motionless. I don't break the silence; I simply watch her until she leans her back against the door, facing me with her eyes closed. 'I wouldn't have let anything happen to you.'

My anger dissipates instantly as I move towards her, taking her hands in mine. 'He did what he had to do to protect himself and me.'

She slowly opens her eyes. 'But he put you in that situation in the first place and he still killed a man.'

'In self-defence.'

'It doesn't matter. How can you stay with him after that?'

'Because he did the right thing in the circumstances and one night doesn't define a person.' *God, I hope it doesn't.*

'He killed a man, Scarlett.'

'Amanda, I won't leave him over this and if you and I are going to be able to get past this, you need to never ask me to leave him again. I don't want to lose you either.'

'Please tell me this isn't about your dad.'

My heart nearly stops beating. *Does she know?*

'It's still so recent. I don't want you to think you need Gregory because you don't. You have me and you've got Sandy.'

I exhale slowly. 'I do need him, Amanda, but not because I feel alone.'

'But how, Scarlett? How? Why?'

'Because I love him. I'm in love with him.'

'Holy shit,' she whispers. 'Come here.' She pulls me into her body and gives me an Amanda bear hug. 'And he loves you?'

A light tap on the door breaks our hold and saves me from having to answer the question I wish I knew the answer to, the question I keep begging my subconscious not to ask.

'Come in,' I say.

A young boy in an ill-fitting suit and too-skinny tie, but with quite a handsome face, is looking at us nervously. 'Erm, I'm looking for Scarlett.'

'Yes, that's me. And you are?'

'Jonathan, Jon, Jonnie Pencey.'

'Which is it?' I ask as he thrusts his hand too anxiously, first to me, and then to Amanda. His hand is clammy and trembling.

'Erm, err, Jon, I think.'

Amanda sniggers and I glare at her.

'Sorry. I'm Jon, I'll start again. I'm the new trainee in the Corporate team.

I've been pulled out of my seat in the Banking team because Corporate needs more support. I was told to see you and help with whatever you need.'

'Right. Who sent you?'

'Neil Wallace.'

'Okay, well I've got a lot of work on so I could definitely use some support. Whose office will you be sharing?'

'Amanda Darling but I'm not sure who—'

'Me?' Amanda all but yells. 'Why do I have to have a trainee? Don't move your stuff in yet, Jonnie.'

With that, she turns on her heels again, and this time, she does storm out of my office.

'She'll come round,' I offer. 'I need to get sorted and I've got meetings most of today but get yourself set up and I'll come to see you with work.'

'Awesome. Thanks, Scarlett.'

Awesome? I walk around my desk and sit back into my office chair. Jon is still watching me when I raise my head from my computer screen to look at him seconds later. 'Was there anything else, Jon?'

'Ah, err, no, sorry.' His cheeks flush pink and he shakes his head before scurrying out of the office.

Finally, I skim the new emails in my inbox. There's one from Neil Wallace inviting me to brunch and separately explaining that there might be a potential sale of the Platinum Spring Hotel Group to a company based in Abu Dhabi but it's highly confidential at this stage. Margaret has sent me a calendar appointment for the meeting I've moved to tomorrow and Gregory's invitation to his interview with *The Times Magazine* is waiting for a reply.

To: Ryans, Gregory
From: Heath, Scarlett
Sent: Monday 9 Nov 2025 9:28
Subject: Re: Times Mag Interview (1pm)

Gregory,

Many thanks for the invitation to your interview today. Unfortunately, I have a brunch meeting which is likely to last until at least 1 p.m. Is this something in relation to which you need legal advice? If so, I could take a call before 11 a.m. to discuss.

Regards,
Scarlett Heath
Director
Saunders, Taylor and Chamberlain LLP

To: Heath, Scarlett
From: Ryans, Gregory
Sent: Monday 9 Nov 2025 9:29
Subject: Re: Times Mag Interview (1pm)

Scarlett,

Whilst it would of course be pleasant to have you watch me be interviewed by *The Times Magazine*, I have perhaps misled you with the subject of my invitation. There will be time during the interview and photographs this afternoon when I would like to discuss the potential joint venture with Shangzen Tek. It would be a helpful and efficient use of my time.

Regards,
Gregory Ryans
CEO
GJR Enterprises

To: Ryans, Gregory
From: Heath, Scarlett
Sent: Monday 9 Nov 2025 9:30
Subject: Re: Times Mag Interview (1pm)

Gregory,

I could be at your office as soon as possible after my brunch meeting but unfortunately, 1 p.m. may be a push. I could accommodate an alternative time this week to discuss the joint venture if that would be convenient? I have also noticed that your previous email was sent from GJR Enterprises. I had originally understood the Shangzen deal was to be executed through your company Eclectic Technologies. Please would you let me know the correct entity as I may need to run a new conflict search?

Many thanks,
Scarlett Heath

Director

Saunders, Taylor and Chamberlain LLP

I purposefully don't tell him that I'll be at the Savoy for my brunch meeting, knowing he's partial to gatecrashing my client meetings, or at least having Jackson stalk me on his behalf.

To: Heath, Scarlett
From: Ryans, Gregory
Sent: Monday 9 Nov 2025 9:30
Subject: Re: Times Mag Interview (1pm)

My apologies, Scarlett, the joint venture will be run through a new company (part of what I would like to discuss with you) but I will be completing the deal on behalf of GJR Enterprises.

    Regards,

    Gregory Ryans

    CEO

    GJR Enterprises

To: Heath, Scarlett
From: Ryans, Gregory
Sent: Monday 9 Nov 2025 9:31
Subject: iPhone

    Regards,

    Gregory Ryans

    CEO

    GJR Enterprises

When I take my iPhone from my tote, sure enough, there's a message waiting for attention.

> I've moved the interview to 3 p.m. I'd like you to come. We can go for dinner afterwards.

I quickly fire a message back. I want to be irritated with his demands and my own acquiescence but the thought of seeing him is making my stomach flutter. It's half-past nine and I miss him already.

> I'll come to the interview but only because you're paying me to.

> Are you quoting Pretty Woman to me?

I grin, remembering torturing him with his first ever showing of *Pretty Woman*. Mm, how I'd like to be curled into his chest with popcorn and ice cream instead of texting him from my desk.

> I'm impressed. One viewing and you know the words already. I usually do yoga on Mondays… for future reference… but I forgot my kit this morning. We have to talk about Shangzen, I can't just indulge your wealthy-man arrogance and not put time on my clock. Dinner would be nice.

Another beep makes me chuckle.

> You have a lot of attitude this morning.

I quickly message what I promise myself is my last text.

> You deserve it!

Then I rest my phone face down on my desk but I can't resist it for more than five seconds when another message comes through.

> Aurora.

I beam, no longer cross or even wanting to be. Then I open my Saunders app and call Amanda.

'You're so lazy!' she says as she answers, referring to the fact my office is about ten paces from hers.

'Yes, but I'm busy. I forgot my kit for yoga, I'm sorry. Can we go tomorrow?'

'Don't be sorry; I only go because you drag my arse. Tomorrow, never, whenever, fine.'

'Great, let's do the morning session.'

'Urgh,' comes through the line before the phone is slammed down.

* * *

Ten forty-five comes around too quickly. I wrap myself in my coat and gather what I need to meet with Gregory so I can go direct from the Savoy.

'Margaret, I'm going to the brunch meeting,' I call, hanging my head around the corner of my office to the secretaries' station.

As I'm walking along the corridor to leave, I hear Amanda gasp dramatically. When I dip into her office, she's sitting bolt upright in her desk chair. Jon, the new trainee, is staring at his feet.

'The skinny tie was bad enough but tan shoes with a grey suit?'

Jon looks like a child who just had his favourite toy snatched by a bully. 'Are they really that bad?'

He notes my presence and looks to me for support, I think, but the best I can do is wince.

Amanda pouts. 'What you wear is the first impression a client gets of you. Insta-judgment.'

'Maybe go with a different vibe tomorrow,' I offer. 'I'm off to a meeting. I won't be back this afternoon so I'll meet you at Iron Monger's Row in the morning, Amanda. Six thirty.'

'Urgh, fine. Fitness freak.'

Neil is already waiting in the executive chauffeur car when I make it out of the office. He's wearing a black, hard-hitting, pinstripe three-piece suit that tells me two things. First, the stakes are high. Second, he's going to flaunt his Head of Corporate title.

'Good morning, Neil,' I say, settling into the cold, black leather of the car.

'Scarlett, how are you?' He shifts his upper body to face me, his lanky legs trapped by the passenger seat in front of him.

'I'm well, thank you. And you?'

'Good, good. We're going to meet with Mr Ghurair. He's the CEO of his family's construction business. Extremely wealthy. His family owns the most profitable construction company in the UAE. Demand is high and they're taking advantage. They're looking to acquire in the UAE *and* they want to break into more western markets.'

'Are they big enough to float?' I ask, hoping for an initial public offering.

'Undoubtedly, but they tend to keep things in the family in the Middle East so I don't foresee an IPO any time soon.'

'That's a shame,' I say, genuinely disappointed.

'Right. Are you ready to bring your A-game, Scarlett?'

My brows rise unintentionally. *Neil Wallace is asking me if I have 'A-game'?*

'All right, all right, I'm just trying to be up with the kids and all that.'

I snort a too-loud laugh as Neil holds open the door to the kerb outside the Savoy. 'Down with the kids.'

'Pardon?'

'It's *down* with the kids, Neil.'

'Perhaps I'll keep my colloquials on the down-low over brunch.'

I laugh again. 'Colloquials? Down-low?'

'It's my son; I'm trying to fit in with him but I really haven't the slightest idea how to mesh with a teenager.'

'Neil, stick to archaic; it suits you.'

'Tell my son that.'

I stop laughing and replace my upturned lips with an expressionless line then straighten my coat.

'Ready?' Neil asks.

'Ready.'

The concierge dips his top hat as we approach the Savoy, one of London's oldest and finest hotels. We walk through grand mahogany doors onto a black-and-white tiled floor. The Savoy never fails to impress me with its sheer grandeur and elegance. A butler makes a beeline for us: grey, button-up coat, top hat, leather gloves and a regal accent.

'Can I help you with your files, madam?'

'Please. We have a brunch reservation but I'd like to leave these. They're confidential so I'll need to—'

'I understand entirely, madam. We'll store them in a locker for you and I'll bring the key to your table.'

'Wonderful, thank you.'

'And your coat?' he asks, taking the ring binders from my arms.

I unravel myself from my coat and place it across his free arm, then straighten my skirt and blazer as Neil hands over his knee-length, black coat and the red scarf that drapes loosely around his neck.

A second Savoy butler leads us to our table in the restaurant.

'Mr Ghurair, your guests.'

'Abdulla, it's an absolute pleasure to see you again.' Neil beams, offering a hand. 'This is Scarlett Heath, the colleague I mentioned to you.'

'Ah, yes, nice to meet you, Scarlett.'

'And you, Abdulla,' I say, shaking his hand. 'When did you arrive in London?'

'I arrived Saturday. I have a good friend who invites me to his football when I visit. He takes care of me.'

Abdulla remains straight-faced beneath his black moustache, despite his friendly tone.

'Shall we?' Neil says, gesturing with a hand for us to sit.

The waiter steps forward to pull out my chair but before he gets to it, I flash my eyes to his and subtly shake my head. He clasps his hands together at his lower back and takes a step away from the table as we sit. Then he moves to place our linen napkins across our laps, starting with Abdulla. I smile my thanks when I catch his eye. I appreciate being wined and dined and having doors held open for me as much as any woman but this isn't the kind of meeting to draw attention to my gender. We're presented with leather-cased brunch menus and remain silent for the short minute it takes for us to choose an order. I don't look for long, opting for the first brunch plate I like to prevent any unnecessary delay or show of indecisiveness.

'Madam, are you ready to order?' The waiter pulls a pad of paper from his black trousers and a pen from the pocket of his burgundy waistcoat.

'Yes. I'll have eggs Benedict on brown, a fresh orange and an Earl Grey tea, black with a slice of lemon. Thank you.'

He moves to Abdulla then Neil and takes our menus with him as he leaves us to talk.

'Abdulla, I was enlightening Scarlett as to the family business on our way here. She was very impressed, as I always am. I think I'm right in saying you're looking to acquire in the UAE and Europe?'

'Yes. Correct. Our focus is Middle East for now. We do not want to be the biggest construction firm in the UAE; we want to be *the* construction firm in the UAE.'

I mentally scoff at the thought of the fun competition authorities would have with an attitude like that in Europe. Neil shoots me a warning glance and visibly relaxes when he's confronted with my best fake smile.

Our drinks are placed around the table. Neil takes a sip of his black coffee after stirring in three brown sugar cubes – it must drink like tar – then gets back to business.

'So tell me, Abdulla, what are your immediate needs?'

Abdulla places his glass of sparkling water back on the table in front of him, then rests his elbows on the cotton cloth and interlocks his fingers.

'I have three companies that I would like to buy. Two are small family businesses that I know well. I can work with the owners. The third is a competitor. I do not like the family, I do not like what they stand for and I do not want them to have an... ah... *say* in how I run my business.'

'Then you either need to negotiate hard and get them out for as little as possible, or we need to think about differentiating the share classes, weakening their power to vote on matters of business,' I say, pausing for a drink of Earl Grey. 'Weakening their power might be enough of a deterrent and they might decide to walk away but failing that, at least you wouldn't relinquish control, as such.'

Abdulla nods but annoyingly looks to Neil for confirmation.

'She's right,' Neil says, although it does little to dampen my irritation.

Three waiters place our respective breakfasts in front of each of us in perfect unison and I tuck into my eggs Benedict, all the while counting to ten in my head. Neil clears his mouth of a forkful of smoked salmon before speaking again.

'We can talk about the detail of how you want to structure the acquisitions, Abdulla, but what sort of time frame are you working to? Three deals is a lot of work; of course, quite how much work depends on the size of company involved, the level of due diligence required and any unexpected issues that crop up.'

'Yes. I recognise that. You are here because I am told good things about your firm, Neil, and I like you, but this is your opportunity to tell me you can meet my needs. If you cannot, another firm will get my business.'

'Of course.'

'I would like to complete at least one deal by end of year.'

I almost choke on my mouthful of English muffin. My eyes flick to Neil's over my glass as I soothe my throat with cool orange juice.

Neil's face is firmly schooled into a poker expression. 'Calendar year end or tax year end?'

'Calendar. The other two by tax year end.'

It's no good; orange won't stop me from choking this time. I can feel Neil's eyes burning into me as I cough into my napkin. There's no way we can commit to that, at least not without more detail.

'We can do it,' Neil blurts. 'It'll take a lot of resource but that's the benefit of a firm of our size and stature; we have resource in abundance.'

No we don't! We're already snowed!

'Yes. I understand that my needs will not be cheap but I think we can come to an arrangement.'

'What did you have in mind?' Neil asks.

'I would like to have someone in control from Dubai... on the ground, I think is how you say. I would like a link between someone in my company and your team in London.'

Neil draws back from his breakfast. He places his knife and fork down and leans back into his chair thoughtfully. 'You want a secondee?'

'Yes.'

'Full-time, in Dubai?'

'Yes.'

I'm holding a forkful of egg midway between my plate and my mouth when I feel two sets of eyes blazing into me.

'Me?' I ask.

'You'd be a perfect fit,' Neil says, his eyes asking me whether I'll do it.

'It would be a good opportunity,' Abdulla adds. 'And in Dubai, the sun always shines.'

I can't deny, it would be a fantastic opportunity. The wealthiest construction company in the UAE. Three more deals likely to follow. It's a huge opportunity.

'How long?' I ask.

Abdulla purses his lips and wobbles his head from side to side. 'We need to discuss money but I think six months. I would like someone in Dubai for deal one in December, then to stay on for the others. They complete in February and March then tidy up. Yes, six months, or bigger, more.'

Six months. Dubai. A massive CV builder. I could be giddy if I let myself. *But what about Gregory?* Leave him for six months, maybe longer. A court case for something I did. My dad's house to sell. Making sure Sandy is okay.

'Why don't you send me some details of the companies, Abdulla, then I can make a better assessment of fees and ways of helping you to meet your time frames? We can have a call to discuss or I can come out to Dubai for another meeting.'

'Yes. I agree. I would like to have a plan in place by month end. If not, I go elsewhere.'

'I understand completely.'

I'm grateful for Neil taking control as my head feels like it might explode. I really can't take any more issues, messes, questions, things to think about. A dull ache builds at the base of my skull. *Can I really pass up an opportunity like this for a man I've known a matter of weeks?* A man who I'm completely and utterly besotted with but who I really don't know is committed to me. A man who right now could be with me through a sense of obligation alone. But the way he looks at me, the way he touches me. He calls me his light. *How can I doubt that he wants to be with me?* Then again, why would he want to be with plain, ordinary Scarlett Heath?

'Madam? Are you finished?'

I straighten my knife and fork to six o'clock on my half-eaten plate of food. 'Yes, thank you.'

'We'll take the bill, please,' Neil says, nodding to the waiter hovering by our table. 'This is on us, Abdulla.'

'Thank you, sir. It sounds like we have a way to move forward,' he says, rising from his seat, holding out a hand, first to Neil and then to me. 'Three weeks. No more.'

I have no idea how much of the conversation I missed, lost in thought. 'It was a pleasure to meet you, Abdulla.'

'And you, Scarlett. I will hopefully see you in Dubai soon.'

'You may well,' I say, feigning confidence in my words.

We watch Abdulla climb into the back of a limousine, then a Savoy butler whistles through his fingers for the next cab in line.

'Actually, Neil, I'm going to stay here and work for an hour. I have another meeting not far away.'

'Okay, well, give some thought to Dubai and we can discuss it further once Abdulla has given me a more detailed scope of work. You know, Scarlett, it would be a good experience for you and great for you to get so close to a new client. It wouldn't hurt your chances of partnership one day to build a relationship like that. And I don't mean to speak out of turn but with what you've been through recently, losing your father, it might be a good time to take a break from London too. I'll leave it with you for now. Think about it.'

'I will,' I say, knowing too well that he'll expect me to go.

Once the car has pulled away from the hotel, I wander back into the bar and nurse a latte for fifty minutes, neither drinking the coffee nor doing any work until Apple's standard ringtone chimes through my iPhone.

'Sandy. I've been meaning to call.'

'But you haven't,' she snaps. 'How are you? I've been worried sick.'

I sigh. Sandy's been more of a mother to me than my own mum ever was. She stayed for more than five years of my life, for a start, and when the going got tough, in my dad's worst days of Alzheimer's, she stuck with us and nursed my dad so I could keep my career, keep making him proud. Neither of them would be proud of me now, not if they knew what I'm capable of.

'I'm sorry. I just didn't know what to say.'

'Girly, I ought to slap your backside. Your dad would kill me for not looking after you properly.'

I smile. 'He really wouldn't.'

'No. He wouldn't. But I ought to look after you better.'

'How are things at Lara's? Do you like the new job?' It's still strange to me that Sandy now keeps house for Gregory's mother.

'Demanding. We're still cleaning up after the party. Stop changing the subject. How are you? I mean *really*, not what you're feeding other people. Tell me the truth.'

'Shit.' The word leaves my mouth without any real intent or conviction.

'Watch that potty mouth!'

'Sorry,' I mutter. 'So Jackson told you what happened, how it happened?' It's also odd to me that Sandy is striking up a relationship with Jackson. And terrifying that, on some level, Gregory's dark web has caught her too.

'Yes, he told me.'

I hold my breath and nervously wait for seconds that feel like an eternity. 'Say something, Sandy, please.'

An enormous exhale comes down the line. 'Genesis 9:6. "Whoever sheds man's blood, by man shall his blood be shed."'

I've no idea whether that's acceptance or confirmation that I'm damned but that's not what's playing on my mind. 'Sandy, please don't hate Gregory. I can stand other people having an opinion of him but not you.'

'Sweets, hate Gregory? I'm saying in his shoes, in the circumstances, knowing everything he knew about his father, what he did, who he was, I can only hope I'd have the strength to do what he did.'

Relief overwhelms me and fills my eyes with tears I can't hold back. I dip my head, aware of my surroundings, and rub my eyes with the back of my hand, conscious that I don't want to smudge black into my cheeks. 'Thank you,' I sniff.

'Scarlett, please don't cry. I want to give you a big, fat Sandy snuggle.'

Sniffing a laugh, I try to compose myself, feeling like everyone in the bar is watching me unravel over my now cold cup of coffee. *Christ, I never used to cry.* 'I've been asked to go to Dubai with work,' I blurt, desperate to change the subject and my melancholy thoughts but actually introducing only my latest dilemma to the forefront of my mind.

'Dubai?' It's more exclamation than question.

'It's for a big client and it could be a good opportunity but... I don't know... I don't think I can go.'

'When?'

'I'd need to leave in December.'

'For how long?'

'Six months, maybe longer.'

'Oh.'

'Yes, oh. The timing couldn't really be worse, what with, well, you know. And then there's Dad and the house to sort out, and... I don't know.'

'And you don't want to leave Gregory?'

I groan, frustrated and increasingly aware that the ache at the back of my head is turning into a throb. 'Let's not talk about it now. I've got to go, Sandy, but I'll call you later in the week.'

'All right, sweets. You call me whenever you need to or want to and if you don't want to in the next forty-eight hours, you'd better call me just because.'

I imagine her fake angry face and wagging finger, the same wagging finger she would shake at me when I was seven years old.

'Okay. I love you.'

'Love you too, sweets. Keep safe and tell that man of yours thank you from me. If anything had happened to you—'

'It didn't. I love you. Speak soon.'

6

The lift doors open to the gold GJR Enterprises wall plaque. The usually quiet floor of Gregory's office block feels occupied. Two men holding what look like camera accessories, both dressed in khaki combat trousers and black T-shirts, are hovering in the glass-lined corridor.

'Mr Ryans's office is just this way.'

I follow Sue, a new receptionist of Gregory's. Her brown bob bounces as she totters along the corridor in kitten heels.

'Yes, I know, thank you,' I say with a smile.

'Oh, of course, you said you've been before,' she says on a nervous giggle, sliding her square-framed glasses back to the bridge of her nose. 'It's my first day and my last job wasn't half as corporate as this. I've been up and down to Mr Ryans's office all morning, helping out the staff from *The Times* – photographers, camera men. Gosh, he makes me so... so... flustered; I'm not used to him yet. The other girls warned me but...' She shrugs and casually wafts a hand by her flushed cheeks.

'The other girls warned you about what?'

'Well, you've seen him,' she says, her hair bouncing in all directions. 'He's so... so... hmm, I need to learn to cope with it, like the girls said. He's my boss, after all. He just looks so... so... oh Lord, I'm being unprofessional again. I won't even last until day two at this rate.' She snaps her head around to face me and stands still on the spot, almost causing me to walk right into her. 'You won't tell him, will you?'

If my head wasn't banging like I've just fallen down a set of concrete steps, I might be narked at Sue's obvious crush but I'm not that primitive or possessive. Instead, I feel empathy for the state of frenzy she's worked herself into.

'Tell him what?' I ask, attempting a reassuring smile.

'Thank you. It's this one,' she says, gesturing to Gregory's open office door.

Gregory's positioned at his desk, the foot of one leg crossed over the thigh of his other and his interlaced, manicured fingers held in front of him at his waist. Cameras, umbrellas and screens cast a purposeful soft light across his olive skin. My feet forget how to walk and I stand, gormlessly, gripping the sides of my ring binder files to make sure they don't fall to the floor with my jaw. One day, I might get used to this man enough to not be blown away by the sight of him but right now, blown away is exactly how I'm feeling.

'Miss Heath, good afternoon.' The tall, flawless blonde I'm used to seeing behind the reception desk at Eclectic Technologies in her figure-enhancing pencil skirts whispers a greeting. 'You can take a seat on the sofa over there. Mr Ryans is expecting you. They'll be taking a break shortly.'

'Thanks.' I tiptoe to the leather sofa and place my files down on the glass table to the side as quietly as I can. I undo my coat and rest it over the back of the sofa then take a seat and watch as Gregory replies to another question from a man whom I assume is a reporter for *The Times Magazine*.

As if he feels my eyes burning into him, he shifts a little in his chair and finds me. His straight lips turn ever so slightly up, then he winks in a way that's most unlike the CEO Gregory. Despite myself and despite my usual ability to remain at least outwardly professional, I beam back at him, quickly biting my lip in an attempt to rein it in. Too late. Every pair of eyes in the room just landed on me until the interviewer continues.

'So, Gregory, the youngest technology billionaire in the United Kingdom. To what do you owe your success?'

Gregory straightens the arms of his blazer, pulling the cuffs of his shirt just slightly in front of the hem of his jacket. It's a move that's terribly him.

'Many things. Hard work, ambition but more than anything, in such a fast-paced environment, it's important to make your sector your life. I live and breathe technology markets around the globe. I know what exists, what doesn't exist and what ought to exist. I understand what businesses and consumers need.'

God, I've missed him. My watch tells me it's half-past three. Seven hours I've been away from him and I'm desperate to run to him and fold myself onto his lap.

This can't be normal. There's no way I could stand to be away from him for six months. *When did this happen to me? When did I become reliant on a man?* For years, I've thought of nothing but work and my dad and now one man has derailed everything I know in a matter of weeks. *My dad.* I lean forward on my forearms and drop my head into my hands, massaging my temples with my index fingers as images haunt me. My dad, pushed down the stairs, frail, bandaged and strapped to machines, fighting for his life from a hospital bed. Alone when Kevin Pearson came back to finish what he started and pull the plug. The image of Gregory as a boy, sobbing as he watched his mother being battered half to death. Gregory just two nights ago, struggling beneath the chain wrapped around his neck – the mark still visible above his collar to those in the know. Eight hours, six months in Dubai. Either would be nothing compared to Gregory serving a life sentence.

Abdulla wants a decision in three weeks. In less time than that, the CPS will make an even bigger decision.

'Are you unwell?' Gregory is on his hunkers in front of me, gently prising my hands away from my temples.

Oh God. Every person in the room watches as I stare at my beautiful CEO. The curt manner he reserves for work is gone and it's just Gregory, *my* Gregory, his face drenched in concern.

'I'm fine,' I whisper. 'I just have a headache.'

He silently questions me, his focus falling to my lips. Knowing I can't, won't, kiss my client in a room full of cameras and a reporter, I pinch my eyes shut and when I open them, his expression is replaced with one of professionalism.

'Francesca, please get Miss Heath some painkillers and a glass of water.'

The receptionist snaps into action but Gregory remains focussed on me.

'Would you like to postpone our meeting?'

'No. I'm fine. Sorry, it's been a long day.'

'Let's see if I can make you feel better tonight,' he whispers so only I can hear, then stands, straightens his jacket and fastens one button in the middle as he walks back to his desk. 'Let's draw this interview to a close,' he says, taking a seat and returning to his cross-legged position.

'Well, I was about to move on to your status as one of the world's most eligible bachelors but—'

'I don't think that would be appropriate. This is an article about business. My personal life isn't the concern of the readership.'

'Err, erm, right. No, of course not.'

'Do you have another question, or are we done here?'

His tone is so abrupt, I actually feel for the reporter. The rare flash of relaxed Gregory is replaced with the brusque white-collar mogul.

My headache wanes under the influence of paracetamol, not in the least bit aided by the flashing bulbs of cameras as Gregory is set in poses at his desk and in the window.

'Can we try that with a smile?' a cameraman asks.

Gregory cocks his head to one side and arches a brow.

'I'll take that as a no.'

'Do so,' Gregory says, brushing one side of his blazer, which I'm almost certain is purely for effect.

Another series of flashes illuminates the room before Gregory announces, 'We're done. Help yourselves to food and drinks, gentlemen. I have another appointment.'

* * *

'How did your meeting about handling PR go with Sydney this morning?' I ask when we're tucked in the sanctity of one of the meeting rooms.

Gregory crouches down in front of my oversized leather chair, turning me away from the large glass table to face him. He runs his fingers down the side of my cheek then drops his forehead onto mine.

'Kiss me,' I whisper.

He presses his lips to mine and I hum, breathing him in. He nips my bottom lip between his teeth and slowly opens his hooded eyes.

'I've been desperate to do that since I left you this morning.'

'Why didn't you say you aren't a bachelor?' The words leave my mouth before my brain has even processed them.

Gregory pulls his head back, his face still level with mine. 'Like I said, it's not their business.'

'But... do you...'

'Do I consider myself a bachelor?'

I shrug, feeling emotionally juvenile but still wanting the answer.

'No.' His tone is matter-of-fact but I'll take it.

I try not to smile but I'm not convinced my attempt is successful.

'Now, shall we get on with this meeting? I was told this morning in no uncertain terms that we absolutely *must* discuss Shangzen Tek.' He steps back against the table and folds his arms across his chest as he presses those perfectly pert arse cheeks onto the edge.

Clearing my throat, I take a notebook from the front of my document folder, keeping my eyes down to lessen the distraction. 'You mentioned a new company.'

'Yes. I'd like to structure the joint venture through a new subsidiary of GJR Enterprises.'

'Have you already agreed the approach with Mr Cheung?'

'I wanted to discuss the feasibility with you first. I want to fully understand the tax implications and how the ownership of the products we develop would work. If this idea comes off, it could provide the software necessary to significantly increase the flight speed of a drone, something that could be very valuable to businesses using drones commercially.'

We're both fully in professional mode. He moves to take a seat on the opposite side of the table from me.

'I assume you're aware that there're fairly tight limitations on the use of commercial drones?'

'Yes, but hurdles can always be navigated. In fact, my thoughts are that the software would probably be seen as more desirable once companies have had an opportunity to explore some of the development areas of the drone.'

I nod, making notes. 'And you understand things are a little trickier in other jurisdictions? The US is particularly unfavourable as things stand.'

'Yes. We're also looking into how we could make the drone safer and more visible. Or at least the new company will. There are always hurdles to surmount where something is innovative.'

'Okay. Well I can come up with a briefing paper for you, specifically covering tax and intellectual property. If you think of any other areas you'd like me to explore in more detail, let me know, otherwise I'll give an overview of the pertinent points.'

'Excellent.'

'When do you need it?'

'Tomorrow would be ideal. Wednesday morning at the latest.'

Picking my head up from my notepad, I try to remind myself he's a client but I can't help my eyes from rolling. *Does he really think I have no other work to do besides his?*

'I'm not trying to be difficult,' he says, reading my mind. 'I'm flying out to Hong Kong early Wednesday morning to discuss the deal with Shangzen. I'd like to have had the opportunity to digest the paper before my meeting with Mr Cheung and his board.'

'I didn't realise you were planning to go away.'

'Scarlett, you know I work away a lot. I thought you understood that?'

'I know. I do. I just thought, what with things the way they are at the moment.'

He leans forward on the table towards me. 'Are you uncomfortable in the apartment without me?'

I hadn't even thought of being alone in the Shard. 'I don't know. I haven't been there alone since—'

'Jackson will be there. I could ask him to stay in a bedroom closer to ours if that would make you more comfortable.'

'That would make me much *less* comfortable.'

'I can't understand why,' he says, his lips slightly upturning.

I squirm a little in my seat, not knowing quite how to phrase my next question. 'Are you actually allowed to leave the country?'

Gregory sits back sharply. 'I've not been charged.' The mood in the room instantly changes and I wish I'd never said anything.

'I could come with you, you know, if you need legal support?' I hate how unbelievably needy I sound.

There's a shimmer of amusement in his eyes. 'I'll only be gone a couple of days. I'll be back by the weekend. We have plans.'

'We do?'

'Yes. It's Opening Meet of the season on Saturday. I thought you'd come with me.'

'Opening Meet?'

'Fox hunting.'

'Like the fox hunting that's banned?'

'Hmm, not exactly. There're rules around leaving fake scent, rather than chasing real foxes, but people still hunt.'

'So you ride horses?'

'I ride *a* horse. Yes.'

My mind floods with images of Mr Darcy and white knights, except it's Gregory's toned pecs beneath the see-through, wet shirt.

'You'll come.'

I bite my gums. 'That's not a question.'

'You're very observant, Miss Heath. You'll need a dinner dress and some country clothes.'

'Country clothes?'

'Yes. I've already arranged for you to see Julia on Thursday evening. She'll find you something appropriate.'

I sigh, more huffily than I really intend. 'I can pick my own clothes, Gregory, and I don't need your Harrods stylist to force unnecessarily expensive brands on me.'

'Fine.'

'Fine?' *Surely I didn't just get my own way.*

'I'll make sure she doesn't tell you the price or brand name of any item.' There's an unmistakeable and frankly irritating arrogance about him.

'I have clothes. You can't buy me something new every time we go out together.'

'Why not?'

Urgh! 'You infuriate me.'

'And your attempt at defiance rather infuriates me,' he muses, forming a steeple with his fingers. 'In fact, I think I ought to take you home right now and teach you a lesson.'

My eyes blink in shock but my heart rate increases at the thought of him spanking me. The feeling of sinful pleasure that only Gregory has ever shown me. 'I can't finish for the day; I have work to do and chargeable hours targets to meet.'

The roll of his jaw tells me he's as tightly wound as I am.

'I wonder if you'll ever do as I ask without pushing all my buttons first.'

'Unlikely.' I close my notebook. 'Unless you give me an incentive.'

'What happens if I do?'

My thighs pulse in response to him. I glance down, expecting to see the throbbing of blood pumping to my sex. My nipples harden against the lace of my bra.

A low, rumbling growl leaves his chest. 'Fuck your targets.' He charges towards me and attacks my mouth with his, pulling me up to stand.

My notebook falls to the floor as I dig my fingers into his thick, dark hair, yanking hard. Frustrated with myself for being so easy to give in to him. Angry that there's so much going on in my head, I can't think straight. Pissed that I'm trapped in a situation and the only way I can think to fix it is to tell the truth but I'm being stopped from doing so.

'Home. Now.'

With one hard grind of his hips against mine, I'm groaning agreement into his mouth and desperate for him to fuck me. Hard. Rough. Ferocious. The way I'm feeling.

'Not here,' he says, although his length pressed up against me tells me he's as ready as I am.

He separates us, leaving me pining and furious. He retrieves my notebook from the floor and watches me pack away my files as he taps his phone screen and holds it to his ear. 'We're ready now,' he snaps.

His eyes are darker than ever.

We leave the meeting room feigning good ethics, walking side by side but not so close that passing staff would suspect our relationship is anything other than CEO and legal advisor. Kenneth opens the rear door of the Mercedes and I crawl inside. Gregory slips into the other side and pins Kenneth through the rear-view mirror until he rolls up the partition between the front and back of the car. It's a look that tells me I'm not alone in needing to vent what's pent-up inside.

'I never thought I'd actually *need* Jackson to come back,' Gregory says.

'How's Kenneth supposed to know your demanding ways after a few days?'

He turns his head on his headrest to face me as the car is maneuvered into traffic. 'My demanding ways?'

I move across the seat, hitching my skirt to straddle his hips, pinning his shoulders to the leather. 'Your isms,' I say, biting his lobe. 'Your quirks.' I dig my teeth into his neck. 'Your obsessive ways.'

He pulls my chin and holds it where my eyes are level with his, his grip too tight. 'There's only one thing I'm obsessed with right now.' He kisses me chastely and pulls the back of my thighs, pressing me tighter to him, letting me feel him grow beneath me. 'You have no idea what you do to me. I can't stand seeing you like I did today. Knowing what I've brought on you. I need you to talk to me and *listen* to me.'

'You've got to stop seeing this as your problem, Gregory. It's *our* problem. And I do listen to you. We're doing all of this your way, not mine.'

He drags his fingers through my hair. 'You shouldn't have gone to work today.'

If I hadn't, I wouldn't have introduced Dubai, yet another dilemma, to my presently screwed-up life. 'What do you want me to do? Let Pearson ruin another life? He's already doing a good enough job as it is without me losing my career too.'

'Don't say that, Scarlett. I won't let him taint you. I won't let my past spoil who you are.'

'He murdered my dad, and I killed him for it. I'd say I'm already spoiled.'

He tugs harder on my hair and bites down on my lip, hurting me in a way I want. 'No,' he growls into my mouth.

My legs part further, drawing me down onto his crotch.

'Keep talking to me, baby, please. I need to know how you're feeling. I need you to be okay. I have to protect you.'

I roll my pelvis against him, desperate to feel him, for us to connect in a way that lets me know he wants me. 'Why? Why do you need to protect me?' *Tell me. Please. Say those three words.*

The Mercedes jerks to a stop and Kenneth drops us at the front entrance to the Shard. The interruption fuels the raging fire inside me. Gregory tells Kenneth to take my files to the apartment once the car is parked then offers a firm hand to help me out. The same hand drags me frantically through the doors of the Shard. The sooner we reach the apartment, the better. As we wait, Gregory glances from me to the lift repeatedly. Eyes dark. Jaw set. The chatter of suits entertaining and tourists making their way up to the viewing platform surrounds us.

'Gregory, I thought that was you.'

The voice belongs to a balding, upper-middle-class suit with a hearty tummy and the scent of wine already on his breath.

'Francis, it's been a while,' Gregory offers in a less than friendly tone.

'How are you, old boy?'

'Well. And you?'

'Fair to middling, fair *to* middling.'

Awkward silence descends and Francis flicks his head in my direction.

'Francis, allow me to introduce you to Scarlett Heath.' Gregory steps to one side and places a possessive hand on my lower back as I shake Francis's hand.

'An absolute delight, I'm sure.' Francis runs greedy eyes from my head to my toes, making my skin crawl.

'Francis is a director of Carter's Private Equity House,' Gregory explains. In other words, Francis has the power to make big investments in business ventures.

Suddenly, it's clear to me why Gregory's entertaining a man he obviously dislikes.

'Yes, I've worked on a deal of yours recently, actually.'

'You're an accountant?' Francis asks.

'She's a lawyer,' Gregory says, his chest puffed to full stretch. 'Excuse us, Francis.' Gregory tosses his head in the direction of our lift, the only one to service the residential floors of the building, and guides me forward.

'See you Saturday then, old boy!' Francis calls, seemingly oblivious to the animosity teeming out of Gregory.

As soon as the lift doors close, Gregory lunges at me, crashing his mouth onto mine, thrusting me back against the wall. My lips part, accepting his warm, wet tongue and welcoming his teeth against the plump flesh of my lips, already tender from the drive.

The lift pings and the doors open on Gregory's floor.

He takes my hand, pulling me from the lift.

'Not fast enough,' he growls before hitching my skirt and lifting my thighs around his waist. He opens the door with one hand and carries me straight through the lounge and up the stairs as I nibble the heated flesh of his neck, drowning in his musk.

He plants me on my stiletto heels in his bedroom then holds my face and lets me see the hunger in his brown pools before he pulls my bottom lip between his teeth and slowly draws back.

'Strip.'

I blink, startled, but my hands respond, unbuttoning my suit jacket.

Surprisingly, the jacket falls and I confidently cast it onto the chaise longue. I feel in control, like I'm reclaiming some of the power I've lost.

Slowly, tortuously, I undo the buttons of my blouse one by one, each time exposing a little more of my lingerie and all the while watching Gregory as his eyes follow my hands. I feel... sexy.

My blouse floats to the ground and I turn my back to him as I roll down the zip of the skirt and push it to the floor, bending forward like a temptress who's actually done this before to lift my stocking-clad legs out of the skirt. Hearing Gregory's heavy breaths spurs me on. I turn my head over my shoulder and part my lips.

'Fucking hell.' He inhales, his palm moving to rub the erection bulging in his trousers. I can't believe how much I want him.

He steps towards me and runs his fingers up the backs of my thighs, then snaps my garter against my leg.

'Ouch!'

'That's nothing, baby; I'm just getting started.'

He yanks me to him, pulling my back to his chest, and slides his hand down my abdomen then finally to my sex, cupping me over my thong. I lean back into him, my hips rising to meet his hand. He turns my chin to face him and I desperately want to kiss him but I'm not quite done being a seductress yet.

Turning, I unwind the tie from his neck, tossing it onto the chaise longue. He yanks my waist towards him and moves to kiss me but I shoot him a warning look.

'That's very daring.' He chastises me but his words are low and husky. 'Alpha Scarlett.'

'You created her,' I say, sliding his suit jacket down his tensed biceps and to the floor.

'And I'll be the one to tame her. That's a seven-thousand-pound suit you just dropped on the floor.'

I smirk briefly then get back to my mission: to torture this magnificent man until he can understand just how furious he makes me. I unbutton his shirt, trailing kisses down his firm chest with each inch exposed, then unhook his cufflinks and push the shirt down his arms to meet his suit jacket in a pool.

As I set to work on his belt and move my hand into his trousers to take hold of his solid erection, his head lazily drapes back.

'Fuck, Scarlett, you drive me crazy.'

He kicks off his shoes when I pull his trousers and boxers to the ground then lifts each leg out and removes his socks at a rate of knots.

'I'm going to show you exactly how much you make me lose my mind.'

I have no choice in the matter. He pulls me to him then lifts my thighs to his waist. My hands lock behind his neck as he unhooks my bra with one hand and I let it fall to the floor. His lips are quickly back on mine and he moves us to the bed, bringing me to sit on his lap.

'Lean back,' he orders.

I meet his demand, exposing myself to him, spine arching in response to his fingers trailing down my chest to the rim of my suspender belt. He releases me then moves my thong to one side, thrusting two fingers into me roughly. I groan and grip the duvet in clenched fists, my hips gyrating, begging for more. He draws back and slides his wet fingers over my clit then rams three fingers into me, rotating his thumb over my swollen bud, his rhythm unforgiving. He wants me to come fast. He wants to show me who's boss. My mind fights against him but my body builds towards an explosive orgasm. My muscles tense with fury, urgency. This is coming; he's making sure of it.

'Gregory!'

'Come for me, baby. Let me take care of you. Let me make things right.'

My breaths are erratic. My hips bucking as his fingers become increasingly determined.

'Gregory! Yes! Yes!' I explode around him on a scream.

His strokes slow, giving my body a chance to return to a state of comprehension.

'Mm,' I moan in sheer blissful loveliness, my eyes closing.

'Oh no you don't.' He rises and pulls my thong down my legs then lifts me back up the bed, planting himself between my thighs, his forearms either side of my head. 'You have no idea how much of a turn-on it is to see what I do to you.'

He circles his hips, pressing his hard, throbbing cock into my navel. I'm instantly back in wanton mode.

'Lift your legs,' he says, encouraging me with his palms beneath my thighs then guiding me to place a leg on each of his shoulders. Before I have a chance to adjust to the position, he thrusts his enormous length deep inside me, both of us gasping.

He holds himself still, closing his eyes, and as desperate as I am for him to take me, I let him have his moment. Then he moves with purpose, pulling out of me and crashing back in, the position of my legs letting him immerse his cock fully inside me on a delicious medley of pleasure and pain.

'You feel so fucking good, Scarlett.'

The sound of his lust and his continuous crashing into me has me quickly building again. My hips rising to meet each drive forward, pushing him deeper.

'Oh God!' I pant.

'Wait.'

I don't know if I can. My head is blurring with my irregular breathing. My insides are pulsing around him. He drives forward with two more punishing blows.

'I'm coming, Gregory.'

'No,' he barks.

He pulls out and flips my body so I'm on all fours and yanks my hips back until I tense with anticipation, waiting for him to give me what he promised. He strikes the globe of my arse and the sting, the knowledge that I mess with his head the way he does mine, lifts me to the fringe of another earth-shattering orgasm. He lands another blow then assaults me with his cock, unravelling my last modicum of self-control.

'Now, Scarlett, give yourself up to me.' Another blow. 'Say it. I need to hear it.'

'It's yours. I'm yours, Gregory.'

He drives into me one more time and holds his position as we both erupt on a yell, our frustrations with each other, with the world, sated. For now.

7

'Amanda, where are you? It's thirty-eight minutes past six.' I end my voicemail on a sigh and continue bouncing on the spongy heels of my gym shoes to fend off the frosty air. I don't need to look to know my exposed shins will be blue and bobbled. I push my phone into the pocket of my zip-up and wrap my arms around my chest.

'I'm here! I'm here!' Amanda pants, bounding around the corner onto Iron Mongers Row. 'You should know my bed is royally pissed off with you. We were having a gorgeous snuggle this morning.'

Despite my irritation and chattering teeth, I laugh. 'Come on.'

We make our way into the hot yoga temple, otherwise known as the basement of a house split into various commercial sublets. Amanda rubs the head of the giant, smiling Buddha statue as she always does and blows him a kiss.

'Always happy to see me,' she purrs.

The changing rooms are empty, the other hot yoga-ites already having made it to the practice room. I take my red pencil dress from my gym bag and hang it inside a locker, then dump my bag, trainers, socks and zip-up and drag Amanda to our hot flow yoga class.

The thirty-seven-degree heat of the room is a welcome blanket around my cold body. Kamal, our resident yoga instructor, peels himself from his mat where he was lying in savasana. 'Ladies, you're late; take up position.'

'Sorry,' I whisper both to Kamal and the rest of the room. We're always late. Correction: Amanda is always late.

'Over there.' He gestures to two mats in the back corner of the room, tucked close together and right under two of the orange wall lamps maintaining the temperature of the room.

'I'm not going there,' Amanda huffs. 'I'll fry!'

'Amanda, stop being dramatic; we're disrupting the class.' I give her a soft nudge in the ribs with my elbow and smile politely at Kamal.

'Yes, you are,' he confirms, adjusting his hairband and pursing his lips.

We make our way to the mats, Amanda grumbling. 'I'll disrupt the class even more when I pass out.'

'You're missing your relaxation time,' Kamal says, walking back to his own mat at the front of the room, notably far away from the heat lamps. 'Remember, ladies and gents, no drinking during the session. We hydrate before and after the class; we don't disrupt the flow.' He addresses us all but only Amanda sighs in response.

'He's kind of hot when he's vexed, don't you think?' Amanda says, thankfully quiet enough that only I can hear as we lay back into savasana.

Shaking my head, I close my eyes, listening to the gentle sounds of animals awakening in the rainforest.

'Clear your mind. Concentrate only on your breath. Deep in, fill your lungs. Gently out.' Kamal's words are soft and controlled.

Clear my mind. *How hard can that be?* I try to picture darkness, emptiness but there are a thousand images flying through my mind: work, guns, Gregory, my dad, Sandy, Dubai. It's day three in the countdown to the ballistics report and this is all *really* happening.

'Let's move to sun salutations,' Kamal directs gently as Eva Cassidy's 'Fields of Gold' fills the room. 'Inhale on the rise. Swan dive, exhale.'

'How are you feeling about everything today?' Amanda asks as we push back into a downward-facing dog.

Exhaling, I push my hips back further to feel a burning stretch in the back of my legs. 'Fine. Same.' I really don't want to discuss Saturday or Gregory's father or police or anything else. For an hour, I'd just like to pretend everything is normal. I snort a laugh as I arch my back and press my hands, hips and toes to the mat: cobra position. I'm not even sure what normal is any more. I've spent so long focussing on other people that I just don't know who Scarlett

Heath really is. Daughter, lawyer, loyal friend. Orphan, insatiable hussy, murderer.

'How was your brunch at the Savoy yesterday?'

My outward breath is much harder than it probably ought to be.

'What? Tell me.'

'Neil wants me to go to Dubai on secondment.'

'What? That's amazing!' she shrieks.

'Shh.' Kamal's glaring at us again.

'Why don't I get asked to go places like that?'

'Would you want to?' I ask, dipping again into downward-facing dog.

'Are you joking? Dubai is like *the* place to be right now. Party and fashion central.'

'Hmm. Well, you might get a chance to go.'

'You are kidding me,' she says, slumping to her mat as I move into cobra again with the rest of the class. 'Why on earth wouldn't you go? You're crazy.'

'Amanda, come on. It's hardly great timing.'

She rises to her feet on an inhale but I'm not convinced her flaring nostrils are due to her hatha breaths. 'Don't ruin your life because Mr Bazillionaire decided to put a bullet in his pop's head.'

I rear, glaring at her.

'Ladies and gents, moving to standing strength positions now.' Kamal is speaking softly but his eyes are burning into Amanda and me.

We move silently into warrior two: back leg straight, front leg bent, both arms held out from our shoulders. All the while, I'm trying to breathe through my anger.

'I'm just saying, now might be a good time to find out whether Gregory loves you back.'

We move into upward warrior two, a similar position but with one arm raised in the air and the other back and pointed to the ground. I follow my fingertips to look up at the ceiling. Salt water trickles down my cheek.

'What if he doesn't?' I inhale the words to myself.

Though I'm sure Amanda doesn't hear me, she does say, 'Then at least you'll know.'

Will I go? Should I tell him?

We comply with Kamal's instruction and move into triangle pose. *Ouch*, this one always hurts my inner thigh but the distraction from other thoughts is welcome.

'Anyway, what's going on with you and Williams?'

'Meh.' She flippantly wafts a hand. 'Just fun.'

I exhale and bend forward between my legs so I'm looking at the top of her head.

'*Really*, it seems like more than fun to me.' My words sound strangely garbled from upside down. 'You've seen him a lot over the last five weeks.'

She lifts her head until she's looking at what must be my very red face and rolls her eyes.

'I'm just saying.' *See how you like it.*

'Actually, I've decided to cool it. I'm not going to see him for a while.'

'For a while. Right. So you do intend to see him again?'

We both stand and follow Kamal's direction to strike chair pose. We bend our legs to a seated position and thrust our arms in the air.

'Shoulders down, don't let them ride to your ears. Relax. Slip deeper on each exhale. In, full. Out, down.'

'Would you stop twisting everything I say, please?' Her words are scolding but there's a faint upturn at the corners of her lips.

'You like him.'

'Stop. I don't want all that *stuff*. I'm not ready to be grown-up and serious. I'm just in a playful place. It's like Carrie Bradshaw says: play in your twenties, learn lessons in your thirties and pay the bill in your forties.'

I smile, remembering our obsession with watching reruns of *Sex and the City* in pyjamas, with a gluttonous stash of chocolate and popcorn, at university.

'That she does.'

'I'm clinging to the last year or so of fun in my twenties.'

'Let's take it to the floor, ladies and gents, and lengthen our spines.' We move down to our mats in response to Kamal's instructions. I'm grateful; my clothes are now sodden with the sweat teeming out of me and my legs are beginning to feel like jelly.

Amanda flops onto her back and sighs, throwing her arms out from her shoulders and letting her head fall to the side to look at me.

'I thought you said Williams is just fun. In which case, doesn't he count as playing in your twenties?'

'Urgh!' She groans, bringing her arms to flop across her face.

The smile that tugs on my lips is quickly wiped away by the sight of a vexed-looking Kamal standing over us. 'Ladies, pipe down or leave. People are trying to get into this whether you are or not.'

'Sorry, Kamal,' we sing in unison.

We endure the remainder of the class in silence and I surprise myself by being able to concentrate on my mind and body instead of everything else going on in the world around me. By the end of the class, I'm feeling completely rejuvenated. Kamal taps his gong to rouse us from the foetal position then we follow his moves, crossing our legs and bringing our hands to prayer position.

'Good class today,' he says with three claps of his hands. 'As always, to draw the full benefit from the class, drink lots of water and eat lots of good fruit and vegetables throughout the day.'

Another drawback to being positioned in the back corner of the room is that we're last to the showers. Amanda tuts and taps her feet in the queue for the four cubicles as if she really wants to get to work. I know better than to fall for that.

The cool air is welcome as we leave the yoga studio.

The result of hot yoga, a warm shower and twenty minutes blow-drying my hair is that my cheeks are flushed even beneath my light covering of make-up.

'Ohhhhh that's soooooo gooooood!' Amanda groans, lifting her face to the sky. 'Starbucks or Pret?'

'Hmm, let's go Pret today.'

'Fabulous! Do you have much on later?'

I sigh. 'I really need to get my head down and draft a paper for Gregory.'

'He puts a lot of work your way, doesn't he?'

'We'll see. It's early days really but he is for now. How about you? Are you busy?'

'Not really. I've been keeping a low profile for a while but my utilisation figure is shocking. There's absolutely no chance of me getting a bonus if I don't put in some hours soon. Do you have anything you could pass my way?'

I watch Amanda's back as she makes her way to the counter of Pret. Working with her is a nightmare. As soon as she gets bored, she stops pulling her weight and keeping to deadlines seems to be her nemesis. But she needs my help.

'Sure. I'll take a look at the matters I've got on and hand a couple over.'

'Great, thanks!' She casts the words back to me over her shoulder then returns her attention to the barista.

I make my way to the next free server, depositing a banana and a bag of almonds on the counter, and ask for a skinny latte.

Amanda has perched herself on a stool in the window with coffee and a bacon and egg bagel. She chuckles when I take up the stool next to her, munching rapidly with hamster cheeks.

'I feel like taking a picture of my breakfast and tweeting it to Kamal,' she says through a half-eaten, nasty blend of egg and bread.

I laugh at the thought of his face. 'For the record, what's going on in your mouth is disgusting,' I say when I'm able to speak. 'You should think about taking smaller bites.'

She responds by wrapping her mouth around as much bagel as she can manage and taking a mammoth bite with a completely satisfied moan.

* * *

After checking my emails, I lock my computer screen and resolve to focus on the Shangzen Tek joint venture paper. I switch my phone to silent and divert my calls to Margaret. I really don't have time for wayward thoughts and distractions today and I really *would* like to cling to my healthy, post-yoga zen as long as possible.

It's almost twelve when I look up from my document for the first time. I've scribbled an outline which Margaret can type up and drafted a short list of colleagues in other departments who I need to ask for input. I unlock my screen to find, unsurprisingly, my email count has risen by double figures. The last three emails are from Margaret with subject lines reading:

Mr Ryans of GJR Enterprises has called, please return his call

Mr Ryans has called again and asked that you return his call as soon as possible

Mr Ryans has called a third time – said it is urgent.

The two emails before Margaret's are from Gregory, both asking me to call him. There are countless missed calls and a text on my phone.

Please call. I need you.

There's a sharp knock on my office door then Margaret appears wearing a rather harassed expression. 'I'm sorry, Scarlett, I know you don't want to be disturbed but—'

'Mr Ryans?'

'Yes. He's called again and he sounds very agitated. I really think you need to call him.'

'Thanks, Margaret.'

She leaves the office, closing the door behind her, and I quickly scroll to Gregory's number in my phone.

'Gregory, what's wrong?'

He sighs, whether in relief or exasperation, I've no idea. 'I need you.'

His words, just like his text, pull on strings in my stomach.

Oh God, they're going to charge him.

'I've been given notice of an emergency Board meeting. Three of my directors are trying to get rid of me.'

My heart rate calms. 'Okay.' I try to shift my brain from the blind panic of Gregory being charged for murder and think about company law. 'I'm guessing when you say directors, you don't mean Williams and Lawrence?'

'No. Nick Henshaw, Tim Marshall and Jean-Paul Gaville – they're directors of a European-focussed subsidiary. It's not big, mostly research and development for gaming software, but I won't be pushed aside, Scarlett, not from any of my companies. I need you to fix this before I fly to Paris and fix it the wrong way.'

'Gregory, calm down. Now's not a good time for you to be losing your temper with people. Okay? Gregory, tell me you've heard me.'

'Okay.'

'Now, tell me the name of the company.'

'Constant Sources.'

'Suffix?'

'Limited. It's a private company.'

'It's incorporated in England?'

'Yes.'

'Good, that makes things a little easier.'

'Scarlett, they know about Saturday.'

'That's why they want rid of you,' I say, stating the obvious.

'It's their excuse. I acquired the company a couple of years ago. Retaining Nick, Tim and Jean-Paul was part of the deal. They've been looking for a way out for a long time, especially Nick. He used to have most control in the company and never really wanted the deal but the company was struggling before I acquired it.'

'Are you at your office?'

'Yes.'

'Stay put and stay calm. I need to get some documents from Companies House then I'll head straight to you.'

'I'll send Kenneth.'

'Okay,' I say, having no desire to challenge him. 'You mentioned Paris; are all three directors based in France?'

'Tim and Jean-Paul are in Paris. They're flying in. Nick lives in London.'

'I'll be with you as soon as I can.'

Shit! Shit! Shit! The incessant headache that I thought I'd escaped today is working its way back with a vengeance. Dropping my head into my hands, I roll my fingers over my temples. I knew it was a matter of time until someone outside our circle found out but *how* did they? *Shit!* If more people find out, Gregory could be ruined, his companies could really suffer and there'll be more than three directors calling for him to be out. *I can't let him lose his companies.* The truth can save him and I need to make him realise that.

'Okay, Scarlett, pull yourself together.' I tap my cheeks too hard. 'He needs you.'

I dart from my office to Margaret's desk. 'Margaret, I need you to get me the Articles of Association and information on the directors and shareholders of Constant Sources Limited and I need them now, please. Can you clear anything that's in my diary for this afternoon too?'

'Of course.'

After quickly throwing things into my bag, I pull on my coat and set my out-of-office reply before closing down my computer.

'Margaret, do you have tho—'

'Here you go.'

Kenneth is waiting when I burst out of the revolving glass door. I bundle myself into the back of the Mercedes and start scouring the constitutional documents of Constant Sources. To my relief, Gregory isn't outnumbered in directorships. Nick, Jean-Paul and Tim will have to take on Gregory, Williams and Lawrence. Then I run through the list of shareholders but before I see the percentage holdings – in other words, the power they each hold to make decisions on behalf of the company – Kenneth opens the door for me. I make quick time into the office block, not sure whether I just think to say thank you or actually say it. The lift doors open to GJR Enterprises and I head straight for Gregory's office, passing the dropped jaw of Francesca. She immediately picks up the phone at the front desk, I suspect to tell *Mr Ryans* that there's nothing she could do to stop the mad woman on a mission.

His office is silent but for the sniffles of a woman who's sitting in a leather chair on one side of Gregory's large glass and chrome desk. He faces her, resting on the edge of his desk, his hands either side of his hips, his fingers hooked over the rim. All eyes in the room turn to me. Williams and Lawrence offer a swift, 'Hello,' which I return without moving my focus from the scene in front of me.

'Are you going to fire me?' the woman croaks through a sob.

'How to deal with you is *not* the top of my priorities, Sydney,' Gregory says through a tight jaw.

Sydney, his PR manager. I don't know what's going on but I feel for her. It's an almost impossible feat to keep this whole mess quiet; too many people are interested in the thirty-year-old CEO who's already made it to *The Times* Rich List.

'Go and clean yourself up but don't go anywhere. This conversation isn't over.'

Sydney nods, another sob escaping her, and scuttles past me, no doubt desperate to be free from the room. I can't believe Gregory has made a woman cry but my anger disappears as soon as I see my CEO sag in defeat. It's unprofessional but my legs carry me to him and my hand reaches out for his.

'Hey, it's going to be fine.'

His eyes lift to mine, wide, surprised, I think, then he casts a look to Williams and Lawrence, who are subtly feigning conversation. I drop his hand and force some objectivity back into my voice.

'Tell me what happened.' I cast my coat on the leather sofa and open my laptop on the coffee table.

Gregory runs his eyes the length of my body greedily before he finally pushes himself from his desk and joins me on the sofa, Williams and Lawrence taking up position on the sofa opposite. 'Nick found out about Saturday.'

'You've told me that much. How did he find out?'

'Does it matter?' Gregory snaps.

I'm taken aback by his reaction but I don't let it show. I'll let that one go on grounds of stress. 'I guess not but I'd like to know if the situation is about to become common knowledge.'

'Sydney told him,' Lawrence offers.

'She what? Why?'

Gregory glares at Lawrence. 'It won't happen again.'

'That's all well and good, Gregory, but now someone who clearly has it in for you knows something that, for very good reasons, you were trying to keep secret.'

Gregory thumps a hand on the arm of the sofa. 'Damn it, Scarlett! Just tell me how to deal with the directorship.' He leans forward, resting his elbows on his knees, his usual confidence and poise broken. I've done this to him. 'I'm sorry,' he mutters.

'Gregory, I know you don't want to hear it but there's an easy way out of this.'

He eyes me nervously.

'Tell them the truth.'

His hands are back in his hair. 'Scarlett, we've been through this. We can't.'

'That's not what I mean.'

He casts cautious eyes to the confused faces of Williams and Lawrence then turns to me. 'Then what do you mean?'

'Tell them why. If you told them about your father, who he is, what he did, anyone with a heart would have sympathy.'

Gregory stands so abruptly, it makes me jerk backwards. 'Sympathy. Do you think I want their fucking sympathy, Scarlett?' His words are a roar that shock me into silence. He charges to the window and stands with his back to me, his arms folded.

I don't know where he's gone but *my* Gregory isn't present in the room. I wish I could read his mind but the reality is, I probably wouldn't like what I'd see. It was a stupid suggestion. He won't open up to anyone so he's not about to open up to three men he hates. I want to go to him. I want to take him in my arms but this is the Gregory I see during the night, the Gregory who wants to be alone in his own dark world.

I need to be objective about this. I need to put him firmly back in the client box and be his lawyer. 'What've they said so far? Have they tried to call a directors' meeting?'

'They sent this letter by email this morning,' Williams says, sliding a document across the coffee table towards me.

'It's a notice to remove a director under the Companies Act,' I say, speaking my thoughts aloud. 'That's a good thing in terms of them knowing that they don't have a right to remove Gregory under the Articles of Association of the company. It does mean they think they have sufficient shares in the company with voting rights to remove Gregory by a simple majority.'

'In fucking English, Scarlett!' Gregory yells, thrashing his arm at his desk, sending a water glass smashing into the wall.

Lawrence jumps to his feet. 'I'm as sure as death and taxes are certain that I brought you up better than this. If you're going to act like an ape, leave this to Williams and me.'

Gregory swings his head from staring at the pile of broken glass and glares at Lawrence, neither one of them relenting.

'It's fine, Lawrence, really.' *I did this to him. He's wound so tight because of me.* 'I was thinking out loud. So here's the intelligible version.'

Gregory resumes a position on the sofa sitting next to me. 'He's right; I'm sorry.'

I throw him a cursory glance but now isn't the time for me to look into the distracting eyes of my man of multiple personalities.

'Forget it. So, I read the company's Articles on the way over here. The Articles govern how directors are appointed and removed from the company. There isn't an express right in the Articles for Nick and the others to remove you, although there would be if... if you're charged.'

Gregory's shoulders tense slightly, then he nods once, his lips set in a straight line.

'Does that mean they can't remove him?' The question comes from an anxious-looking Williams.

'Well, it means they can't remove him in their capacity as directors but they're either ignorant of the possibility or they've looked at the Articles too.'

'The former,' Gregory grunts.

'That gets us to the Companies Act. The legislation gives shareholders the right to remove a director. There are rules around how to exercise that right, which Nick clearly hasn't followed looking at this letter. He hasn't given sufficient notice first off so he couldn't hold the meeting today to remove you. Are you with me?'

Gregory nods again, stroking his chin between his index finger and thumb.

'Right, so based on technicalities, we can at least delay things from today.'

Gregory leans back on the sofa, unbuttoning his suit jacket and resting one ankle across the knee of his other leg. 'A delay isn't good enough.'

'I know. What I need to understand is how many shares they have in the company, their percentage holding. They need a simple majority vote to remove you under Section 168.'

'A simple majority being more than 50 per cent?' Lawrence asks.

'Yes. Exactly.'

'Bloody hell!' Williams snaps, taking his turn to rise from his seat. 'They have 18 per cent each.'

'54 per cent as a group?' I ask for confirmation. *How could Gregory have let that happen?*

Gregory nods but his face is expressionless, controlled. 'Does that mean I'm screwed?'

'It means—' *On top of everything else, now I have to tell him he's going to lose...* Someone switches on the proverbial light bulb in my recently overactive mind. 'Wait!' I rummage through my papers and pull out the company's Articles. *Please, please, please.*

My eyes catch the clause I hoped I hadn't imagined. *Thank you, God!* I slouch back, sinking into the sofa, and exhale the pressure that's been building in my throat.

'What?' Gregory's tone is clipped but he's restraining his temper.

I sigh with overwhelming relief. 'You have a Bushell and Faith clause in the Articles.'

'A what?' he asks, irritation lining his voice.

'A Bushell and Faith clause. You've got enhanced voting rights on the matter of your removal.'

'English, Scarlett.'

'Sorry. Your shares count for three votes each when there's a vote to remove you as a director. How many shares do you have?'

He leans forward, his hands interlocked, his elbows resting on his knees. '25 per cent.'

I feel myself grin. 'Your shares count as seventy five votes. They can't remove you.'

'Are you sure?' Williams asks.

'Yes. I'm sure.' I turn to Gregory, who's resting his forehead in his hands, and slide Nick's letter across the coffee table, moving it into his field of vision. 'Tell him to go fuck himself.'

Gregory's head darts up, as shocked as I am at my potty mouth. Then he turns on that half-smile of his and I'm putty. 'I'll do just that. You should watch your language, lady.'

'So Sandy tells me,' I say. 'You don't have to attend the meeting today either.'

'Oh no, believe me, I'll be at that goddamn meeting and Nick Henshaw will be told exactly *how* to fuck himself.' There's nothing funny about the blackness of Gregory's irises now. 'What time is it?'

Lawrence checks his shiny, gold Rolex. 'Half-past eleven.'

'Right. Scarlett, can you throw together a letter of resignation before twelve?'

My brow furrows, questioning.

'Not for me,' he confirms, rising from the sofa and fastening one button of his suit jacket then arranging his cuffs so that his pale-blue shirt hangs ever so slightly longer than his slick, charcoal jacket. 'Nick Henshaw will be resigning as a director at noon.' He leaves his words hanging as he makes for a dramatic exit from his office.

'Gregory, wait.'

He turns to face me just before he reaches the door.

'Are you sure that's wise? Whilst Nick is a director and shareholder of the company, he won't do anything to damage his own investment. If you force him to go, he could expose you. If he does that, it's not just the reputation of this company that would suffer.'

Gregory swallows. There's a shred of doubt in his mind. 'Trust me, he won't be doing that.'

He opens the door and leaves the room, then just as quickly reopens the door. 'Scarlett, in case I forget to tell you later, you are one *amazing* woman.'

Despite the raging fire burning in my cheeks, my heart bursts. *God, I love him.*

* * *

'Here you go.' I hand the letter of resignation to Gregory. 'Just needs a signature.'

He folds the letter by three and tucks it into his inside pocket.

We take the lift as a foursome down to the twenty-seventh floor and make our way to the boardroom. The three men already sitting at the far end of the oversized mahogany table stand as we enter. Gregory doesn't offer his usual introduction, nor does he exchange pleasantries, but he inclines his head, gesturing for me to take a seat to his left at the head of the table.

I dislike the three directors already. Scouring their faces, I attempt to determine who's who. One of the men does actually look French in a way I can't quite pinpoint. He has a slight frame and golden skin; he's not at all bad looking. His hair is swept back, black with just the smallest sign of introductory greys, his thick, black eyebrows as yet untarnished.

'Are you going to enlighten us?' One man leans forward on the oval table and stares at Gregory whilst glancing in my direction. This must be Nick, the ring leader. Mid-forties and broad, he clearly looks after himself. He's not good-looking but he is striking. A woman would be forgiven for taking a second glance. His tousled, dirty-blond hair suits his tan which is, at best, uncommon for November in England. His blue-grey eyes are dishonest and cold but strangely handsome at the same time.

'This is Scarlett Heath, my legal advisor.' Gregory checks his watch as he speaks, a small demonstration of how highly inconvenient this little gathering of Nick's is. 'You summoned us, Nick; let's move this along.'

Nick scoffs, raising a supercilious smirk to the ceiling. In my periphery, Gregory is focussing, straight-faced, on the nemesis at the opposite end of the table. There's no love lost between these men, that much is clear.

'We're here to tell you that your time as our liege has come to the cliff's edge... and I'm about to kick you off.'

'Spare us the melodramatics, Nick,' Williams snarls.

'We've learned about your little adventure on Saturday night, Gregory, and we're here to remove you as a director of our company before you get banged up and drag our name down with you.'

I flinch at his words. He really is a nasty piece of pie. I'm actually excited to watch this unfold and see his vindictive plan fall to shit around him.

'Hmm, yes, I've been informed of your knowledge.' Gregory leans back in his black leather chair, his elbows resting on the arms of his seat. 'I'm also aware of how you acquired that knowledge.'

Nick squirms. *There's a reason Sydney told him.* Williams and Lawrence similarly rest back into their directors' chairs. They know and they also know that Gregory just took the upper hand. But I'm not the only person in the room who's still in the dark. Jean-Paul raises his thick brows at Nick. Finding no answers, he turns to look at the man I presume is Tim. As Tim's shoulders rise, his second chin wags a little from side to side.

'How I came to find out is beside the point,' Nick snaps, clearly rattled. 'The fact is, you killed a man and you can't direct a company from a prison cell. So, why don't we get this over with and vote. All those members in favour of removing Gregory Ryans as a director, please raise your hand.'

Nick shoots up his hand as the three men at my end of the table remain stone-faced, although there might be the slightest curling at the corner of Gregory's top lip. Tim and Jean-Paul are uncertain, their hands hovering, lifting and dropping as they look from one another to Gregory. I open my mouth to speak but Gregory drops a hand to my knee. He wants to wait; he wants to know whether Tim and Jean-Paul will turn coat.

'Gentlemen, how do you vote?' Gregory asks calmly.

The men look to each other one more time and then to a snarling Nick.

'I'm sorry, Gregory, but Nick's right. If you're convicted, the company will suffer.' Jean-Paul doesn't want to do this but in his shoes, I might feel compelled to do the same thing. He raises his hand, followed by the sheepish climb of Tim's hand.

Now it's my turn to watch that smug face twist. 'Actually, Nick, forgive me for breaking up your fun but the other directors won't be voting. Neither in their capacity as directors nor as shareholders. You see, you have no right to remove Gregory from the Board today.'

'Excuse me?' *Oh yes, this is fun.* He despises me already, as I do him.

'Well, removal of a director under Section 168 of the Companies Act requires a period of notice, which you haven't given.'

'Ridiculous, we're all here; there's a quorate meeting. The vote stands.'

'I'm afraid you're mistaken. However, let's suppose for a second that you are correct and the hands around the room reflect the voting position.' Nick's head follows my gaze as I, rather dramatically, turn to each man at the table and count the number of hands held, finally settling back on Nick. 'Three. I'm afraid you don't have an ordinary resolution.'

Nick finally draws down his hand and laughs heartily, sardonically. 'Well, pretty little legal advisor, you should've gotten a better degree. Let me point out the facts for you. The three raised hands represent 54 per cent of the shares in this company. We just passed an ordinary resolution.'

My body seems to move faster than my mind as I push back my chair and move to the other end of the table where I lean on one hand, my face close to Nick's. I slap the company's Articles on the table in front of him. 'You might want to read Article 9, pretty little pig.'

I watch as realisation sinks in to his pea-size brain. He raises his head and looks first directly at Gregory, then to me. I can't help the smug grin that pulls on my face.

'I have a first-class honours degree from Cambridge and a distinction in legal practice. I'm not new to this game, so I suggest you don't try to outsmart me at my bread and butter.' I hold his stare until he blinks, then tap the Articles of Association with my index finger. 'You can keep those.'

Williams is clearly suppressing a laugh as I strut, somewhat unprofessionally, back to my place by Gregory's side. He squeezes my knee quickly under the table before standing and fastening one button of his jacket. 'Here's what's going to happen. Tim, Jean-Paul, I don't hate you. In fact, I don't care enough for either of you to like or dislike you. But I do respect the work you do for this company and I know how much you care for it. I also know that you've followed like sheep as Nick has tried to take a personal stand against me. So I'll ask you once and only once and you'll answer me now. Do you want to side with him and sign your resignations today, or do you want to walk out of this room, keep your positions and swear never to cross me again?'

Tim speaks first. 'I'm with you, Gregory; I always have been. I just didn't know what to do.'

Nick mutters something under his breath but it's not loud enough to reach our side of the table.

'Me too, Gregory, I'm sorry. Really. Truly. I'm sorry.' Jean-Paul looks on the brink of tears as he speaks but there's no empathy from Lawrence or Williams. I'm inwardly delighted by their solidarity.

Gregory doesn't acknowledge the apologies; he's too busy burning his black eyes into the blue-greys opposite him. He reaches into his inside pocket and removes the resignation letter, then flattens it on the table. 'Pen, Scarlett.'

I hand him my pen, which he fleetingly scrutinises before placing it on top of the letter. *Arrogant arse, what's wrong with my pen?* 'Nick, this is your letter of resignation and an expression of your request to have the company buy back your shareholding.' He lifts his eyes back to meet Nick's. 'Sign it.'

Nick throws his head back, laughing. 'Why the hell would I want to do that?'

I'm holding my breath, waiting for Gregory to pounce. But he doesn't. Instead, he fiddles with his shirt, bringing it back to its usual position, just breaching the end of his jacket sleeves. 'You'll sign it because you don't want me to tell your wife that you've been fucking Sydney.' His words are calm. *That's what he held back from me.*

'Motherfucker!' Nick is yelling but he's walking to our end of the table.

'No, Nick, your mother is one person I definitely *wouldn't* fuck.'

Gregory leaves the room, slamming the door behind him. I wait for Nick to sign the letter, then he storms out too. There's an awkward air in the room whilst the other four men consider each other in silence.

'I'll leave you to it,' I say, realising as I carry my documents out of the board-room that my legs have the strength of sponge.

After bringing myself back to life with splashes of cold water in the ladies', I make my way to Gregory's office. His chair is turned to face the bustle of London, marred by low-hanging clouds.

'Hi,' I say, making my way to him.

He rotates his chair a little to watch me, his hand wrapped around a glass half-filled with what looks like Scotch.

'It's the middle of the day.'

He holds his glass up, swilling the contents. 'Join me?'

'Actually, yes.' I offload my documents to his desk, separating the signed letter of resignation from the pile, as he brings me a crystal glass filled with the orange-brown liquid.

He resumes his position, staring out of the floor-to-ceiling window, and pats his leg. 'Get here.'

I should go back to my office but as it's *his* work I need to finish, I guess he just trumped his own instructions. I climb happily onto his lap, leaning into his chest, and sip my Scotch, letting the fluid heat the back of my throat. This is a most unlike Gregory thing to do at work and massively inappropriate of me but his hot breath on my neck quashes my rational thoughts. He nibbles the skin, then my lobe, and I hum my contentment.

'Another rough day,' he says.

He draws my chin to face him with his Scotch-free hand. Pulling my waist tighter, his mouth meets mine. It's a triumphant kiss. We've fended off another attack. But our war against Gregory's demons is far from over.

'Sorry, I'll come back.' Williams halts midway between the door and Gregory's desk.

'Oh, gosh, no, I'll go.' I make to leave Gregory's lap but he holds me to him as I wriggle uncomfortably.

'Neither of you need to go.'

Williams brings a drink and sits on Gregory's desk next to us, his long legs crossed at the ankles. He drops a hand to his friend's shoulder, then sips his Scotch. We look out over the River Thames in silence for the time it takes us to finish our drinks.

'I need to go,' I eventually admit to myself on a sigh. 'I have a slave-driving client who needs a document for his meeting first thing.' It suddenly hits me that Gregory is leaving for China tomorrow morning.

I don't know how to cope with everything that's going on without him.

Gregory tugs on my waist as I try to stand, then casts a glance at his friend.

'I need to get on,' Williams says. 'Thanks for today, Scarlett.'

Turning as much as I can in Gregory's tight hold, I waft a hand in the air. 'It's my job.'

'Come home and work,' Gregory whispers into my neck. 'I don't want to be without you tonight.'

I drop my head back, exposing my throat. 'Hmm, as tempting as that sounds, I'll get much more done in the office.'

'What if I promise not to talk to you until you're done?' He parts his lips as he sucks on my skin.

'Hey, don't mark me,' I say, wriggling from his touch, feeling cold at the loss of contact.

'I'll mark you if I want to.' He presses his lips to my neck again. 'It just so happens that I don't want to today.' I don't need to see him to know he's grinning against my flesh. 'Come home, please.'

Pressing my lips against his, I nod my agreement, not wanting to break our contact.

'Do you have everything you need?' he asks, lifting me to my feet.

'Yes, I've got my laptop.'

After punching two buttons on his phone and declaring, 'We're ready,' we're leaving the office, side by side, business personas firmly rooted in place.

'Why didn't you tell me about Sydney?' I ask when we're in the back of the Mercedes with Kenneth weaving us in and out of the London traffic. I want to know why he's even considering keeping her at the company when he seems ruthless in every other aspect of his business life. Admittedly, he did sort of offer Tim and Jean-Paul an olive branch but I suspect that's because they do a good job of managing Constant Sources.

'What about her?'

'Erm, that she's sleeping with Nick.'

'It's not that I didn't tell you. It wasn't something you needed to know.'

'Have you slept with her?'

He scowls at me. 'Her ex-husband used to mess her around, and she's got two young kids. Now Nick is preying on her, making her promises he's got no intention of keeping, making a fool of her. I *helped* her; I didn't sleep with her.'

I sit back against the leather seat and watch traffic through my window feeling suitably admonished, ridiculously and pathetically jealous. There's something else I didn't know about Scarlett Heath: she's got a nasty jealous streak.

We finish the journey in silence and when Gregory lets us into the apartment, he takes himself straight into the kitchen area.

'Are you sulking?' I ask.

He downs the glass of water he's poured from the fridge filter. 'No. I'm giving you what I promised: space to do your work.' He places his glass down on the black, granite worktop and looks at me. 'But if you keep up with the attitude, I won't be responsible for losing control and stripping that red dress right off you.'

He really has no idea how much I'd like him to lose control. Or maybe he does.

'Go!' he demands, raising a finger in the direction of his office.

I nestle into the big, black leather chair and tuck myself under Gregory's contemporary, white desk. I laugh to myself – more black and white to surround my man who definitely operates in the grey. Black and white is who I used to be: addicted to rules and boundaries. Not any more. Not since this CEO swanned into my pitch and broke down my sense and sensibility. My world used to operate at *content enough* but he's shown me how to live at *mind-blowing*, off the scale one minute and crashing to unbearable lows the next.

It's irrationally, disgustingly addictive.

Five hours in, emails dealt with for the day and Gregory's paper almost complete, I twist my hair into a messy bun and push a slide through to hold it in place. My eyes are starting to sting so I put on my glasses and resolve to be finished in thirty minutes.

Right on cue, as I'm carrying out an arms-raised, celebratory stretch, a perfectly toned body clothed in a fitted, black T-shirt and low-rise, dark jeans appears in the doorway. 'If I'd known I wouldn't get to touch you 'til this hour, I would've never agreed to give you space.'

'I'm done.'

'Glasses?'

'Only when my eyes are tired.' I pinch the corner of the cat frames to remove them, feeling a little exposed.

'Hot.' His voice is laced with sex and my body's already responding. My sex tingles, my chest fills, my shoulders roll back in my chair as he strides towards me. I leave my glasses where they are. 'Very naughty secretary.'

I smile but can't help wondering whether he likes his secretaries *that* way; they're all uncommonly pretty and they drool at his feet when they see him.

He stalks around the desk and turns my chair to face him. Hunkering down in front of me, he lifts my chin with his index finger until I'm looking him in the eye. 'Stop those cogs whirring. I don't notice other women. Not any more. I have eyes for one woman.'

I nod but inside, I'm praying that really is true.

'Stop overthinking, Scarlett.' He pecks the tip of my nose. 'Only you, baby.'

He kisses me gently once, then deepens the contact. Strong arms lift me to my feet without breaking our contact. In my heels, I don't need to reach so high to wrap my arms around his neck and he doesn't need to bend as much as usual. Holding me with firm hands on my waist, he performs a slow, beautiful grind of his hips against mine.

'Each time I kiss you, it's like kissing you for the first time.' His words fall onto my neck. This is going to be Miss Me Sex: a reminder of what I'll be missing whilst he's away. He nibbles my lobe, then my neck, and sucks gently. 'I want people to know you're mine whilst I'm gone.' I know what's coming and I know he's asking permission. There's no way I want to be marked for everyone to see but his lips drive me crazy. I lean my head slightly to one side. Taking his signal, he clamps his lips down on my skin and begins to draw the blood to the surface, sending my insides into a tailspin.

'Proud of yourself?' I ask when he lifts his head to face me.

There's an air of amused satisfaction about him. 'Perfect.'

'You're insane.'

'And you're insatiable,' he says on a pulse-inducing grind.

'You created the problem.'

'And I'll be the only person to fix it, baby.'

His mouth is back on mine and firing on all cylinders, licking, stroking, sucking. He breaks our contact to turn me and draw the zip of my dress down my back. He lifts the hem up my body and throws the dress to the floor.

'You look fucking amazing in red.' His eyes absorb the red bra and matching French knickers I chose this morning.

'Kiss me,' I whisper and *boy* does he, drawing his hand down the nape of my neck as he does, leaving goosebumps in his wake.

'I want you to remember this when I'm gone. How good it feels,' he says.

He means China but a sombre feeling swells in my chest. What if it ever had to be longer? What if we were talking about months or years?

I miss him so much already, it physically hurts. And everything is uncertain now but deadlines are looming. The decision of the CPS to charge Gregory or not. Neil and Abdulla needing a decision on Dubai. I'm crumbling inside and I don't know how to tell him. He has enough to deal with, more than he'll let me know.

8

'Please don't look at me like that.'

I can't help it. I know how pathetically needy it is but I don't want him to go. He leans down and plants a kiss on my brow. I push myself up on the bed and bring my face to meet his. He smirks at my greediness before placing his lips on mine.

'I'll buy you a treat,' he says through a grin.

'I'm not a child.'

'Then stop behaving like one.' He winks, making me smile briefly. 'I've got to go.'

'I know.' And I do know. I've always put work top of my priorities – well, just below my dad. He would've never knowingly stood in my way.

'It's just... what if...'

'What if I'm charged?'

I twist my fingers in my lap.

'Baby, it was self-defence and that's why it's taking so long. You heard John Harrison. If the CPS thought I was a danger to society, I'd be charged. But they don't, I'm not, and I won't be charged.'

'Gregory, you don't know that.' My eyes feel heavy as I continue staring down at my fingers. 'What if in a few days...'

'I can't put my life on hold, Scarlett. I have a business to run.' He places a hand over mine, holding my fingers still. 'And I won't put *us* on hold. I'll be back Friday and we'll enjoy our weekend together, okay?'

I nod but inside, I know nothing has changed. 'I'll see you Friday.'

'See you soon, beautiful.'

I have to use this time. Three days to get my head straight without any forget-the-world sex or angry sex or miss-me sex, without the distraction of this excruciatingly stunning, infuriating man. Time to process everything: me, Gregory, us, my dad, the investigation, Dubai.

My life really has become complicated since I met the man who still in so many ways is a complete mystery to me, the man who's taken complete control of my mind and body and sent my head and heart into the battle of all battles. The man who won't let me in and the man who really might not be in love with me. *Who am I kidding, these three days are going to be mental torture.*

My alarm draws me out of my muddled thoughts. Reaching over to the bedside table, I silence the phone then get ready in the luxury of solitude and opt for a fitted, black dress and a soft-damson blazer with black heels, then curl the ends of my hair.

Amy has already arrived when I make my way downstairs.

'Good morning, peach,' she sings as she busies herself, her oversized jumper swishing at the thighs of her leggings as she rubs the already gleaming worktops of the kitchen back to super-sparkle. 'You look very nice. Would you like coffee?'

'Please.' I plonk myself on a stool at the island.

'Strawberries and yoghurt or something warm for a change?'

I check my watch. 'I probably have time for something warm.'

'Eggs? Bacon? Porridge?'

'Porridge would be nice, thank you.'

She stops scrubbing and pours me a coffee from the filter machine. 'Let's see... hmm... seeds, nuts, berries, honey, banana?'

'You spoil me, Amy. Seeds and honey sounds great, please.'

'Right you are. Did Gregory get off okay?'

I nod through my coffee. 'He left early, about five, I think.'

She shakes her head. 'I don't know where that man gets all his energy.'

'How long have you worked for him?'

'Gosh, maybe five years. I used to just clean but he's hopeless. He'd work all hours, get up at the crack of sparrows to exercise with that nutty driver of his and never eat – well, never eat or eat rubbish. You know they put all kinds of fat and salt and sugar in food in those fancy restaurants.'

I giggle to myself; she sounds just like Sandy. 'What about the women he's lived with? Didn't they cook for him?'

Amy throws her head back in an almighty chuckle. 'Sweetness, that man has never been with a woman long enough to move her in. You're special to him, I can tell.' She raises her brows with a grin that draws my smile up to my ears.

'You'll get the sack for spouting rubbish like that,' Jackson chirps before he limps into the kitchen in sports shorts and a polo. 'And I'm not a nutter.'

Amy twists her damp tea towel and whips it across Jackson's legs.

'Argh!' He bends forward gripping his injured leg and hopping.

Amy's quickly by his side, panic-stricken.

'Only joking!' Jackson stands with a cheeky grin.

'You are a nutter!' Amy slaps his shoulder and moves back to stirring porridge. 'I hope you don't expect me to feed you after that performance.'

'My man said I could have his breakfast this morning.'

Amy tuts at the ceiling. 'Well, if the boss calls it. Eggs?'

'Poached please, flower.' He hops up to a stool next to me. 'You don't mind me being here for breakfast, Scarlett, do you?'

I laugh through my coffee. 'You have more right to be here than I do, Jackson, and don't pretend he hasn't told you to babysit me whilst he's gone.'

'He said nothing of the sort,' he laughs.

'No crutches today?'

'Nah, it's healing up nicely already.' He proves his point by flexing his injured leg then straightening it flat and flexing it again. 'I'd like to be driving again next week.'

'Isn't that a little soon?'

He scoffs and shakes his head. 'If I don't get back soon, I think Kenneth might lose a limb.'

'One porridge with seeds,' Amy announces, placing the steaming bowl in front of me. 'You can put your own honey on to taste.' She pushes a very pale-looking substance towards me.

'Manuka?' I ask, reading the label. 'Oh, one of those healthy things.' I hold the pot up in front of my face.

'It has superhuman properties, apparently. Gregory insists on it, won't have any other kind. Crackers if you ask me. It's ten times the price of ordinary honey.'

'Hmm, tastes okay, I suppose.'

I gobble up my porridge, drink my coffee then finish up getting ready for work.

'Ken's downstairs. Do you have his number?' Jackson asks, still munching his way through poached eggs on toast.

'Gregory put it in my phone last night.'

'All right. Call me if you need anything. Let's try not to do anything to make the crazy fool jump straight back on that jet home.'

I roll my eyes to the ceiling. 'Yes, Dad.'

'There's no need for cheek, girl. I'll be at Lara's this afternoon seeing Sandy but I'll be back tonight.'

My eyebrow instinctively rises.

'Get out of here!' Jackson snaps, clearly suppressing a smirk.

Kenneth drives me to work where Margaret has left a latte on my desk with my mail. I've got one conference call this afternoon, otherwise I can get my head down into some documents.

First, I dial my favourite contact at the firm.

'Hey, foxy lady!'

'Hello yourself. Gregory's been his stubborn self and made me another appointment with the Fashion Police at Harrods tomorrow. Come with me?'

'Now, now, don't be like that; Lucas was a delight, the cute little thing.'

'You mean when he wasn't stealing our carbs and telling me I make designer dresses look like a sack of potatoes?'

She laughs and I know her head will be thrown back in her chair. 'He didn't say that; he just said, "Ew, darling, that's all wrong."'

'Same thing. I need another evening dress and some country clothes.'

'Country? But you're City.'

'Yes, apparently *City* doesn't work for fox hunting.'

'Fox hunting! Bloody hell! Where?'

'No idea. The country somewhere.'

'Oh my God.'

'Yup. So you'll come to Harrods tomorrow? We could have a girls' night in with a bottle of wine after.' I silently beg her to say yes and not leave me in the apartment alone.

'I'm there.'

'Great, thank you. Now let me work out how on earth I'm supposed to disconnect this call.'

There's no need. Amanda's obviously sussed this damned technology and the line goes dead.

Abdulla Ghurair's work keeps me distracted for most of the day but the space-from-Gregory thing really isn't going to plan. I miss him immensely. By lunchtime, I'm starting to wonder whether he'll have landed in China yet; he must be close. Will he call me or text me to let me know he's landed safely? I have a wave of irrational fear that something could've happened to him mid-flight and I'm exceptionally grateful when Outlook flashes a reminder on my screen that Neil and I have the distraction of a call with Abdulla at two thirty.

With one ear engaged on the call and the other listening for any sign that Gregory has landed safely in China, I continually check my emails and text messages but nothing comes. Then I'm dragged away from my distractions by the inevitable matter of a secondment to Dubai. Abdulla seems set on the idea of me being the secondee. Neil doesn't say a final decision hasn't been made but thankfully buys us a couple of weeks before we have to confirm that request because, as he explains to Abdulla, there are more pressing matters to deal with in the first instance. I can breathe a sigh of relief for now but I'll have to make the decision imminently. The way I'm feeling, beside myself with complete nonsensical and unfounded worry, tied up in knots at the thought that I'm missing Gregory so much already, I might not make it to Friday with my sanity intact. There's no way I can accept the secondment.

Suppose I decide not to go. *Would it really be that bad?* I refuse a potentially enormous client and let Neil and the firm down. There's no way around it; if I don't go, I'll be placed indefinitely in the not-concerned-about-the-interests-of-the-firm bracket.

I call Jackson just after four.

'Scarlett? Is everything okay?'

Suddenly feeling very silly, I confirm that there's really nothing wrong. 'I was just wondering if you've heard from Gregory?'

'You really have it bad don't you? No, I've not heard from him. He should touch down shortly: half-past four, quarter to five, give or take for wind and what have you.'

'Thanks, Jackson. Are you with Sandy?'

'I'll let you know if I hear from him. And she's right next to me. Would you like me to put her on?'

'Erm, yes please, just for a sec; I'm at work.'

'Scarlett, sweets?' Her bubbly voice is my ultimate reassurance.

'Hey, Sandy. How are you?'

'Not bad. I'm just having a couple of hours' break before I get started on dinner. Are you all right?'

'Mmhmm, sure. Are you enjoying your break with Jackson?'

Sandy scoffs. I imagine her rolling her eyes at the phone. 'That's really none of your business, missy. Get back to work.'

'Enjoy the rest of your break,' I sing, receiving a puff of air before Sandy hangs up.

My iPhone rings. Quickly grabbing it, I see a number I don't recognise. 'Scarlett Heath,' I say.

'Scarlett, it's Amy here. Would you like me to make you dinner this evening?'

'Oh, hi, Amy.' I try my best not to let my disappointment show. 'Erm, no, gosh, it's fine. I'll make myself something.'

'Scarlett, darling, this is my job. Now, what would you like? I do a mean fish pie?'

'A mean fish pie sounds wonderful, thank you.'

'Excellent, I'll leave it in the oven so you just need to reheat it whenever you get home. Pop it on 180 for half an hour; that should do it.'

'You're a star, Amy.'

'I know,' she chuckles. 'I'll most likely be gone when you get home but you can get me on this number if you need me. Otherwise, I'll see you in the morning.'

Is this what life with Gregory would be like? Me completely dependent on him, tracking his movements, dealing with his staff?

A last-minute meeting drags me away from staring at my silent phone. It's almost eight fifteen by the time I get back to my desk, so I do a final check of my emails and decide to call it a day. I text Kenneth and he's waiting outside when I step out into the blustering wind and rain.

Following Amy's instructions, I set my mean fish pie off heating in the oven and take a shower, coming back to the emptiness of the lounge that now feels bigger than ever, and curling up on the sofa in my oversized jumper to eat my dinner. Everywhere I go, my iPhone comes with me. Still nothing. The feeling of unease I have is increasing and it's not just because I've not heard from Gregory. This is the first time I've been in the apartment alone for any length of time. I've never stayed here alone and my mind is beginning to wander to the spot of the floor which was covered in a crimson pool on Saturday night.

I used to feel like this as a child when my dad was working the night shift. *What I wouldn't give to know Sandy was in the bedroom next to me tonight.*

I squeal when my phone beeps to announce a text.

> How's my girl? I miss you.

Biting my bottom lip in an attempt to slim the excessively wide smile spreading across my face, I reply.

> Your girl is missing you too. I'm wishing it was Friday already.

> Me too, baby. I'm heading out for a run before breakfast. Sweet dreams, don't let the mites bite.

I laugh to myself.

> I think you mean bed bugs, baby. The saying is don't let the bed bugs bite.

> There better be nothing biting you except me.

* * *

Bolt upright in bed, I pant, my palm instinctively feeling my chest. There's no hole, no blood, no bullet. My nightdress is soaked, my hair stuck to the back of my neck. Glancing around the dark bedroom, I realise I'm alone, I'm safe. My shoulders stop heaving as my diaphragm regains control, expanding and contracting with my lungs in a regular pattern.

Retrieving my phone from under the pillow, I learn it's after five in the morning. There's little chance of me going back to sleep and I'm not sure I can face it. I take myself to the bathroom and splash cold water over my face and in my dry mouth. Then I find my gym clothes in my section of the walk-in; we really are going to have to do something about expanding my space if I stay here. Clad in Lycra, I slot my phone around my arm in a holster and traipse to the gym room.

The cross-trainer and treadmill feel a little ambitious in light of my lack of sleep, so I opt for the spin bike; at least I can warm up a little first. Ne-Yo's 'Closer' fills my ears and my legs begin to find life. Ten tracks into my workout playlist, my legs are most definitely awake, sprinting to the chorus of each track and keeping a steady pace to the verses. A bead of sweat tickles my face as it rolls to the end of my nose. I'm happily too tired to think about anything other than turning my legs to the beat in my ears.

When I hit sixty minutes, I climb down from the bike and cross my foot over my opposite knee, bending to stretch out my glutes.

'Couldn't sleep?'

Jackson stands in the doorway dressed in sports shorts and a vest.

I wipe the back of my hand across my brow to mop up the influx of sweat. 'Not the best night's sleep I've ever had,' I admit, switching legs to stretch the other side.

He flicks his head to the lat pulldown machine on the non-mirrored side of the gym. 'Do you mind if I join you?'

'Not at all.' I finish my leg stretches and lie down on the spongy gym flooring to do some bums and tums.

Jackson grunts on each yank down of the bar. After his set of ten, he smacks a fist into the punch bag that's suspended from the ceiling by a metal frame. His lats look fierce.

'How's the leg?' I ask, making my way over to him.

He looks at his injured thigh with pursed lips. 'I'll let you know later. I'm going to try some exercise on it today.'

'Jackson, I was wondering if you would teach me some stuff. Just some punches, that kind of thing, on the bag.'

Jackson eyes the bag, then me.

'I'd just feel better if I knew how to defend myself a little.'

He nods twice, then shakes his head. 'He'll never let anything come near you again, trust me.'

I sigh. 'I appreciate that he thinks he can control everything, Jackson, but there are some things he can't stop. We've seen that. I know Pearson's gone. I know *that's* over. But I'd just feel better.'

'Come on then. Show me your fist,' he says, standing on the opposite side of the punch bag to me, holding it still.

I clench my fist and hold it up.

'You'll break your knuckles if you punch like that, kid. You do it like this.' He demonstrates, forming his own fist, then takes my attempt and adjusts my thumb position. 'That's better.' He resumes holding the punch bag. 'Let's try a hook. You need to swing from your shoulder, that's where you'll get the power.'

I swing my hardest punch at the bag. Jackson holds it still.

'Lift your elbow a little and punch through the bag, not at it. Carry your arm right through the impact.'

'Like this?' I throw my hook at the bag, shaking my fingers after the impact to stop the sting.

'Atta girl! Nice hook! D'you want to wear the gloves?'

I nod quickly with a giggle. 'Yes, please.'

My cardiovascular system has had a serious workout by the time we finish. I collapse in a heap on the spongy floor with Jackson looking on, laughing. My face feels like the savannah in the heart of summer. Even if I had the strength to do it, I don't ever want to move again but a hand pulls my arm, forcing me to stand on my jelly legs.

'You need to stretch those arms and your back.'

'Jackson, I can't. I can't breathe.'

He laughs but lifts my arm across my chest. 'Stretch.'

Another man to boss me around. Jackson and Mr Controlling are a good pair.

'He cares for you, Scarlett.' Jackson's voice is low but he's staring at me intently.

'Do you really think so?'

'He's crazy about you, kid. But I'm not sure he knows it yet.'

'How can he not know whether he cares for me? I don't understand him. One minute, I feel like I'm just in his way; the next, he says he's missing me.'

'This is new to him. Now there's so much other shit going on too but give him time to work it out and he'll get there.'

I really hope so, but there's as much chance of Gregory deciding he cares for me as there is of him deciding he doesn't care enough. His words come back to me: *so she can move on.* What does that mean? Does he want me to move on or is he really just afraid of letting me see who he really is? He said he wishes I wanted to leave but he won't tell me to go. I don't want him to be with me through obligation, through owing me a debt. I want us to be in this together. But sometimes, it feels like he pushes me away. If we weren't in this position, would I be contemplating damaging my career by not going to Dubai for a man who really might not want to be part of the same team?

'Sandy seems happy,' I say, desperate to change the subject and my wayward thoughts as I move to a tricep stretch. 'You make her happy.'

Jackson looks at me with eyes lit like I've never seen on him before, wide, sparkling espresso browns, just a shade darker than his glistening skin.

'I try,' he says, trying to be all butch, but there's no mistaking the slight curl of his lips. 'How're you holding up with everything?'

'I'd be lying if I said well. I can't stand the thought that I've killed a man but what's eating me up more is watching Gregory suffer for my wrong.'

'You know, Scarlett, he doesn't see it like that. He dragged you into all this and he wants to fix it for you. Darlin', that man's mind has been black as long as I've known him. But not with you, for the first time. I don't know whether he's more afraid of losing you, getting you caught up and hurt in his next mess, or you feeling the way he has for years.'

'I don't want him to blame himself.'

'I know, kid, I know. He'll fix this case. It won't go to trial but he needs your help with the rest.'

'The rest?'

'If he's going to stop hating himself for what he thinks he made you do, you need to show him you've accepted it.'

'But I haven't. I don't know if I can.'

He takes my hand and encourages me to sit on the weight bench beside him.

'I've killed, Scarlett,' he says. 'In the forces. It was my job but don't think it's easy to kill a man and not have guilt follow you around like a black dog. Especially the first one, that takes some getting over.'

I've never really delved into Jackson's past but I suddenly feel an overwhelming desire to know more about Gregory's protector and Sandy's new love. 'How *did* you get over it?'

'By reminding myself why I did it. I killed not just for my country but to save the men I was serving with and to save myself. That's how I live with it. In that situation, to kill was the only option.'

I know I killed Pearson to save Gregory. What I don't know is how much of me took that shot in revenge. For Gregory. For my dad. For me.

The only thing I'm sure of is that having Gregory with me gives me the justification I need.

One more day until he's back. One more day closer to the ballistics report that will prove a murder took place in this apartment.

Day five.

9

'You look so peaceful when you sleep.'

I smell him before I see him, his fresh, minty scent. My eyes open to him gazing down on me, his forearms either side of my head, holding his weight.

He smiles and rests his body down between my legs, the weight of him on my stomach telling me he really is home. I lean into his touch as he brings his palm to my cheek.

'How was your trip?' I ask, my words sleepy.

'Shh, we'll talk in the morning. Now, I just need to feel you.'

His tongue slides across my top lip and into my mouth, meeting mine. I've missed this taste so much. He nudges the tip of my nose with his then moves to my neck, trailing kisses down to my collarbone.

'My mark is fading,' he says between delicious presses of his lips against my skin.

'I don't need your mark any more; I have you.' I let my head fall back, giving him full access.

His breath is hot. 'You do.'

He kisses me in the way that tells me he's going to make love to me, slow and gentle.

'Three days felt like forever,' he mumbles against my skin.

Give him time to work it out. Tonight, in this moment, I think and hope that Jackson could be right. That faith alone is my reason to stay.

* * *

'Up you get.' Gregory's holding a cup of hot coffee, staring down at me.

'Tired,' I grumble.

'Ja, well if you will let men into your bed at all hours...' He hands me the coffee with a wink that would floor me completely if I weren't already lying down.

'Don't you ever sleep? What time is it?'

'Early. We've got a long drive. Chip-chop.'

'*Chip*-chop?' I ask on a raised brow as I swing my legs over the side of the bed.

'Exactly.'

I chuckle as my South African leaves the room. *I wish playful Gregory could be here always.* Although that would probably mean I'd lose the angry, earth-shattering-style fuckings. As much as I love sweet Gregory, I think I'd miss those now I've had a taste. Maybe a medley of Gregory's multiple personalities isn't too bad.

I hop into the black leather of the Range Rover in my newly purchased country get-up. 'Just another unnecessary car then?'

'It's very necessary. I have a lot of stuff and this has the boot space for a lot of stuff.'

Shaking my head, I strap myself into the seat, feeling like I'm sitting on top of a mountain as Gregory pulls out of the basement car park. He pushes a button on the cockpit-esque dash and Thirty Seconds to Mars' 'Kings and Queens' blasts through the speakers. I lean back in my seat and watch him as he settles into a needlessly fast but smooth drive out of the city.

'It was a week ago today,' I find myself saying. 'Should we even be doing this: going away for the weekend, being... normal?'

His knuckles tighten on the wheel. 'Scarlett, normal is the absolute minimum you ought to have.'

'We met because I agreed to help you with a hostile takeover. Three weeks ago, my dad was murdered because of that. Seven days ago, I shot a man in the head. And any day now, my boyfriend might be charged for my crime. Which part of that is normal?'

He focusses straight ahead but his expression shifts to one that's pained.

I rest my elbow on the window ledge, propping up my temple. 'I'm sorry, I didn't mean that. I just wish you'd stop telling me what I should have when what you really mean is you think I shouldn't be with you. I don't think that, Gregory.'

He shakes his head without moving his attention from the road. 'You should have better, Scarlett. I just don't seem to be capable of walking away.'

'You know what, Gregory? Screw your sense of obligation.'

The car screeches and I grip the edge of my seat as we swing off the motorway onto the hard shoulder. *This is becoming a dangerous habit.*

'That's what you think, Scarlett: that this is all because I feel trapped by circumstance?'

I shrug, looking out of the window at the grass verge, anywhere to stop him from seeing my clouded eyes.

'That's not why.'

I turn to him now. 'Then why?'

He drags a hand over his face. 'I'm not like other people. There're things you don't know about me.'

'So tell me. Take a chance on me. Let me in.'

He silently opens and closes his mouth, then rests his head back against his seat. 'I wish you could see what's good for you. You're smart, funny and beautiful; can't that be enough of a reason?'

'I guess it'll have to be, for now.'

After two hours, two service station coffees and me feeding Gregory bite-size chunks of apparently the worst smoked salmon and cream cheese bagel he's ever had in his life – a tad dramatic – concrete has been replaced by increasingly lush green. He pulls us off the motorway and we wind through roads flanked by hillside and evergreen trees.

'Where are we?' I ask, tearing myself from the unfamiliar sight of undisturbed nature.

'Derbyshire.'

'It's so green. Beautiful.'

'It is.'

'Then why do you have that look on your face? What's wrong?'

'Nothing. I was thinking.'

'Thinking about what?'

He turns to face me briefly then focusses forward again, taking us through a sharp bend. 'If I told you, I'd be saying it rather than just thinking it. Defeats the objective, wouldn't you say?'

A huffy sigh reveals my frustration. I really hope this weekend isn't going to be antagonistic Gregory the entire time.

After a ten-minute silence of continuous weaving through the countryside, he speaks. 'This whole thing is quite pretentious, Scarlett.'

'Why doesn't that surprise me?' I say on a petulant scoff.

He ignores my childishness, despite the increased tension in his jawline and the tight sinews in his neck that look too damn sexy. 'There are rules and customs. The only members of the hunt are male.'

'Are you trying to tell me this will be a chauvinistic affair?'

'Actually, yes. It can be. I'm going to be with you but just keep your wits about you. The women can be—'

'Cliquey? Bitchy?'

'Both.' He's deadpan. 'They like money, they don't like new faces and they'll absolutely hate a beautiful young woman.'

I smile inwardly but it's my concerned look that Gregory finds. 'You've brought me to the lions' den.'

'Yes. I always come alone so you'll be a bit of a surprise to them too. I'm just saying... I don't know what I'm saying. If they get too much, you can leave them. I'll be back as soon as the hunt is done and we'll have a nice dinner tonight.'

His back straightens and his eyes widen as if he's had an epiphany of some sort. He hits two buttons on the dash and the music makes way for a ringtone.

'Old boy, where are you?' It's Williams.

'Almost there. Is your sister with you?'

'She is.'

A sweet voice chimes through the speakers. 'Hi, handsome.'

'How are you, Charlotte?'

'All the better for hearing your voice, Ryans.'

He laughs, a manly and attractive sound. 'Your purposeful attempt to make me uncomfortable is failing, Charlie.'

A very girly giggle fills the car.

'I'm bringing someone to meet you today.'

'Yes, I've heard all about your *girlfriend*.'

Gregory shuffles in his seat. She's succeeded in her goal. A laugh escapes from my stomach.

'Hi, Charlie,' I say.

'Oh, shit, sorry! I didn't realise I was on speaker.'

'Mouth, Charlie!' Gregory snaps.

'Fuck, sorry!'

I laugh harder now, my head thrown back against the seat. The feeling is a relief from days of angst.

'Charlotte, that's enough,' Williams says, though his smile obvious in his voice.

'Charlie, can you just show Scarlett the ropes today?'

'Yes, of course. I'll keep her away from the pack hounds; that's what you're actually asking, isn't it?'

He relaxes. 'She can look after herself but you know what it's like when a new hound infiltrates the group.'

My jaw hits the floor in shock. 'Am I a hound in this scenario?'

'I think we'll go. See you both soon.' Charlotte's amusement is clear in her tone.

'That didn't come out right.'

'I should hope not, Mr Ryans.'

He shoots me a sideways glance and a smirk. 'You're hot when you're angry.'

I fire him my fiercest playful pout. This is better than fighting.

We round another tight bend and the top of a most extravagant stately home comes into view.

'Wow.'

The stone building is as big as a palace. Maybe even bigger. The top of each pillar is decorated with a small, gold dome and each of the multitude of windows is framed in gold too. The courtyard veers off to rows of stables and a huge fountain trickles in the middle of the open space. I look right as water shoots high into the air and sprays down into a lake beside the house.

Gregory drives up to large, iron gates. 'Ryans,' he says into the intercom. We drive a gravel path, passing stone gargoyles and lions, climbing towards the magnificent building. 'Welcome to your home for the night.'

'We're staying here?' I gasp, my head still turning around the huge expanse of grounds and the enormous structure towering over us.

Gregory pulls the Range Rover into a spot on the gravel then stretches his arms back over his headrest. The exposure of his toned chest draws my eyes away from our surroundings.

'Like what you see?' he asks on a grin.

I nod and my dry lips part. He grabs my chin between his index finger and thumb and brushes his lips over mine on an inhale. His familiar scent and the feel of his soft, smooth flesh drive my senses wild.

'I don't want to fight with you, baby. I just want to spend time with you, away from London, the apartment, all of it.' He nuzzles his brow against mine, our noses melting.

'Okay.'

A knock on the driver-side window propels me back to planet normal. Gregory snarls but his expression lightens when he turns to see the face at the window. She looks like Williams, just a very attractive, female version. Gregory unhooks my seatbelt, then his own. As soon as his feet hit the gravel, Charlotte wraps her arms around his neck. He hugs her back, a rare display of emotion. 'This is Scarlett,' he says, taking my hand and encouraging me to his side.

'Hi, Charlotte. It's nice to meet you.'

She throws herself forward and plants a kiss on my cheek, startling me but making me smile, part uncomfortably, part because I like her immediately.

'Would you calm down?' Williams says. 'Forgive my little sister; she doesn't get out much.' He leans forward to kiss my cheek. Then takes Gregory's hand in a firm shake. 'How was China?'

Gregory nods brusquely, his CEO persona in full swing. 'The deal is on.'

We're joined by a young man in *Pride and Prejudice* style get-up. He takes our bags on the shake of a hand from Gregory, no doubt accepting a note, and heads through the courtyard into the palatial home.

'Mr Ryans, we're up here.' The voice belongs to Kian, one of the attendants from Gregory's farmhouse-cum-mansion in Surrey, his luxurious property outside the city, complete with land, dogs, staff and a triple garage full of motorbikes. My mind drifts to a memory of him kitted out in leathers and the feel of my legs wrapped around his lean hips as we burnt up the country roads around the farm. 'How was your drive, sir?'

'Not bad, Kian. How does he look?'

We climb the incline to where a string of horse boxes and four-wheel drives are lined up along a dirt track, and men in various stages of undress are hopping into jodhpurs and black blazers.

'He's looking really good, sir. I've had him out every day this week. He's ready for the season.'

We wait to one side whilst Kian retrieves the grand, shining, black horse from the box labelled *GJR*. Gregory moves straight to the horse, stroking the length of its mane, then its back. 'Good work, Kian. He looks great.'

'He's riding well too, sir.'

'All right, saddle him up.'

'Yes, sir.'

Gregory glides his hands down my shoulders, his palms coming to rest in mine. 'I need to say hello to a few people. Why don't you go down to the breakfast room? Charlotte will be there. The hunt starts just to the right of the last horse box there. Come up and see us off, then you can do whatever: look around the house, take a walk. If you get fed up, you can always go back to our room. The reception is in the courtyard. They'll help you.'

'Mr Ryans, you're stressing unnecessarily. I'm a big girl; I'll be fine for... how long will you be?'

He shrugs. 'A few hours, maybe. We'll head back early afternoon before it gets too dark. They'll announce in the house when we're on our way. The ladies tend to watch us back in.'

'Sounds *very* pretentious.'

'It is *very* pretentious, but these men are money: private equity, hedge funds. Sometimes, it pays to play their games.'

I nod, understanding completely that this is business more than pleasure.

He plants a kiss on my brow. 'Have I told you how good your arse looks in these trousers?'

I smile. 'You just did.'

He turns me by my shoulders and points me in the direction of the breakfast room, slapping my bottom as I walk and receiving an over-shoulder scowl in response.

The large, wooden door is held open for me by another young man in period dress: a thigh-length waistcoat, baggy, knee-length trousers with pulled-up socks and a frilly cravat. The dining room really is something special. The ceilings are high and adorned in intricate architecture. Four very grand, gold and crystal chandeliers hang from the ceiling above the white-clothed tables. The impressive, arched windows on two walls flood the room with bright light.

'Scarlett, over here!' Charlotte jumps up from her seat at a table with six women who all look like they've been dressed by Julia and Lucas. Her dark-blonde waves bounce on her broad but slim shoulders. She really is striking in that kind of edgy, model way.

'Ladies, this is Scarlett,' Charlotte announces as I take a seat at the table. 'She's with Gregory.'

I glance around the table, smiling as I say hello. I recognise one of the women: scorned Stella from Lara's party last week. *This should be fun.* Her dyed, blonde hair is swept up in a French roll and clip, her natural, tight curls spraying out at the top. She takes a purposeful sip of champagne, eyeing me as she does, then places her lipstick-stained glass next to her Eggs Royale.

'Nice to see you again, Stella.' Even though it really isn't. Five minutes in this woman's company on Saturday was enough for a lifetime.

She sits taller in her chair, her back perfectly straight. 'Two events in one week; there's a first.'

'Stella, stop!' A woman with black hair, lacquered away from her face at the sides, smiles at me: a disingenuous smile if I ever saw one. She waves a hand in the air and a waiter comes immediately to our table. 'This here's Scarlett; she'll need some breakfast too.' Her accent is decorated with a hint of North American but she's obviously lived in England for a long time.

'Just tea is fine, thank you,' I say.

'English Breakfast, madam?'

'That would be great, thank you.'

'I'm Caroline. And never mind Stella; she's just a little shocked, as we all are.' She wags her head slightly and brings one side of her hair over her shoulder. 'Gregory's the eternal bachelor.'

'We see him with plenty of women but never with the same woman twice.' Another woman with flushed cheeks, possibly from champagne, throws in her twopenn'orth.

I don't need to look to know Stella is still burning holes into me. Well, this is *just* lovely. Subtly checking my watch, I realise I've been here a full seven minutes. The hunt hasn't even begun yet. Three hours is going to be torture.

'Don't you all look just wonderful?' An elderly lady is making her way towards us gingerly, using a stick to take her weight. She shuffles, more than lifts, her brogued feet forward.

The lady to my right, dressed entirely in black, with pearls draped around her neck – a departure from the seemingly staple shirt and gilet – leans into my ear. 'That's the Duchess.'

'Thank you, erm...'

'Florence.' She seems to be the only sincere one at the table. 'Try not to let this lot get to you,' she whispers. 'They're all after Gregory. They're like wolves for money and the fact he's a young, strapping body and a fine face to match sends them into a frenzy.'

'No hope of me winning them over, then?'

'Would you want to?' She laughs so boldly that even though it's a short-lived sound, it makes her whole body wobble.

'Probably not. But it'd make my day and night a little easier.'

'You're not part of their circle, darling; I'm afraid they won't be making it easy for you.'

'They're about to start,' the Duchess announces in a voice that matches her frailty, when she finally reaches our table.

'Come on, Scarlett,' Charlotte chirps, dancing out of her seat.

'Are you coming?' I ask Florence, who's sipping her tea.

'Oh good Lord, no! After thirty-odd years of marriage, you'll get bored of watching it. I'll be happier here.'

We make our way up the hill to where a group of English foxhounds is being controlled by two men in red blazers and hard, black, velour-coated hats. The other hunters come cantering towards the pack, all dressed in black blazers, cream jodhpurs and black hats fastened beneath their chin. I scour the faces and eventually find my strapping knight, sitting with pride atop his stallion. *Mr Darcy really has nothing on Gregory Ryans.*

'Gregory looks as good as ever.' The whisper finds my ears but I turn left and right and can't locate the owner.

'It's so exciting!' Charlotte says, giving my shoulder a giddy nudge. It really isn't but I smile at her before locating my knight again.

Those piercing, brown eyes are looking right at me.

'You okay?' he mouths.

I nod and curl my lips as high as I can force them. He doesn't need to know I'm having an utterly shit morning, being talked about both behind my back and to my face and thrown daggers by rich women in expensive clone clothes, one of whom just happens to be Stella, who I've already come to despise.

A third man in a red blazer holds a black stick in the air and everyone, including the pack of hounds, falls silent. 'The scent has been laid. Let us commence the season. Good hunting, fellows.' With that, the foxhounds head out with the red coats. Gregory knocks his heels into his stallion and sets off, flanked by Williams.

We stand, some women doing far too overzealous waves, until the hunt is out of sight.

'Gosh, that was fun.' Charlotte is back at my side, smiling in the way Williams does, charmingly, defying any person not to smile back. 'Should we go back to breakfast?'

'Actually, I was thinking about taking a walk around the grounds.'

'Good idea. I'll come with you.'

I know I need to smarten up my miserable face but I really have no desire to be here. 'Excellent.'

She thrusts her arm through mine as I walk with my hands in the pockets of my gilet. We make our way past the house, to a lake and into the fields beyond, strolling leisurely, intentionally killing time.

'My brother said you're a lawyer?'

'Yes, I am. I work for him sometimes.'

'He said. And that's how you met Gregory?'

'Yes.'

We both turn sharply when the water feature shoots high into the sky and sprays down into the lake behind us. 'What do you do?'

'I'm in my final year of uni. I'm studying Classics so God knows what I'll do when I graduate.' She laughs.

'Do you enjoy it?'

'Mm, yep, but I'm ready to leave. Did you feel like that towards the end?'

'I guess so. I was looking forward to working and making my own money. Funny.'

'Why's that funny?'

'Because given the chance, I'd go back. Life's much easier at uni. You've got the rest of your life to work long hours.'

'But you enjoy being a lawyer?'

'Yes, mostly. It has its moments.'

She nods thoughtfully. 'I think I'm ready to be out of my parents' control *and* my brother's shadow. My parents think he did everything right and I do everything wrong.' Now her head is shaking. 'He drank, he had sex, he did whatever, but it's different with me. If they even *think* that I'm doing something wrong, even though he probably did it, I'm hauled over the coals. It really pisses me off. What pisses me off more is that I listen to them too. My friends will be going out, doing whatever, and I think, *what would my parents say*? I just want to go a little crazy, you know?'

I nod. I never did either. Gregory is the most exciting thing that's happened in my life. *Be careful what you wish for.*

We walk until the house is almost out of sight, only the tallest peaks poking through trees behind us.

'You could probably have a worse big brother. Williams is pretty cool.'

'When he's not being uptight.'

Williams, uptight? There's a rarity. My mind wanders to Amanda. Maybe she brings out light-hearted Williams.

It's starting to drop cold, the November sun being replaced with an increasingly grey sky.

'We should head back.'

The concierge, in period dress like the rest of them, shows me to our room, guiding me along dark stone corridors which are lit romantically with five-prong candelabras and soft wall lights. He opens the bedroom door with an enormous, black key, then places it in my hand and leaves me to my own devices.

The room is amazing. It's got a medieval feel. A large, four-poster bed stands proudly in the middle. The walls are adorned with luxurious, deep-red fabric. The bed is laid with red and gold silk, a black velour throw swept across the bottom. The furniture is dark, antique-looking wood: a chest of drawers, a wardrobe, an ottoman and two bedside cabinets. I open a door and walk along a short corridor, flanked by decoratively carved wardrobes, then I reach the bathroom. It must be half the size of the main room. A large, freestanding, ceramic bath takes centre stage with little else in the room. I open a door to the right, which leads to a big mirror and his-and-hers sinks. Beyond the sinks, another door opens into a wet room with a monsoon shower. *This is incredible.*

My phone beeps, drawing me back to the bedroom to find it. A missed call and two messages from Amanda.

Are you having fun?

Then an hour later:

So is Ed there?

Just fun, my arse! If she'd just stop being so stubborn and admit what's blatantly obvious, she could be here to save me from the torture of a night with these women who want to throw daggers at me.

He's here. With his sister. She's nice. I wish you were here.

She fires back a message as if she's been staring at her phone, waiting for my response.

He said he was taking someone. He didn't tell me it was his sister! Not that I'm bothered. I have a date.

A date with who?

His name is Alex. Hot.

I laugh to myself, shaking my head. She's desperate for me to tell Williams.

Have fun then. Let me know how it goes.

* * *

Charlotte and I reach the start point just as the hunt is returning. Gregory and Williams are laughing together as they ride back side by side. *How can he manage to be so calm when I feel like the world is crashing down around me?* The red coat who commenced the hunt calls, 'Farewell' to the huntsmen. The other red coats guide the pack of hounds away and the hunters begin to dismount.

Gregory stalks my way on his horse, halting in front of me, his fine self towering. He removes his helmet and pulls a hand through his dark hair, ruffling some life back into it.

'Get here,' he says to me in that way he does.

'Up there? You've got to be kidding!'

The horse plods towards me and turns so I'm looking at Gregory's boot. He shuffles back on the saddle. 'Turn around.'

With a frown, I do as he instructs and turn my back on the horse. Then I'm hauled up by my arms on a girly squeal. I lift my leg and he places me down between him and the front of the saddle. 'That wasn't so bad, was it?'

'It's so high!'

'High is best, Scarlett, I've told you this.' He plants his helmet on my head and turns me to face him. He tightens the strap under my chin and pulls my hair over my shoulders. 'I didn't think anyone could look good in one of these. I was mistaken.'

He kisses me chastely on the lips then kicks his heels into the horse and we shoot away from the stares and whispers of the group, into the dusk. Gregory holds the reins around me and presses his chest into my back. The wind bellows in my face as we ride faster, so fast, I feel like I'm flying. I should be terrified. I've never ridden a horse, let alone ridden one at this speed. But I couldn't be more content, I couldn't feel safer, wrapped in his arms.

'Whoa, boy.' Gregory tugs the reins as he speaks to the stallion and our pace falls to a trot. He guides us to a tree where he commands the horse to stop. He turns my chin to him and relieves me of the helmet, reaching for a branch above him and clipping the helmet to it. Moving my hair across one shoulder, he presses his lips to my neck, sucking, nibbling. 'I want to make you happy, baby. I want to see you smile.'

This is what *I* want. Only him, just us.

I lean back into his chest, giving him easier access to my skin. His mouth glides up my sensitive skin, along my jaw, and meets mine.

'You do make me happy.'

'Turn around.' Guiding me and taking my weight, he helps me manoeuvre until we're sitting face to face.

He tugs me towards him and kisses me, our tongues indulging in the taste of each other. Holding the branch above us with one hand, steadying himself, he lifts my legs around his waist. I pull back to see his face, stunning in the last fading light of the day, his dark, lust-filled eyes locked on mine.

Yes, this is definitely what I want. These moments when he sees and feels nothing but me. When I'm his, completely. This is the place where everything makes sense.

With balled fists gripping his blazer, I pull him to me. He releases the branch and drops both hands to my back as my hips roll against his.

* * *

Kian is waiting by the horse box when we get back, most of the others dispersing or already gone. 'Good hunt, sir?'

'Yes, thanks, Kian. You prepared him well.'

I swing a leg so both are on one side of the horse and let Gregory lower me by my underarms to the ground before he jumps down himself. He pats the horse before Kian takes over control. I watch as he strips down to his boxers under the light of the horse box, his toned body making me wanton again. He really has turned me into an insatiable temptress and I enjoy every second of it.

'Like what you see?' he says with a smirk as he fastens his belt buckle over his jeans then pulls his Barbour jacket over his jumper.

'Always,' I say, returning my teeth to my bottom lip.

Shaking his head, he says, 'Come on.' He lifts his arm and I tuck into his side beneath it.

'What happens now?' I ask.

'Now it's brandy and cigars to debrief.'

My face contorts at the thought. 'Is there an alternative option? Brandy isn't my favourite.'

'No, baby, it's just the men.'

'Oh. So I get to hang out with all the women who want to fuck you again?'

'Is there any need for the French?'

'I just like our bubble. Breakfast was horrible, Gregory; they looked at me like I have ten heads and it's clear all those women want you. I know I sound petulant but—'

He halts us and turns me to face him but I'd rather look at my new Hunter wellies. 'Look at me.'

I continue to look at my feet.

'Look at me, *please*.'

I lift my head.

'I'm here with *you*. Only you.'

My eyes find the floor again. 'I know, it's just—'

'No just. I'm yours. Only yours.' He lifts my chin with his index finger the way he does, forcing me to look at him. 'Yours.' He plants his lips on mine, a long, lingering, worry-forgetting kiss.

Does he tell me he loves me in these moments? Is that what he's saying?

10

My gown has already been taken out of the dress bag and hung up in the wardrobe. I rummage through the leather weekend bag that Gregory said we could share. I find his Bluetooth speakers and place them on the bedside cabinet, pairing them to my phone and putting my song list on shuffle.

The monsoon shower is so good, I have to drag myself out. I wrap myself in my kimono and rough-dry my hair before taking sections and blow-drying it straight, securing one side over my shoulder with a crystal and pearl comb. I'm almost done with my make-up when I hear the bedroom door close.

Gregory's eyes have a brandy sheen when he appears at the door to the bathroom but he doesn't seem drunk or even tipsy. He runs his attention from my head to my toes and his brandy sheen is replaced with desire. If I hold his stare, I'll relent. I look instead at the object he holds in his hand.

'What's that?'

He holds it up. 'It's tradition. It represents the fox's tail.'

'Oh, of course, silly me. I should've been able to see that from the bunch of black feathers on a stick.'

He grins roguishly and moves towards me. He casts the feathers aside and grabs my arse cheeks, pulling my hips into his.

'No, Gregory. You'll ruin my make-up.'

He lifts my legs around his waist and sits me onto the marble unit. 'But I can kiss you here,' he says, drawing my kimono over my shoulders and taking my nipple in his mouth. 'Don't fight me, Scarlett; I've wanted to be inside you all day.'

'No, Gregory. I know where this leads and that's me having to redo my hair and make-up which I don't have time to do before dinner.'

He lifts his head, staring at me, his cogs in overdrive. 'So I can't put my lips on you and I can't touch your hair?'

My goddamn body is going to betray me and tell him to do whatever the hell he wants in whatever way he wants. I keep my lips firmly pressed shut and shake my head.

His brows furrow, then that roguish grin is back. He pulls me forward, my legs reflexively gripping his toned hips, and fixes those devastating browns on me, walking us to the bedroom. I give in. I move to drop my mouth to his but he pulls away.

'Your rules, Scarlett.'

He sets me on my feet in front of the four-poster bed. He looks up to the horizontal post above my head, then to my feet and disappears to the wardrobe. He comes back with my black stilettos and bends to put them on my feet.

'What are you, Prince Charming now?'

'I'm just giving you what you asked for, princess.' Smouldering, hooded eyes meet mine. I've no idea what's going through that complicated mind of his but I can't wait to find out.

He stands and slips the silk belt of my kimono, pulling me into him. I lift my hands to his neck but he places them back at my sides. 'No touching. Your rules.'

He pushes my kimono back over my shoulders to the floor, leaving me naked in my heels, then draws his fingertips up the sides of my body painfully slowly, before lifting my hands above my head. Goosebumps form on my skin as he wraps the silk belt twice around each of my wrists then threads it around the bed frame, binding my arms. I tug gently. They're secure.

The only other time he's gotten kinky in this way, I was the catalyst, too. I came home from Harrods with bags for me and one bag for him, containing a corset and stockings. I'd dressed in them and the new heels he'd bought me for Lara's party. I'd lain out on his chaise longue waiting for him to come to me. The thought of that night, how he blindfolded me and made me feel and smell everything intensely, has me squirming, my chest lifting and exposing my breasts.

He takes a step back and scrutinises his work. 'Perfect.'

He removes his tie. I know where it's going. His mind has conjured up the same memory as mine. I bite down on my lip to suppress the tension building between my thighs as he moves to the bed behind me and passes his tie across my eyes, knotting it at the back of my head. I'm nervously waiting. Vulnerable and desperate but anticipation making me wild. I can hear him moving around the room but I can't see a thing. Everything goes silent, then Shakespeare's Sister's 'Stay' fills my ears. *God, this is sexy as hell.* I'm already squirming, craving his touch. I let my head hang back, my arms pulling on the silk belt.

He starts with my toes. Soft, tingling feathers. They move up my lower leg in slow, controlled swirls. I swallow the desire that's built in my dry throat. The sensation climbs, circling my thigh, working higher. He reaches my hip, so close to where I want him, and my back arches so I'm tugging on my restraint.

My breathing quickens. The strokes move to my navel and spiral torturously up my abdomen. The feathers move in a soft line between my breasts, up my sternum. My muscles tense, my lungs unable to function. I silently beg him to move to my breasts and gasp when I feel the feathers tickle the full perimeter of my plump flesh then caress my nipple. I moan, my chest rising towards him, and I feel my clit swell, tingling. I shuffle my feet further apart. The desire to have him inside me is overwhelming. Every nerve ending in my body is coming to life.

This facet of him – the one that's dark and draws out a side of me I've never known – is as irresistible as the knight who kissed me under that tree against the backdrop of the setting sun.

My lungs fill with air when the feathers move to my shoulder and slowly down the length of my arm, finding places I've never been touched, driving me insane. He circles my wrist then pulls the feathers through my fingers, a most oddly sensual feeling. I'm completely under his control, bared to him. And instead of feeling exposed, I feel hot as hell.

The tingling glides to my neck. My arms yanking at the bed frame. The feathers caress my heated face and move down the skin of my throat, then my opposite arm, before coming back to my other breast. He draws a circle around the hard end, pausing as I pant and writhe. This is crazy but it's happening. He hasn't even touched me. I haven't felt his lips. I haven't felt his skin on mine, yet my hips are lifting as my insides begin to tense, my muscles crying out to feel him. I lick my lips at the thought of him naked in front of me, his erection waiting to fill me.

The caresses move across my waist.

'Please.'

I can't take any more. The feathers trace my hip then stroke my thigh, swirling around my lower leg, down to my foot. He draws the sensation through my toes and draws a line straight back up my thigh.

Now. It has to be now.

My head is fogging, my insides are pulsing. Then he does it. He draws a line straight down my centre, the feathers answering the prayers of each frantic nerve in my sex and I scream his name as my legs go weak and an orgasm shudders through my body.

'I love watching you come for me, Scarlett.'

Jesus, the sound of him saying my name has me writhing again. I want him inside me. I want him to continue the heady euphoria of my climax. I need to feel him come inside me.

'Gregory, let me feel you.' My words are barely audible.

The tie is pulled from my eyes and I open my lids, rewarded with a look of desire.

I take in the sight of his proud, angry erection against his stomach and groan.

'Fuck your rules!' He lifts my thighs around his waist and rams himself into me with a bark. I cry out with sheer pleasure, my painful yearning satisfied. He holds us still for a moment, taking my weight. I let him settle his throbs then move my hips, needing to feel him. He draws out and drives back in relentlessly until we're both on the edge.

'Please, Gregory!' It's one continuous orgasm but my insides are crying out to peak again, to feel the high.

'Come for me, baby.'

The most profound climax rips through every vein in my body and I implode. 'Gregory!' As I scream his name, his hips buck, pushing him brutally deep.

His teeth clamp down on my shoulder as he bursts inside me.

Once his breathing has returned to normal, he holds me up with one arm, pressing our sweaty chests together. He unties my wrists with his free hand, my limbs falling around his shoulders, weightless.

'How did you do that?' My words are weak mutterings into his neck. I don't need to look to know he has a smug grin on his face. Right now, I don't know whether to hate the other women he's been with or be grateful for the many skills he's acquired, the skills he uses to show me a new world.

* * *

My energy levels match my enthusiasm for attending this dinner, with all the predatory eyes I know will come with it. Gregory takes himself to the shower whilst I set about fixing my hair and finishing my make-up. I slip into a black lace thong and strapless bra then ponder how the devil I will get this Diane von Furstenberg over my head and face without unravelling everything I've just fixed.

I'm grateful that Gregory is tucked in the bathroom as I fumble my way, not at all gracefully, into my one-shoulder gown. I adjust the one long sleeve at the wrist, untwisting it all the way up to my shoulder. The gown hugs every curve of my body, the front sweeping the floor even in my heels, the back trailing slightly. I touch up my red lips and spray myself in Coco Mademoiselle, then carry out a final once-over in the floor-length mirror.

'You look unbelievable.' He's leaning against the doorframe, his hair slicked back, his three-piece dinner suit impeccable. He quite literally takes my breath away. We stay locked in a heated stare until my lungs cry out for oxygen.

'Shall we go?' He lifts an elbow for me to slide an arm through and leads me from the room, his strength preventing my trembling legs from giving way beneath me.

The whispers and scrutinising eyes of both men and women are even more uncomfortable than I've been imagining they would be. There're more people for dinner than were here this morning: at least eighty, maybe more. As we walk into the grand reception room, we're presented with a tray of full champagne flutes. Gregory releases my arm to take two glasses, giving me a chance to absorb the majesty of the old room. Red satin drapes across the large, arched windows, drawn back in the middle by gold rope ties. A concert harpist is playing an almost gothic melody as the log fire roars beside her. Whilst most people stand in their finery, snacking on canapés and sipping champagne, I see Florence talking to a silver-haired man with a matching beard and moustache, a hefty middle, both sitting on tall, wooden thrones. The thrones are upholstered in thick, red linen and match variations of the same chairs scattered around the perimeter of the room. I'm handed a glass of champagne on a reassuring smile before Charlotte and Williams make their way towards us. We have a chance to quickly exchange greetings and gush about dresses before the Duke and Duchess are announced to the room. The poor Duchess really looks beautiful in her royal-blue two piece but she shuffles in clear discomfort. The Duke guides her subtly by the elbow, bending his lanky frame a little to give her support. He thanks the hunt for returning for a fifty-third consecutive year, reminisces about tales of his father, then on completion of his speech, announces dinner.

We make our way into another, even grander – if that's possible – room. A nudge in my side knocks me into Gregory. His arm flies up protectively and I lean into him, thrilled that Stella is scowling.

'Ever so sorry, Sarah.'

'Scarlett,' Gregory growls at her, a reaction that pleases me immensely. She flashes my delectable gentleman a dazzling smile that isn't returned, then narrows her focus on me before continuing her strut to her table.

I'm relieved to be perched between Gregory and Williams for dinner. After the Duke says grace for the room, game terrine is placed in front of me. I spread a thick layer over my oat cakes and waste no time settling it into my empty stomach. It really is scrumptious.

'Good?' Gregory asks.

'Delicious,' I say, after clearing my mouth.

He's stolen away from me during our main course to indulge another affected woman in conversation. This one is Adriana, the pretty and much younger wife of Francis, the private equity investor Gregory seemed to dislike when he introduced us in the Shard. Francis studies me a little too closely as I eat my venison, whilst Adriana throws her head back on a fake laugh and touches Gregory anywhere she can reach despite the fact he hasn't said anything funny.

By the time my crème brûlée arrives, I'm too full to even attempt it. Gregory's now in a business conversation with Francis but Adriana's hungry eyes continue to watch him. I'm beyond fed up.

A different loud, flirtatious laugh makes me lift my focus from the piece of thread I'm playing with on the table. Charlotte is clearly tipsy and behaving as though she's overly interested in a middle-aged man who's admittedly quite handsome in a silvering fox kind of way but far too old for her. It's actually a little creepy if I'm honest, the way he's touching her hair and feigning interest in a story about her watch, which she got for her eighteenth birthday. That it was just three years ago doesn't seem to faze him.

'Want to get some air?' Williams is leaning in, his hushed tone for only my ears. He seems as truly pissed off as I am.

'Love to,' I admit with the first genuine smile I've offered this evening.

As I make to stand from the table, Gregory's hand clamps around my wrist, his face filled with concern. 'Are you okay?'

'Yes.' My tone is sharper than I intend. I force my lips into a soft smile for the other eyes around the table but speak through my teeth. 'I'm fine. I'm going to get some air with Williams.'

'I'll come out in five minutes.'

'No rush.' And I mean it. He's ignored me long enough; why change his attitude now? Christ, he has me up and down like a yo-yo. One minute, I'm high on life and him, feeling like I have everything I'll ever need and want. The next, the possibility of a break, an opportunity to get my head straight in Dubai, doesn't seem like a bad idea. But I'm afraid. Afraid of what I could lose if I go. Those highs. My reason. My sanity. The reality that we're on day seven of the countdown to the ballistics report comes crashing to me. We're on borrowed time until those findings.

'How do you stand this every year?' I ask Williams.

The cold air feels nice on my hot, irritable skin.

He leans forward, resting his elbows on the wall of the veranda. 'It drives me half-insane but we've got some good business contacts here.'

'Charlotte's sweet.' I fold my arms across my chest, the cold beginning to bite.

He shakes his head then drops it to look at his feet. 'She's the reason I'm out here.'

'The flirting?'

'I don't know what's got into her this last year or so. It's like she's found sex.'

I smirk, knowing the feeling.

'I was going to bring Amanda,' he says, flicking a questioning eye to me. 'I didn't want to bring Charlotte after last year.'

I don't know which statement to respond to first. I want to dig a little about my best friend and what happened last year sounds quite intriguing too. I resolve to tackle both. 'What happened last year?'

'Long story short. She got drunk, got flirtatious then got dragged to bed kicking and screaming.'

'By you?'

'Gregory. He looks out for her and bollocks me when I screw up looking after her.'

I want to ask why he wasn't looking out for his little sister himself but I move on to my next intriguing topic. 'Did you ask Amanda to come?'

'I was about to when she told me she didn't want to see me any more. Something about her and space and learning lessons.'

I roll my eyes. 'She'll see sense.'

'Right!' He pushes himself up as if someone just shot him with adrenalin. 'Back to fending off the wolves.'

I internally laugh at the thought that he has to fend dirty old men off his twenty-one-year-old sister whilst I'm struggling to fend a load of floozies off my thirty-year-old man.

'Can I escort you back, my lady?'

'Actually, I'm going to enjoy this fine weather a little longer.' I lean forward, replacing Williams in his spot on the veranda and watch a shooting star glide through the crisp, black sky until it disappears.

'Are you going to tell me what I've done wrong or am I going to have to guess?' His velvet words reach me just before his dinner jacket is draped across my shoulders, still warm from his body. I inhale his scent and pull the jacket tighter around me. 'I've been ignoring you,' he says when I don't answer.

'Acting like I don't exist and entertaining Adriana, you mean.'

'It's just business, Scarlett.'

'Please tell me what *business* Adriana is in,' I snap, turning to leave the veranda.

'Hold the fort,' he says, grabbing my arm back.

Despite my irritation, I tell him, 'You mean hold the phone.'

'Whichever,' he says resting back on the veranda. I resume my position next to him. 'She's in the business of *if I don't keep her happy, I don't keep her husband happy* and her husband is a very wealthy man.'

'Her husband's a sleazy dick.'

He laughs, a warm sound that causes me to let out a short laugh too. 'He is a dick.' He nudges into my shoulder and drops a kiss on my cheek. 'Dance with me?'

'You don't deserve my moves,' I say stubbornly whilst tuning into the sound of the band covering Sammy Davis Junior's 'Mr Bojangles.'

Taking my hands, he pulls me to him. 'I'll see your moves later. Right now, I really want you to dance with me.'

He raises my right hand in the air with his and I shuffle my left palm to his shoulder as he turns us to *bo-oh-oh-oh-oh-oh-jangles.*

'I'm not sure you have much in common with a man in shabby clothes with a dog.'

'I have dogs at the farm.' He smiles, the kind of smile he reserves for me. Liquefying.

I feel his body tense before he leaves me so abruptly, I almost stumble to the floor. It takes me seconds to regain my balance and process Gregory surging from the veranda into the reception room where the man Charlotte was flirting with is leading her by the hand up the grand staircase to the bedrooms.

It happens quickly. Gregory reaches them at the top of the stairs. Charlotte staggers back as Gregory pins the man by his throat to the wall, just out of view of the rest of the room but not those at the bottom of the stairs and not me, making my way towards the commotion.

'What the fuck do you think you're doing?' Gregory is seething, his muscles bulging beneath his suit, his words a strong, South African bark.

'Take your fucking hands off me!'

Gregory reaffirms his grip on the man's throat and slams his head into the stone wall again. Seeing the ruthlessness in his black eyes, I'm reminded of what Gregory is capable of. His rage will kill this man.

'Gregory! Stop!' I yell, then move towards them, trying to shift into Gregory's field of vision.

His dilated pupils find me and soften but then his face contorts and he slams the man's head against the wall again. 'Don't ever lay a fucking hand on her. Do you hear me?' Head meets stone again. 'Do you fucking hear me?'

'Yes, Christ! Let me go!'

Gregory drops his grip and the man falls limply to the ground.

'You mad bastard. She's gagging for it.'

Williams comes out of nowhere and grabs Gregory's fist before he lands a blow. 'I've got it, Greg; get out of here.'

'You shouldn't have left her with him,' he snarls at Williams as he yanks his arm back, still glaring at the heap of man on the floor.

A million thoughts are crashing through my mind and I can't get a handle on what just happened. His rage.

Two deep, brown pools move to consider me. I have nothing to say.

'I've suspected for a while that he was in love with his best friend's sister. Seems obvious now, don't you think?'

I turn to find the smug face that owns that whisper. Stella.

'Well, that he's fucked her in any event.' Her lips are curled into a snarl. She's the final straw in this whole godawful day.

Gregory steps towards me as the other guests go back to their own business.

I hold up a palm. 'Don't. I've had just about all the humiliation I can take.'

I barge past him, walking quickly, almost running the corridor to our room. Jealousy burns through my entire body, worse than this morning, worse than when any other woman has looked at him because this is different. He was like an animal, so protective and... possessive.

I sit on the edge of the bed and make soothing circles with my fingers at my temples. I really might be going insane. I don't know how much more I can take of this man: his hidden truths, his lies, *our* lies, *our* deception.

Does he love her? Is he fucking her? The rational side of my brain is screaming *no* but the other has been crying out for him to say those three words to *me*.

The bedroom door closes but I refuse to look at him.

'Scarlett.'

'Don't talk to me, Gregory. I don't want to hear it.'

He stalks towards me, his feet moving into my line of sight. 'Hear what? That I'm not sorry I just stopped that arsehole taking Charlie to bed?'

'No. I don't want to hear the why.'

He bends now, putting his hands on my knees, and lifts my chin with his index finger in that goddamn tender Gregory way.

'Those women, all of them, they want you. I've been fighting the pack all day. Then you ignore me to flirt with Adriana all night. And don't tell me it's just business; she was all over you. To top it off, you let the entire world know that, that... Do you love Charlotte?'

He laughs like I'm a silly little girl and I want to slap his stupid, arrogant, beautiful face.

'Scarlett, angel, she's a kid. She's like a sister to me. I've known her since she was a toddler. I'm not in love with her but I look out for her. Like a brother should look out for a sister. And Williams...' He stops and shakes his head. 'Williams does a pretty shitty job of it sometimes.'

'Stella said... Have you... have you slept with her?'

He pushes up from my knees and sets about undoing his bow tie.

'And what about all these other women? Have they... have they *had* you?'

'I'm not dignifying that question with an answer.'

'That's a yes.'

He throws his dinner jacket onto the bed and makes his way to the bathroom. 'No. That means stop behaving like a fucking child.'

I know it's irrational and I know how pathetic I must look but the weight of today, the weight of everything, is crippling my chest. I move to the wardrobe and retrieve my bag, throwing my clothes, shoes and anything else into it. I need to get out of here. *I'm losing my mind.*

'Scarlett.' His voice is soft and quiet as he leans in the doorway to the bathroom, watching me pack.

'I'm going, Gregory. I don't know why you brought me here.'

He stalks towards me topless, all moody and sexy as hell. *Damn myself for looking!*

'Where do you think you're going to go?'

Shit! I can't drive, neither can he and I'm in the middle of nowhere. Throwing my deodorant into the bag, I thrust the whole thing against the bathroom wall, frustrated and defeated.

I flinch as he rests his hands on my shoulders and lowers his head so I'm forced to look into those devastating eyes. 'I brought you here because I wanted to spend the night with you. I have a funny way of showing it, I know. I messed up. Again. And I'm sorry.'

I swipe my wet cheeks with the back of my hand and storm into the bathroom with less conviction than I had just moments ago.

Once I've showered and put on my nightdress, Gregory comes into the bathroom and showers quickly. We brush our teeth, each of us casting occasional glances at the other in the mirror above the his-and-hers sink but neither of us speaking.

I crawl under the bed covers with no intention of speaking to him or touching him, leaning as far on my side of the bed as I physically can without falling out. But his strong arm wraps around my waist and pulls me into his chest. My body caves in.

'I hate that I make you unhappy,' he whispers into my neck.

'You do.' I squirm into his chest. 'But you've also shown me a new kind of happy.' *And there's my dilemma, Gregory Ryans: I'm a mess with you but I think I'd be a bigger mess without you.* 'And maybe, *maybe*, I overreacted.'

He nuzzles into my neck. 'It's not just about tonight. I get it.'

I roll over to face him, my head resting on his pillow. 'This isn't easy on either of us, especially you. And I know you want to tell me you won't be charged but we can't know that for sure. I don't want you to take the blame for me, Gregory.'

His face contorts in contrast to the tender fingers he trails down my cheek. My chest flutters as he opens his mouth to speak. I wait.

'I just wish the decision would come sooner rather than later.'

A piece of my heart breaks as I swallow my waning faith. 'Me too.'

'Can I kiss you?'

I nod and he lowers his lips to mine.

'Gregory.'

'Hmm.'

'If you could try not to make every woman you meet want to sleep with you, it would really make my life a whole lot bloody easier.'

'I'll do my best,' he says, his chest rising against mine as he smiles into my hair.

11

'Rise and shine, baby; you need to get dressed. We need to get back to London.'

I roll onto my back with a moan. 'Why are we in such a rush?'

He looks over his shoulder from his perch on the end of the bed where he's pulling on his boots. 'As much as I could look at that fine naked body of yours all day, I want it in *my* bed.'

Oh! 'Is that right?'

'That's right.'

'And what if I say no?'

He crawls onto the bed and lies above me, all dark jeans and tight, black t-shirt, with twinkling irises gazing down at me.

'You won't,' he says, his minty breath too close, making it difficult for me to find sensibility.

'Oh, really?'

'Really, because I happen to know you can't resist me.'

I have to force my hands to stay by my side instead of going rummaging under his T-shirt. 'Hmm, you've got me. It's your modesty; I'm so hot for it.'

In one fast move, he pins my hands to my sides with his legs and thrusts his tickling fingers under my arms.

'Get off me, Gregory! Get off me!'

I squirm beneath him but he doesn't relent. My squirms turn to screams and as his tickling increases, a belly laugh takes over my body. I'm heaving and panting but he still keeps going. 'Stop! Please, stop!'

He halts his assault and I heave air into my chest. 'Will you quit with the attitude?'

'I don't have an attitude!'

'Wrong answer.' The tickle torture recommences. His fingers are attacking my skin again and I'm squealing in response until the squealing turns back into a rib-aching laugh.

'Stop! Please! Stop it!'

'Will you be nice to me?' This time, he won't give me a second to think; his fingers continue driving my fit of giggles. *God, it feels good to laugh.*

'Yes! Yes. I'll be nice to you.'

He flashes me his most mischievous grin, white, perfect teeth and all. 'Good girl. Come on.' He jumps off the bed and offers me a hand.

'What're we doing?'

'*You* are going to get dressed.' He pulls me towards him and drops a kiss on the tip of my nose. 'Then I'm going to take you home and make all of this up to you. Today is all about Scarlett.'

'You mean, you're apologising to me?'

He cocks his head to one side on a playful pout. 'Do I need to show you who's boss again?'

I shake my head quickly. 'So do I get to choose what we do?'

'Erm, no. I said today is all *about* Scarlett, not *up to* Scarlett. But don't worry; I plan on making up to you *all* day. What else are Sundays for?'

Sunday. Day eight.

'What's wrong, baby?'

'Nothing... I was just thinking—'

'That John Harrison told us five to seven days. I know.'

'How can you be so calm?'

'It's life, Scarlett.'

'I'm not even going to pretend I understand that comment.'

'Look at me. Stop biting your lip. Tell me what else John said.'

I shrug.

'He said the longer it takes for the CPS to make a decision, the better. We're another day closer to putting that night behind us, Scarlett.'

I wish I could believe that, I really do.

* * *

Gregory spins the Range Rover into a supermarket car park and leaves, returning with a bag of shopping, which he drops into the back seat.

'Are you cooking for me?' I ask, unable to hide the surprise in my voice.

He casts his head over his shoulder and reverses out of the space, then knocks the car into first gear and shoots out of the car park at Gregory speed.

'I'm feeding you,' he says, watching the road ahead with the smallest upturn of his lips. 'Well, I might be; that really depends on you.'

By the time we reach the Shard, I really am hungry but I can't tell which is the bigger cause: my empty stomach or the man next to me. Gregory opens the door for me and as soon as we're in, he casts the weekend bag aside. My back is pressed against the wall of the lounge and he takes me by surprise, his tongue making a delicious sweep of mine. I'll never be able to resist his touch, his taste. I accept his attack, groaning into him. He circles his already hard crotch against my skinny jeans and pulls my body into him with one arm at the small of my back, the other at the nape of my neck. I liquefy in his hold as he takes command of my body. I know who's boss and I don't care. I willingly relent control.

In one easy move, he lifts me, my legs wrapping around his lean hips. He carries us to the walk-in shower and plants me on my feet whilst he turns it on.

'I'm hot from the drive,' he explains. Not that I need an explanation; I'll take any opportunity to see his sublime naked body. He releases my hair from its messy knot and pulls it through his fingers. 'I'll never have my fill of you.'

'Good,' I whisper into his parted lips. 'I think I'm going to like make-up sex,' I tell him.

'Baby, I like every kind of sex with you.'

Once we're showered and sated, for now, he dries every inch of my skin and towel-dries my hair, letting me see tender Gregory, the Gregory that most people never get to meet. He takes my hand after a chaste kiss on my brow and leads me to the walk-in wardrobe in all our naked glory. He slips into a pair of dark denim jeans and fumbles around locating my underwear drawer. That heartbreaking half-smile is plastered on his perfectly angular face when he turns, dangling a black, lace thong in the air from one hand and a black, satin eye cover in the other.

'Wait for me in the bedroom. Wearing these. *Only* these.'

I have no idea what he's planning but something tells me I'll like it. I do as he says, making quick working of hanging my head upside down and blasting my long locks with the hairdryer. I coat myself in shea butter then slip on the black thong and make my way to our bed, crawling backwards up the sheets, already turned on with anticipation. When his footsteps approach, I slip on the blindfold as he told me to do. Just the sound of him, knowing he's in the room, has me wriggling and turning my fingers in the satin bed throw.

I quell my excitement, digging my teeth into my bottom lip, then the sound of him is drowned out by The Verve's 'She's a Superstar.' The guitar hits my ears first, followed by the beat of the bass drum and when the beat drops for the smooth voice, I can feel Gregory near me. My nerve endings are tingling like the strings of the electric guitar. His hands part my thighs, his touch and the soft kiss of air between my labia set off fireworks at my no-doubt drenched vulva. His mouth strokes my navel, sucking, nibbling, his bare body caressing mine as he works up to my neck.

'Open your mouth.' He words are low and drenched in sex. 'We're going to play a game.'

I'd ask him what the game is but my brain refuses to send a signal to my lips. I open my mouth, my heart rate already rising.

'You're going to guess what I put in your mouth.' He's hovering over me now, his breath close to me. 'If you guess right, I'll feed you.'

'If not?'

'You'll go hungry.'

I know he doesn't mean for food. He'll refrain from the only thing that can sate the hunger I'm feeling right now in my spinning head, my fluttering chest, my knotted stomach and my throbbing entrance. The stakes are high.

'We'll start easy.' He lowers himself so the weight of his hips is pressing his erection onto my abdomen, his torso held on his arms. 'Open.'

Cool, wet, smooth. He slowly sweeps something across my lips. The tip of my tongue slides forward to meet it. Mm, sweetness. I swirl my tongue around the tip of the fruit, lapping up the syrupy juice. Then the fruit is gone. I want more.

'Strawberry.'

'Good girl.'

The strawberry is back on my lips. I reach out my tongue again, this time finding Gregory's mouth wrapped around the berry, lowering the fruit into my mouth. I bite into the strawberry when his mouth presses against mine. We chew and swallow, then he sucks the last drop of flavour from my bottom lip.

Jesus, that's erotic.

He draws back, exposing my lips, my face, my chest, leaving me squirming, bereft beneath him, desperate for his touch. I go to move my hands to his hair but his hands clamp down on my wrists and place them back to my sides.

'No touching.'

I twist my fingers into the bed throw, my hips mirroring the circular motion.

'Another?' The lust in his words is a match for my wanton state.

I shake my head, meaning to nod. 'Yes.'

'Yes, what?'

'Yes. Please.'

I smell it before I taste it, the rich and bitter blend piercing my heightened senses. 'Chocolate.' The word leaves me on an exhale, breathy, pleading.

'That won't do, Miss Heath.' He pushes himself up, the scent disappearing, his weight lessening between my thighs.

'No. Wait.' My need to feel him against me, to have my senses driven crazy, is agonising. 'Dark. Dark chocolate.'

He lowers himself but not all the way. I could scream. I need to feel him. The smell is back, driving through my nose and clouding my mind. 'Orange.' I lick my lips. 'Dark chocolate with orange.'

He lowers his hips, grinding his erection onto my stomach. I moan under his weight. Then his chocolate-covered finger is in my mouth. The only part of him I can take. And I do. I close my mouth around the base of his finger and draw back slowly, relieving him of chocolate, taking the richness with the subtle taste of salt from his skin and dragging the most erotic sound from him.

I'm gripping the bed throw, my back bowed, heat travelling up from my core. I lift my hips to feel his pressure against me. His chest lowers, rubbing against my breasts. He's touching every part of me, making me ravenous.

He lifts his torso, cool air taking the edge off my burning urge to have him.

'Next.'

Oh God! How much more can I take?

I concentrate on calming my raging desire and focus on the intensity of the building Evanescence track playing in the background.

'Open.'

My head is filled with the power of the female voice, the piano, building strings reflecting the mounting tension in my muscles.

His mouth. Salt. The sea. He's taking over my mind, my body, my pounding heart, my pulsing thighs. My fists clench, my hips push into him and I bite down on his lip.

'The sea.' It's not an answer. I can't think of the answer.

His mouth leaves mine. His torso lifts from my chest. Despair kicks my brain back into action.

'Oyster. Oyster.'

'Good girl.'

He lifts my leaden head by the nape of my neck. My mouth automatically opens and takes the saltiness, the oyster sliding down my throat, the ice-cold wetness soothing my dry skin. I know what comes next. I push my shoulders into the mattress, my spine arching in anticipation. My panting breaths return, my hips thrust up to meet his shaft. He waits, the seconds torturing my frenzied mind.

Then his tongue makes a delicious sweep of my top lip and drops into my mouth. I dig my fingernails into the skin of my palms as he grinds against me on a low, rumbling growl.

'Gregory, take me.' I don't recognise my voice. Hoarse. Sex-filled. Shameless.

'Not yet. I'm savouring every move you make, every pant, every thrust. This bursting in your chest.' He places his hot palm against my heart. I can feel it thudding against him. His touch, his scent, pushing me to euphoria. 'Last one.'

I wait, drowning in expectation. My body on fire, writhing beneath him, begging for him to quench my yearning.

The frozen cube stings my flesh.

'Ice.' My word is barely audible, obscured by short, desperate breaths.

I open my mouth, expecting to taste him but he slides the ice down my chin, in a line down my neck and onto my chest. He draws a circle around my full breast, then lets the ice bite my hard nipple. He trails the cube down my abdomen, my body moving in waves beneath him. I'm contracting between my legs in the knowledge that he's working his way down. My orgasm is near, my entrance painfully aware of its emptiness.

He reaches my navel with the ice melting against my burning skin, his lips getting closer to my flesh as the cube diminishes. My hips gyrate without rhythm and I bite my lip to stop myself from crying out. He continues to move the cube but not down; he draws to the side, caressing my thigh.

'Gregory, I need you. Let me have you.'

The ice changes direction, working back up my thigh, onto my stomach. He brings it to rest on my belly button and I feel a drop of ice water lick my skin as it falls to my hip. Then he parts my labia with his fingers and attacks my raging bud with his mouth. I cry out in shock and delight. I've waited too long.

'So wet.' I feel his words on my centre.

'Gregory. Take me *now*.' I'm brazen and I don't care. He's taken everything I have, built me to the point of explosion, and now I need to let go.

'You win, baby.' His voice is carnal.

He kneels between my thighs and lifts my leg, kissing every inch, throwing my head further into a cloud of lust when he reaches the inside of my thigh. My mind is flashing bright colours. I think I'm going to black out. His tongue strokes me, one delectable line up my centre. Then those sweet kisses are back, his lips falling in a line up my navel, my stomach. He draws a circle around my nipple before sucking it into his mouth. The muscles of my vulva start clenching. I'm there and this is going to happen with or without him inside me.

'I love seeing you like this. You're such a fucking turn-on,' he growls.

He pulls my bottom lip hard between his teeth then absorbs my gasp of painful pleasure.

Kneeling up, he lifts my hips, my back bowing towards him. He pulls a hand down my sternum, my stomach, then returns it to my back and smashes into me on a mind-blowing, punishing drive that makes me scream.

'Fuck, Scarlett, you feel fucking amazing!'

This is the last assault on my senses I can take. He moves in controlled, deep circles, holding my hips so he's pushed as far inside me as physically possible. My hips lift to meet each roll of his. His exquisite rhythm never falters as the weight of him, the sensation of him filling me takes me the final inch to the orgasm that's going to overpower my entire body.

Oh, Jesus! My hands are in my hair, pulling my roots as my head shakes from side to side. 'Gregory! Harder!'

He drives into me ruthlessly until I can feel him throbbing inside me. He's ready.

'Come for me, baby; let me feel you.'

I lose all control as my orgasm overpowers me. Every drop of need and desire bursts from within me, hitting me in ferocious waves, washing me up in another world. His hips buck ruthlessly, his shaft pulsing as his climax hits on a round of expletives.

My body flops, completely satisfied and utterly spent. He swirls his hips slowly until he stops contracting, then drops to his back, rolling me on top of him. I take off my blindfold and watch my truly mesmerising man, sweating and panting beneath me.

'I accept your apology.'

'That's the most beautiful smile I've ever seen.' He strokes my damp hair from my face and wraps his arms around me, pulling my face into his neck.

I bury the urge to tell him I love him. My heart is just not strong enough to hear that the feeling is one-sided. Instead, I place my hand over his chest and hope that inside, he feels the way his actions suggest. He pulls me tighter into him and strokes lines up and down my back with his fingertips.

'Aurora.' He speaks with just a whisper in my ear but that whisper is all I need to hear. It's his own way of letting me know he cares.

I close my eyes and drown in utter contentedness, breathing him in, feeling his soft touch on my skin.

Then I panic. This could end any time now with one knock on the door, one phone call, one police car.

12

I'm ravenous when I wake. It's dark outside, the flashing, red lights of aeroplane wings passing the window are the only light I see, yet I know I haven't slept for long. I'm alone. I pull the white, cotton bed sheet around me and go in search of food. I can hear the clattering of pans in the kitchen and the low hum of The Script playing through the sound system. Gregory's oblivious as I tiptoe down the stairs, watching him flip a block of cheese from the fridge with one hand and catch it in the other before locating the grater. Who knew the sexy CEO could cook?

He looks at ease, laid-back even in his dark, low-rise jeans and fitted, white T-shirt. As much as his expensive, tailored suits drive me crazy with desire, his casual look is insanely hot, too. I plonk myself on the bottom stair and watch him move, grinning from ear to ear when he eventually spots me.

'Hungry?' he asks, holding up an oven tray with garlic bread.

'Starving.'

He drops the garlic bread onto a wooden board then sets it on the breakfast bar between two placemats. 'Good.' He pats a stool invitingly. 'I'm so hungry, I could eat a cow.'

I giggle as I totter to the stool, perching myself on top of it, arranging the bed sheet around me to spare my graces. 'Horse. You're so hungry, you could eat a horse.'

He pauses, holding a pan aloft above the sink. 'Why would I want to eat a horse?'

'Erm, well, I don't know. That's a good point. I would also rather eat a cow than a horse.'

'So I'm right then?'

'Well, no. The saying is *horse*.'

He shrugs and proceeds to strain penne pasta.

'What're we having?'

He pours the drained pasta into another larger pan which is already bubbling on the induction hob, then stirs the contents of both pans together and finishes by spooning the pasta onto two plates and tops each with parmesan.

'I like to call it Al Italiano Meato Pasto by Gregory.' He plants the plate in front of me and drops a kiss on my temple.

'Just rolls off the tongue,' I say.

He reaches for a slice of the garlic baguette and gives me a lopsided smirk that nearly knocks me from my stool. Laid-back and damn sexy. I could get used to this Gregory. I feel black thoughts creeping up on me and I have to fight them back down, focusing on my forkful of pasta, blowing on it then putting the whole thing greedily into my mouth. I'm hit by tomato, garlic, herbs and the intense flavours of cured meats. 'Mm, super good. I didn't realise you could cook.'

He finishes chewing his mouthful of food. 'I can't. Al Italiano Meato Pasto by Gregory is the only dish I know.'

I laugh again at his elaborate Italian accent with a hint of South African twang. 'Who taught you?'

'No one really. It just sort of happened. Would you like wine?' He reaches for an open bottle of Malbec and two wine glasses.

'Yes, please.'

He pours, then sits back on his stool. 'I spent some time in Italy. In the early days, when I was trying to get GJR off the ground in Europe. I kept ordering dishes similar to this.' He looks down at his plate. 'Kind of. They were better presented in Italy.'

'You lived in Italy?'

'Of a sorts. I was in Italy for three months but I moved around the big cities. I spent most of my time in Milan.'

'I'd love to go to Italy. Wander the cobbled streets in a white, cotton dress. Sip espresso with the locals. Ride a scooter.'

'Let's take tomorrow off.' His face is absolutely serious.

Swallowing, I ponder the idea. 'I can't just take the day off.'

'Yes, you can. Let's spend the day together, just us.'

'But... well, I... I have work to do. I can't just leave my clients in the lurch and... you could be, we might be, you could be charged any time.'

He pulls my stool towards him so my knees are pressed between his. 'I want us to have a normal day. No shit. Just you and me.'

'Okay.'

'Okay?'

'Okay. I'll email Neil after dinner.'

Neil. Mr Ghurair. Dubai. I smile at my astounding CEO. There's no way in hell I'll leave this man by choice. For the first time, I'm hopeful. Hopeful that he's falling as hard for me as I have for him. Hopeful that no news of the case by day eight means we might escape charge. Maybe, just maybe, this could work.

'You need to eat some of that,' he says, inclining his head towards the plate of garlic bread.

Giddy with the light feeling in my chest I ask, 'You think you have garlic breath, don't you?'

'I don't think. I know. Eat.' He picks up a slice of baguette. 'Open.'

I do as I'm told, laughing as my mouth is stuffed with potent garlic bread. As I'm slowly churning through the mouthful, the intercom to the apartment rings.

With furrowed brows, Gregory eventually goes to answer the intercom. 'Ryans.' The colour drains from his face, leaving a grey, concerned man in its wake. 'Send him up.'

He hangs up the receiver and before I can ask who's here, he's pressed his phone and he's pacing as he waits for the person on the other end to pick up. 'Jackson. Yes. Did you know? Now.' He hangs up and I hear Jackson making his way into the apartment from his self-contained wing. 'Baby, I need you to do something for me.' He lifts me from the stool and plants me on my feet. 'I need you to go upstairs and stay up there until I say otherwise.'

'What? Why? Who was that?' I sound concerned and I am. 'What's going on, Gregory?'

'Scarlett, please don't challenge me on this. I don't know what's going on yet.' He grabs my wine glass and plate, holding them out for me to take. I'm gripping the bed sheet around me with one hand so even if I wanted to take both things from him, I couldn't, but refusing is the one thing I can control. His stern, set jaw is telling me he won't relent.

With a scowl, I snatch the glass of wine from him and stomp through the lounge and up the stairs.

As much as I don't want to, I try to do as I'm told. I exchange the bed sheet for leggings and an oversized jumper and tie my hair into a rough knot. I make up the bed. But the distractions are short-lived. I want to know who's downstairs and why our night together has been hijacked. Silently tiptoeing to the top of the stairs, I hear male voices. Gregory. Jackson. And a voice I recognise but can't place. Taking another three stairs, I pause and listen.

'I told you to tell me if there was anything else I should know, Jackson.' The third man's words are low and controlled but there's no mistaking the anger driving them.

'I told you everything you needed to know,' Jackson says.

'There's nothing to tell.' Gregory's tone is clipped. 'The pair of you need to stop trying to pull the fucking wool over my eyes.' The stranger is growling. 'NABIS have told me the story doesn't add up. Their report is on the record. I've done what I can but now I don't have a choice; I have to investigate it properly. No matter how this ends, it won't end with me losing my fucking job so what's on the record needs to be looked into. I need to bring people in for questioning and it would be a lot fucking easier for me to fix if I know what I'm dealing with.'

'NABIS have got it wrong. It happens,' Jackson snaps.

'What the fuck is NABIS?' Gregory's pissed but there's something else in his voice: concern, I think.

'Ballistics,' Jackson and the stranger say together.

The stranger starts to speak again, now composed, matter-of-fact. I know who it is. 'The report is back from Ballistics,' DI Barnes explains. 'Ballistics are—'

'I know what fucking ballistics are; tell me what the report says.'

'Sit down.' Jackson's words are softer now.

'I'm fine where I am.'

I need to hear this. I slide down two more steps to where I can see them in the lounge. Gregory is standing in the window, his back to the other two. Jackson's perched on the end of a leather chair, his recovering leg outstretched in his stonewashed jeans. DI Barnes sits back into the sofa.

'Calm down, Greg.' Jackson attempts to placate him.

DI Barnes pulls a hand through his greying, black hair then rubs his dark stubble. 'Ballistics say the gun was fired head on and that it was fired from a distance of at least two meters.'

The room falls silent. Gregory stands deadly still in the window and all I can hear is my own laboured breathing. Even when I thought the worst, I managed to convince myself on some level that the report would show Pearson was shot, then the CPS would agree with a finding of self-defence. It didn't occur to me that NABIS would implicate me.

'I've done my best with what you gave me. I thought we might be able to stop it but consider this your advance warning. When Trina gets this tomorrow, she'll be over it like a hawk.'

'You said she was off the case,' Jackson snaps.

'She is but she's hovering. She's got a point to prove. She doesn't like me; she hates the system. She's looking for a big case to make her mark. She transferred to the city from the regions and she'll stop at nothing if she thinks there's a scandal.'

'There is no scandal.' Gregory is measured as he unfolds his arms from his chest and shoves his hands into the pockets of his jeans. 'That report proves nothing when three people are telling you what happened. So I shot the bastard on an awkward angle. What does that prove?'

DI Barnes rises from the sofa, glaring at Gregory's back. 'There were four people in that room. One is dead. One was locked in a tussle with the victim, making it impossible for him to take a shot from two meters. That leaves two others. Jackson was shot and bleeding. Did he get up, retrieve the gun, walk from the door to the middle of the lounge, and shoot your father?' He takes two steps forward so he's closer to Gregory's tense back. 'Now I know that didn't happen, because there was no blood between the door and the lounge. That leaves one other person in the room and only one conclusion to be drawn.'

Gregory turns now, fast and furious, his entire body tensing, making him seem taller and broader than normal. 'She had nothing to do with it.'

I did. And I can see clearly now. This was supposed to happen. Gregory made me follow his plan when I wanted to tell the truth but now he can't deny the evidence.

It's time. It's time to put a stop to this. It's time to free Gregory from his past and tell the truth.

I stand and walk down the remaining steps, no longer worried about my presence being heard, mentally preparing myself for the admission I'm about to make.

'Get back upstairs!' Gregory roars, my entire body jumping back.

'No.' I'm resolute. This is the right thing to do. I'm sick of the lies. I listened to him before, when he convinced me this would go away. Not now. They have evidence.

'Scarlett, get back upstairs, now!'

'Stop speaking to me like that. It's time, Gregory. I won't stand by and watch you go through this. I couldn't live with myself if anything happened to you.'

'Scarlett, I won't tell you again. Get back up those fucking stairs, now!'

'Do you have something to tell me, Scarlett?' DI Barnes positions himself between Gregory and me.

'Yes. I do.'

'No, she fucking doesn't.' Gregory is irate. His eyes are wild, possessed. In three strides, he reaches me. He drops his shoulder into my waist and hoists me up, leaving me kicking and screaming against his back as he drags me upstairs.

'Well, at least I know what I'm really dealing with now.' DI Barnes stands then and moves close to Jackson, his mumbles almost inaudible above my screeching.

'Put me down!' I'm screaming at him, punching at his lower back. Then I'm thrown on the bed in the first bedroom we come to. 'Why did you do that? Why won't you accept that I need to do this?'

'Fuck!' He's pacing the floor, both hands locked in his hair. Each time he glances at me, his eyes are bulging. He's trying to control himself but fury is driving him. My body jumps as he lets out a roar of exasperation then pounds his fist into the back of the bedroom door, puncturing the wood.

I don't know what to do or say so I sit on the edge of the bed, motionless.

'Why can't you just understand that this is something I have to do?' His tone is calmer now but he's still fighting his anger. He shakes off his already colouring and swelling hand as if pounding the door was a tickle.

'Because you won't talk to me. You won't let me understand. Take a chance on me, Gregory. Let me in.'

He drops to his knees in front of me, shuffling between my thighs, then he lifts my chin with his index finger until I'm looking into desolate eyes. 'Everything in my life before you was screwed up. I've spent my life trying to make up for everything I've done wrong and trying to move on from my past. But it haunts me. It's haunting me now. Can't you see that I expect us to go wrong? I know we will because that's what I do. I damage things and people.'

I open my mouth to speak but no words form. He expects us to fail. It's like he won't even try to defy the odds. My eyes fall to my fingers in my lap as they turn around each other.

Gregory lifts my chin again. 'Look at me. I wanted to hurt him. I wanted to kill him. You pulled that trigger but I'm the one who loaded the gun and forced you to fire. I screwed up and I'll spend every day for the rest of my life hating myself for dragging you into this. I didn't protect you. I let who I am hurt you.'

'Please don't say that. I picked up that gun to save you. I wanted you to be free of your past and I wanted revenge. You didn't drag me into this, Gregory. I had my own motives.'

'Motives that I inflicted on you. My past, my demons. I live with them every day and I won't... I couldn't live with myself if I did that to you. I'm dark, Scarlett. I'm fucked up. And I keep telling you that you deserve so much more than *me*.'

I swallow the lump that forms in my throat. 'And I keep telling you to stop saying that. You aren't like him; you aren't like your father. You deserved better than *him*.'

He shakes his head. 'You. Are. Incredible. You're strong, beautiful and smart. And I'm too damn selfish to let you go. I'm too selfish to let you have a happy life without me. But you should walk away and at some point, you'll see that. That's why we have to do this my way. Please.'

So she can move on. Anxiety strikes my chest and pressure builds behind my eyes.

'Gregory, I *am* happy with you. You're the only thing that makes me happy any more.'

He shakes his head again with a slow blink. 'Please don't ever say that. It breaks my heart to hear you say that. I've brought you so much upset.'

I take his divine, messed-up face in my palms and look him directly in the eyes. 'And you've shown me a new world, an unbelievable world where I'm alive. Truly alive. You do make me happy. Happier than I could've ever imagined before I met you.'

He shakes his head again. 'If anything ever happened to you, I'd kill myself, Scarlett.'

'Hey! Don't you ever say things like that! Do you hear me?'

'Please, Scarlett, you have to let me clean up this mess. The mess that I've caused.' My heart is breaking as he gives me what I suspect is just a taste of the depths of his pain.

I can't promise to see this through. But for now, I'll give him what he wants.

'You do deserve me,' I whisper, dropping my lips to his. I feel his head shake but I hold his face to mine, pouring every ounce of love I feel into him, until he relaxes into my kiss.

We won't fail. I won't let us.

13

Jackson let me fool around with the punch bag for ten minutes when I first came into the gym. Today's lesson focussed on teaching me to kick like a man... as opposed to a girl. Now I'm dripping in sweat on the spin bike, keeping a steady pace in the verses of the dance tracks he's playing through the sound system and sprinting through the choruses. Jackson is hollering at me to go faster. It feels good. Through each leg turn, I vent my frustration. We're back to where we were a week ago, overshadowed by uncertainty. But now the question isn't only whether the CPS will charge Gregory; it's also whether they'll charge me. I can't rely on self-defence. There was no glass in my side, no chain around my neck, killing me. There were only two things. The first, and I think or hope the most prevalent, was my need to protect the man who unequivocally possesses my heart. The second was the black streak of revenge coursing like tar through my blood.

John Harrison KC really does have his work cut out.

When my chorus ends, I drop the pace of my rotations and push back on my hands, sitting up straight and filling my lungs.

I open my eyes to see Gregory, back from his run, his grey T-shirt stained with sweat, his hair wet and slicked back. Anything I was thinking just got lost in the Land of Lascivious.

'Keep turning, Scarlett,' Jackson hollers, pausing midway through a bicep curl.

A smug half-smile washes over the face of the reason my legs feel like spaghetti. I force myself to keep going, picking up the pace with the beat of the music, but I can't take my eyes off my fine specimen as he removes his earbuds from his ears then peels his top from his hot, damp skin and over his head. Every muscle in his chest moves. If I was in paradise with just this man, there's no way I'd ditch the Adam to my Eve for an apple. This is why God made men, of that I'm sure.

'Like what you see?' *Arrogant arse.*

Ignoring him, I drop my head to sprint through the chorus but can't help a cheeky little glance up through my lashes.

He straps himself into boxing gloves and sets off swinging at the bag. *Fuck me gently!* His back twists, turns, stiffens, releases with each punishing blow. I think, I know, my jaw is hanging loose. When I realise that the tune in my ears is already part-way through the next chorus, I force my feet to spring into action, much to Jackson's amusement.

When I hit thirty minutes, I climb down from the bike and move to the area where there are mats, mirrors and exercise balls, to stretch. I make sure my leggings and Climacool T-shirt are where they should be, then reach up high and bend from my hips to touch my toes. When I rise, I take my legs wide. I reach up again and drop my hands to the ankle of my right foot. It feels so good, I hum. Then I repeat the same move, bending to meet my left ankle. The pounding of gloved fists against the punch bag stops. Peering between my legs, I find Gregory unashamedly standing next to the punch bag, arms folded, watching my arse.

'Like what you see?' I say with a smirk.

The Velcro of his gloves is ripped open and he's on me in a flash. He wraps his arms around my waist and lifts me, my back pressing against his chest as my legs flail in the air and I squeal. 'Damn right I do.'

We leave Jackson laughing on the leg press. He's obviously feeling stronger. I'm laughing too as Gregory darts up the stairs carrying me like I weigh nothing. He flicks on the shower then plants me on my feet, spinning me to face him.

'Such a temptress.' His hands are already under my T-shirt, lifting it over my arms. His mouth is on mine before my top reaches the floor. We kick off our trainers. This is going to be an extension of his high-energy workout. An endorphin fuck: killing my pain and taking me to Gregory euphoria all at once.

* * *

'Which one?' I scan the row of Gregory's supercars in the basement car park.

'You pick.' He stops walking, adjusting the cuffs of his high-end designer jacket.

'Let's try one I haven't been in before.' I have no idea about cars but I do recognise the Ferrari emblem. 'Ferrari,' I say with a smile.

He bends and adjusts the bottom of his dark jeans over his leather boot. 'I don't think so.'

'Why not? I've never been in a Ferrari.'

'Are you getting a taste for fast cars, Miss Heath?'

'Everything high and fast, right?'

He moves towards me, engulfing me in his firm arms. 'That's my girl.' He drops a kiss on my brow. My inner princess swoons. 'But we're not taking the Ferrari because the key in my pocket is for the Aston Martin.'

'If you had the key the whole time, why did you let me pick?'

He shrugs and drops a hand into mine, walking us towards the DB9 as it bleeps and flashes. 'Because winding you up is fun.'

I scowl at his back as he ducks into the driver seat.

We get to Lincoln's Inn with relative ease, rush hour having subsided. We walk the corridors of the old building in silence, my grip on his hand tightening as we get closer to John Harrison's office. Another dramatic switch from light to dark in our turbulent relationship. One minute, we're making love like animals in the shower; the next, we're on our way to see a lawyer about a murder charge.

I make to knock on the antique office door but Gregory grabs my hand and turns me to face him. 'Before we go in there, I want you to promise me that we're doing this my way. No attitude, Scarlett, do you hear me?'

'And by attitude, you mean *truth*?'

He sighs and bites my nose, I suspect half-playful and half in exasperation. 'By attitude, I mean that kind of insolence. My way, Scarlett. Don't make us fall out on our day off.'

'Some day off.'

'What did I just say?' He bites the tip of my nose again. 'Attitude.'

He raps on the door and John chirps, 'Come in.'

'Gregory, if John knows the truth, he'll be prepared.'

'Now then, old boy, good to see you again.' John stands from behind his desk as Gregory opens the door, deliberately cutting me off.

'Mr Harrison,' Gregory says with a curt nod.

'Take a seat, take a seat.' John wafts a hand at two leather chairs then lifts a pile of documents from his desk and dumps it on the floor so we can both see him when he resumes his position. 'Tea? Coffee?' He flicks his wrist in front of him and assesses his Breitling. 'It could be time for a pastry, could it not?'

I feel Gregory tense in his seat, heat emanating from him. 'We're fine. Can we discuss my case?'

John is visibly taken aback and must think better of ordering himself a drink and a pastry. 'Righty-ho, old boy.' He shuffles through some papers on his desk. 'Ah yes, here she is. The ballistics report.'

Gregory crosses one ankle over his opposite knee and drops his shoulders from their position around his ears. 'It suggests my story doesn't add up.'

John's eyes are wide. 'Dare I ask how you already know what is in the report despite the fact your lawyer received it thirty minutes before you arrived?'

Gregory brings his hands to a steeple. 'Best not.'

John drops the report on the desk in front of him and leans back in his chair, his upper body mirroring Gregory's. 'Right you are. In that case, the report suggests to me one of two things. In the first option, three witnesses, including the accused, were mistaken about what they saw and did. In the second, someone else took that shot.'

They stare at one another across the desk, neither one willing to be the first to break contact. Eventually, John blinks.

'As I have told you before, I'm defending *you*; I am not protecting a third party.' He shifts his focus to me and back to Gregory. 'If you want me to help you, you need to give me the facts.'

'You have the facts, Mr Harrison.'

'Are you telling me the report is wrong? Because if that is your proposed defence strategy, old boy, you might as well put yourself in shackles and chains and cart yourself off to hell now.'

I close my eyes but the image of Gregory in a prison cell won't be blocked out. I take two deep breaths and when I open my eyes, Gregory's watching me. He moves a hand subtly to my knee and I accept it, placing my chilled palm across his warm skin.

'What are the options?' He speaks to John without moving his attention from me.

John sighs. 'Well, you can change your story. The danger being, you look like a liar. If it goes to court, you have already lost the jury. Or, you can stick to your story. Then you have three statements, assuming none of those statements change, arguing against a ballistics report. If you risk the latter, there is a good chance the prosecution will start digging for the person who really took that shot, scrutinising the forensic evidence more closely, interviewing acquaintances.'

This is falling apart and there's only me who can stop it.

'Of course, I will continue to look for holes in procedure. That is a technical way out but I am yet to find anything.'

Gregory takes my hand, squeezing it until I open my eyes. 'Scarlett, would you leave us, please?'

'Excuse me?'

'Attitude,' he says under his breath. 'Five minutes. This isn't a discussion, Scarlett.'

'No.'

'Scarlett. Go.'

John rises from his chair and makes his way towards me. 'If I may say, Scarlett, I think it could be helpful for me to have a chat with your boyfriend alone.'

Seriously? Now they're in it together. Unbelievable.

With a giant scowl, I leave the room and go in search of the ladies'.

Business taken care of, I tuck my shirt into my tapered trousers and wiggle the material at the calves, adjusting them so they fall just above my pointed heels. My reflection seems older than it did two months ago. So much has happened; so much is happening. Things were so simple when it was just Dad, Sandy and me. That feels like the life of an entirely different person and right now, I don't know which Scarlett is best. Old Scarlett had a father, a career she could be proud of, morals. New Scarlett is confused, up and down on a daily basis, a liar, a murderer. But she has a man she adores. A man she's so utterly infatuated with, she's about to throw away a huge opportunity at work because she can't stand the thought of leaving him. A man who could be carted off in cuffs at any moment for a crime he didn't commit.

He's standing outside John's room, leaning one hip against the wall and holding my black wool coat across his arm. 'Ready?'

'You're done?'

'Yes.' He opens out my coat for me to slip in my arms, then turns me and fastens the buttons to my neck. He drops a kiss on the tip of my nose. 'Right. What're we doing with our day?'

'Are you joking?'

'Scarlett, I'm not letting this whole thing keep dragging us down.'

'What happened in there?'

'We agreed to request another ballistics report.'

'Can you just request another ballistics report?'

'Well, we aren't changing our story and the report doesn't *match* our story, so John's going to make a case for it. If not, we'll go independent.'

I mull the idea over for a moment, trying to get things clear in my head. 'Let's say we get a second report.'

'We are.'

'What if the report comes back exactly the same, which, let's face it, unless they're utterly shite at their job, it will do.'

'Was there really a need to swear then?'

'Stop changing the subject, Gregory, and yes. Since meeting you, I've found a lot of reasons to swear so please let me indulge my new vice.'

He steps towards me and wraps his arms around my lower back. I turn my head because I know I'll see hooded eyes if I look at him and I'll completely lose my train of thought.

'Look at me.' His words are heavy.

'No.'

'Look. At. Me.'

I do. His eyes are filled with desire. 'I like that I give you a reason to swear... in some departments. In others, please watch your dirty fucking tongue.'

I laugh at his forced hypocrisy. 'Can we be serious for a minute? If both reports say the same thing, Gregory, you have two damning pieces of evidence to rebut. They make you look like a liar.'

'True. But if they're both different, they completely undermine each other. John still thinks that if it's an obvious case of self-defence, given my father's history, there's a good chance the CPS won't even charge but if they did and the case went to trial, their reputation would suffer because of the conflicting evidence and it would be hard to refute our story and my claim of self-defence.'

'But we have no way of knowing and now it's another week of waiting.' I take an enormous breath that doesn't settle the tightness in my chest. 'Gregory, why did you get the ballistics report early?'

He sighs. 'I've told you. Barnes is an old friend of Jackson's. It was a heads-up.'

'He was angry.'

'Well, he's conflicted. He has to investigate a friend. Relax, baby, this is our day. We can't change things.'

As if that's supposed to make me feel better. I throw my arms around him and bury my head in his neck that still bears the faint evidence of that fatal night because I really don't know what else to do or say.

'I won't give up without a fight, Scarlett. I'll make this right. You'll see that what happened, what we did, was right.'

He closes the passenger door to the DB9, locking me inside, then slips into the driver seat. 'Right, what do you want to do?'

'Mm, let's go for a walk. Let's go to Primrose Hill.'

'It's freezing.'

'You're a big baby, Gregory Ryans. We're wrapped up.'

He leans his head back against the headrest with a sigh, then looks at me. 'One condition. We don't talk about the case or anything to do with it. Just us for the rest of the day.'

I open my mouth to speak then press my lips shut again.

'What?'

'I just... You mentioned your father's history like it's on record. Do you mean... was he arrested for... for what he did to Lara?'

His eyes noticeably flick away then back to me before he speaks. 'He has a record. Now, can we stop or am I going to have to take you home and spank that pert little arse of yours?'

I gasp, then follow it up with a laugh. 'So if I don't talk about Saturday, we get to go to Primrose Hill. If I *do* talk about Saturday, I get a spanking? Hmm, I'd like to talk about Saturday, please.'

He shakes his head with a laugh and pulls out into the road too quickly. A full afternoon of relaxed Gregory. I'm giddy with excitement.

He turns into a street near Primrose Hill Road and parks up. He lifts the collar on his coat and buttons it up to his neck.

'Miss Heath,' he says, offering me a hand to step out of the car. Two scrutinising eyes fall to my high heels. 'Didn't think this through, baby, did you? Looks like we'll have to take you home for a spanking.'

I actually belly chuckle and it feels amazing. When I'm sufficiently composed, I pull two blue dolly shoes from my handbag and hold them up, my opposite hand resting on my hip. 'A true London girl *always* carries her flats.'

He holds me up with an arm under my shoulder whilst I switch my shoes and throw my heels back into the car. I mirror him in pulling up my collar and fastening the gold buckle at the neck.

We walk up Primrose Hill Road hand in hand, passing a row of white town-houses and local shops with a quaint, homey, village feel. Gregory Ryans and Scarlett Heath do normal. Maybe old Scarlett and new Scarlett don't have to be worlds apart.

'Mm, smell that.' Freshly baked French sticks fill wicker baskets on a table outside a small Parisian café, a red canopy blowing in the breeze above them in case of rain. 'I love the smell of fresh bread.'

'If we survive the cold to the top of the hill and back, we can come here. Frost bite or no frost bite, I won't keep my lady from her fresh bread.'

I nudge into his side as he blows his fingertips for effect and hunches his shoulders.

At the bottom of the hill, a brilliant-white Scottie dog comes running towards us and jumps up at Gregory's leg. I expect him to bat it away but instead, he bends and fusses the dog.

'Oh dear, I'm sorry. She gets excited and I'm not quick enough to catch her.' The Scottie's owner is a petite, elderly lady whose mink coat is drowning her body.

'It's not a problem at all,' Gregory says, giving his Most Charming Man impression. 'How old is she?'

The owner is next to us now, beaming back at Gregory. 'Older than she thinks. Like me.'

She's not flirting?

'You're only as old as you feel, wouldn't you agree?' He stops fussing the dog and stands.

'Hey, you got a saying right!'

Now I'm smiling. Gregory winks at me and it's hard to know who's swooning more, me or the little old dear.

'We'll let you both get on,' Gregory says with another dashingly handsome smile. 'Have a good day.'

'And you.' She turns to me and drops her gloved hand to my arm. 'You hang onto him, young lady.' She leans into me as far as she can and I lean down until her mouth is next to my ear. 'He's a hottie.'

I laugh, for the second time a total belly chuckle, and wave as the little old dear and her Scottie move on.

'What was that about?' Gregory asks as I slip my arm through his.

'Girl talk.' I lean up and plant a kiss on my hottie's cheek. 'Race you!' I set off running up the hill before he answers but it only takes him a second to catch up. He sweeps me from my feet without breaking his stride and keeps running up the hill. His breathing isn't even laboured when he puts me down just shy of the top. Then he takes two more big steps to make sure he reaches the peak before me.

'You cheated! I would've won if you hadn't picked me up.'

'Get here.' Those magnetic, brown gems burn into mine. I go to him and let him wrap me in his arms. 'How did I find you?' He drops a kiss on my brow, then turns me, dropping his arms over my shoulders, pulling my back into his chest. We look out over the city in the quiet calm of the hilltop. *I'll make you fall in love with me, Ryans.* I pull his arms tighter over my shoulders and drop my head onto his forearm.

'That's the zoo,' I say.

He nods his head, then drops his mouth to my neck, inhaling deeply.

'And Canary Wharf.'

His lips gently suck my skin.

'St Paul's Cathedral.'

His tongue slides up to my jawline.

'The Gherkin.'

He kisses my lobe.

'The London Eye.'

He draws a line of kisses along my jawline.

'And that's home,' I say, looking at the Shard.

He twists my head to face him and covers my lips with his. I shift into his chest and wrap my fingers through his hair as I breathe in his rich, fresh scent. He pushes my hair over my shoulders and his fingers gently tug me into his body.

He turns us slowly on the spot, faster and faster still until my lips peel away from his and I throw my head back, giggling, my arms outstretched above my head. A moment of total and utter happiness amongst our anguish.

He slows our turns, then spins us once in the opposite direction, which makes me smile. My dad used to say that was the only way to counteract the Dizzy Duck Effect created by spinning over and over in one direction. This is exactly where I want to be. In this moment, nothing else matters except Gregory and me. The thief who stole my heart, me his accomplice and willing victim.

He slides me down his body to my feet then strokes my hair back from my face and pecks the tip of my nose. 'You're cold.'

I shake my head. If I am, I'll ignore it because I don't want to go. I don't want our bubble to burst.

'Let's get coffee.' He lifts my hand to his lips then guides us down the hill.

We take two stools in the window of the French bakery. 'We're going to need lots of fresh baked bread,' Gregory says to the waitress as we take off our coats. 'And two coffees. Americano for me: black, no sugar.'

'Latte for me, please.'

'Would you like anything with your bread?' she asks with a gentle French lilt. 'Cheese, olives, oil and balsamic, meats?'

'All of that.' Gregory's polite but distracted. I have his complete attention. He pulls my stool towards him so my knees are pressed between his thighs. We eat and talk, we laugh, in this exact position for almost two hours. It's easy and right. We talk about everything and nothing of consequence. Gregory rubs a rogue drip of balsamic from my chin when it falls and pays the bill without entertaining my protest.

Dusk is already descending when we leave the café and stroll arm in arm back towards the car.

'Oh, I love this bookstore.' Slipping out of his arm, I go into the traditional store, every wall lined with hundreds of books, and head straight to Classics. 'This is my favourite of all time,' I say, holding the book in front of my chest.

'*The Count of Monte Cristo?*'

'Yes, it's so wonderfully tragic.'

'Agreed.'

I cock my head to one side with a raised brow. 'You've read *The Count of Monte Cristo.*'

'Of course. It's a classic. Do you want it?'

'No, I have it at home.'

He pouts then snatches the book from me and takes it to the counter, handing over a two-pound coin.

'Now you have a copy for your new home.' He hands me the yellow paper bag, rests an arm around my shoulder, and points us back towards the car.

He wants to share his home with me. He looks and acts like he loves me. But he doesn't say it.

I'm risking everything for you, Gregory. Please let me in.

* * *

Amy has made boeuf bourguignon and left a note to say it's in the oven. It smells delicious but I'm still stuffed from the bread feast at lunch.

Gregory pours us both a glass of water from the fridge and slides mine across the breakfast bar to me. It seeps into my veins, cool and refreshing. He fiddles with the remote to the sound system and Des'ree 'I'm Kissing You' plays through the entire apartment. He takes a glass of wine to draw us a bath and calls me to join him once I've undressed and hung up my clothes. I sit in the bath, leaving space for Gregory to lower himself into the bubbles behind me. His movement makes the candles in the bathroom flicker as he pulls me back into his hard chest and begins soaking and squeezing a flannel over my skin.

'Tell me about the women: the women at the hunt, other women.'

I feel him tense against my back. He stills for a moment, then slides the flannel across my chest.

'I don't want to piss you off; it's just, I know you must have been with a few. I guess I'm curious. Have you ever... been in love?'

He exhales and squeezes the flannel again. I leave the silence hanging between us, waiting to be filled.

'The night of your father's funeral, you asked me to help you forget. Do you remember?'

I nod, not wanting to speak because this is new and I don't want to say the wrong thing and close the door.

'You wanted to have sex with me so that you didn't think about anything else. To help you block out the pain.'

I'm beginning to understand. I nod again.

'I've spent my life trying to forget, Scarlett, and it never worked. Not until you. Those women, all other women, they've meant nothing to me. I sleep with women, I work, drink, run, all to try to forget. It never works.'

I shuffle in the water so I'm resting between his legs, my chin on his chest, looking up at him. 'What do you want to forget?'

His expression changes; he's putting up his walls. I've found out everything I'm going to. For now. I crawl up his body and press my lips against his, thankful that he's shared at least something.

He's never been in love.

He pulls his hands through my wet hair and kisses me, his tongue working around mine in slow, smooth circles. My hips roll against him in response. I move my hand to his length and find him already hard. He groans into my mouth before I break our contact and slide down his wet skin. His hips rise, lifting his shaft out of the water. I look up at him and find hazed eyes. He wants it.

I turn my tongue around his tip and listen to him moan. Then I nibble the skin at his navel and down each of his thighs until he's pushing his pelvis up, inviting my mouth. I make him wait, trailing a finger up his sack until I cup him, applying pressure to his base and lightly stroking his back entrance. When his hips buck higher, I take him in my mouth, sucking the head then seizing as much of him as I can. I close my eyes and concentrate on taking him deep until he's touching the back of my throat. He thrusts his hands into my hair and pushes further into me. I take a deep breath and accept him, opening my throat. Then I swallow.

'Fuck, Scarlett!'

I draw back up his length and flick my tongue across his sensitive spot, then slide back down, taking him deep again.

'Fucking hell!'

He's pulling my hair, holding me still and pushing himself deeper into my mouth until my eyes are watery. His need for me turns me on beyond reason. Drawing back and wrapping my hand across his base, I swirl my tongue around the end of him and pump up and down with my fists, feeling him build beneath me. He throbs and swells further, his scrotum tightening. I remove my hand and withdraw my mouth. Then I step out of the bath and, feigning nonchalance, dry myself off with a towel.

'You are fucking kidding me, lady!'

I wrap the towel around me then throw him a minxy grin over my shoulder. 'I was promised a spanking.'

'Oh, now you're *definitely* getting a fucking spanking!'

'Is there a need to swear, Mr Ryans?'

He practically jumps out of the bath, his erection red and menacing. I squeal in delight as he yanks me up from the waist, my thighs locking onto his hips. He lays me down on the tiled floor and unties my towel. 'You want it hard?'

I bite my bottom lip and nod enthusiastically, already flooded with antici-pation. Jerking my legs apart with his knees, his dripping-wet body hovers as he takes my wrists above my head, securing them with one hand. There's no need. I have no intention of doing anything but accepting him. Rough. Brutal. I want him.

He moves the other hand to my sex, cupping me first, my hips already moving in response to him. His fingers enter me and stroke my G-spot. He brings them to his nose, then his mouth.

'You always taste so fucking good.' His words are throaty and dry.

He attacks my rock-solid nipple with his mouth and clamps down his teeth, sending a spike of lust through every nerve ending in my body. He takes the other in his teeth and slowly pulls back, extending my hard end. Then he moves his mouth to the fullness of my breast and sucks, drawing blood to my skin, marking me as his.

He sucks and nibbles his way down my stomach, finding my clit. My back arches as I reel from his carnality. He bites until I'm crying out. An indulgent, yearning cry.

I drag my fingers through his soft hair and he rises sharply as he growls. 'Hands.'

I quickly throw them back above my head and watch him drive into me.

'Gregory!'

'You like that, baby?'

I nod, shake, whirl my head. 'Yes.'

He powers forward again, a hedonistic and utterly mind-blowing drive. I close my eyes and try to control my erratic breaths and tensing muscles. Then his hands are on my waist and he's flipping me onto all fours. He spreads my knees and pulls my hips back towards him, then lifts my hands to the rim of the bathtub.

'Hold on.'

I do. I grip the rim tight, bucking forward when his hand strokes my centre.

He yanks my hips back to him then pounds his cock into me, sending me forward on a scream. He pulls me back to him and draws out slowly. Then his palm comes crashing down on the globe of my arse with a growl. It hurts but my hips push back, begging for more. He strikes again and I take a deep breath, expecting. He waits. I feel exposed and desperate, but deliciously so.

'Gregory.'

'You want me, baby?'

'Please. Yes.'

He hammers into me, hitting my end, lifting me to a euphoric fog. He pulls out slowly, excruciatingly slowly, then crashes back into me and I groan as my body starts to pulse. Then his palm comes down again, followed by a brutal thrust.

My insides are in blissful turmoil. My rear stings but there's something about his power, his control, that's driving me crazy.

'More!'

He yanks my hips back as he pounds into me. 'Fuck, Scarlett! You feel so.' Crash. 'Fucking.' Crash. 'Good.'

I throw my hips back as he thrusts again. 'Gregory, I'm there!'

'Not yet.' He slaps my arse again and rams into me. I can't take any more. My body clenches, inside and out.

'Now, baby.'

He crashes into me again and I come undone, reaching an overpowering climax. He drives again and his warmth fills me.

'Jesus!' He squeezes my hip bones as he pulses and bucks into me, no longer controlled at all.

I hang my head between my arms as he circles, bringing us down. My body is drained, panting and weak.

He wraps an arm around my waist and pulls me back onto his lap, where he rests his head in my neck, his sweat mixing with my own. We sit together until our pants subside and my blazing heart returns to a steady beat. I lean my head back against him, shattered. I could sleep right here on the tiled floor.

As I close my eyes, he lifts me and takes us both back into the lukewarm bath water. He rubs us both down, then lifts me out of the bath and dries my body, smiling as he moves the towel over me.

'Boeuf bourguignon?'

I nod faintly.

Dressed in a short, teal nightdress and matching silk kimono, I find Gregory downstairs dishing out boeuf bourguignon and wild rice, wearing a pair of black lounge pants, *only* black lounge pants, bare-chested and truly tantalising.

He lifts me onto his lap on a stool and we eat like that, wrapped in each other. When we're done, I rinse our plates and stack them in the dishwasher.

'I need to work for a while, angel.' He's apologetic but I recognise that I've had him to myself almost all day and I bet he hasn't had a day off work for a very long time, if ever. 'I'll work here, on the sofa.'

'Okay. I'll read *The Count.*'

He takes the middle of the sofa facing the lights of the city set against the dark sky and pats the corner for me to sit. As I slide down the leather arm, he lifts my thighs across his legs. I snuggle into his arm and start reading *The Count of Monte Cristo* for probably the tenth time in as many years. He dims the lights with a remote control to a cosy level where we can both still read with ease, and grabs his laptop. I sneak glances at him, watching his stoic business face and the occasional twitch of the muscle in his neck as he concentrates. Sometimes, he catches me and flicks his eyes to my book, telling me to read. I giggle each time and start reading again. It takes me over an hour to get through the first chapter. Being so close to his naked skin is more than a little distracting.

With a sigh, he leans forward and sets his closed laptop on the floor. 'Read to me.'

He lifts me to my feet then lies down, his spine against the back of the sofa. He pats the cushion resting on his forearm, and I climb back onto the sofa in front of him, pressing my back into his chest and my feet between his warm legs.

I read to him. I read until his head falls into my neck and his breathing slows. Then I carefully lean forward and drop the book to the floor. I hit the off button on the remote control and nestle against him.

'I love you.' I know he can't hear me but I whisper just in case. If he can't hear me, it can't tear another piece of my heart when he doesn't say it back.

14

I take the spare bagel that Amy has wrapped in tinfoil for me and pop it into my tote, then tie my coat over my red dress and slip my feet into heels.

Gregory's in full business mode, his manner brash as he speaks into his phone. Laid-back Gregory may be gone but the plus side is that I get to see him in my favourite blue suit. I watch his lean frame move down the stairs, everything about him refined, from his perfectly moulded hair to his polished shoes.

'Update me at ten and not a minute later.' He disconnects and drops the device into his inside pocket. 'Ready?'

I follow him to the lift, calling goodbye to Amy, trying not to think about tearing that suit off him. He folds one arm across his chest and moves his opposite hand to his chin. The lift suddenly feels small and I'm hot. I exhale and tap my foot. Then I'm flung back against the wall, my hands above my head, and attacked by his mouth as he grinds his hips against my stomach. He's hard.

When the lift pings, we both dart upright. I step onto the marble floor with a wobble and Gregory turns back to adjust himself in his trousers. I smirk as he strides to my side. We dip our heads to the concierge and step onto the street.

'Jackson!' I call excitedly. He's out of the car and holding open the door to the back of the Mercedes. Gregory's lips curl slightly as he walks around to the other side of the car and climbs into the back seat. Jackson knows just how Gregory likes things to be done.

'Good morning, Scarlett.' Jackson beams at me as I climb into the car with him holding his hand on the rim of the doorframe in case I should bump my head.

'Nice to have you back.'

'It's nice to see you've finally accepted being chauffeured.'

Gregory is back on his phone but rests one hand on top of mine in the middle of the seat as we cross to the north side of the Thames. I could fool myself into thinking this is a normal day.

I deposit the still-warm, spare bagel with Paul on my way into the office. He looks grey and cold this morning but he's as polite as ever.

My phone rings as I'm walking the corridor towards my office and as I'm midway through taking off my coat. Fumbling to do two things at once, I manage to answer.

'Mr Ryans, what can I do for you?'

'Are you stealing food from me to feed the homeless?'

'Erm, it was only a bagel. I thought—'

'Two things. First, you need to be careful. Do you know that man?'

'It's, he's Paul. He's sweet. He's always outside the office block.'

'Regardless, you need to be careful, Scarlett. He has nothing.'

'I don't—'

'Second, do you want to help him?'

'Yes. Of course. He was kicked out by his parents, he's young and he's... polite.'

'Where does he go at night?'

'There's a shelter he goes to: a soup kitchen near Liverpool Street Station.'

'And his name is Paul what?'

'Erm, I don't know.'

'All right. Have a good day. And stop stealing my food.'

Just like that, he hangs up the phone.

Before my computer even beeps to life, Amanda bounds into my office.

'Who are you and where's Scarlett Heath?'

I look around as if something in the office will clear my confusion.

'Since when does the Scarlett Heath *I* know take a day off?'

'I'd gladly have taken another too.'

'Seriously, where is *my* Scarlett?' She plonks herself onto the edge of my desk and pushes the latte Margaret has left towards me. 'What did you get up to?'

'Walked. Talked. Ate.'

'You're literally beaming. Your hair looks pretty like that.'

I instinctively touch my roughly pinned-up hair. 'I call it the I-didn't-want-to-come-to-work style.'

'This really is a whole new you. So, how are things? Have you heard any more from the police?'

She catches me off guard. The ballistics report says someone other than Gregory took that shot. It implicates me; that's why Gregory is demanding another. We're back to an excruciating countdown.

'Nothing concrete yet.' It's not a lie, yet I feel guilty.

'Soooo I called Williams on Saturday night.'

'You did?'

'I had a godawful date with a mind-numbing prick and it made me think that maybe *fun* isn't so much fun after all. We're going out for dinner on Friday.'

'Am I allowed to say I told you so?'

'Really rather you didn't.'

I snortle unattractively. 'Fair enough.'

'I have a proposition for you.' There's a glint in her eye. 'How about we ditch yoga and go out for lunch.'

'You've twisted my arm. One o'clock?'

'Amaze! And we're still on for drinks Saturday?'

'Oh, I forgot.'

'Scarlett, it's been in the diary for an age. We haven't seen Luke properly in forever.'

Luke Davenport, my university ex and now a good friend.

'Erm, yep, we're still on.'

She practically skips back to her own office as it dawns on me that the ballistics report could be back before our night out. It might never happen. Shrugging off the thought, I bury my head in documents for Mr Ghurair. It's been a week since our brunch and I know I have to give Neil my decision about Dubai. I am, without question, avoiding him. I wouldn't leave Gregory with the case looming over us and I won't leave him whilst there's any chance he's falling for me as deeply as I've fallen for him. But telling Neil that I'm willing to disappoint a potentially huge client on a whim... Well, best-case scenario is he's unhappy but understanding. The worst-case scenario is he's *really* pissed. Either option is likely to be career-limiting.

I've done half of what I intended to do by the time Amanda grabs me for lunch and my newfound reluctance to work, coupled with Amanda's never-present desire to work, means we talk our way through two hours before making it back to the office.

I open my office door, unbuttoning my coat, and jump back when I raise my head to see Gregory standing in the window, tall and broad, his hands in the pockets of his perfectly cut trousers.

'What're you doing here? How did you get into my office?'

His expression gives nothing away. 'Your secretary let me in.'

'You can't be here, Gregory; I have confidential files everywhere.'

'I told her it was an emergency.' His tone is flat.

My stomach sinks and my heart stops beating in my chest. I can hear my own heavy breaths in my ears. 'What is it?'

'Sit down.'

I close my office door. 'Just tell me, Gregory. What's happened?'

'I wanted to tell you so you didn't hear it from someone else, that's all.'

'Tell me what?' My voice is louder than intended.

'My mother and Sandy have been taken in for questioning. Well, asked to go to the station.'

'Sandy! Why? What do they want with Sandy? Oh God, she'll be beside herself. It's me, isn't it? They suspect the truth.'

He moves towards my frozen body and encourages me to sit on my desk. 'It's routine. That's why I wanted to come here. I knew you'd panic. You heard John Harrison. Going against the ballistics report was going to lead to another dig by forensics and more questioning. Barnes has to investigate, that's all. Sandy knows all of us and it's obvious why they'd want to question my mother. It means nothing.'

I slap his hands away. 'How can you say that? Pulling Sandy in is *not* routine. She doesn't know you, not really, and you're the suspect. She knows me and she knows Jackson.' I lift my hand to my mouth, shaking my head. 'I've got to get to the station. I need to see her.'

'Jackson's with her. He took her down there and he's waiting to bring her back. She'll be fine, Scarlett.' He rests against the edge of the desk beside me. 'They know. They know or they suspect.' He inhales deeply, his broad chest expanding. 'They found a partial print on the gun. John Harrison called to tell me. He told me about Sandy and my mother too. They're struggling to identify the print but they will.'

'Okay.' I feel sick but eerily resolute. This is going to force his hand. They'll identify my print and Gregory won't be able to protect me any longer. We'll have to tell the truth.

I'll be charged and they'll find out. I didn't just kill for love; I killed for vengeful love. Me, my dad's daughter and the unrequited love of the little boy who haunts my sleep.

'I think you should go.'

He rears, frown lines wrinkling his face.

'I've got work to do, Gregory, and you can't be in my office with all these files.' I gesture to the rows of shelves lined with ring binders and correspondence files.

Standing, I walk with confidence to my desk chair. He eventually rises from his perch, watching me. I slide on my glasses as if they might hide the feelings I'm so desperately trying not to show, then click New and feign typing an email, conscious as I do that he's scrutinising my every move.

'Let's go home. Together. I don't want to leave you alone.'

I bite down on the inside of my gums and take off my glasses, dangling one tortoiseshell arm between my fingers. 'I'm fine, Gregory. Like you say, it's routine. Jackson's waiting for Sandy. It's all just... dandy.'

'Dandy?'

'Yes. Dandy. I'll see you later.' I pop my glasses back on and make up a sentence as I type, focusing intently on my screen. 'The longer you stand there staring at me, the later I'll be.'

'Fine. Have it your way.'

'I will.' My words fall on his back as he storms out, slamming the door behind him, making me jump and the thin walls rattle.

Alone, the enormity of what's happening takes hold. I lean back in my chair and stare at the ceiling, begging the dams in my eyes to hold back the ensuing river. *This can't be happening.* Seven weeks ago, if someone had told me I'd be sitting in my chair now, distraught because the only mother I've ever known is being questioned by the police in connection with the murder of a man I killed, I'd have laughed. Then I would've told that person they have a very vivid imagination.

But here I am. A hostile takeover under my belt. My old boss locked up for assault. My dad dead. Sandy working for a woman I hardly know because I couldn't give her a job. I'm in love with a morally grey man with a past so dark, he won't dare reveal it. And I'm a murderer. Now everyone I love is being dragged under the bus with me.

No matter how long I lean back in my chair, staring at the ceiling, I can't locate Scarlett Heath. She seems so far away, further even than my rapidly disappearing sanity. And I'm wondering now whether the real reason I haven't given Neil my decision about Dubai is because deep down, a part of me thinks it could be a fresh start, a clean slate. But a flight won't hide me from a murder charge. That's just about the only thing I can be certain of right now.

I'm trying to pinpoint the last time I knew myself and the only place I get to is the boardroom. My pitch in the boardroom of Eclectic Technologies. I wonder whether it would've been better for everyone if Gregory hadn't walked into my life.

That thought kills me.

Finally, the dams disintegrate and two silent tears drip from the corners of my eyes. This will break us. Now. Next week. Next month. When I'm rightly behind bars for killing a man. This will break us because one person's love can't defy the order of the world alone. My silent tears build to a sob and I drop my head to my arms on my desk. Despite everything, I need him and I hate myself for being *that* dependent woman.

I ignore my ringing phone. I don't want to speak to him. I can't. I've got no idea what I want to say and I'm afraid of anything that might leave my mouth. I'm not thinking straight. It's getting late, the sky is pitch-black and the sensor lights are out in the corridor. Wiping tears, and no doubt mascara, from my cheeks with the backs of my hands, I sit up and grab my phone as it starts to ring again.

But it isn't Gregory.

'Sandy, are you okay? I'm so sorry. I'm so, so sorry.' My tears are flowing from a bottomless well.

'Oh deary me, stop that. I'm fine, it wasn't so bad. Quite exciting in places, really, like being a police show.' I know what she's doing but I can't muster a smile.

'Were they nice to you?'

'That Barnes is a nice chap. He knows Geoffrey.'

'DI Barnes. I know.' *And there's something highly coincidental about that.* 'Was there a woman too?'

'Oh, yes, she was a nasty piece of work but nothing I couldn't handle.'

'What did they ask you?'

'Nothing of much consequence: how I know you, Gregory and Geoffrey, whether I think you and Gregory are in love.'

'Enough to do anything for each other is what they really mean.'

'They implied things, yes. But I told them you always do what's right, Scarlett. They, erm, they asked me how your father died.'

'Did they... were they... did they make a connection?'

'No, I explained he had Alzheimer's.'

I hadn't realised my shoulders were up by my ears but now they sag. 'I'm so sorry you got dragged into this. I'm sorry for everything.'

I can hear Jackson in the background; he sounds like he's talking on his phone.

'Are you home?'

'I'm at the Shard. I'm going to stay here tonight with Geoffrey.'

'You call him Geoffrey.'

'That's his name.'

'He'll always be Jackson to me.'

I can hear a soft smile in her voice. 'I thought I might see you here.'

I stand and walk to my office window. 'I'm still working.'

'Scarlett, you can't possibly be concentrating with everything that's going on. Come home. It's late. Gregory tells me his housemaid has made salmon en croute. That'll be nice, won't it?'

'You're not going to lure me back with salmon en croute.'

'Well, what if I made you some pancakes?'

'Sandy, you've just been to the police station and questioned. You must be exhausted. Let Jackson look after you. Go put your feet up.'

'It'd be a lot easier to relax if I knew you were okay, sweets.' I can hear her moving, then her voice drops to a whisper. 'I'm worried about you. Gregory said you two had words.'

I sigh. 'Sandy...'

'I'm here, sweets.'

I pause, debating whether to share the truth. 'I don't want to go home.' A lump forms in my throat and I swallow hard to prevent it from rupturing.

'Oh, Scarlett, I know you love Gregory, it's written all over that pretty little face every time I see you but if you need some space, if you want to get away, you can stay with me. Or if you don't want to stay at Lara's house, I can stay at home with you... at our old home.'

'I'm fine. I'm being silly. I'm going to go and finish my work. I'm glad you're okay. I really am sorry, Sandy.'

'Now you listen to me, missy: you're *not* to blame for all this. You've gotten yourself mixed up in something... someone—' She stops herself before she says what I know she's thinking. I know because everyone will be thinking it. Amanda has said as much. And however idiotic it might seem, I can't stand people thinking badly of Gregory.

'He's a good man, Sandy. This isn't his fault.'

'I wasn't going to say—'

'Yes, you were, or at least you were thinking it. I get it, I do. But there was nothing we could do. Maybe he made a mistake taking over that company and maybe I made an even bigger mistake helping him.' I offload with an odd sense of relief, finally articulating what's been eating me up. 'If I'd walked away, he might've never gone through with it. But I understand why he needed to. That deal was his vengeance, Sandy, and I... I... with Dad, when he... I can understand how desperately he needed to take revenge.' I'm close, too close, to telling her everything. This is Sandy, Sandy who'd stand by me no matter what, probably the only person in the world who would. 'Sandy... I know because that night, I wanted revenge too. I hate Kevin Pearson for everything he did to Gregory and Lara and for what he did to Dad. Gregory isn't to blame for all this.'

'Neither of you are to blame for that man trying to kill you all, Scarlett.' Her words are louder, almost shouting, cutting me off.

'Sandy—'

'Enough! Young lady, what if he hadn't been shot? What then? Geoffrey was already hurt. That man would've killed him and I'm sure he would've killed you too. So stop! Just stop it!'

'Sandy, it wasn't Gregory, it was—'

'Stop it now! I won't listen.'

My eyes are on fire, my hand clamping my open mouth shut. The line is silent but for Sandy's breathing and I realise mine has stopped but my heart is thudding in my chest. My lungs fill on a gasp. 'You already know Gregory didn't take that shot. You know.'

'I have to go, Scarlett.' The call beeps to an end.

I don't go back to the Shard. I sit in my desk chair as I've done all day and lean back, my head turned to one side, staring at the orange lights flicking on and off in the high-rise buildings nearby. Sandy knows our dirty little secret. She knows and now she has to lie too.

* * *

Jackson kicks open the door and a gun fires. He falls to the floor, blood immediately pooling around his leg. A scream lingers in the back of my throat but fails to make it to my mouth. Frantic and with shaking fingers, I attempt to tie a tourniquet around his punctured thigh.

Gregory and Pearson crash out of the bathroom, bashing against the walls, growling, snarling. They're trying to kill each other. They fall into the gym room and I'm staring helplessly when they burst back through the door, eyes wild, raging, as they thrash around the floor. Pearson pulls a chain tight around Gregory's neck, causing the skin beneath it to flame red. He's struggling to breathe. The chain is killing him and all I can do is watch in horror.

Jackson shouts, screams at me to retrieve the gun he dropped to the floor. I can hear him but my limbs refuse to move. He tells me the safety is off, to use two hands and only fire if I have a clear shot. I pick up the gun but Gregory's broken free and Pearson's body lies lifeless on the floor. Gregory slumps back against the wall to catch his breath, then forces himself up to make sure Jackson's okay.

Pearson moves in the background. I'm sure of it. My feet carry me towards him. Then his arm is raised, the gun aimed directly at Gregory.

I pull the trigger, the bullet bursting through Pearson's skull almost instantaneously with the bang of the gun and the reverberations through my arms.

I'm sitting on the sofa, staring into darkness. The distinct smell of lilies invades my nose. There're voices behind me, numerous male voices, mumblings at first but the sound sharpens.

'Greg, we can clean this up. Don't be fucking stupid!'

'I said no. This is my past and I'll fucking kill myself before it haunts her. Call the police, Jackson.'

'Motherfucker! What the fuck is wrong with you?'

'Jackson, look at her. For Christ's sake! She's not like us. She's better than us, better than both of us.'

'That might be so, kid, but she can be better than us without anyone going to fucking prison.'

'No one's going to prison. It was self-defence. I shot him in self-defence.'

'You're crazy. I'm not gonna help you ruin your fucking life!'

'Jackson, if we don't do this, her life will be ruined and I'll have another fucking life on my conscience. The only way she'll get through this is if we do it through the police and she realises that what she did wasn't wrong. I'll be cleared. This will end and she can leave me if she wants to; she can move on knowing she did the right thing.'

'Then I'll make damn fucking sure you're cleared, you crazy bastard.'

'Right. But it has to be the police.'

'You've known her two minutes, Greg.'

'Enough. No matter what happens, she can walk away if she wants to but this way, she won't have to wonder every fucking day for the rest of her life whether she should've done it. I know what it's like to live with a shadow, Jackson, and she doesn't deserve that.'

Jackson's exhale is long and considered. 'Wipe down her hands in case they check for powder residue.'

I gasp as I'm awoken by a cleaner tapping on the door to my office.

'Can I empty your bin, Miss?'

I wipe my mouth with the back of my hand. 'Yes. Of course. What time is it?'

'Just before seven, Miss.'

Shit!

My phone screen is full. Twelve missed calls, three voicemails and a stream of text messages. He's been awake all night.

Double shit!

Firing off a message to tell him I worked through the night and fell asleep is not going to cut it but I send the message anyway.

The phone rings almost immediately. I'm not ready to talk to him. My brain still hasn't processed yesterday's developments and now it has to decipher what's real and what's fiction from my nightmare. They can't be real memories. I don't remember any conversation about police; I only remember Gregory telling me what I had to say to them, making me repeat his version of my statement verbatim.

The ringing cuts off then starts up again. With shaking fingers, I type a message.

I'm fine. I'm sorry I didn't call. I just need some space.

They're there again, those words, lingering. *She can move on.*

I drop my phone into my handbag and pull on my coat. I want to leave the office before people start turning up but Gregory won't have left the apartment yet. Unlocking my laptop from the docking station, I slip it into my carry case and head to a coffee shop.

The barista brings a large latte with two extra shots and an almond croissant to my table and I mutter my thanks. I tear a couple of bite-size chunks from the pastry then push them around the plate.

I keep coming back to the same conclusion. *He's doing this for me.* He's putting himself through the uncertainty, the stress, because he doesn't want me to live in a world where I feel trapped like he does. This isn't about him wishing he'd killed his father or about him wanting to punish himself because he brought this on me. This is about him making sure that I can move on, without the weight of my conscience, without wondering if I did the wrong thing. Is that different to me moving on from him, leaving him? *She can leave me if she wants to.* Does that mean he won't leave me?

My wandering mind snaps back to real time. He's in my face, speaking through his teeth.

'Never. Do. That. To. Me. Again. Do you understand? Anything could have happened to you. For fuck's sake, Scarlett, I've had Jackson driving around the city; I've been to your office block. It was fucking irresponsible and selfish!'

My chair scrapes against the tiled floor as I stand, my eyes wide, my mind working on stringing together a pissed-off retort. My skin heats under the eyes of impatient suits queuing to be served, irritated baristas and the handful of seated coffee-drinkers.

'Why didn't you call or message? Sandy said... Christ, it doesn't matter what she said. You should've come home.'

'So now you're conspiring with Sandy too. What did she say?'

'She said you didn't want to come home. God, I thought. If you'd have done anything stupid, if you'd harmed yourself, I don't know what I would've done.' He's shaking his head, his eyes squeezed shut.

'Gregory, stop being ridiculous. I can't believe you think I'd—'

'How the hell am I supposed to know either way if you don't call?'

I fold my arms across my body instinctively as I cast my eyes around the space. 'Could you please stop being neurotic?' The words grate through my gritted teeth.

He sighs; his shoulders sag. 'Things have been hard but... but I thought that as long as you and I were okay, we'd get through it. It broke my heart to think you wouldn't come home to me, Scarlett.'

And the look in your eyes just broke mine.

'I feel suffocated, Gregory. There's so much going on and I don't know how to deal with it. I want to be strong for you. I know everything is worse for you; even though I don't want you to, you're taking the blame. I just need space to think. Away from it all.'

The question of Dubai pricks my mind again.

He steps towards me, the feeling of his warm palms on my cheeks soothing me. 'Baby, I'd rather you were honest with me. I'd rather see you messed up and be able to take care of you than not see you.'

I look up and find two apprehensive but gentle eyes questioning me. 'That's just it. I don't want you to have to take care of me. I don't want to be another burden for you.' I look away from him, internally cursing the tears spiking the backs of my eyes.

'Look at me.'

I don't.

'Baby, look at me, please.'

Swallowing away the impending rush of tears, I do.

'I need to ask you something,' I say.

'Anything.'

'That night. When it happened. Were you thinking about not calling the police?'

His gentle fingertips stroke an imaginary strand from my brow. 'Where's this come from?'

'I had a dream and you were talking to Jackson, shouting at him, telling him you had to call the police because it was the only way I could move on. Did that happen?'

'Yes.'

His arms move to my back, preventing me from stepping away from him.

'Why? Why would you put yourself through all this if you could've cleaned it up and forgotten about it?'

'Do you really need me to answer that?'

'I think I do.'

He sighs as he finally takes a seat in the dark wood chair opposite mine and pulls my chair to the side of the table next to his. I sit down, letting my knee graze his as he unbuttons his grey blazer. He picks up my hand and entwines my fingers in his.

'I've lived my whole life carrying around regrets and what ifs. I've told you before, my world is dark. I've screwed up; I've failed people. But you, you're like this bright light. You're smart, you're sassy, you're too damn gorgeous for your own good. You live in a different world to mine and I'm not going to mess up your life too. I refuse to let that happen.'

'But it would mess up my life if I couldn't be with you.' I mumble the words, watching his fingers draw shapes around mine.

He stops drawing and grips my hand. 'Don't say things like that, Scarlett. You'd be fine without me. You'd be better off without me. But I know that night is eating you up inside. I can see it. I know what it looks like to turn black from the inside out. You need confirmation that you did the right thing.' He lifts my hand, pressing my fingertips against his lips, then he looks me in the eye. 'You did the right thing, Scarlett, and when this is cleaned up, the right way, you'll see that. I promise you'll be able to move on.'

'It sounds like you're breaking up with me and you just can't say it straight.' A shiver runs the length of my spine.

His Adam's apple moves slowly up and down his taut throat. My stomach falls and I hold my breath. 'That's not what's happening, Scarlett. I've told you before, you'd be wise to walk away from me but I'm too selfish to tell you to go. I wish I wasn't; I wish I could find the strength to let you find someone right for you. But I can't let you go.'

'I don't ever want you to do that.'

His eyes are fixed on mine as he retrieves his dancing phone from the inside pocket of his suit jacket. 'Sydney, what now? Which one? Fuck integrity. Give them more. However much it takes, just fix it.'

The phone is pushed with bitterness back into his suit jacket. He reaches for a piece of my uneaten pastry and pops it in his mouth, sucking the tip of his index finger then his thumb as he stands. 'Let's go.'

I pull on my coat and gather my things. 'I need to go home for a shower,' I say, following his back as he navigates the tables of café.

He turns his head back over his shoulder to deliver a sexy half-smile and twinkling eyes. 'I was counting on it.'

'You're coming with me?'

'I most certainly am, Miss Heath.' He holds open the door and gestures for me to step onto the now bustling street before him.

'So you listened to me when I said I needed space then?'

He suddenly grabs me, nudging me back against the Mercedes. My squeal has yet more people tuning in to this morning's *Gregory Show*. He leans into my neck, with no regard for his surroundings, his breath hot on my skin. I close my eyes and breathe him in, his familiar scent making me melt against him. 'I listen to your body language. We established a long time ago that what you say and do often don't tally.'

I smile, remembering our first night together. How he drove me insane with desire in our own private box at the theatre. A torturous three-hour performance. Then, my biggest conflict was whether I let myself get close to a client. Now, there are so many conflicts torturing me, I've lost my grip on life. And as much as I hate myself for it, I can't stop the thought lingering that this all started with Gregory, the man I love. He thinks *he's* screwed up. I don't even think MI5 could solve the mixed-up puzzle in my head right now.

He steps back, the exposure to the cold air reminding me of our position in the street. Subtly adjusting his blazer to cover himself, he inclines his head, gesturing for me to climb into the back seat before he slides in next to me.

'Change of plan, Jackson. Back to the Shard.'

'Sure thing.' He flicks an eye to me through the rear-view mirror and shakes his head with a smirk when I huffily cross my arms. Whether it's intuition or the silent understanding between these men, Jackson rolls up the partition screen.

Once the screen hits the roof, Gregory moves a hand under my arse. 'Get here,' he says.

I fight it at first.

'Lady, do not anger me more than you already have.'

'*Me* anger *you*?'

He lifts me to his lap and hitches up my dress so I can slip my knees either side of his legs and rest down onto his lap.

His smouldering eyes have been replaced with big, brown, teddy-bear eyes and he strokes my hair behind my ear in that way he does. 'Don't ever be afraid to come home to me, baby, please.' His voice is genuinely pleading. 'You have to always talk to me. Do you understand?'

I decide against pointing out the irony of that statement, instead nodding my head, leaning into his palm.

'Say you understand.'

I turn my lips to the warm skin of his hand. 'I understand.'

'Good girl. Now, not only did you terrify me last night by going missing—'

'Oh, Gregory, get real; I was at the office, for Christ's sake.'

'Your attitude is going to get you into even more trouble than you're already in. Are you trying to piss me off?'

'Are you trying to piss me off?'

'Fuck, Scarlett, no one can make me as angry as you can.' He yanks my hair at the nape, pulling hard, jerking my head back, and lets out a primal growl as he bites the plump flesh of my breast over my dress.

I lunge forward, dragging my fingers just as hard into his hair, and crash my lips against his. *God, I love and hate this man all at once.* He meets my attack lick for lick, suck for suck. He pulls my arse further onto his hips so I can feel his cock knocking at my throbbing door. He's ready to fuck me just as hard as I need to fuck him. A battle of wills, a fight of love and war, the deepest darkness and the most profound light going into the ring together.

'You're so confusing,' I snarl.

He slides his hands up my body over my dress then cups my breasts in his palms, circling the tender mounds. I want him to take it off, to rip it off. I groan, thinking about him touching my naked flesh, moving inside me. He pushes his hips up, letting me feel his erection harder against my sex. My fingers grab at his thick, dark locks, pulling his head to my throat. I yank in frustration. *How can something so good be so difficult and fucked up? Why can't we just be together, happy, normal?*

He runs his tongue up my neck, nibbles my chin, then bites my lips harshly. The car jerks, rocking me against his solid crotch, teasing me through my thong. We both turn to look out of the tinted window. The traffic is stationary, a bumper-to-bumper jam of red lights. I turn my gaze from the stream of cars to Gregory as he curses beneath his breath. 'I'm having you now and you're going to take everything I give you.'

'You infuriate me, Ryans.'

'Baby, the feeling's mutual. Nobody defies me continually. No one steps out of line and gets away with it like you do.'

'Maybe if your lines weren't so unreasonable, I wouldn't cross them.'

His fingers shove my thong to one side and invade me. My head rolls back as his thumb draws a slick circle around my clit.

'Can Jackson see us? Can he hear us?'

Gregory's only response is to drag his fingers forcefully against my G-spot with an animalistic growl. Whether he could hear us or not, I don't think I'd have the strength to stop now.

'You're always ready for me. Even when you think you're pissed at me, you always want me.'

I cry out as my body responds to his punishing fingers and his rough grip on my breast. *Damn him. Damn me and every goddamned thing that I can't control.*

His words, his touch, his velvet, lust-filled voice, his smell. Everything about him consumes me. I drop forward and bite his neck, my mouth and teeth working up to his ear. I pull his lobe through my teeth and push my hips down, taking his fingers deeper inside me, greedy to feel the pressure of his tense, fisted hand against my entrance. He works his fingers in circles, pressing harder when he strokes my spot, and keeps the rhythm of his thumb in sync. My hips start to move, slow and controlled.

'Gregory.'

'Is that what you want, baby? You want me just there?'

I nod through my heady breaths.

'Tell me. Tell me, baby.'

I can't. I can't breathe. I bite my lip, not wanting to submit to him. Pushing my hands to the ceiling, I lift my hips and he holds himself as I crash down on him, finally feeling his cock filling me. Through the rear window, I can see the face of the driver in the car behind and rows of traffic around us. No one can see us but the knowledge that they're there has a strange effect on me. More people who just can't leave me the fuck alone.

I rise and pound down on Gregory, taking him to my end.

He pulls my hair again, forcing me to look at him. 'Tell me.' He grabs my hips, grinding me against him in the rhythm he wants.

I relent to his command. 'I do. I don't want to but I need you, Gregory.'

I'm on the cusp of falling apart in every way. He grabs my arse roughly and spreads my cheeks, his fingers applying pressure to my rear hole, the move stretching my vulva and increasing his friction against me.

'Oh, God, Gregory.'

He lifts me and yanks me down, impaling me on his angry cock.

'Fuck!'

He holds me still.

I lean into him, grabbing his hair. Taking him in, the feel of him, the pressure of him against my clenching insides. I'm pulsing around him but I can feel him too; he's not far away. I need more.

I attempt to move my hips but his hands grip me tighter. He's too strong for me.

'Fuck me,' I demand, dissatisfied, impatient, irritated, annoyed.

He doesn't move as I shift my head to look into his smouldering eyes. He's enjoying this.

My mouth drops open, needing to scream but knowing I can't.

'I love watching you like this. Desperate for me. You're so fucking beautiful.'

'Please, Gregory.'

He releases his grip and pushes his pelvis up. Our mouths lock as we moan into each other. I slowly rise and bear down on him, hard.

'Jesus!' he barks.

I rise again and crash down on him, feeling him reach the top of me. He takes hold of me, moving me round until we settle into a fast, deep, mind-blowing rhythm.

'I'm close.' My words are hoarse.

'Let go, baby. I want to feel you come for me.'

He moves us faster until my body can't take any more. I throw myself forward and bite his chest through his shirt. My hips thrust uncontrollably as he continues to turn his swollen shaft inside me. My scream is muffled but it takes him to the edge. He slams his cock up into me and throws his head into my chest, his fingers digging painfully into my waist. He fills me as quietly as his release will allow.

* * *

I can't bring myself to look at Jackson as he holds the door open for me in the basement car park. The three of us ride the lift in silence. It must be written all over my face. I feel ravished, dirty in a way that's a total turn-on. My vexation is now lost in a sea of lascivious thoughts.

The lift pings at the sixty-fourth floor but my mind is in a state of trance, thinking about *that* fuck. In the middle of the road, in the heart of London, with Jackson in the front seat. Gregory's hands rest on my shoulders and he guides me out of the lift. We follow Jackson into the apartment, Gregory moving me forward with his palm on the small of my back.

'I'll take these to the office,' Jackson says, holding up my laptop bag and documents.

'Thank you,' I manage.

'Hello, darling, you must be shattered. Gregory said you worked all night.' Amy takes in my tousled hair.

'Erm, yes, I've got a deal on.' That isn't a lie. I was working on Mr Ghurair's upcoming deal but I miss out the part about spending most of the night doing not much at all, my head in a spin.

'Can I fix you something to eat?'

'She needs breakfast, Amy,' Gregory answers for me. 'Go take a shower,' he says to me, 'then come and eat.'

As much as I'd like to argue with him and fire off some smart quip, I'm suddenly drained. I take myself off, not because he's directed me to do so but because I actually do need a shower. I needed a shower before he made me all sticky between the legs. Now I *definitely* need one.

I scrub myself clean, then roughly blow-dry my hair before dressing in a pair of leggings and an oversized jumper. Gregory is in his office when I tiptoe across the landing.

'Fuck Nick! He's not getting a penny.' Through the ajar door, I can see the top of his head, his leather chair facing out of the window into the low, autumn-winter sun. 'I'm paying people off left, right and centre right now as it is. I'm damn sure that bastard isn't getting anything. Tell him if he wants money, he should get out and fucking earn it.'

He slams the phone down on the desk and drags a hand furiously through his hair.

Slipping through the door, I ask sheepishly, 'Is everything okay?'

It's a stupid question really, and one with an obvious answer, but he lifts his head calmly. 'It'd be good if the CPS made a decision sometime soon.'

'It would.'

He rotates his chair sideways as I move towards him and I crawl onto his lap.

'Is Nick Henshaw trying to fight his termination?'

'It was a resignation, not a termination, and yes. But he's not going to get anywhere with it. He's just an itch.'

'And the other people you're paying off?'

'Press. I don't know how they've found out.'

I lean my head into his chest. 'I guess these things make for good gossip.'

'Ja, but Sydney said she hasn't seen the interest so high and all at once like this before. She thinks someone talked.'

'Nick?'

'I can't see it. He might not be scared of me telling his wife about Sydney but he knows better than to test me.'

I close my eyes. I don't even want to know what that statement alludes to.

He leans back, the leather chair rocking a little. 'But the only other people who know are the police and... people who wouldn't say anything.'

'Us. Sandy and Jackson. Your mum and Lawrence. Williams and Amanda. The guys in Jackson's team that night. Would they say anything?'

'Not a chance.'

He sighs. 'What about Amanda?'

I sit back quickly, my hands pushing against his chest for leverage. 'Of *course* she wouldn't. She's my best friend, Gregory.'

'All right.' He plants a kiss on my brow, then lifts me to my feet. 'Breakfast. Now. Go.'

15

Practising corporate law means accepting that your life will be a constant navigation through peaks and troughs. One day, you're riding high on the buzz of closing a deal or taking a cheap thrill from getting one over on another lawyer. The next, you're back to mundane documents or a pissed-off client because your opposite number has managed to screw you in a negotiation. It might be fair to assume therefore that I'd be seasoned to life's highs and lows, might even put them within one of those vague stereotype categories like *normal* or *ordinary*. But life with Gregory is like taking up an extreme sport. Not like diving or skiing. More like cliff diving or ice climbing without a harness.

The thing is, I'm addicted. I'm addicted to the adrenalin rush, the thrill of being with him. Bad days, in fact, utterly shit days, like today, make the high days like Monday at Primrose Hill and Wednesday's kinky home-working day, seem even higher. He's in my veins, he's in my blood and I'm starting to think he might be the only thing keeping my heart beating. But I don't know how many more days like Tuesday, Thursday and today I can take. I find myself sitting at my desk, as I am now, wondering whether it's all worth it. What I'm wondering right now is whether those three words I'm so desperate to hear him say would justify everything.

Yesterday had started like any other day. We woke at five thirty and Gregory went straight out for a run whilst I worked out in the gym with Jackson, quizzed him about Sandy until he blushed then moved on to the spin bike, making way for Gregory and his fine torso to beat up the punch bag. We had morning kinkiness which meant I had to take breakfast on the move. Jackson dropped me at my office, where I deposited a second bagel with Paul, albeit with a scowl. I still haven't forgiven him for snitching on me, telling Gregory which coffee shop I was hiding out in on Wednesday morning.

The cliché goes, *bad luck comes in threes*; well, my first bout came via email. It pinged through to my inbox around nine thirty. I was finishing off the latte Margaret had left on my desk and Neil Wallace's name – accompanied by a rather awkward-looking headshot – appeared on my screen. Mr Ghurair was apparently very impressed with the due-diligence report I prepared for the first in his series of imminent deals. *Concise, commercial, pragmatic.* That's what Neil wrote. I'm not sure if it was a direct quote. Then came the catch. Because I've done such a concise, commercial and pragmatic job of the due-diligence report, Mr Ghurair is now not just keen but adamant that *I'm* the person to take up the Dubai secondment. Neil tells me he needs my decision by Friday next week but it's obvious he still thinks I'll do what everyone expects and say yes. That's why he isn't pushing and that's why telling him *no* will be ten times worse than if I was any other lawyer under his management.

I was still pondering the prospect of Dubai when Gregory's name danced across the screen of my phone.

'Hey, baby,' he said. I knew from his tone that it was about the case. 'I'm about to join a conference call but I wanted to let you know John Harrison called. The results on the second print from the gun are going to be back tonight or tomorrow.'

Just like that. That's how he delivered the news, as if it was completely within the scope of ordinary. Perhaps it is in the scope of *our* ordinary. I'm beginning to understand the parameters of *our* normal are much different to the average person's. I thought about that for most of the day. Even when I wasn't thinking about it as the main event, it remained a subplot in my mind all afternoon. I worked on Gregory's joint venture with Shangzen Tek – at least that's one thing that seems to be ticking over according to plan – but at six thirty, I gave in. I couldn't sit at my desk and feign normal any longer. I also didn't want to go back to the Shard and continue the charade. So I wandered. I had no aim in mind, I just headed west and found myself in Covent Garden where the Christmas lights – a giant Christmas tree hung with red LEDs, and an enormous, sparkling white reindeer – drew crowds of tourists doing early Christmas shopping.

It was after nine when I took Jackson's call and he came to pick me up. He dropped me at the entrance to the Shard after I insisted I really couldn't come to harm navigating the vestibule and one lift. He watched me into the building before heading off to see Sandy.

Gregory was on his phone, still in his navy suit, his crisp, white shirt open at the neck, one hand tugging at his hair. He paced in front of the lounge window, the city lights bright behind him.

'They asked about her? About her specifically?' His voice was raised and laced with something, irritation or anxiousness perhaps, but he wasn't shouting. 'That much is on police record, Mother; they were bound to bring it up. Did they... did they ask how she—'

He took a deep breath as he listened, his upper body rising and expanding. Then he slumped, defeated, onto the edge of the sofa and leant forward with his elbows on his knees.

'They're trying to establish motive. Trina? She's supposed to be off the case.' He shook his head and his cheeks puffed out with his breath. 'Look at it this way: the CPS are going to see that this whole thing has sent that sick bastard where he belongs.'

Sick bastard! I've heard him growl those words once before, in exactly the same way. Last time, they were aimed at Jack Jones, my old boss and the man Gregory beat until he confessed to sexual assault. Gregory was beyond livid then too.

Quietly, I placed my bags down on the floor and pressed the front door closed.

'Stop crying. Please. I *know* that. I'm sorry you got dragged into this and I'm sorry that they brought her up. Yes, I know she has a fucking name and I'll do everything I can to keep her out of this, you know I will.' He stood up abruptly, then turned and found me on the opposite side of the lounge, not daring to move from the doorway. His irises were black and piercing. 'You're drunk,' he snapped into the phone. 'Stop drinking. Now? Fine. Stop drinking, I'm on my way.'

'Hi,' I said. It was all I could think to say. His rage was clear.

'I need to go out.'

'Now?'

He walked towards me and dropped his lips to my nose roughly. 'Yes.'

He collected a set of keys without saying another word and he was gone.

I thought I heard the front door open and close in the middle of the night but he never came to bed. I don't know what time he came home. The first I saw of him was in his sweat-drenched, grey T-shirt this morning when he returned from his run. When I asked if he was okay, he lied. 'Never been better,' he said. Then he showered and spent most of the journey into work on his phone to Sydney, agreeing to ever-higher sums of money to keep the press schtum.

Now, I'm sitting at my desk, turning my pen between my fingers, mulling over the events of yesterday, wondering who *she* is, why Lara was questioned and fighting with Gregory about her, and why Gregory is so desperate to keep her name off the case. He can't say he loves me, he tells me to leave, then he tells me he can't walk away. The only thing that's certain is there are things he isn't telling me.

How long can we continue like this? What if my love isn't strong enough for us both?

Dubai. A break and a clean slate. I'd be giving up an opportunity for nothing if he won't let me in. Six months, a year from now, would I be left regretting my decision not to go?

I think about whose print is on the gun and I will the phone to ring to put an end to the uncertainty.

My phone lights up on my desk an unknown number.

'Scarlett Heath speaking.'

'It's Gregory.'

'Oh. Hi. Your number didn't come up.'

'I'm not on my own phone; the damn roaming is knackered.'

'Roaming? Where are you?'

'I'm in Frankfurt, baby.'

'Frankfurt. Frankfurt, Germany?'

He chuckles. I'm not in the least bit amused. He's hardly spoken to me for the last twenty-four hours and now he's in bloody continental Europe.

'Something came up and I had to fly out. I'm going to try to fly back tonight but it might be tomorrow. Depends how long things take here.'

'Oh.'

'Listen, that's not the reason I called. I have some good news.'

'Do we get good news these days?'

'Well, good in our screwed-up way.' He laughs and despite myself, I let out a short, sadistic chuckle. 'The print on the Glock was Jackson's.'

My sense of humour fails in a nanosecond. 'That's a good thing?'

'Yes, angel, it means you're not associated with the gun. John thinks it helps corroborate our story. The police know that Jackson has handled the gun in the past so it makes sense for his print to be on there. It doesn't necessarily implicate him because it's only one partial print; it doesn't look like he gripped the gun. Do you see?'

'Ah, yeah, I guess. So it doesn't put Jackson in the frame?'

'No. And it means no matter what the results of the ballistics report are, there's no evidence to back up anyone else being involved. Our stories still all point to me pulling the trigger.'

Still he fails to understand why that doesn't please me. Not even a little bit. Not at all.

'John thinks this will be over soon, baby. He thinks the CPS will make a decision early next week.'

I sigh. 'We need to be realistic, Gregory; that decision might not be the end – it might only be the beginning.'

'Baby… breaking… tomorrow… tunnel.' The line goes dead.

16

My eyes open to the indulgent sight of Gregory's naked torso hovering above me. Messy hair and day-old stubble. The weight of his thighs resting against my pelvis and two big, brown, teddy-bear eyes staring into mine. 'Good morning,' he says, with that devastating half-smile.

I've woken in paradise. Then I remember I'm still pissed.

'Is it?'

'Cryptic Scarlett. How I've missed her.' His thumb strokes my cheek then he drops his mouth gently against mine, his soft lips lingering, rousing me from my sleepy fog. 'You look adorable when you're sleepy.'

'Stop with the sex sword, Gregory. You just took off.'

'No, I went away on business and I don't want to come home to a fight.'

'You dropped the fingerprint result on me, *by phone*, right before hanging up.'

'I didn't hang up, I lost signal.'

'Same thing.'

'It really isn't.'

'And what about Thursday? One minute, you're arguing with your mum about some phantom woman, then you're running out to calm your mum down. Who is she?'

'My mother? Rarely who she says she is.'

'You're not funny.'

'Then why are you smirking?'

'Because you're making me. Stop being evasive and tell me who she is.'

His face contorts for a second and I think he might tell me. 'You're adorable when you're taking a tantrum.'

I scowl. 'This isn't over, Ryans.'

He leans his head to one side and raises a brow. 'No?'

I squirm beneath him and grab his pert arse cheeks with a squeeze, digging my nails into his flesh. 'No.'

'I beg to differ, Miss Heath.'

He attacks the sensitive skin at my sides and under my arms, making me scream with laughter. 'Is it over?'

'No!' I squeal.

He jumps backwards, grabbing my ankle between his legs and tickling the middle of my foot. I put a brave face on for as long as possible but it's no good. It's so bloody ticklish, my squeal bursts from me again. I wriggle and yank at my foot, trying to kick, squirming in the bed sheets, but he's too strong. He grips my ankle and then his quick-moving fingers are on the uber-sensitive skin beneath my toes.

'Stop! Stop!' I scream.

'Say it's over.'

I shake my head vigorously.

'Scarlett Heath, I have a sex weapon and you know I'm not afraid to use it.'

My ribs are aching and I think I might actually pee. 'It doesn't look like much of a weapon to me.'

He stops. My giggles subside and he dives forward again, his weight shared between my legs and the forearms propped at either side of my head. 'I'm going to show you exactly how much of a weapon it is. I want my morning fuck.'

'I want your morning fuck too.' I take a deep breath and surge forward with all my might, throwing him to his side and diving from the bed. 'But you're not getting it after that!'

I run from my side and round the bottom of the bed, making it to the door before he grabs me. He wraps a muscled arm around my annoyingly light waist, halting me with ease. I thrash around, legs and arms air-running, and eventually, I get enough leverage to burst from his arms. I'm giggling so much that my arms and legs can't crawl more than a few feet along the wooden floor of the landing.

He's laughing too, the most wonderful, playful sound, as he flips me onto my back, the rosewood cold against my skin. He hovers over me, his weight fully resting on his arms, making the muscles flex. I raise my head and bite his bicep.

'You're so gorgeous when you giggle,' he tells me.

I look down to find his cock ready, naked and swollen. Digging my fingers into his arse, I yank him down towards me until his shaft is pressing against my navel.

He raises two playful brows. 'Hungry this morning, aren't we?'

I bite my lip... *I really am.*

* * *

Rather than taking up my usual position between Gregory's legs, I slide down into the opposite end of the bathtub and tie my hair in a messy knot. He might have escaped me whilst we frolicked on the landing but I have some questions to ask and I'm not going to let him grope his way out of answering them.

'How was Germany?' I break him in gently.

He lifts his arms from the water, steam rising from his skin, and rests them on the sides of the bath. 'Dry. I had to meet with a business contact from the States who happened to have a meeting in Frankfurt so I agreed to meet him there.'

'Anything I can help with?'

'No. Nothing legal, just business, or future business, rather. I like to have my irons in a lot of pies.'

A giggle escapes me, despite my want and need to be serious. 'You surely know that's incorrect.'

'What's incorrect?' I can't be certain but I think I detect the faintest air of a knowing smile around his lips.

'You either have irons in the fire or fingers in pies, baby. You don't have irons in pies.'

He turns his head from one side to the other, contemplating. 'I guess that wouldn't make sense, would it? I mean, the irons would just ruin the pies.'

'Right.' I smile on a shake of my head.

'Would you get over here?' He moves a hand to his toned pec, indicating for me to take up my usual spot. I fight the urge to move in and lie back against his chest, instead leaning back a little, letting him know that this woman is putting her foot down. *Now there's a saying he might understand.*

'Are we going to talk about Thursday?'

He moves his hand back to the rim of the bath, his upper body purposefully wide and strong. 'What about Thursday?'

'Don't play games, Gregory. You were angry on the phone to Lara, then you left almost without a word. Next thing I know, you're on a flight to Germany and you wouldn't have even called me if the fingerprint trace hadn't come back.'

'I would've called you.'

This man is infuriating. I sigh and bend my legs, burying my impending scream of exasperation beneath the bubbly water. When I slide back up, he hasn't moved.

'Who was the woman you were talking about on the phone? Lara was upset, that was obvious. So who was it and why did the police mention her?'

I lose him. He's still looking at me but he isn't present. He drifts to somewhere else, somewhere I'm not invited to go.

'Why won't you talk to me?'

'Why do you keep pushing me, Scarlett? Can't you accept that I have a past and that I want to forget it? I want you to be my future. Untarnished.'

'So the woman is part of your past? From South Africa?'

'Enough!'

I jump, surprised by his growl, water lapping at the sides of the bath as I move. 'Don't hate me for trying to break down your walls, Gregory. I want you to let me in. Can't you see that for us to have a future, you need to be open and honest with me? Let me understand you. Let me understand everything that's going on. *I* need to make sense of it all too.'

Pulling his knees up and leaning forward, he cups his hands and splashes water in his face and over his hair, then pauses, holding his hands in his dark, wet locks.

I wait. Hoping.

Eventually, he lies back again and leans his head against the wall tiles, his eyes closed. 'Let me take you to dinner tonight.'

Would you open up to me then, my beautiful, conflicted man?

'Somewhere nice, just us.'

'And when you say *just us*, what you mean is no talking about the present or the future, which you can't seem to grasp is based entirely on the past.'

'Jesus, Scarlett, I don't even know what that babble means. I'm just asking you to come to dinner with me. As my gorgeous, sexy, infuriating girlfriend.' He slips a foot between my thighs and starts moving it up to my centre.

I slap it away, causing a splash. 'Oh no, you don't! You're not using sex to ignore me again.' I climb out of the bath and wrap myself in a warm, white towel from the heated rail. 'And no. I won't come to dinner with you. I have plans.'

He leaps out of the bath as quickly as he can without slipping on the bubble-greased base. He yanks my towel off me and picks me up, my back against his chest, plonking us both back into the hot water, in our usual position. He pins me against him until my wriggly limbs relent.

'We're going to dinner,' he says, reaching for a flannel, soaking it and squeezing the water across my chest.

'I genuinely have plans. I'm going out with Amanda and Luke. I promised.'

'Luke, your ex?'

'Luke, my *gay* ex, yes.'

He nods his approval of Luke's sexual preferences against my neck. 'Cancel.'

'No. I can't ditch my friends, Gregory. I've hardly seen them since we met.'

'So?'

'So I'm not cancelling. We'll do dinner another night.'

He bites the bottom of my earlobe sharply. 'Where are you going?'

'For drinks.'

'Just drinks? No food?'

'Just drinks.'

'Is that wise? I'd prefer if you have dinner.'

I turn to face him and realise he actually *is* serious. 'I'll eat before I go.'

'Fine, but something substantial. I don't want you drunk.'

'Erm, I'll be drunk if I want to be, thanks all the same.'

'Fine, then I'll come too.'

I try to push away from him in protest but he holds me to his chest and resumes casually soaking and draining the flannel.

'You aren't invited.'

'Then don't get drunk.'

'Fine. I'll get tipsy. Better?'

He shrugs against me and I can feel my temper stirring.

'Where are you going for drinks?'

'Why?' My tone is petulant but I can't help it. 'So you can follow me?'

'I won't be following you, Scarlett.'

'Ha, so you'll have Jackson follow me.'

He squeezes the flannel against my chest and drops a kiss to my temple, my temper instantly dampened.

'Actually, no. Jackson is taking Sandy out tonight for a special dinner.'

'A *special* dinner?' My head fights against his palm, trying to catch him smirking. 'Let me see you. What *special* dinner? Oh my gosh, he's not going to... You don't think...?'

He shrugs against my back, still keeping my head faced towards the bottom of the bath.

'Damn you, Gregory Ryans, tell me!' I wiggle my feet in tantrum, splashing water over the edge of the tub.

His chest jerks against my back as he laughs. 'I can't; it's a secret.'

'Oh bugger off, Gregory!'

I stomp out of the bath as he throws his head back, laughing.

'And I won't tell you where I'm going tonight and I *will* get drunk!'

'You won't need to tell me where you're going, angel; I'll find out when I drop you off.'

Snatching my towel from the floor, I stalk out of the bathroom, internally screaming at my *oh-so-bloody-humorous* billionaire.

17

The last proper night out I had, as in not after work and not rushing home to look after my dad, was far too long ago, which is obvious given the show I make of getting ready. From the appointment with the beauty salon to smarten up my waxing, washing and creaming my skin, giving all twenty nails a base coat, three colour coats and a top coat, and blow-drying my hair into a mousse-induced, high-volume do, I manage to fill the day.

'You're going to be late.' Gregory appears, leaning against the doorframe of the walk-in wardrobe, watching me flick through my dresses in a fluster.

'So now you do want me to go out.'

'No. I'm making conversation so that I can enjoy the view.'

Looking down at my black, lace thong and matching bra, I bite my lip to stop my grin from giving me away. I'm still feigning my earlier mood. I shouldn't have to be the one to apologise.

'Smart Guy's a conversationalist now?'

'Shh, your mouthful of attitude is ruining my moment.'

I select a black, fitted dress with spaghetti straps that's probably a little too short. In fact, I've only ever worn it once *because* it's so short but Amanda convinced me to spend too much money on it during a dry martini-fuelled shopping trip and given it *has* been a long time, I should make the effort. I bend forward, fully aware of the lace thong slipping between my cheeks, and rummage through shoe boxes, knowing too well where the strap shoes are that I'm looking for but enjoying the torture I'm inflicting on Mr Unreasonable.

'Keep going, Miss Heath. Please keep going and give me a reason to come over there and spank that arse until you'd rather scream my name than go out.'

I'd always rather do that but now isn't the time to flatter his ego.

With purpose, I slip my feet into my heels and buckle the thin straps at my ankles, then slide the tight dress down over my breasts, wiggling my hips as I pull it down to my thighs.

'Are you planning on coming to bed with me?' he asks.

I flash him a dirty scowl.

'Right. Fine. Then you can take that negligee off right now.'

'Excuse me?' My hands move to my hips for maximum effect.

'There's no *way* you're going out in that excuse for a dress.'

'I think you'll find I am.'

'Take it off, Scarlett.'

'Quit treating me like a child, Gregory.'

'Then quit acting like one.'

'I hate it when you say that to me.'

He moves towards me. 'I can take it off or you can.'

'No.'

He grabs my hand and pushes it against his length, hard beneath the dark denim of his jeans. 'Do you feel that? I'm not having other men looking at you and getting a hard-on, Scarlett. Take it off.'

Oh how I'd love to stay home and fix his problem.

'Fine.'

'Fine.'

As soon as I manage to wiggle free of the dress, I throw it in a heap on the floor and start rummaging again through the hanging clothes. 'There's nothing I want to wear.'

'You really are cranky tonight, Miss Heath; what's gotten into you?' It's a rhetorical question, more to make his point than actually obtain a response, so I don't bother offering one. But I am insanely cranky; that I would both have to agree with and blame him for.

'Here.' He holds out a black, strapless all-in-one, fitted to the waist, with tapered bottoms. 'This is nice. It's sexy and sophisticated and other men won't be able to see my spanking target if you bend over.'

Despite myself, I giggle, and take the jumpsuit from him.

* * *

'You look stunning,' he says as I descend the stairs to the lounge. 'Ready?'

I nod, afraid to speak in case I accidentally forgive him for the list of things that've made me mad at him in the last few days. He slips a grey blazer over his black T-shirt and pulls on his leather ankle boots.

We drive to Clapham in the Range Rover. A thoughtful choice of vehicle for two women in heels. He beeps the horn once and Amanda comes running, tugging down her short, raspberry dress as she moves. She slips into the back seat, still fastening her jewellery. 'You look yummy, hunny,' she says, popping her head through the gap between the front seats to give my outfit the once-over.

'You too. New dress?'

She winks with a grin. 'It's allowance day.'

Gregory shakes his head. Amanda still gets a monthly allowance from her father and Gregory finds it as unbelievable as I do. Gregory worked hard for everything he has. At twenty-eight, he wasn't living on Daddy's money; he was a multimillionaire. This is just another reason my boyfriend and my best friend can't seem to get along.

'Chelsea please, driver,' she says, Gregory's jaw tightening in response.

'Are we meeting Luke there?' I ask to change the subject.

'Mm,' she says, using her teeth to hold her bracelet in place as she fastens the lock. 'And Shelley. Emily and Harry said they might see us out.'

'Lawrence's niece?'

'Mmhmm.'

'Perfect. It's been weeks, no, probably months, since I've seen Shelley and it'd be nice to see the others if they make it. Where does Shelley live since she moved out of your place?'

'Mm, near Monument, I think. I haven't seen her for a few weeks either. She met a new guy, blah, blah.'

Luke is waiting on Kings Road, bouncing on the spot in dark jeans, waist-coat and blazer, a sign of just how cold it is without a cloud in the late-November sky.

Amanda bounds out of the car and runs into Luke's arms.

'Thanks,' I say, unbuckling my belt.

As I turn to leave the car, Gregory grabs my wrist.

'Kiss.'

I turn and look into those devilishly handsome, brown eyes. *Stay strong, lady!* With a deep breath, I snatch my hand away and open the car door.

'Scarlett Heath, don't you dare get out of this car without kissing me.'

'Thanks for the lift.' I step into the road and slam the door shut.

He reaches me before I've even managed to walk around to the pavement on his side of the car. He grabs my thighs and flips me upside down so I'm dangling in front of him, my head inches from the ground.

'Jesus Christ, Gregory! Put me down!' I check my strapless top to make sure nothing's fallen out and thank God for my adequate but not large breasts. 'You're insane, do you know that?'

I glance up to find everyone on Kings Road staring at the ridiculous scene and Luke and Amanda crippled with laughter. *Traitors.* He eventually flips me back upright and holds my waist until I'm steady on my feet, then he leans me against the side of the Range Rover, the cold metal against my back making me shiver. He locks his thighs against the outsides of mine and subtly presses his crotch against my pelvis.

With his index finger, he lifts my chin. 'It's never acceptable for you to leave me without a kiss. Do you understand?'

The air has escaped my lungs so I nod my response.

'Say you understand.'

'I understand.'

'Good girl.'

And then he kisses me, slowly, deeply, passionately, in a way that lets me know what will be waiting for me when I get home and tells every other man on Kings Road who I belong to. Forgetting my surroundings, I moan into his mouth as his tongue lightly grazes mine and I pull his waist into me. I'm dizzy when he eventually peels his lips away.

'Call me when you want to come home.'

'I'll get a taxi; it'll probably be late with these guys.' I flick a hand in the direction of Amanda and Luke, who've finally stopped laughing.

'What did I just say?'

'I'll call you,' I say.

'Thank you.'

Slipping between Amanda and Luke to keep my bare shoulders warm, I watch him drive away.

'Jesus, Mary and Joseph! Who. Was. That?'

I close Luke's open mouth with the tip of my finger. A rogue strand of hair falls from his carefully styled honey-blond and rests across his brow. He could be a model.

'*That* is Scarlett's billionaire client,' Amanda confirms.

'I actually have a stiffy.' Luke moves in front of Amanda and me and pushes his crotch forward. 'Really! Feel it!'

That's all it takes to send Amanda back into hysterics.

'Bloody hell, Luke, must you constantly remind me that you preferred taking baths with every man on Cambridge's rugby team rather than me?' I say with a shake of the head.

Luke drapes an arm across our shoulders, encouraging us towards the red canopy at the entrance of the bar. The queue of people to the left of the entrance stare as Luke dips his head to the two hefty doormen and we walk straight in.

'I confess, the changing room orgy was a particular fantasy of mine,' Luke says as we ascend the staircase.

'Scarlett! It's been too long!' Shelley jumps from the booth she was nestled in and, as fast as her four-inch heels and body-con dress will allow, she hurtles towards me.

'I always forget how squealy she is,' Luke says, leaning into my ear. 'Drink?'

'No need! No need! We have Grey Goose and Bombay Sapphire and every mixer you can think of.' Shelley throws her arms around me and yanks me into her suspiciously larger-than-usual chest.

'Hi, it's so nice to see you. Shelley. Shelley, I can't breathe.' I peel myself away.

'Whoopsies!' She giggles. 'Come. Come. I want you to meet my new guy.' She drags my arm, jerking it in the socket, and pulls me through the bar. I smile apologetically as a man I've been forced to bump into snaps his head quickly to look at the culprit.

Shelley's new guy is stocky, with broad shoulders that seem part-muscle and part-just mass. He rises from his seat at the far side of the booth and leans over three ice buckets full of alcohol and mixers to shake my hand and drop a kiss on my cheek. I clock the Tag decorating his chunky wrist, the cuffs of his shirt clearly rolled back for effect.

'I'm Dan,' he shouts across the pounding bass of the music.

'Scarlett,' I yell through a smile.

'Vodka or gin?' Shelley asks, holding up both bottles as she drops into the padded leather booth with a thump.

'Gin, please.'

Self-poured, or rather Shelley and Dan poured, measures are dangerous. Drink four has been pushed in front of me and they're already clouding my head. Emily and Harry have turned up and, after telling me again how I must drag Gregory out for drinks 'just one time ever,' they work the room, happily socialising with the wealthy cohort.

'I need to slow down,' I say to Amanda as I wince through my first mouthful of the strongest mix yet.

She's fiddling with her phone as she mumbles her agreement.

'Is everything okay? You've hardly touched your drink.'

'I'm just pacing myself,' she says, putting her glass to her lips but taking the smallest sip.

'Okay, who are you and what have you done with my best friend?' I nudge into her shoulder and receive a dim smile in return.

'It's nothing. Really. I'm just feeling a little green. I thought I'd be fine after one or two drinks but this is my first and I just have no fancy for it.' She leans into the booth and nudges her glass away. 'Let's dance!'

It must be the four lethal gins because I feel like I can actually dance. I lift my arms above my head as I move in time to David Guetta's beat.

'I love this tune!' Amanda yells, suddenly revived.

My waist is attacked by two man-arms.

'Shots!' Luke screams into my ear. He drags me backwards to the bar where a row of six tequila shots is being poured.

The barman sets a slice of lemon across each glass then dishes out three salt shakers.

Amanda goes first, licking the side of her hand and tipping salt on top. Nothing stands in the way of Amanda and tequila. For me, on the other hand, this is a bad idea. Beyond bad. Tequila and I go together like pink and green, oil on a fire, tomato juice and a white shirt. The ending is predictable. Option one is wasted. Option two is sick. Option three is a combination of one and two. And there isn't an option four.

But I haven't been out for a while.

'God help me,' I say, licking my hand, pouring over salt and clinking my shot glass with Amanda's and Luke's.

'Cheers!'

The salt bites in such a way that I actually *want* to chase it with tequila but... *good Lord*, that stuff is vile. I dig my teeth into the slice of lemon and suck as hard as I can, my head shaking, my feet stomping against the floor.

'Yeah, like old times,' Luke says, slamming his empty shot glass onto the bar with a satisfied slurp. 'Next!'

'I couldn't do it. The smell is making me queasy! How do we drink that stuff?' Luke and I both dart our heads to look at Amanda, who's holding her full glass of tequila mid-air.

'Since when did you become a prude?' Luke asks.

'I just can't. You have it.'

He shrugs, takes the glass from Amanda and rearranges the row of glasses on the bar so that he and I each have two left.

'Luke, I can't. I'll be ill. I'm already drunk.'

'Nonsense, Scarlett, we used to drink more than this on a weeknight at uni. Man up!' Luke says with a wink, the irony of his statement not lost on either of us. He presses a shot glass into my hand as Amanda lines up the camera on her phone.

'Cheers!'

'Oh, crap,' I mutter, just before I lick the salt, neck the shot and suck hard on my second slice of lemon. 'Oh it hurts!' My feet stomp again and I shake my head, which only adds to the increasing fogginess in my mind.

'Last one,' Luke sings, seemingly unaffected.

'Luke, I can't!' I protest, rubbing my chest as if it might quell the burning sensation.

'Pipe down, Scarlett, it's only one.'

'One that'll have me running to the toilet.'

Amanda flashes her camera at us again as we carry out the same procedure and my feet stomp on the floor a third time.

'All right. I'm going on the prowl,' Luke announces, without even so much as a flinch from his final hit of tequila. 'Coming?'

'No, thanks. I'm going to go and find my sea legs,' I say, conscious that I'm having to concentrate too hard on putting one foot in front of the other as I walk back to the booth.

'Are you going to vomit?' Amanda asks, eyeing me cautiously as she slips into the booth beside me.

'No.' I laugh. 'I just need a minute.'

'You sure? I know what you're like with tequila.'

'Yet you still inflicted an extra shot on me?' I raise a playful brow and she giggles with a shrug.

'I thought it would be good for you. You seem... less... well, happy tonight.'

'Oh, Amanda, please don't start. I *am* happy. There's a lot of stuff going on but I'm not unhappy with Gregory and I know where you're going with this.'

She turns to face me, lifting her knees sideways onto the leather seat. 'Just hear me out.'

My fingers locate a glass, mine or someone else's, and turn it in circles until my head decides it's too dizzy to watch anything rotate. A sudden need to swallow comes over me, then my stomach settles again.

'I can see what he has to offer. He's attractive, anyone can see that. He's wealthy. He's obviously smart to have gotten to where he is.'

I lift my head and find two sympathetic eyes looking back at me as she rests her head against the back of the booth, her auburn hair falling across her shoulders.

'But?'

'But, he's not right for you, Scarlett.'

'Excuse me?'

'I know you. You're one of the nicest people I know, probably will ever know. You never do or say anything wrong, Scarlett, and suddenly he comes on the scene and—'

'And what?' My words reflect the sharp bout of anger I'm feeling. She's got a matter of seconds before I refuse to listen to any more.

'I don't trust him. I don't trust him and I don't like what he's doing to you.'

I stand, shuffling awkwardly around the table to escape the booth. I'm not listening to this and I'm not starting a fight with my best friend over it either.

'He's dark, Scarlett. He's cagey.'

I turn on my heels, fighting against unsteadiness to face her. 'Why don't you just spit out what you're trying to say, Amanda?'

'Do you know why he really killed Kevin Pearson? You just accept that his father came after him, tried to kill him for no reason and Gregory shot him.' She stands now and braces herself on the table with two hands. 'Not just shot him, Scarlett, shot him at point-blank range. Cold-blooded murder.'

'Shut up. Shut up!' Tears spring to the back of my eyes and the words are on the tip of my tongue. I want to tell her. I want to tell everyone that Gregory is a good man and I am the cold-blooded killer. And that I know why I did it. I might not know everything, not yet, but what I *do* know is I shot Kevin Pearson because otherwise, Gregory would be dead.

The room begins to sway with the mix of tequila, fighting with Amanda and the crashing home of the stark reality that I'm a killer. I'm no longer ordinary Scarlett Heath who plays by the rules. I killed another human being and I'm letting the man I love with every single cell in my body take the blame. A man who can't tell me he's fallen for me too. A man who despises himself so much, he wants to be punished for my crime. My chest is suddenly tight and painful as I try to take a breath in. I slap a hand against my chest in an attempt to ease the pain. I need air.

Pushing through the full room of people, I make my way to the exit. At the staircase, I hear her calling my name and find enough strength to stop and tell her not to follow me. I watch my blurred feet take the staircase as cautiously as my murky mind, breathless body and unsteady legs will allow. Downstairs, I find the smokers' area outside and push my back against the cold brick wall, my lungs finally filling with air.

Without thinking, I dial his number and as I wait for him to pick up, the tears fall and sobs burst from my chest, relieving the pressure.

'Are you ready, baby?'

I try to speak but I can't. I hold the phone to my ear, willing myself to gain some composure but it won't happen. I'm sobbing uncontrollably, the eyes of smokers on me as I slump to the ground on my hunkers.

'Scarlett? Scarlett, what's happened? Where are you?'

The words leave my mouth in chokes, breaking through my tears. 'I don't know who I am any more.'

'Baby, please, where are you? What's happened?'

'Nothing. I'm fine.'

'You don't sound fucking fine, Scarlett. Has someone hurt you? Where are you?'

'No. No one's hurt me.' I press my finger and thumb into the corners of my eyes to stop the tears but it works only momentarily, then another sob breaks the silence. *No one except you, Gregory.* 'I don't know what to do.'

'I'm coming to get you. Where are you?'

'I'm at the same place you dropped me off.'

I can hear him moving quickly and I hear the rustle of keys, then the bang of a door.

'Are there people around you?' His voice is stricken with panic.

'Yes. I'm okay. I'm in the smokers' shelter outside.' I sniffle back another onset of tears.

'I'm getting in the car, baby. I'll put you on speaker. Stay on the line for me. Can you do that?'

'Yes. Gregory, people think you're... that you're a bad person, that you're bad for me. I can't stand it. I can't stand that people think badly of you because of me and what I did. How can I do that to you?' The sobs come back again with a vengeance. I press my face into my hand to mask myself from onlookers.

'I don't care what other people think, Scarlett. I only care what you think.' I hear a horn sound down the phone. He must be driving like a man with rage. 'Do *you* think I'm a bad person?'

'No. But I think... I don't know what I think.' Pressing my fingers to my lips, I look to the roof of the outdoor canopy.

'Scarlett? Are you there?'

'Yes. I'm here.'

'Keep talking to me, angel. I'm almost there.'

'I think we're bad for each other, Gregory. People should be together because they bring out the best in each other, shouldn't they?'

'You do bring out the best in me, Scarlett. You make me feel like a decent person. I've never felt like a decent person before. You give me more purpose than anything else in my life.'

My eyes fills again and now I don't know if it's because I want to hold him and tell him that I understand the pain he locks away – at least I *want* to understand – or if it's frustration because I'm so utterly and completely lost.

'I make people think badly of you, Gregory. I make you angry. I make you do things you shouldn't have to do. And you make me— I just don't know how I got here. I don't know who I was or who I am any more. I'm outside a bar in

Chelsea crying and wasted. Since when do I behave like this? I... I don't know anything any more.'

'You know you love me.' His words are calm and quiet. A test.

'I do love you, Gregory. But I don't know who you are either because you won't let me in.'

'You do know me, Scarlett. You do.' The panic is back in his voice, despite knowing I'm safe. 'No one has ever known me like you, understood me when I can't say the things I think and feel. No one has ever come close to breaking down my walls. Only you, baby.'

'You say these things and it makes me think— Gregory, I don't even know if you love me.'

I pause, waiting, but he doesn't say a word. His heavy breath comes down the line and my heart aches in my chest.

'How can you do and say things like I'm yours and I'm your purpose and not know if you love me?'

His silence gives me the obvious answer. He tells me what I need to hear for now, until this whole mess is over. He wants me to be able to move on. That's why the police: so when we're over, I'll be able to accept his plea of self-defence as my own, if it works. He doesn't want me. I won't keep waiting, humiliating myself. He's been forced to stay with me and that's not what I want.

'Gregory?'

'Yes.'

I take a deep breath, my shoulders chugging back against the cold brick wall. 'I've been asked to move to Dubai with work. For six months. On secondment.'

Silence.

'I'm going to go, Gregory. I'm going to go to Dubai. So if you love me, tell me now.'

'Scarlett!' Amanda shouts as she lands in front of my face, making me drop my phone. 'I was looking for you. Ed's come to pick me up. We'll drop you home.'

I shake my head and press the heel of my hand against my brow as it begins to throb. I look up and try to focus on Amanda but she just won't stand still.

'Oh, God, Scarlett, are you going to be sick?'

I nod my head then somehow stand and take two steps towards the corner and throw up. I heave as it just keeps coming.

'Scarlett, I'm sorry. I didn't mean for us to fight,' Amanda says as she holds my hair back.

Then my legs give way and I'm being lifted through the smoking area, back inside and along the corridor to the front of the bar.

'I'll get the door,' Amanda says.

'I've got it,' Gregory snaps. He opens the door, still holding me against his chest, then sits me down into the passenger seat of his Lamborghini and buckles me in.

'Look after her.' I can't open my eyes but I know if I could, Gregory would be glaring at Amanda. 'I don't like you, Gregory; you've broken her. But I want my best friend back and it seems like you're the only person who can fix her.'

The car door is closed and I lean my head against the cold window before the driver door is opened and shut and the car is moving.

18

My head feels like concrete. Actually, it feels like it's been bashed by concrete. Concrete that's been dropped from the top of a skyscraper and landed sharp edge down, perfectly in the centre of my skull. I don't dare move. Opening my eyes seems like an impossible feat, one which should be attempted with extreme caution. Despite my effort, my lids are just too heavy to peel back and expose my no doubt bloodshot whites and constricted pupils to the world.

My mouth is dry but strangely tastes of mint. With monumental effort, I roll from my foetal position to my back and straighten my legs. That small act alone sets off a bass drum in my temples and at the bottom of my skull. Groaning, I move my hands to my face and slowly, very slowly, behind the safety of my fingers, I open my eyes. They feel sore, bruised even, as I rub life into them with my fingertips. When I've amassed the courage I need, I drop my hands to the duck feather pillow above my head and expose myself to the sunlight creeping through the sides of the crushed silk curtains. It comes to me slowly, my brain reacting to each new detail as I turn my head around the bedroom. The large, Georgian sash bay window with soft beige cushions turning the ledge into a seat is hidden by the teal curtains. The abstract art on the walls. The large, gothic hanging mirror. The familiar, soft brown-black leather sofa in one corner of the room and the matching ottoman at the bottom of the king bed I'm lying in. Gregory is perched on the end of the bed resting his elbows on his spread legs.

I push myself up to sit, holding onto my head with one hand to stop it from falling off, and groaning under the strain of the small movement. I'm wearing a silk nightdress that I don't recall putting on.

'There's isotonic water on the side table,' he grumbles without looking at me.

There are also two white pills. I assume they're paracetamol but right now, I don't care what they are; I'll try anything. I pop them on my tongue and wash them down with the disgusting, pink isotonic drink.

'You brought me to the farm?' I ask, once my twisted face has returned to normal. The same twisted face I pulled after those lethal shots of tequila.

He turns to look at me over his shoulder. He looks like crap. In a very hot, Gregory kind of way, he looks like he hasn't slept at all. 'You said you couldn't be at the Shard.'

'Oh. Why?'

'You said you couldn't be where it all happened.'

I search my memory and come up empty. 'I'm sorry, I didn't mean to cause such a faff.'

He leans forward and pulls his hands through his hair.

'And I'm sorry for getting drunk. I know you didn't want me to... to make myself vulnerable. It just sort of happened.'

'Scarlett, I wouldn't ever want you to get that drunk. I didn't know where you were. You were so upset, I thought that something had happened to you. You *were* vulnerable.'

'I know.' I turn the glass of pink liquid around in my lap.

He moves his full body, lifting one knee onto the mattress, and rests a hand on the duvet on top of my leg. 'It wasn't just about you being vulnerable. I knew this would happen. You've been carrying too much around and I knew if you got drunk...' He shakes his head and disappears somewhere. His eyes are distant. 'The truth always comes out in drink.'

And the penny drops. 'Gregory, I swear I didn't say anything to anyone. I wanted to. But I didn't.'

He looks up at me now, his face the image of confusion.

'Amanda and I had a fight. Oh, God, Amanda. I just left her! I was so angry, I walked out of the bar and left her.' I dart from the bed, searching for something: my bag, my phone.

'Amanda's fine, Scarlett. Williams picked her up.'

'Williams was at the bar?' I slump down on the sofa, defeated after my brief, unsuccessful search. 'I really don't remember that at all.'

He sits up straight, his eyes still distant but the cogs of his mind whirring. 'What do you remember?'

Let me see. 'Dancing. Then bloody Luke wanting to do shots. Amanda wouldn't do hers so I had three.' My body shudders. 'Amanda and I argued. That's why I left. I was angry and upset and... I...' I glance quickly up to him and find two irises set on me, scrutinising my words. I hate myself for being so needy.

'Go on.'

'I just wanted to talk to you. I missed you and what Amanda said...'

'What did she say?'

I look at him, into those big, dark-brown eyes, the angles of his face, day-old weekend stubble lining his jaw. The guilt comes back.

'I remember crying.'

He nods.

'Oh, God, I was sick! I was sick outside the club.' My hands move to my mouth. 'I can't believe I did that. I'm a disgrace. That's hideous.' My head shakes as I close my eyes, my entire insides cringing. 'I always used to be the sober one. The one helping everyone else throw up, dabbing mascara from other girls' cheeks. What's happened to me?'

'Being drunk, even being sick, doesn't make you a bad person, Scarlett.'

'Oh, no. My nightdress.' I tug the silk around my body. 'We went to the Shard. Was I sick there too?'

'In spectacular fashion. I showered you there and changed you into some leggings and a shirt.' He motions to my clothes, on top of a folded duvet on the floor. 'You were frantic in the apartment. So I packed some things and drove here.'

My eyes flick from the bed to the folded duvet on the empty space next to me on the sofa. 'You slept on the sofa?'

'I was worried you'd be sick again.'

I can feel my brow furrow. 'Why didn't you stay in the bed with me?'

He sighs, his shoulders sagging. 'You really don't remember what you said to me on the phone last night?'

My heart rate rises as panic descends. 'What? What did I say?'

'Nothing you shouldn't have said, baby. I just wish I'd given you the answers you needed.'

I try to remember what I said but my slow mind just can't function.

'Get here.' He flicks his head for me to go to him and there's nowhere else I'd rather be. I crawl onto his lap and he holds me to him, pressing my head into his neck and dropping the most gentle of kisses on my brow.

* * *

Gregory drags me out for a walk. We walk for hours with his dogs, Bramble and Buster. They run and bark playfully in the crisp, hangover-curing air but Gregory is distant. All day, I have the feeling that he's put up an invisible wall. When he touches me, my skin doesn't spark; when he speaks, his voice is melancholy rather than warm. Getting drunk, forgetting everything for a few hours, really wasn't worth it.

Kian comes to meet us when we arrive back at the farm. His head is covered in a thick, wool hat and his insulated, fleece gloves make him look even more youthful than he is. His wellies are almost as muddy as Bramble and Buster, who he directs to the back of the house to be washed down.

I kick off one wellie with my opposite foot but the other is stuck. Gregory sits me back onto the window ledge, bending and flexing the boot until he's able to free my foot. He helps me out of my winter coat and hangs it up with his Barbour. When I pull off my gloves, he presses my hands together between his and blows hot breath onto them.

'I'm sorry, Scarlett, for everything I'm not.'

'What are you talking about, Gregory?' I know today of all days, I won't hear those magic words but I still want him to know. 'I love you, just as you are.'

He drops his lips to my brow and pulls me tighter into him. Maybe I'm becoming resigned to the fact he won't say what I want to hear because this time, it doesn't shatter me. Or maybe it's because I need to start accepting that we're a CPS decision away from the end of us.

Kian's been in the lounge and struck up the open log fire. I sink down onto the sofa and bring my legs into my chest. Gregory disappears and returns again with two cups of hot tea. Then he slips down onto the sofa next to me and wraps his big, comforting arm around me, pulling me into his side.

We drink our tea in silence, staring into the roaring fire.

'Gregory, I am sorry.'

'Baby, we've all been there. It's done. Stop worrying.'

'If that's how you feel, why are you so... off? What did I say to you last night?'

'Nothing you shouldn't have said.'

'Stop saying that. Please. What did I say?'

He sighs but squeezes his arm tighter around me. 'You said a lot of things. A lot of honest things.'

'Gregory.'

He sighs again. 'You said you think I'm bad for you. That you don't know who you are any more. Is that how you feel?'

I shrug under the weight of an overwhelming sense of guilt.

'Scarlett?'

'Yes. I don't think you're bad for me, I didn't mean that. But I— I'm struggling to get a handle on things, yes and I...'

'And you what?'

I shrug.

He lifts my chin and turns my head to face him. 'And what?'

I don't dare defy the intensity of his gaze. 'I'm scared that we've gotten ourselves into this situation because of circumstances. I mean, look at us living together. That was never supposed to happen but you felt like you needed to protect me.'

'We've discussed that, Scarlett. I asked you to move in with me for more reasons than protection.'

Just not love. I suddenly have no energy to continue the conversation so I turn away from him and bring the back of his hand to my lips, leaning into his side, shielded from his scrutiny.

'You also told me you want to move to Dubai.' His words are little more than a whisper.

Holy shit! I dart upright and face him. 'I told you about Dubai? God, Gregory, I never meant to tell you like that; that's really shitty of me. It's been playing on my mind—'

'I got that.'

'No. You don't get it. I haven't mentioned it because it's only a secondment and I've decided not to go.' Panic is clear in my shaky words. 'If I said that last night, it was drink talking. I haven't told my boss that I won't go yet but I've already made the decision.'

'Shh, calm down, baby. I... I've been thinking about it a lot today and I think maybe you're right.'

'What? No.'

He strokes my fallen hair back behind my ear. 'So much has happened. It would give you time to think. Space. Like you've been saying you need.'

'You...' The words are crushing my chest. 'You want me to go?'

'No, Scarlett. I don't want you to get trapped in a dark world, in my world that you don't... You deserve better. You deserve knights and flowers, a man with a good heart. A man who can feel the way any man should around you, like he's the luckiest man alive, and make you see that, give you the fairy tale.'

I hold my hand to his chest. 'Gregory, yours is the only heart I'll ever want. Please believe me. I know you think you can't let me in but you can. I don't ever want to leave. I don't *want* the fairy tale.' A single, silent tear tickles my cheek as it worms down my skin like the sliver of doubt in my mind. *Is he protecting me from him or him from himself?*

'Hey, shh. Okay.' He wipes the tear away and we both jump as his phone starts ringing. He leans away from me to retrieve the phone from the opposite arm of the sofa.

'It's for you,' he says, handing me the handset.

'Me?' I glance at the screen and see Jackson's name. I rub a hand across my cheek and calm my breathing as Gregory takes my free hand in his. 'Hello?'

'It's Sandy, sweets.'

'Oh, hey, Sandy. You and Jackson share phones now, do you?'

Sandy giggles and it's that sweet giggle that she reserves for when she's really giddy. Just about the only thing that could improve my mood. 'We'll be sharing a lot more than that soon.'

'Huh?'

'I wanted to tell you in person but I don't want anyone else to know before you.'

I plant my tea cup on the floor then sit bolt upright on the edge of the sofa. 'What? Tell me what?'

I can just imagine her, eyes twinkling, brown cheeks flush, an arm wrapped around her ribs. 'Geoffrey asked me to marry him and I said yes.' She laughs, utterly, blissfully happy.

'Oh my gosh, Sandy! I can't believe it! That's amazing! You make such a lovely couple. Jackson is a good guy and you... oh my gosh, he's so lucky to have you.' My eyes fill and for the first time in as long as I can remember, they're wet with happiness. 'Oh Sandy, you're going to make me cry. I'm so happy for you. I really, really am.'

'I'm so happy. Geoffrey is wonderful.'

'And it's so soon, so romantic; he's completely swept you off your feet, hasn't he?'

'It's a dream,' she says, her smile obvious in her words.

I sit back into the corner of the sofa and Gregory resumes his hold around my shoulders. 'Tell me *everything*. How, when, where? I knew he was a closet romantic. Wait until I see him.'

'Oh deary me, I'll have to sit down.' I hear her fumble around in the background. 'We're staying at The Ritz, can you believe it? I don't know how he afforded this.'

I raise an eyebrow in Gregory's direction. I suspect I know how and I love him even more for it too.

'We walked around Hyde Park in the afternoon yesterday and then Geoffrey had booked a table in the restaurant. Can you believe we ate at The Ritz?'

I laugh, sharing in this wonderful woman's happiness. 'Go on, go on.'

'Well, I had a smoked salmon terrine to—'

'Sandy! Stop teasing me! I don't want to know what you ate.'

She laughs a hearty, Sandy laugh. The type that'll have her small belly jiggling and her fingers covering her mouth. 'All right. All right. Well, we had coffee and petits fours after dinner. He was getting all sweaty. You know, I was starting to worry about him but he had a big steak for mains so I thought maybe it was just the meat sweats.'

'Sandy!' I try to sound stern but my chuckle gives up my game.

'No, this is part of the story, I promise. So there he was, sweating, but we still had coffee in our pot and well, I won't be going to The Ritz again any time soon so I fully intended on getting my money's worth—'

'Sandy! Get to the proposal!'

'Right, yes, that's where I was going. So I moved to pour another cup of coffee and when I turned back around, he was on one knee. It took me a second, mind you, to realise what was happening. One minute, he was in the chair next to me and the next... pop! So there he was on one knee in the middle of The Ritz... can you imagine? And he said it'd been a whirlwind of drama but more happiness than he's ever known. And then he just said it... he just asked... Sandy, will you be my wife?'

'Aw, Sandy, that's perfect. Really, it is. I hope you had some fizz.'

'Oh, yes, well, Gregory actually had already arranged to have a bottle sent to the table. Such a kind man.'

'Hold on a second. Gregory knew?' I sit back and look at his suppressed smile.

'Well, yes, that's why I had to call. I wanted you to be the first to hear it from me. You see, Geoffrey needed to ask Gregory and Lara for the time off.'

I scowl and turn a playful pout on Gregory. 'Are you staying there tonight?'

'Yes, we've just had a late cream tea. Geoffrey's calling it a mini-moon.'

'And is it too early to ask when the big day will be?'

'Oh, when we can afford it. Not for a long time. We're just happy being engaged for now. It sounds a little silly doesn't it, engaged at our age.'

'It really doesn't, Sandy. It sounds just right.'

'It feels just right, sweetheart. It feels just right. Well, I'm going to go and find Geoffrey. I bet he's stealing the free shampoo.' She laughs again, another belly-aching sound. 'Bye, darling.'

'Bye, Sandy. Have a good night.'

'I'm sure we will.'

I shake my head and shudder at the thought of Jackson and my stand in mum-cum-best friend having a *good night* together.

As happy as I truly, genuinely am for Sandy, a small part of me is jealous. She's known Jackson less time than I've known Gregory and they've agreed to spend the rest of their lives together. I push the thought from my mind and focus on the man next to me.

'I can't believe you knew and you didn't tell me,' I say, flicking the phone at Gregory, who catches it in one hand.

'I told you they were going for a special dinner.' There's a cheeky glint in his eye.

'That's hardly the same as saying, "Scarlett, Jackson is taking Sandy to The Ritz tonight to propose."'

'Why are you talking like that?'

'What? You don't like my man voice?'

'Stop it!'

'I don't know what you mean; stop what?' I say, keeping up my not-at-all-manly man voice.

'It's really unattractive. Are you supposed to be me? I don't sound like that.'

'Ja, ja! *Pasop Boet!*'

In a swift movement, he grabs me and throws me to the other side of the sofa. He clamps my foot between his knees, pulls off my sock and starts tickling. I squeal and wriggle and he worms those horrid, nimble fingers to the crease beneath my toes.

'Do you relent?' he asks.

'No!' I scream.

'Sure?'

'Yes! Okay! Yes! Stop!'

He pauses then but I can't stop a smirk from rising to my lips.

'You tickle like an octopus with no tentacles!' I say in my fake-Gregory voice.

'I would never say that,' he says.

'Ja, ja.'

The tickling starts again. Relaxed Gregory is putting in a rare and undoubtedly fleeting appearance.

Life is pretty screwed up.

19

'I don't want to go back to the city; I love it here.' As I say the words, I put the overnight bag Gregory packed for me into the back of the Lamborghini.

Gregory runs his hands from my shoulders down my arms and plants a kiss on the tip of my nose. 'Work is in the city, baby.'

'I know. I just like our farm bubble. I could actually convince myself that the case isn't hanging over us here, that life is normal.'

'Normal isn't something you're ever going to get from me, Scarlett.'

That's becoming very clear.

He presses his lips against mine, leaving my mind to wander as they linger.

Reluctantly, I peel myself away from him and sit in the front seat. He burns through the rush-hour traffic, weaving, speeding, generally driving like a man on the edge. At the Shard, we both quickly change into suits and switch to the black DB9, which Gregory feels is more businesslike than the yellow Lamborghini. Probably true.

He drops me at work after waiting impatiently for me to pick up a bouquet of flowers on the way in. He shakes his head as I hand Paul the spare bagel Amy wrapped up for me, then he heads off to a meeting in Brighton, south of the city. As I watch Gregory swerve away from the pavement into oncoming traffic, thoughts of Dubai and the imminent CPS decision hit me with the force of an express train.

I dump my coat and take a big swig of latte, then set my laptop and screens to life and take the flowers I bought in the direction of Amanda's office. I get two pencil-skirt-restricted steps into the corridor before being met by an incoming Amanda. She looks pale and not her usual vibrant self, which I put down to her choice of black dress. Her usually flowing, auburn hair is pinned back from her face into a messy knot at the back of her head.

'These are for you,' we both say in unison, me holding up the bunch of white roses and lilies as she holds up a bag decorated in peanut M&M's and a label stating she's been to M&M World.

We share the shortest of laughs, then both declare our apologies.

'Coffee and choccies?' Amanda asks, wiggling the yellow paper bag in front of me. 'Like old times?'

'Love to.' I take the bag from her and hand over the bunch of flowers which she holds to her nose, inhaling deeply.

'Beautiful,' she declares. She retrieves her own coffee from her office and brings it to mine, where I've already spread the contents of the M&M goodies across my desk. 'Peanuts for me.'

I throw her the bag of peanut M&M's, which she catches with one hand and happily tears into once she's settled into a chair next to my desk. I open a brown bag of traditional M&M's and moan theatrically around a blue.

'What's it about the blues?' I ask.

'They taste so different to the others,' she says.

'Couldn't agree more. So good. Listen, Amanda, I don't want us to fall out. Especially not over a man. We always said that would never happen.'

'Me neither. I'm sorry, Scarlett. I know he makes you happy and Ed and I had a long conversation on Saturday. He helped me understand some... stuff. He told me about Lara and the abuse. And I get it. Kind of. I at least understand why Gregory would hate his pop. And I know he's not all bad.'

I snort and sip my coffee. 'I'll take that as a ringing endorsement.'

She laughs. 'I might even like him in time.' Then her face turns serious. 'Look, he makes you happy and you're no fool. I just want you to be careful, okay? Don't get yourself hurt.'

'I'll do my best.' *But at the moment, that seems highly unlikely.*

'Has he told you how he feels yet?' She asks the question with her attention focussed on her cardboard cup, then takes a sip of coffee.

'You mean, do I think he's in love with me?' I sigh and lean back into my desk chair, taking my latte with me. 'I wish I knew, Amanda. He hasn't said as much but then when we're together, especially when we're... you know... it's like I'm the only important thing in the world to him. He says things like he's under my spell and he can't let me go but he's never told me he loves me. And there are other things he's not telling me. There's always something lingering that he either can't or won't share with me.' I try not to think about the Dubai conversation and whether there's part of him that wants me to leave.

It's my own doubt. I caused that situation.

'He certainly looked like a man in love on Saturday. He was crazed, Scarlett.'

I shrug, feigning impassiveness but beaming inside. 'Time will tell, I suppose.'

'And what about the case? Ed said there's still no charge; that's a good thing, right?'

'The KC thinks so. The police questioned Lara and Sandy so they're obviously considering the strength of Gregory's motive versus self-defence.'

'But it was self-defence, right?'

I shoot her a warning stare. She's *still* questioning Gregory's motives. 'Amanda.'

'No, I know, I—'

'Let's leave that there, okay?'

'Well, they obviously don't consider him a threat to society. Otherwise they'd hold him.'

'True. Hopefully, it's all a good sign.' But there's a tightness in my chest and an increasingly heavy ache at the base of my skull.

'Scarlett?'

I rub my breastbone. 'Hmm, sorry, what was the question?'

'Dubai.'

I exhale slowly, exasperated, and rub my aching temple. 'I've decided not to go but I haven't told Neil yet.'

'Really?'

'Yes, really. Don't look at me like that and please don't say whatever it is that you're thinking.'

She pulls an invisible zip across her pursed lips. 'Neil isn't going to take that well.'

'Not at all. And he really hasn't pushed me for a decision even though the proposal has to be with the client by Friday.'

'Because he thinks you'll go.'

I nod. 'Precedent says I never refuse, so I guess he's assumed I'll drop everything for work, like I always do. Right, enough about me; did you and Williams spend the night together on Saturday?'

'Yes. No. He stayed over at my apartment and we shared the same bed but we didn't sleep together.' She slips a red peanut M&M into her mouth. 'It was nice, actually. We spooned. He cuddled me all night and it felt right somehow to wake up with him on Sunday.'

'Are you together?' I ask across my cardboard cup, then sip the milky coffee.

'Hmm, we haven't really said. We've just decided to date. Start again and see whether there's something else.'

'Besides just fun?'

She smiles. 'Besides just fun.'

'Sooooo, Sandy and Jackson got engaged on Saturday.'

'What? That's so fast! I mean, fab and all, but *really* quick.'

'You think so? I guess it is but if you know, you know, right?'

'Still. Super quick. When do you think they'll get married?'

I whirl my hand in the air as I clear my mouth of a yellow M&M. 'Not for a while, she said. I think it's the money thing really and then other stuff, like where they'll live. Sandy lives with and works for Lara and Jackson needs to be where Gregory is. They've got some things to work out, I guess.'

'You must be happy for her.'

'I really am. She's spent her life looking after me and then Dad; she deserves to have something else, someone to love her in a romantic way.'

'How are you coping with that? Your dad, I mean. Everything else has kind of taken over, hasn't it? But it's still so close.'

'Honestly, I don't know how I feel. Everything that's happened lately is just a massive blur.' I killed a man and whilst saving another's life, I don't know how much of me killed to avenge my father's murder.

My fate could be decided any moment now. I glance at my phone but there are no calls or messages showing on the screen.

'I know that I miss him,' I sigh. 'I miss him like mad.'

Amanda darts forward in her seat and presses a hand against her chest. 'Oh, crikey, I feel so sick.'

'Where's your stamina?' I laugh. 'At uni, you could've done 500 grams before you felt sick.'

She retches then and puts her other hand over her mouth.

'Shit, you're not playing.' I grab the bin from under my desk and push it in front of her just before she vomits.

I pull two tissues from the box on my desk and hand them to her. She wipes her mouth and her brow, then slumps back in her chair.

'Are you okay? Do you want me to get you some water?'

'No, I'm fine.' She sips her coffee. 'I feel better now. It just came over me so quickly. This stupid bug. I've thrown up every day for a week. I just can't shake it.'

'Amanda, if you've been sick for seven days, you need to see a doctor. Do you have a temperature? Let me feel.' I move to her and place the back of my hand on her forehead the way my dad used to do to me. 'You actually feel okay.'

'I know. It's not constant. It comes and goes. I've tried taking something to settle my stomach but nothing works.'

'Erm, I hope you don't mind me asking but is it, erm—'

'Coming out of the other end?'

I laugh a little. 'Sorry, it's not funny; you're just so blunt. Is it?'

'No. No diarrhoea.' She laughs too and pops an M&M into her mouth as I look on with a furrowed brow.

'And you're not off your food?'

'No. Well, actually, certain things but not M&Ms.' She grins.

'Bloody hell, Amanda, you don't think you could be—'

'Pregnant!' She jumps up from her seat. 'Holy shit!'

'How hasn't this occurred to you?'

'Jesus, Scarlett, now's not the time for a lecture! I can't be. Can I?'

'Well I don't know, do I? Have you had unprotected sex?'

'I'm on the pill; you know I am.' She slumps back down in her seat and rubs her chin with the tips of her fingers. 'I missed one or two pills but I took them the next day; I doubled up. That's fine, right?'

'I'm sure it is. Calm down. Let's go to the pharmacy after work. You can come back to the Shard and take a test.'

She nods her head quickly. 'Gregory won't be there, will he?'

'We'll go at five thirty on the dot. He'll still be working.'

* * *

We could've caught the bus or the Tube but Amanda's legs turned to jelly in the pharmacy and I didn't think they'd carry her to a station, so I hailed a black cab instead and settled her into the back, pale-faced and silent. I try to check in with Gregory but wind up leaving a message on his voicemail to tell him I'm already on my way home and I was just wondering whether the CPS or John Harrison had called. I know they haven't, otherwise I would've heard from him, but I really wanted to make sure Amanda and I had the all-clear to go back to the apartment without interruption.

We line the three different brands of pregnancy tests along the breakfast bar. Fortunately, Amy's left for the day. I read the boxes as Amanda concentrates on breathing and sipping her water on a stool. This is alien to me. Some test within hours, some within a day, the pale-blue boxed test takes a week for an accurate result.

'I assume this means a week from conception, rather than having to hold the pee stick for a week?' I internally laugh at my own joke but it doesn't seem to register with Amanda. She continues to stare into the distance over the rim of her glass, oblivious to the fact her hand is gently cupping her stomach.

'Are you ready?' I ask. 'They seem straightforward. Pee on the stick and wait.'

'I can't, Scarlett. I can't do it. What if I *am* pregnant? Pops would kill me.'

'Amanda, *if* you're pregnant, your dad won't kill you. In any event, you're a grown woman; he really has no say in things.'

She flips her head to look at me. 'No say in whether I keep it, you mean?'

'Amanda, that's not what I said. We don't even *know* whether you're pregnant. Come on.' I scoop up the three sticks, leaving the confusing boxes and instructions behind, and hold out my hand, guiding her across the lounge to the downstairs bathroom.

I look around the room, remembering the violence that took place in here just over two weeks ago. The mirror that was broken and used by Pearson to stab Gregory has been replaced. Everything looks normal. I shake away the thoughts of that night as I close the door behind us. 'Okay, you need to control your pee; don't blurt it all out in one go. You need to trickle and swap these in and out.'

She sighs, lifts up her dress, pulls her black thong to her knees and sits down on the seat. 'I've got stage fright,' she says, looking down between her legs as if it might encourage the stream.

'You've taken a pee with me a thousand times; just do it. Here.' I wave the first test at her, then the second and the third.

'Done.' She holds the wet sticks out for me to take.

'You *are* joking. There's no way I'm touching those things. Sharing a bathroom is one thing. Fondling your pee sticks is a whole other level.'

She laughs. It's a nervous laugh but it's a laugh nonetheless and I'll take anything to lighten the tension. She lies the sticks face up on the marble sink and washes her hands.

'Right. So now we just wait?' she asks.

'Yep.' I lift myself up to sit on the marble unit next to the sticks and Amanda lowers the lid on the toilet seat, then perches herself on top.

All our years of knowing each other and I can't think of a thing to say. I bounce my foot anxiously and cross and uncross my legs as the seconds tick by.

'I know you must be wondering,' Amanda says, staring at the marble floor tiles.

'I'm not.' I am.

'If I *am* pregnant, I do know who the father is.' She lifts her head now to look at me.

'Williams.'

She nods subtly, then looks at her watch. Ten seconds. We both move to stand in front of the tests, staring as the marks appear.

'What do they mean? Scarlett, what do they mean?'

I stare at the developed lines. All three sticks in agreement. Then I turn to look at my wide-eyed friend.

'You're pregnant.'

She steps back and drops down to the lid of the toilet. 'Holy shit!'

We exhale in unison. Then she speaks again. 'Holy shit!' Her eyes lock on a spot on the floor. 'Holy. Fucking. Shit.'

'You're going to have to learn to control your potty mouth.'

She looks up at me and we both laugh but her face contorts and her laughter turns to tears. For the second time today, I find myself grabbing tissues for my best friend.

I hunker down in front of her, bracing myself with my hands on her knees. 'It's going to be fine. Really. You'll be such a fabulous mummy.'

Her shoulders chug on a sob but she pulls back her tissue to reveal the slightest upturn of her lips. 'You think so?' She sniffs.

'Are you kidding? A little red-haired girl in a pretty two-piece and tiny little princess heels, following you around for babyccinos. I *know* so.'

I wrap my arms around her and pull her into my chest until I feel her lungs return to steady breaths.

'How about I make us a nice cup of tea?' Taking the tissues from her hand, I dab away her running mascara.

She nods. 'I'll be out in a minute.'

I leave the bathroom smiling. I haven't only convinced Amanda; I've also convinced myself that she can do this. She can be a great mum and Williams will stand by her; he's a good man.

'Gregory!'

His face is possibly paler than Amanda's shocked, already fair, skin. His grey blazer and tie have been cast over a stool. His white shirt is unbuttoned so just a few rogue hairs are on display and his sleeves are rolled back up his forearms. The most animated part of him is a wild pair of eyes as he holds up an empty pregnancy-test box. My head is telling my mouth to speak but no words are forming. I want to tell him they aren't mine but there's a small devil on my shoulder wondering how he'll react, wondering how he'd feel about *forever*.

'What the fuck, Scarlett?' His voice is a notch below shouting but his fury is obvious. I have my answer. A million thoughts race through my mind as my mouth opens and closes silently. He visits children in the paediatrics unit of a local hospital every quarter and he supports the children's charity, Dreams. I've seen him with the children, happy, playful. His reaction isn't about children; it's about him being trapped with me.

'You told me you were on the pill!'

'I am on the pill.'

He throws the box on the breakfast bar and thrusts a hand into his hair. 'You haven't had a period since we've been together.'

'Excuse me?'

'You haven't.'

'Are you accusing me of something, Gregory? Because if you are, you'd better just come right out and fucking say it.'

'Well, are you on the pill?'

'You *arrogant* arsehole. As if I'd try to get myself pregnant. That's what you're accusing me of, isn't it? Trying to trap the billionaire! Well, news fucking flash, Gregory, I'm not trying to tie you into something you clearly don't want. I don't love you for your money and the way you're behaving right now makes me wonder why I love you at all!' I bite the inside of my gums and remember that we aren't here alone. 'Does the thought of forever with me really terrify you this much?' My entire body trembles with anger and a shattering pain in my abdomen.

The toilet is flushed and the bathroom lock jiggled: Amanda's warning. I stare at Gregory, unwilling to be the first to break. But his focus shifts over my shoulder as the bathroom door opens.

'Amanda.' His voice is barely audible. I watch the transformation as his jaw unlocks and his hands drop to his hips as he walks to the window.

'Let's take a rain check on the tea,' Amanda says quietly, kissing me on the cheek.

'Please, Amanda, stay,' Gregory says, turning from the window, looking much more composed. 'You don't have to leave because of me.'

She smiles fleetingly at him and I love her for the effort, especially when his little performance has probably terrified her. 'I have a few calls to make; I should be going.'

'Williams won't react like that, Amanda,' I whisper, stroking her arm. 'He won't.'

She feigns a smile. 'Thanks, for today, tonight, everything.' She pulls me into a hug, then leaves.

'Amanda,' Gregory calls, grabbing his blazer from the breakfast bar, 'let me take you home.'

He leaves her little choice, already across the lounge and holding the door open for her.

* * *

After showering, I choose a spare room and slip under the covers of the double bed. Despite the early hour, I find myself drifting off to sleep when the door opens and light from the landing creeps into the room.

'Scarlett?'

I keep my eyes closed, being careful not to over-squeeze them and make it obvious that I'm awake. The bed dips as his weight rests down on the opposite side to mine. I feel him move close to me, checking whether I'm asleep. Satisfied, he pulls the duvet higher up my arm and presses his lips to my temple. As he lingers against my skin, I breathe in his familiar scent.

He sits up but doesn't leave the bed.

'I'm screwing this up more than I could've even imagined. I'm not afraid of forever. I'm afraid of doing to you what I've done to everyone I've ever really cared about. Hurting you. Failing to protect you, like I already have.' He sighs. 'A baby just like you would be incredible. Your perfect nose, those soft, red lips, your sparkling, green eyes, so bright and full of life. A little girl with your mind, even your sassy attitude. But you don't want that with me, Scarlett. Not really. Another little person for me to mess up. You were right on Saturday. I just need to make you see that.'

He leans in and presses his lips to my temple again.

'Aurora,' he whispers before his weight lifts from the mattress.

'Gregory.'

'Yes, baby?'

I speak without moving to face him. 'I don't know how much more I can take. You pick me up, take me higher than I've ever felt. Then you break my heart, you break me and I just don't know if I can keep crawling back to my feet.'

'I know.' He sighs. 'I'm going to stop hurting you. I promise.'

'Gregory, if the CPS decides to charge you, I'm telling the truth.'

If we break, the last thing I'll do is make sure you're free. The thought kills me but it's a real possibility and I need to start recognising it.

The truth can set him free, finally.

20

KC John Harrison called late morning to say the new ballistics report is back. The findings are broadly the same, the shot was taken at a distance, but there are new anomalies. The CPS decision is going to come this afternoon. I put in a last-minute half-day of leave, although I might as well have put in a full day for the amount of work I got through this morning. I packed up my things on the stroke of twelve thirty and now I'm sitting in the back of the Mercedes as Jackson drives us to the Shard, the tightness in my chest and the throb in my head more prevalent than ever.

This is it. Today is the day I pay for what I've done. Retribution for my vengeance, Gregory's vengeance. Punishment for letting my desire for Gregory talk me into a hostile takeover and everything it brought on my father and my friends. Whilst it's scary as hell and I've got no idea what my future will hold beyond today, I have a sense of rightness, a sense that I'm about to do the right thing. That's who I am: plain, black-and-white Scarlett Heath. And whatever comes, I'll accept it knowing that Gregory is alive and that he'll finally be free.

The CPS will make its decision and Gregory will understand that, despite his best efforts – efforts that I'm truly grateful for – he couldn't protect me from this fate. He won't be punished for a crime I committed.

He might never rid himself of his demons – he's already spent thirty years trying to do that – but he won't sit in a prison cell replaying that night over and over again for the next twenty-five years of his life.

After a brief exchange of pleasantries and congratulations for the engage-ment on my part, Jackson slipped into the driver seat in silence and we've moved through the city roads that way. His attention fixed forward, not casting a glance at me in the rear-view mirror like he usually does, not looking for conversation. He drives with one hand on the wheel, his other elbow resting on the window frame, his fingers pressing against his temple, a rare display of stress. He cares for Gregory, I think more than he's comfortable showing.

People move through the streets beneath the overcast sky, phones to ears, hands in the pockets of winter coats, some eating lunch on the move, some walking with purpose, files in hand. I take it all in, absorbing the colours, the buildings, the sights and sounds of normal life. I have the same sense of surre-alism that I had the day of my dad's funeral. As Sandy and I rode behind the hearse, life altered, changed irrevocably, yet passers-by were oblivious, going about their business as if the world hadn't slipped into a different realm, a darker reality. And now, whilst I accept that today could be my last day of free-dom, they don't look on or stop to stare. It's like nothing's changed, as if tonight, Gregory won't be charged for murder then freed by my confession and tomor-row, I won't be sitting behind bars, the public protected from my vengeful actions.

But Gregory will be free. And before I go to the station and make my state-ment, I'll tell him that he has to move on. Not from me – that much will be simple. But he has to take a chance on the next woman who falls in love with him. He has to accept that it *is* possible for someone to love him, all of him, messed up, dark and all. Otherwise, it'll all have been for nothing. Saving the little boy I see in my dreams, worthless.

'Hi,' I say when I open the door.

Gregory leans forward on the breakfast bar, resting his two large hands on either side of the worktop. He's already removed his tie, my favourite tie, the one he wore the first time I saw him. The same crisp, white shirt is unbuttoned at the neck and the same navy suit rests perfectly on his broad shoulders, the way it did that first day in the boardroom. A rogue hair hangs across one eye as he looks up at me: a sign his fingers have been pulled through his hair more than once. He looks tired and troubled but still makes my heart race and my abdomen pull taut.

'Tell me you've changed your mind.' His voice is hoarse, desperate. 'Please, Scarlett.'

I don't answer at first. I stare, lost in his soul, drinking him in. I want to remember every beautiful inch of him, the way he holds himself, the way he makes me feel when he looks at me, and the way fire ignites in my chest when he wants me. 'I haven't,' I say and watch his head drop forward. 'I don't need you to like it, or accept it, but I do need you to respect my decision. This is the right thing to do, Gregory.'

'I don't like it and I don't accept that it's the right thing to do. You know I never will. But I will *always* respect you, Scarlett.'

I nod silently and make my way to the staircase.

'But promise me one thing,' he says.

'What?'

'If the decision is no charge, you'll accept it; you'll accept that the decision is *ours*. That we were on the right side of the law. And you'll move on.'

Tonight we're done, either way. 'We need to prepare ourselves for—'

'Just promise me, Scarlett, please.'

'I promise.'

I don't change from my black pencil dress. I don't know what's appropriate to wear when you get arrested but as ridiculous as it seems, I want to look smart. I want the confidence that these clothes give me. I *need* the confidence, the strength to follow through on my convictions, no matter the consequences. I drop to my knees in the walk-in wardrobe and for the first time, I ask my dad for strength. He'll know I'm finally putting right my wrong and I need him to look in on me and take my next steps with me, to carry me wherever I need to go. I know that I was right to take that shot. I know because I saved Gregory, I saved the little boy from my dreams and one day, I hope I'll have saved the man I love, truly, in every way he needs to be saved. But the black streak in me that took the shot in revenge – revenge for my dad, revenge for the deep-rooted pain I know Gregory harbours inside him – my dad wouldn't approve of that. That's why the decision will be to charge Gregory, and later tonight, me.

When I'm done, I take an overnight bag from the top shelf of one of the wardrobes, the same bag Gregory packed when we went to the hunt. It's hard to plan for the unknown but I place leggings, jeans, a T-shirt and two jumpers into the bag. Then I rummage through my underwear for cottons: plain, appropriate for a prison cell.

'What're you doing?'

He leans against the doorframe, watching me pack.

'I thought I'd put some things together. I want to be ready to go to the police station. If I wait... I can't wait. It has to be straight away.'

'Scarlett, please, I'm begging you not to do this.'

I can't look at him because I can't see those wide, pleading eyes. My conviction is spent on going through with my decision; I don't have a reserve to deny Gregory.

'I need you to leave me to do this.'

He goes and I finish the bag, adding a toothbrush, toothpaste and face wipes. I zip it up and slump to the floor with it in my lap, suddenly exhausted.

Now we wait.

Time passes by; slowly but surely, the minute hand of my watch moves clockwise until my legs find the strength to make my way downstairs with my bag in tow. The hallway is dark with the early night sky, the soft-blue floor lighting guiding me to the staircase. I turn to take in the spot on the floor where Gregory made love to me, wild and delicious. Then murmuring voices draw my attention. At the bottom of the staircase, I leave my bag and walk into the open lounge, the floor heating warm under my stocking-covered feet.

Lara stands in the window, Lawrence leaning back in the chair closest to her. Sandy and Jackson hold hands on the sofa. Williams sits on a stool a little further out of the group at the breakfast bar.

'We all care about him,' Lara says, her sullen eyes full of worry and sympathy.

I don't want them here but I understand that it's not my place to tell them not to be. Instead, I nod and as ludicrous as it sounds, even as the words are leaving my mouth, I ask if anyone would like a cup of tea.

'I can make tea,' Sandy says, rising from the sofa.

I hold my hand up in protest. 'I want to.'

As I fill mugs with boiling water from the tap, Gregory appears at the bottom of the stairs, putting the headphones of his iPhone into his ears, then pulling up the hood of his running jumper.

'You're going for a run?'

He doesn't reply. Instead, he turns his glazed eyes away from me and leaves. After making everyone tea – whether they asked for it or not and in whatever colour and sweetness combination I decided upon because their requests fell on my numb brain – I busy myself cleaning the benches of the kitchen. Amy has been and gone, I assume because Gregory told her to leave, but I still clean the immaculate surfaces. When I'm done, I decide to clear out the fridge, throwing things that are close to their use-by date and shuffling others: all completely unnecessary and thankless tasks. Sandy tries to stop me but she takes one look at my face and goes back to sit next to Jackson.

The cleaning stops me from hearing the occasional words of the others but the silence is deafening and the reality of losing Gregory tonight makes me sick. The prospect of prison pales into insignificance against the increasing sense of fear: the fear of losing this man, of never feeling his touch, never having a life with him, no matter how twisted. The thought of becoming his in mind and body, by law. The thought of maybe one day having a boy that looks just like the one from my dreams. Nausea rises past the lump in my throat and I dart across the lounge into the bathroom to purge the unbearable reality into the toilet.

All eyes analyse my movements back into the lounge. Gregory is back from his run, his focus trained on me. He swallows hard as he pulls out his headphones, then he bounds up the stairs, three at a time, and I hear the bathroom door close.

Filling my water glass, I fumble around in kitchen drawers and cupboards until I find paracetamol and take two tablets. As the cold water strikes my chest, the phone rings. I jump and turn to face the staircase where Gregory stands, freshly showered. He casts a glance my way before retrieving the phone from its holster and putting it on speaker, then resting it on the coffee table in the middle of the five nervous faces waiting to share our news.

'Gregory Ryans,' he says. His voice is absent of any conviction for the first time since I've known him.

'Gregory, John Harrison here.'

I walk around the breakfast bar, holding on for support until I'm on the side of the lounge. Then I close my eyes, bracing myself.

'John, have they come to a decision?'

'They have, old boy. They said the evidence was inconclusive. The ballistics reports suggest your story is off but there are discrepancies between the first and second reports that undermine their evidentiary weight. The print findings support that no other person took the shot and three witnesses say as much. Furthermore, the CPS does not perceive you to be a threat to the public. As such, it has decided it would not be in the public interest to charge.'

I don't think I hear the words at first. But I hear them when Gregory asks John to repeat them.

'No charge, old boy, no charge.'

My stomach drops out of my body and my legs lose strength. Gregory gives thanks to John Harrison and when I open my eyes, he's staring down at me. He's real and he's free. *We* are free. He hasn't been charged. I didn't confess. We did the right thing. Pearson went to hell for the lifetime of hurt he inflicted on so many people. Gregory's alive and if he'll let me, I'll spend the rest of my life trying to fix him. I watch my hand as if it doesn't belong to me as it reaches out for his heart.

It beats.

My chest explodes and my legs give way as uncontrollable sobs take over my body. Two weeks, three days. The agony seems to have been much longer. My knees crash against the wood floor and I break down, emotionally, physically.

Two big, strong arms encase me and pull me into a firm chest. I wrap my arms around his shoulders, clinging like I'll never let him go, and give myself over to tears.

'I love you. I love you so much,' I sob into his shoulder, not caring if I never hear it back.

He sweeps me up, one arm under my legs, the other pulling my head into his neck. 'Jackson, can you—'

'Don't worry, I got it, kid.'

I feel Gregory nod but I can't lift my head from his shoulder. I need to hold him to me; it's the only way he feels real. Without saying another word, he carries me up the stairs to the first spare room he comes to, where I spent last night. He kicks the door shut behind us then sinks, his back sliding down the wall and as I sob against him, his chest chugs. He holds me to him, kissing my head between sharp breaths. I lean back to peer into his wet eyes.

I believe. I believe that one day, he'll accept that I love him and he'll love me back.

I push my lips against his and breathe in his freshly showered scent. 'I love you, Gregory Ryans. I love you with every cell in my body. I always will.'

'Scarlett.' He holds my face between his two hands and continues to sob as if years of wanting to cry, years of hurt and anger, have been unleashed. I throw my arms around his neck as my heart breaks for him.

'Shh, baby, I'm here,' I tell him, the way he has held me and said those words.

The sound of his tears is a breakthrough and heartbreaking all at once. I kiss his brow and down his jawline and it's my turn to take his face in my palms. 'It's over now.'

He shakes his head as his pounding heart begins to calm. 'If I'd lost you—'

'You didn't,' I say. And then I kiss him.

He kisses me back, pressing my lips against his with his hand on the back of my head. *He does love me.* He pulls away, stroking my hair, my face, my body and when his lips meet mine again, his hand slides down the zip at the back of my dress. He lifts me as he stands and pulls the dress up over my arms then moves his eyes over every part of my body. I lift the hem of his T-shirt and pull it over his arms. He pulls me against his naked chest.

We need this. I need to feel his love the only way he can show me. Right now, he needs to know that I stood by him, that I have faith in him because he *is* a good man.

I unbutton his jeans as he releases the clasp of my bra. I slip the bra over my arms and roll down my stockings as he pushes down his jeans and boxers, standing before me in all his stunning glory. He lifts my legs around his hips then lowers me to the floor. His eyes are fixed on mine as he pulls down my black thong then hovers over me, his weight resting on his forearms and between my legs.

I take his face in my hands and smile. He doesn't return my smile; he continues to look intently into the depths of me, then lifts his pelvis and, with one hand, guides himself between my legs. He swallows my groan as he presses his mouth to mine, his eyes squeezing tightly shut as if in pain.

This isn't the relief I was expecting.

He holds still at first and I give him time to take what he needs. Then he starts to circle his hips, his mouth moving in sync. It's slow and sensual but this isn't lovemaking and it isn't relief. It's something else, something I can't quite describe. Something terrifying and haunting all at once. My eyes well with tears as he fills me and opens his eyes to mine. He's not here; he's somewhere else, without me. His emptiness chills me to the core.

This might be the end.

21

It's been a strange week. Gregory has made love to me every night like it's his last. Each time, it's been passionate and slow. Tentative, like I'm the most delicate thing he's ever held. No expletives, no roughness or kinkiness, just pure, unadulterated lovemaking, beautiful in a way that's every bit as earth-shattering as the explosive orgasms he's so good at giving me. But unnerving. Neil Wallace flew out to Dubai the day after the decision, which means I haven't had a chance to speak to him yet and give him my answer. Or rather, tell him his assumptions are wrong. A conversation I think I need to have in person. The old Scarlett wouldn't have turned down the opportunity, nor the request of a new client. But I don't know where she is. I don't know exactly when she left but this Scarlett is different. There's no way in hell I'll ever do anything to put myself in a position to lose Gregory. I can't, not now I know how much it scares me. He's my anchor. The centre of the new version of me. The core of sense, the only thing that joins all the messed-up pieces together. I don't need Dubai or anything else. There's one thing that matters to me, one person, one man. I love him and so long as I have him, I'll always be happy in our world, as dark and twisted as it is. Whilst I'm dreading it, I *will* let Neil Wallace down.

I smile to myself as I apply my make-up. On Thursday, Gregory came back from an oh-so-normal run and to our oh-so-normal bedroom, sweaty and so goddamn hot, and told me that he wanted to take me somewhere on Saturday: tonight. He's been planning a surprise for two days and I can't wait to finally find out what it is. He sent me to Julia at Harrods and we picked out a gown. I have no idea *why* I need a gown but I decided to make it my surprise to him. Refusing to put it on his account, I bought it myself, the most extravagant thing I've ever bought. I think my first car actually cost less than this dress. Okay, so it was only a little runaround but it had a purpose beyond one night. Yet, oddly, and against all my sensibility, I'd rather have this dress.

I stand back from the floor-length mirror and assess my finished look. I've got to admit, for me, I look good. Fantastic. It feels like how the other half live, honestly.

The long, black, lace sleeves are finished with an extravagant pearl and crystal cuff. The front of the dress is high and square and hugs my skin perfectly until it pools at the floor. The train at the back pulls the front against the shape of my legs, which are looking lean in high, strappy heels. Then the pièce de résistance: the drooped back, cut out to just below the waist. I turn my back to the mirror and cast a glance over my shoulder, biting down on my lip. My pinned hair shows off the open back and the necklace Julia picked out is dazzling in the light. A square-cut diamond rests on top of the square neckline at the front and a platinum chain sparkles all the way down to the middle of my back where three pearls run into another square diamond. The necklace I did have to use Gregory's account for but only as security. Julia said she'd make an exception to the rules and allow me to loan the precious stones, on the basis that Gregory's account would back it up.

There's a gentle tap on the dressing room door. 'Scarlett, are you ready?'

I run my Chanel red over my lips one last time and open the door. 'Ready, Jackson.'

'You, ah, you look lovely.'

I take a deep breath as my heart thumps in my chest. 'I hope he likes it.' Looping my arm through Jackson's, I let him lead me down the staircase. 'Are you going to tell me where we're going yet?'

'I'm under strict orders not to.'

I shake my head and smile. I knew the answer before I asked the question.

My insides tie themselves in knots as we drive through the city in the Mercedes. I dismiss the signs for London City Airport until there's no alternative but the airport being our destination. Jackson drives across the tarmac surface until a private jet comes into view. On its side, GJR Enterprises. He rounds the jet in the Mercedes and a red carpet appears on the other side. He stops the car at the edge of the red carpet. I look around but don't see Gregory.

Jackson opens my door and offers his hand to me in his usual black suit and black tie. I take it with a nervous smile, stomach sick with excitement and anticipation. Jackson chuckles as my wide eyes silently thank him, my mouth incapable of releasing words.

'Your man,' he says, closing the car door and turning me to look towards the steps of the plane, no longer empty.

My heart explodes in my chest, my head in a spin, my legs weightless. He moves his palm to his heart. I take him in, all of him: his tall, perfect body, his immaculate dinner suit and bow tie, his slicked-back hair.

'Holy shit,' I say beneath my breath.

I can't move. I can only stare in awe. His lips turn into a knowing half-smile and he mouths something, which I can guess is, 'Get here.'

I'm aware of the eyes of airport staff and Jackson on me as I find the ability to move one foot in front of the other. Lifting my dress at the side with one hand and holding onto the stair rail for strength with the other, my eyes follow two sparkling, precious, brown stones, lured by their magnetism.

He holds out a hand which I take as I climb the last step to him and when I stand before him, he whispers, 'Aurora,' just loud enough for me to hear.

'My very own Richard Gere,' I say.

'My very own stunning woman.' He lifts my fingers to his lips and melts my heart.

'Where are we going?'

That cheeky half-smile is back. 'To the opera, baby. I want you to know the fairy tale.'

I suppress the irrational fear that he means for one night, before the end.

'*La Traviata*?' I ask.

'If it's good enough for Julia Roberts.'

'It's a good offer for a girl like me.'

He winks and nearly knocks me from my feet. 'Shall we?'

I nod, air having escaped my lungs, and follow him into the jet. It's just like I would've imagined: an almond burr and biscuit leather interior. We're greeted by an air hostess who offers two glasses of champagne from a tray. I thank her and take a sip, a huge grin rising on my face. It's Pol Roger 2002, the bottle

Gregory ordered the first time he took me to dinner, the night of his thirtieth birthday.

He takes my hand and leads me through a channel flanked with four beds, curtains closed across each of them, then through two cream suede curtains into the main area. Four large recliner seats and two cream leather sofas sit on top of a red carpet and there's a small bar in the corner at the far side of the room. Another air steward stands behind the bar, his beige chinos, white shirt and red pocket handkerchief a match for his female colleague.

'Good evening, Miss Heath,' he says.

'Good evening.'

Gregory rotates one of the large chairs to face another and gestures for me to sit, then takes the seat opposite me.

When I do, I lean forward, holding up my champagne flute. 'To moving forward in our own little world,' I say.

For a second, the sparkle drops from his eyes and his brow furrows, then with a straight face, he clinks his glass against mine.

'To the most incredible woman I'll ever know,' he says.

Our moment is interrupted by the pilot's voice coming over the speakers. 'Good evening, Mr Ryans, Miss Heath. It looks like we might catch the sunset over Europe. The skies are clear all the way to Rome. We should touch down in a little over two hours. Enjoy the flight.'

'Italy?'

Those devastating eyes are shining again alongside his smug smile. 'It's the only place to watch the opera without subtitles.'

I throw my head back with a giddy laugh. 'You're crazy.'

The pilot announces we've reached our cruise altitude, then Gregory rests his champagne flute on the table attached to the side of his seat. 'Get here,' he says in that way he does.

Without hesitation, I unbuckle my seat belt and climb onto his lap, my arms wrapped around his neck as we fly through the burnt-orange sky to Rome.

* * *

A limousine is waiting at the airport and we're swept away to the opera house, where we're met at the door and escorted directly to our private box. High, because it's Gregory. Another glass of champagne is poured and small, Italian canapés are brought to the table in our box: mini caprese salads, small bruschetta, crostinis with olive tapenade.

Gregory sits with his knee pressed against mine and takes my hand as the lights fall, the band strikes up and the stage curtain rises, revealing the opening scene of a courtesan's party. I nip his fingers in mine enthusiastically as Violetta sings for the first time.

'She has a wonderful voice,' I whisper.

Part way through the first act, I look back to him and find his eyes on me rather than the stage. They aren't sparkling; they're saying something else. It's unsettling. I push the thought away and turn back to the stage but something in the way he looked at me plays on my mind as the tragic love story unfolds.

'Is everything okay?' I ask him in the interval.

'Perfect,' he says, kissing the back of my hand.

I shuffle from my own seat to his lap and rest the palm of my hand on his cheek. Then I press my lips against his and hold them there, breathing him in, soaking up the feel of his lips on mine. 'Thank you.'

'No. Thank you, beautiful girl.' He strokes a rogue hair from my updo away from my face. 'For showing me a new way.'

Our foreheads meet, then our eyes, then our mouths. We only stop kissing when the lights go down for the start of act two. The curtain rises and Alfredo's country home is revealed. I watch contentedly as the on-stage couple find each other in a space where they can be together, where their past lives are forgotten.

I feel Gregory's breath on my neck before I hear his words. 'Ever since the day when she said, "I want to live only for you," I seem to live in heaven, unmindful of the world.'

I draw a deep breath and turn to him. 'You speak Italian?'

'Among other languages.'

'But what about Al Italiano Meato Pasto by Gregory?'

He smirks.

'I still have so much to learn about you,' I say with a smile.

He squeezes my hand in his.

I pick my moment carefully and when it comes, I turn, leaning back to his ear. Pressing my cheek against his, I translate Violetta's words on a whisper. 'Love me, Alfredo, love me as much as I love you.'

His eyes close and his shoulders rise and fall with his breath but those three words don't come.

One day, Gregory Ryans, one day.

Our limousine is waiting and shoots us straight back to the jet after the show.

'You really are mesmerising, Scarlett Heath,' Gregory says as I lie into his chest on our return flight. 'Kiss me.'

I happily oblige, getting lost in him. His hand moves to the nape of my neck and pulls my mouth against his, making me groan, desire stirring between my legs. I slip my hand inside his blazer and feel his firm chest through the thin cotton of his dinner shirt. His tongue parts my lips and my chest lifts, pushing my breasts against him.

'I want you in my bed,' he says, breaking our kiss fleetingly then parting my lips again with his ravishing tongue.

'I want to be in your bed,' I confess.

* * *

Jackson has already drawn up the screen in the Mercedes and doesn't bother to open the door for me, leaving Gregory to lead me into the back by the hand. Before the car pulls away from London City Airport, I'm pulled onto Gregory's lap and my mouth is taken by his.

Jackson drops us at the entrance and I'm too concerned with the perfect man dragging me inside by the hand to wonder where Jackson goes. I giggle as Gregory tugs me through the entrance to the Shard and bounces his feet impatiently as we wait for the lift.

The doors open and he punches in 64. He glares at the doors, waiting for them to close, then he pushes my back against the lift wall. He lifts both my arms above my head and holds them in place with one hand, then pushes his mouth against mine, biting, sucking and tasting just like him. A taste I can't get enough of. I match him with each nibble and each stroke of his tongue. The need to have him inside me is already unbearable.

The lift pings and Gregory's impatience is evident as he roughly handles the door lock to the apartment. Then he pulls me to him with his hands on my arse and moves us inside, kicking the door shut behind him, then pressing my back up against it.

'Gregory, I want you,' I pant.

'Oh no, baby, not tonight. Tonight, I'm going to cherish everything about you.' He holds my face in his palms and gazes into my eyes. 'The way you move.' Kiss. 'The way you feel.' Kiss. 'The way you shout my name when I make you come.' Kiss. 'And I want you in my bed.'

His words drive the hunger in my sex. Anything. Any way. I'll take him as he is. However he likes. Because my head is already dizzy with burning lust and desire.

He drops his hand into mine and leads me upstairs. I watch his back move beneath his dinner jacket as I follow him into the bedroom. In front of the sleigh bed, he turns me, my back to his chest. He runs his fingertips from the palms of my hands at my sides, up the length of my arms and drops a kiss on each of my shoulder blades. I'm warm but his touch makes the hairs on my body stand on end. He works the clasp of the platinum diamond chain around my neck as he trails kisses across the top of my back.

'Be careful with that; it's loaned on your account.'

He leans forward and lifts the open chain from my body. 'As it should be. We can talk about you paying for the dress yourself.'

He lays the necklace on the chaise longue and dims the lights in the room. Then Kenny G's 'Silhouette' fills my ears. My feet remain firmly planted on the spot he left me but I watch as he removes his bow tie, shoes and socks and stalks towards me.

God, I want him.

He reaches me and presses his body against my bare back. 'You really are captivating, Scarlett Heath.'

His teeth meet my lobe, then his tongue works down my neck and his lips brush my back. Moving one sleeve from my shoulder, he drops a kiss on my newly exposed skin, then follows the same pattern on the other side. He bends as he trails soft kisses and hot breaths down the length of my spine, locating the small zip beneath the draped material of the dress at the top of my coccyx. The zip is released. Standing, he pushes the garment from my shoulders and brings it to pool on the ground.

He studies me for a moment, unashamedly casting his eyes over my entire body, from my heeled feet, up the length of my thighs, my navel, my breasts, my face. His eyes are black, seductively so, when they meet mine, then move to my lace thong. 'Everything about you...' he says, only just loud enough to reach my ears above the music.

He steps towards me and with his palm on the small of my back he pulls me into him, my eyelids closing when his lips meet mine.

'Open your eyes, baby. Keep them open the whole time. I want to see you. All of you.'

I do as he asks but there's desperation behind his words that brings with it a feeling of panic deep in my chest – *is this the end?* I hold my breath until the feeling is drowned out by the swirl of his tongue. When he releases me for long enough, I move back and undo each of his shirt buttons. One. By. One. Never taking my open eyes from his.

My hands rest on his naked chest and I inhale deeply at the feel of his hot, firm skin, my fevered desire building. Pushing the shirt from his arms, I press my breasts against him as I unhook his cufflinks and let the shirt fall to the floor. He leans in and takes my neck with his mouth, breathing, sucking, licking.

'I want to leave my mark on you,' he says and in my moment of indulgence, I nod, moaning when I feel him drawing blood to the top of my skin.

I grind my pelvis against his crotch and feel him hard in his trousers. My hands move to the fastening and when I draw down the zip, I press my hand inside, cupping his solid piece over his boxers. With a groan, he bites my lobe, the sound reverberating between my legs. I step back and push his trousers down his legs. He lifts his feet to free himself. I kneel up and take the rim of his boxers in my teeth pulling them down to his thighs, using my hands to take them to the floor. His hand moves to the back of my head. Encouraging me.

I need no encouragement. His proud erection is enough to have me licking my lips.

I cup his scrotum and stroke a finger from his back entrance to the base of his hard-on. Then I draw my thumb up his length and move in a circle over his tip and most sensitive spot. As his hips flex, I move my tongue to the hard bottom of his penis and drag it to the top, then on his groan, I wrap my mouth around him. My tongue circles his end as I suck and taste him. My hands move to his arse cheeks, my nails digging in. When I've made him wait long enough, I pull him into me, pushing my lips as far down as I can go, opening my throat and taking him to the back.

'Scarlett!'

I move my mouth back slowly then plunge forward quickly, again digging my nails into the skin of his arse. His hand moves to my hair and yanks as his hips pull back and push forward again.

'You're amazing.'

I feel him tensing and move my hand to his sack, working every part of him. His hips lift in time to the sweeps of my tongue across his tip as I lap up his precome. I pump his length with a firm grip as I continue to suck and lick the top.

'Jesus, Scarlett, that's so fucking good.'

I quicken the pace and the pressure. Both his hands pull at my hair and hold my head still to absorb his careful thrusts. His thighs tense, his arse clenches, his cock starts to pulse. I work him harder and faster until his movements lose their rhythm.

'Fuck, Scarlett, I'm there.'

A little more pressure. A little quicker.

'Fuck!' he barks as he pours his warm liquid into my mouth and I accept it with a quick swallow. He hangs his head back briefly, then looks down through heavy, sex-filled eyes and lifts my chin with his index finger, my legs following my gaze to stand.

'That wasn't part of the plan.'

I smile and push my body against his as he strokes the sides of my face. Then with one easy move, he lifts my legs to his hips and takes me back to the bed, laying me down with my arms above my head, and crawling between my thighs.

His perfect torso hovers above me as he drops his lips to my wrist and licks, kisses and nibbles the full length of my arm, sending my nerve endings into frenzy. At my shoulder, he works his way along my collarbone, then my neck, my other collarbone and up the entire length of my other arm.

'Open your eyes,' he whispers, with his face hovering over mine.

I let my hazel-green eyes meet his hooded browns with a contented sigh.

'Good girl.'

Taking his weight on one arm, he traces my jawline with the fingertips of his other hand, then strokes a thumb across my parted lips. 'The way you feel. The way you move.' He dips his head and presses those magic lips to my neck, then my chest bone. My back arches in anticipation before his mouth clamps down on my already hard nipple, biting gently, pulling the skin through his teeth. My insides are yearning to feel him. I wriggle my hips against him.

'Not yet,' he murmurs around my breast, the hot breath making my heart beat in my vulva.

He cups my other breast in his hand before he takes the nipple in his teeth. My hands reach for his hair. He moves his tongue to the centre of my abdomen, then draws a line down my navel, his hand exploring the skin to the side of my stomach. The feel of him on those areas that are rarely touched builds euphoria in my mind. His tongue trails down to the top of my wanton sex but he moves past it, sucking, licking, nibbling my thighs and pressing his lips down every inch of my leg to my feet.

My hips squirm and I grip the bed sheets with balled fists. He switches feet, and moves his mouth up the length of my opposite leg. When he reaches my sex, he lifts his body over mine, pressing his hard shaft against my navel. He gazes into my wild eyes and I can't wait. I push my hips against him and press my mouth to his, assaulting him with my tongue, twirling in circles around his. He withdraws, leaving me exposed and desperate. He shuffles down the bed and parts me with his fingers, the air on my bud making my body tense beneath him. Finally, he tortures my centre with a delicious lick that has me groaning. He turns his tongue expertly around my clit, dipping into me then back to my clit, lifting me higher with each sweep.

My back bows; my hands ball into fists. With a thrust, his fingers are in me, moving in, out, around, in perfect rhythm, synced with his tongue moving over my throbbing clit. I shake my head from side to side and I bite down on my bottom lip between pants, erratic breaths making me feel faint.

'Gregory! I'm going to come.'

I grab his head and pull his hair as he builds the rhythm of his fingers and my impending climax.

'Holy shit!'

My hands fly to my hair, dizziness, desire, my pounding heart taking me to the peak. He pushes those fingers harder and faster and with one last magnificent swirl of his tongue, I explode around him, screaming his name. My legs fall, lifeless, to my sides as I take deep breaths, trying to draw oxygen into my clouded brain.

'Open your eyes,' he says, hovering over me.

That same sense of uneasiness I felt in the opera house comes back. I push it away and wrap my arms around him, pulling him into me. My tongue dips into his mouth, tasting my own saltiness from his lips. As my arms explore his back and my tongue works around his, he slips his erection, back to full throttle, into my accepting sex and moves in tantalising circles, already lifting my unrelenting orgasm back to a high.

We swallow each other's groans, eyes open and locked, our mouths refusing to part. He smiles around my kisses and the moment of uncertainty melts into raw emotion. For me, love. His hips circle and move his cock with slow, purposeful grinds, controlled, just the way Gregory Ryans CEO takes care of his business.

We kiss to the brink until my body begins to lose control again and I can't hold our contact.

'Gregory!'

He speeds his hips now building with each thrust.

'Fucking hell!' he barks. He bursts into me with one final push, completely unravelling.

He gazes down at me and I stroke a loose strand from his sweaty brow as he slowly turns inside me, bringing us down. He kisses the tip of my nose, then rolls us so I come to lie on his chest. I kiss his pecs and turn my fingers around his bare skin.

22

First, the smell of coffee. Then the realisation that I'm in bed alone. Then the sense that someone is in the room. My eyes open to the most beautiful face I've ever seen and I smile as I slide back up the bed, sitting in only the white, cotton bed sheet.

'Time to get up. We don't want to be late for lunch.'

'Lunch. Lunch? Oh crap.' I take the coffee from him in two hands. 'What time is it?'

'Eleven thirty. I let you sleep as long as I could.'

I rub my eyes and realise I'm still wearing last night's make-up. 'I guess it was a late night.'

'We'll leave at one.'

I nod and smile, waiting for him to drop a kiss on my nose or my brow or touch me. But his dark eyes are seemingly a match for his mood: serious and troubled. He leaves the room and leaves me feeling confused. But this is Mr Screwed-up and Neurotic. Nothing should surprise me.

After showering, I ponder what to wear to an engagement lunch and settle on a dusty-pink blouse, tied at the neck, coupled with a dusty-pink-and-grey tweed skirt. Gregory finishes tying his shoelaces, then adjusts his shirt, tucking it neatly into the top of his navy chinos. He turns when he hears my heels clip-clop down the staircase and pulls the cuffs of his shirt just so, slightly longer than his dark-grey blazer. He looks divine. As ever. I lift my chin, waiting for his kiss but it doesn't come. He twirls the curls in the bottom of my hair in his fingers with a furrowed brow, then steps back from me, distant in every sense.

'Is everything okay?' I ask.

He swallows, deep, audibly. 'Fine,' he says through a set jaw.

'Fine?'

'Fine,' he says with a smile that fails to reach his eyes. Last night was one of the best nights of my life – *the* best night of my life – and today, he's *fine*. There I was, hopelessly assuming that after the CPS decision, those peaks and troughs might stabilise. No chance.

Pulling on my coat, I follow him out into the hall. *One day*, I tell myself. But my conviction is waning.

There's an uncomfortable silence in the Ferrari the entire way to Lara's house. It isn't until we pull onto the gravelled driveway and the big, white house comes into view that I start to think I might understand why Gregory is in a foul mood. We haven't been here since *that* night. I hug the bottle of Krug in my lap into my stomach without consciously needing the comfort.

An overly cheery Lara bounds towards us and pulls us, one at a time, into her chest, as the Ferrari is driven away to be parked.

'Mother,' Gregory says, in no better mood with Lara, it would seem.

'Smarten that face up, young man. Scarlett,' she sings. 'Come here.'

'Thank you for inviting us, Lara.'

She slips her arm around my waist and takes the Krug from me, handing it to Gregory, who's already carrying a large bouquet of flowers. 'Nonsense, Sandy would've refused lunch without you.'

She skips into the house before us, her black wide-leg trousers catching in the breeze to be displayed to their full advantage. She subtly checks her white blouse in the hallway mirror and pushes some volume into the roots of her hair.

'Sandy.' I throw my arms around her and squeeze her as tight as I can until her sweet giggle escapes her chest. The one person I will always know I can rely on, no matter how bad or how dark life gets. 'These are for you.' I motion to the champagne and flowers Gregory holds and turn my attention to Jackson, kissing him on the cheek as Gregory does the same to Sandy.

The men shake hands and follow behind Sandy and me as I swoon over her shiny ring. A thin, platinum band with one sole, modest princess-cut diamond. 'It's beautiful.'

I turn my eyes around the large, oval dining table as chateaubriand is served. Sandy looks as uncomfortable as ever as she's waited on but happier each time Jackson speaks to her, nudges her, nips her hand in his. Williams has brought Amanda with him and whilst they look happy, there's an air of unsureness passing between them. But they smile and laugh in a way that tells me they'll be just fine. Lawrence is more concerned with the food than Lara and her demand for attention but he has a certain playful sparkle in his eyes when he shakes his head at yet another story.

I smile as I look on at those closest to me and those who, maybe one day, will be.

I can feel Gregory's eyes burning holes into my side. He's hardly touched his meal but his knife and fork are still, together at six o'clock on his plate.

My smile disappears on a sigh. 'Are you okay?' I ask for the fourth time this afternoon.

'I'm fine.'

'Fine. You've been *fine* all afternoon.' As I place my cutlery at six o'clock to reflect Gregory's stubbornness, a phone ringtone sounds.

Gregory checks his inside pocket, then Williams does the same. Amanda doesn't bother, nor does Lawrence. When no one owns up, I push out my chair and check in my handbag to find Neil Wallace's name dancing across my screen. *Damn it!* He wanted to submit the Dubai proposal on Friday but I left him a voicemail to say I wanted to discuss it with him first.

'I'll call him back,' I say, silencing the call and resuming my position at the table. 'Sorry about that.'

The others fall back into easy conversation whilst I silently question the steely eyes to my right.

Why can't we just be happy like everyone else?

I can feel a lump forming in my throat. Confusion. Hurt. I've no idea any more. I just can't read him unless he's *showing* me what he thinks, physically. Then his words contradict everything I feel in those moments. I need more. I can feel my eyes beginning to sting as I swallow down the lump.

He takes my hand from my lap and lifts it to his lips, then stares as he bends and strokes my fingertips; everything about the move is sombre.

Please, Gregory, let me in.

After lunch, we move to take coffee in the lounge and my phone rings again.

'Sorry, it's Neil, I need to take this.'

As I lift the phone to my ear and press to receive the call, Gregory reaches for the phone. 'Scarlett—'

I place my hand over the receiver. 'I won't be long, I promise. Neil, hi.'

'Scarlett. Got your email. Fantastic news.'

Making my way along the corridor of Lara's mansion to find a quiet spot, I cast my eyes back over my shoulder and shake my head in frustration when I find Gregory's scrunched forehead and unreadable expression still on me.

'Sorry, Neil, my email?'

I dip into a smaller, but equally stunning sitting room with teal, textured wall paint, elaborate cream-and-gold floor-to-ceiling curtains and a collection of mismatched but perfectly complementary fabric chairs and sofas surrounding a sheepskin rug.

'Yes, this morning. I'm thrilled you're accepting the secondment, although I confess, I hadn't realised it was still in question. Mr Ghurair is quite insistent that you're the right person for the job.'

'I... erm...' I try to focus. I'm lost.

'Oh, don't be modest, Scarlett. This will go a long way for your prospects at the firm.'

'I accepted the secondment.' It's clear he thinks that much. *What email?* 'Neil, forgive me, I'm just a little confused.'

'Did you have a big Saturday night, Scarlett?' He laughs. 'Well, I don't want to keep you on a Sunday; I just want to check you're okay to fly out this week so I can confirm with Abdulla?'

'This week... Sorry, Neil, can I call you back in one minute?'

'Yes, of course.'

Hanging up, I pull up the sent items in my email folder.

To: Wallace, Neil
From: Heath, Scarlett
Sent: Sunday 29 Nov 2025 8.44
Subject: Dubai Secondment

Good morning Neil,
    I just wanted to let you know that I have put a lot of thought into the Dubai secondment opportunity and I would like to accept.

Please let me know the arrangements.

Regards,

Scarlett Heath

Director

Saunders, Taylor and Chamberlain LLP

Gregory.

The lump that's been lingering in my throat is back with a vengeance and my eyes are stinging. I catch an escaping sob with the back of my hand to my mouth then swallow the lump and stand up straight, accepting reality.

'Scarlett.'

Neil's voice is like a punch to my gut, crippling. I move my free hand to the back of a beige velour chair for strength.

'Neil. When can I fly?'

'As soon as possible is best for Abdulla. How long do you need?'

'Can you get me on a flight tonight?' My voice is breaking. 'I'd like to get started straight away.'

'Tonight might be a push. Take your time, do whatever you need to do and I'll ask Aisling to book you a flight for tomorrow.'

'Great. Perfect. Let me know the details.'

'Thank you, Scarlett, Abdulla will be pleased about this.'

'No problem, glad I can help.'

Once the call is disconnected, I fall into the beige seat, stunned. *What just happened?*

Gregory didn't do this. Why would he? After last night, after the CPS decision. We're far from perfect but I assumed we could work on that now that things are settled. Maybe that's it. Maybe now there are no excuses and he's afraid to let me in. I snort at just how pathetic that thought is... *He just doesn't love you.*

In the ladies', I splash water over my face and dab away the mascara from under my eyes. My grey skin is almost translucent in the mirror.

Jovial conversation continues when I slip back into the lounge. I scan the room quickly; I want to see his reaction before he has a chance to think and put up the wall of whichever personality he feels like presenting today.

One glance. That's all it takes.

He turns from the window, his skin the colour of the pending rain clouds outside. His face and neck are taut and every sinew in his neck is displayed when he swallows. The cup in his hand rocks against its matching saucer. We hold our stare until Gregory looks down to his saucer and back to me. *Ashamed? Embarrassed?* He ought to be. Too fucking pathetic to tell me straight.

'Everything okay?' Amanda asks from the leather chair closest to me where she's drinking tea and flicking her eyes between Gregory and me.

'Absolutely.' I move to the table between the sofas and chairs to collect a cup of coffee. 'Just Neil, he wanted my answer about the Dubai secondment.'

'So is he mad that you're not going?' She casts her eyes to Gregory but his back is now turned to the room as he looks out at Lara's acres of land, his shoulders around his ears.

I sip my coffee and try to calm my nerves and keep my voice even. 'Actually, I am going. He didn't leave me much choice.'

I watch Gregory's shoulders rise and fall with his breath. *Even now, I don't want people to know his underhand tricks; I don't want people to think badly of him. I'm such an idiot.*

'Shit! When do you leave?'

'Tomorrow.'

* * *

I hug everyone when lunch is finished but I keep my arms locked around Sandy and Amanda because as much as I can talk to them on the phone, absent an emergency, I won't be holding them for six months. I leave tomorrow, that much is certain because Gregory made certain I couldn't get out of it. Going to Neil was conniving but I have to hand it to him, it was the best way to make sure he got what he wanted. Rid of me. He got the CPS decision, made sure I could move on like he'd intended the moment he got the police involved that night. Then he pushed me away.

The question I don't have an answer to and the question I ponder through our stubborn silence all the way back to the Shard, is why bother with last night? Last night, I believed, more than ever, I even thought I *saw*, rather than just hoped, that he loves me.

I get that he has to let me in. We have hurdles to surmount. But I thought we'd have a clear run now, stand together, have the chance to fall in love, know everything about each other without darkness or obligation looming. What's clear to me now is his shadows run deeper than one night.

The silence of the car serves to heighten the tension but I won't ask him here, now. I want to see his face when I ask him, *why?*

He holds open the door to the apartment. I don't look at him but I feel him scrutinising every move I make. He watches me from the centre of the open lounge as I pour a glass of water from the fridge filter and sip. The car ride home gave me time to think about what I wanted to say but now, face to face with the man I love, I'm lost for words.

Katrina Martin was right in the interview room three weeks ago. A perfect stranger could see it when I couldn't. This is unrequited love.

'Are we going to talk about this?' he asks, as if he hasn't already spoken a thousand words.

There's a shift in his expression to something that resembles pity. The look churns in the pit of my stomach and cripples my chest. Then my eyes sting and there's nothing I can do to stop the silent tears from rolling down my cheeks.

'Why?' I whisper with no strength in my words.

He takes a step towards me, his arms raised like he's going to touch me. I jerk away from him.

'Don't touch me. Don't you dare touch me.'

'Scarlett, please don't cry.'

'Just tell me why. Why are you so desperate to get rid of me?'

His head falls to his chest and he looks up at me through burdened eyes. Despite everything, I want to hold him.

'You were right, Scarlett, when you said we're bad for each other. Except you're not bad for me.'

'Then why push me away?'

'For your own good. You should be with someone ten times the person I am.'

'Fuck you, Gregory, and your fucking righteousness.' My tears turn to spitting anger. 'You're a coward. You don't love me and you've made damn sure you can get rid of me without having to tell me that. The last three weeks have been a joke, haven't they? In fact all of this, two months, since the start. You wanted me to help you with your hostile takeover but you didn't anticipate my dad being murdered as a consequence. So you stayed, felt like you had to, thought you'd let me down gently, eventually.'

'Scarlett.'

'No. You didn't think I loved you enough to kill a man, did you? That's a game changer right there. You had to keep me here until the case went away. Now you can finally get what you want: rid of me.'

'Just hear me out.'

'Oh, you mean discuss something with you? The way you discussed stealing my phone and emailing my boss behind my back?'

He sighs and rolls his set jaw. 'I wanted you to have space, away from me, away from all the shit that I brought on you. Time to think about whether you want to be with me. I want to give you the chance to walk away.'

'Bullshit! You're not giving me a chance; you've sent me halfway across the fucking world. What is there to think about, Gregory? I love you. Everything bad has gone away. Why now? Why after last night? I thought... I thought...'

'Last night was selfish, I know. And I'm sorry. I wasn't ready to lose you. I wanted you to have one night, and... I wanted to have one night. I wanted you to have the fairy tale you deserve.'

I snort and shake my head. 'I deserve? When are you going to realise that *you* deserve it *too*?'

He takes a deep breath and furrows his brow, looking almost pained.

'Scarlett, there're things that you don't know about me and if you knew them, you wouldn't want to be with me. You'd run.'

'Is that what this is about? Are you afraid if I know, I'll leave you? Because, Gregory, I don't want to go anywhere or be with anyone else.'

He pulls his fingers tightly through his hair. 'No! Damn it, Scarlett, you should go. Can't you see that's exactly why things had to be this way?'

'So I have no option but to leave.'

He lifts his chin and looks blankly at me. The lost boy from my dreams.

'Tell me. If this is about giving me space to realise I want to be with you despite whatever it is you won't tell me, explain. Make me understand. Tell me what I need to know to make up my mind.'

He stares. Unrelenting. Silent.

'No. Because this is about me leaving you, Gregory. Call it how it is. You don't want me to think and decide to be with you. You want me to go. For good.'

He reaches out to me and for the briefest moment, I think I see panic on his face. 'I do want to tell you and God, Scarlett, I want to love you. Each time you've looked at me, desperate for me to tell you I love you, I've wanted to. It's broken my heart to hear you say it and not say it back to you.'

I step towards him. 'Then say it. Tell me you love me. Tell me everything.'

He closes his eyes. 'I just... can't.'

I drag in three long breaths and tell him, 'Fuck you, Gregory.'

* * *

He's sitting on the coffee table in the lounge staring out to the black sky when I carry my suitcase downstairs.

'Where are you going?' His words are devoid of emotion, of fucking humanity. I can't stand to look at him.

'I'm staying in a hotel tonight. I fly tomorrow. Let's not drag this out.'

He stands now and I shudder. I'm just about keeping it together but if I feel him or smell him, I'll crumble.

'If I wanted to come and see you?'

'Don't. Spare me the let's-be-friends and it's-not-you-it's-me speech. Just let me go.'

The pressure behind my eyes is building again and the lump in my throat is making it hard to breathe. *I need to get out of here.* I reach the door, struggling to hold it open and manoeuvre my suitcase, which makes me want to cry out in frustration. In my frenzy, I miss him come up on me. He lifts the suitcase to the hallway. He doesn't touch me but he stands close. Too close.

'Scarlett...' My name rolls off his tongue in a soft, desperate whisper. *But desperate for what?*

There's nothing left to say.

He exhales, long and shallow, then there's a shift in his mood, in the air. 'Please be safe.'

I look at him now. I fix my eyes on his. 'All this time I've been hoping you were in love with me.' I shake my head as a change settles over me. 'You know what, Gregory? You *don't* deserve me. And not for whatever reason you keep telling yourself, whatever secrets you keep. You don't deserve me because you can't see what's standing right in front of you.'

In the lift, I stare at the closed doors, my hand across my chest, making sure my heart is beating because at least part of me just died. Another part of Scarlett Heath, gone.

He was my constant, the anchor in my new world, the reason for everything that's happened in the last two months. The only reason I knew I could get through it.

Now he's gone and I don't know who I am.

Nothing makes sense.

I'm alone and I'm terrified.

* * *

MORE FROM LAURA CARTER

Another book from Laura Carter, *Tainted Love*, is available to order now here: https://mybook.to/TaintedLoveBackAd

ACKNOWLEDGMENTS

Given this is a second book in a trilogy, I'm going to keep the acknowledgments short but sweet, because all the people mentioned in book one have continued to indulge me and support me through this book, too. I remain immensely grateful. Thank you!

I've toyed with not adding acknowledgments to this book at all but I figure there is one big mention I need to include and that is to you, gorgeous, fabulous reader, for sticking with the Billionaires of London series. Your investment of time and support means the absolute world to me. I hope I haven't let you down and that you want to go on to see this trilogy conclude in Tainted Love.

Thank you from the bottom of my heart. LC x

ABOUT THE AUTHOR

Laura Carter is a top 10 Amazon and internationally bestselling author of romance and romantic women's fiction. She lives with her family in Jersey, Channel Islands.

Download your exclusive bonus content from Laura Carter here:

Visit Laura's website: www.lauracarterauthor.com

Follow Laura on social media:

instagram.com/lauracarterauthor
tiktok.com/@laura.carter.author
facebook.com/lauracarterauthor

ALSO BY LAURA CARTER

Brits in Manhattan

The Law of Attraction

Two to Tango

Friends with Benefits

Always the Bridesmaid

Billionaires of London

Ruthless Love

Twisted Love

Tainted Love

Standalone Novels

Fake It 'til You Make It

Stuck in Paradise With You

Table for Three

Catch a Falling Star

In This Together

The Wild Card Series

A Rookie Mistake

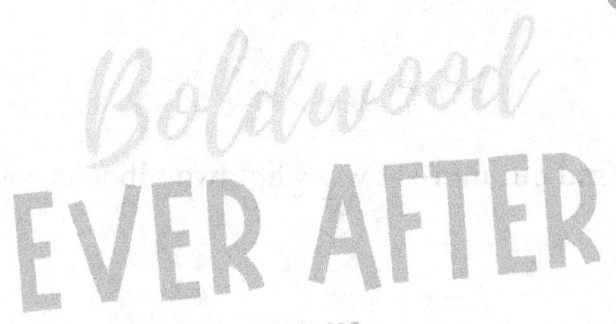

Boldwood
EVER AFTER

X♡X♡

JOIN BOLDWOOD'S
**ROMANCE
COMMUNITY**
FOR SWEET AND
SPICY BOOK RECS
WITH ALL YOUR
FAVOURITE
TROPES!

SIGN UP TO OUR
NEWSLETTER

HTTPS://BIT.LY/BOLDWOODEVERAFTER